Fatally FLAWLESS

SALEEM ROBERTS

THE TMG FIRM

New York

The TMG Firm, LLC
112 W. 34th Street
17th and 18th Floors
New York, NY 10120
www.thetmgfirm.com

Fatally Flawless
Copyright © 2017 Saleem Roberts
Published by The TMG Firm, LLC

For more information about special discounts for bulk purchase, please contact The TMG Firm at 1-888-984-3864 ext 12 or publishing@thetmgfirm.com

ISBN: 978-0-99835-656-3
Library of Congress Control Number: 2016963023

First The TMG Firm Trade Paperback Edition October 2017
Printed in the United States of America

This is a work of fiction. The names, characters, businesses, places, events, and incidents are the products of the author's imagination or utilized in a fictitious manner. Any resemblances to actual persons, living, dead, or actual events are purely coincidental.

Cover created and designed by Maximus Graphix.

This book is dedicated to the memory of my mother, Juanita Roberts. I believe by some twist of fate, she's played a major part in the amazing journey of creating *Fatally Flawless*. I can't wait to see her next lifetime. Xoxo.

—Saleem Roberts

Caught in the Lights

Who am I supposed to be? Am I the person people think they see when they look at me? Are any of us? We wear three hundred dollar jeans to look rich when our pockets are empty. We wear Gucci and Chanel frames, but they are just shields to cover up the pain. When we are dressed up at the club, we hold our heads up high. You can't tell us anything. But when we are drunk back at the crib we lower our heads in shame telling ourselves I want more out of life than 'hood fame. I know I should have paid my electric bill, but those new Prada sneakers from Neiman Marcus were calling my name. Shit, I had to have them so that all of my niggas would say that they're insane. Appearances are everything in the 'hood, and one can't ever be seen as a lame. So who are we? Spiritual young people raised properly by our parents. But in the 'hood ignorance is bliss. We are obsessed with a high-priced lifestyle we can't afford. In the 'hood designer clothes get old fast. We do things by any means necessary to keep an abundance of new shit. So who are we? A hip-hop nation lost in the whore of Babylon we call the 'hood. I know I should get my life together and go back to school we say to ourselves. But that can wait until next year. Such and such is having a party tonight, and everyone is going to be there. So who are we? A bunch of young adults trying to hold on to our glory days...big kids scared to grow up. We drink and shop too much and roll way too many blunts. We party all of the time to numb the pain trying to escape reality. The clock is ticking and time is running out. So we must all finally grow up!

—Saleem Roberts

Chapter 1

MYA'S RULES: BACK TO SCHOOL BLUES

Mya Campbell - 17 years old

September 9, 1997

Seventeen-year-old Mya Campbell rides calmly down Lancaster Avenue headed toward Overbrook High School. This is her first day as a senior. And after a long, wild summer, she cannot wait to get back to her stomping grounds as one of the Fabulous Three, aka the Baddest Chicks in school. Mya's mother, LaTanya, a no-nonsense corporate lawyer, drives cautiously, snug in the plush tan leather seat in her new, white E-Class Mercedes, dressed in a sky-blue Donna Karan pantsuit, her long wavy hair pulled back in a ponytail. LaTanya cuts her hazel eyes smugly at her only child who has her same features: buttermilk light-skinned complexion, full pouty lips, and a button nose. Looks are the only similarity between mother and daughter. LaTanya turns the car stereo off. Mya had been blasting. *It's All About the Benjamins* by Puff Daddy and The Family. Mya sucks her teeth and thinks, *Oh God, I know what's coming next. She's about to talk my head off.*

"Honey, make sure you sign up for the advanced SAT prep class. You have less than half a year before the SATs, and you need to be ready."

"Mom, it's only the first day of school. I ain't thinking about that right now," Mya retorts with a frown [on her face]," as she begins to apply MAC lip gloss to her full lips, gazing into a small pink compact.

"I ain't is not grammatically proper. How many times do I have to tell you not to use that ghetto slang? Mya, listen to me. You need to start thinking about your future ASAP. Your grades were average at best last year, and Overbrook's reputation is not in good standing. If you would have gone to Lower Merion High School as I wanted you to, you'd be a shoe-in for Howard University or Spelman. But you know how to work your father like a snake-charmer," LaTanya snaps, roughly turning the corner on 59th and Lancaster Avenue.

"Mom, you're trippin'."

"Am I tripping when I pay your extravagant credit card bills? You are not queen Mya. You may have your father wrapped around your little finger, but not me, little girl."

"Mom, I'm almost grown. I'm graduating this year."

"Please, I don't care how much you smell yourself or how many little thugs you're running around with."

Her mother's words stop Mya in mid-sentence, a look of shock on her face.

LaTanya smirks at her sarcastically as she pulls in front of the large tan-and-brown brick building that is Overbrook High School, "Yeah, I know all about those no-good niggas you're running around with," she continues.

"Mom, whatever. I don't have time for you and your accusations now," Mya says while practically running out of the car, slamming the door behind her.

2

LaTanya quickly pulls off without saying goodbye.

Mya straightens the skin-tight hot-pink Versace jeans and halter top she's wearing. She puts on a pair of big white Chanel sunglasses to give her face an air of mystery. The four-inch strappy Chanel sandals reveal a perfect pink pedicured size-seven foot. Her long, soft black hair blows in the early-morning breeze as she approaches the thick crowds of urban teenagers waiting to get into school. Guys with fresh haircuts look official posing in Moschino t-shirts, colorful Polo Sport short sets, and Iceberg jeans. Girls sporting their best summer outfits are spread in little cliques, rocking Coogi dresses, and colorful Moschino and Versace.

But Mya and her squad are different. They had long made an art form of ghetto-fabulous fashion. They do it as if for an expensive music video: name-brand divas from head to toe. They were the fly girls that everybody watched and talked about. Even the haters had to give it up. Mya walks through the thick crowd as if Halle Berry showed up at school. Niggas' eyes light up and mouths water at the sight of Mya's firm breasts and round ass as she confidently struts by as if she owns the place, as a queen would greet her subjects. Girls size her up.

Mya spots a group of four senior girls who can't stand her. They are thorough but not as bad as Mya's squad. *Kareema's still rockin' those old Gabbana sneakers, and TeTe's weave is a wreck as always,* Mya thinks as she sizes the broads up under her dark shades. She puts on her fuck 'em-girl look and tosses her mane like Naomi alone on the runway, throwing a devious smirk their way. "Yes, the bitch is back," she whispers, purposefully sashaying by them, almost colliding into them as if in a road rage.

All four girls put on their screw-face expression. Kareema's eyes bulge from her head when she notices

Mya's gear. Mya knows that she's looking, relishing every second as if drinking an ice-cold Pepsi.

"Is that my bitch?" a loud voice screams. Mya turns to see her two best friends in the world. Takia and Raven smile brightly heading her way.

"Baddest chicks in the house," Mya shouts, running to embrace the only girls she loves and trusts with sharing her bad-hair days, acne breakouts and pictures of her wearing braces in eighth grade.

They embrace in a tight three-way hug, all eyes on them. Mya steps back to survey her friends' look. Image is everything.

"What's up Mya?" Takia asks smiling, her pretty caramel face flawless. She rocks the honey-blonde, layered Mary J. Blige look. Mya approves of the form-fitting white Dolce & Gabbana shirt and jeans she wears, and shiny snake-skinned knee boots from Head Start on Chestnut Street. Takia steps back just a bit so that Mya can get a better look at her outfit. Takia eagerly seeks her approval like a child needs a mother's love.

"What's up, miss shy girl?" Mya asks, playfully pushing Raven, the quiet brain of the squad. She has the smoothest mocha-brown skin and slanted eyes and long straight black hair down to the middle of her back. People say that she looks like Chilli from TLC. Guys always say that she's the baddest dark-skinned girl whom they'd ever seen, and with an IQ bordering genius level. Petite and bow-legged, she certainly was the sexiest nerd Mya had ever seen. She looks stunning on the first day of school in a sheer yellow Fendi t-shirt with its double-F logo, super-blue denim miniskirt, and black stiletto knee boots. The Supremes are now officially back together.

"Show Mya your arm, Raven," Takia demands, nudging her.

"Girl, what I get on my body is my business. Don't tell me you got Mally's name tattooed on you," Mya hisses. As she looks at Raven's left arm, there it is; a red heart with Mally Forever going through it.

"Raven, you stupid. Getting' that nigga name on you."

"Me and Jamal been together for three years. I'm in love with him," Raven argues.

"That was ninth grade. We're grown women," Mya retorts as she adjusts her Chanel frames.

That nigga can't-do nothing for you. It's time you started thinking about gettin' this money."

"Raven, stop playing in the minor leagues."

"I do just fine gettin' mine."

Raven rolls her eyes.

"Look what that boah Hakim bought me," Takia giggles, flashing an iced-out Movado watch, sitting pretty on her wrist.

Mya and Raven's eyes light up. "That's hot," they both squeal. "That ice is shiny," Raven smiles.

"Yeah bitch, it's shiny, now it's time to get you some," Mya announces as the school bell rings.

School security guards in uniforms open the doors. Students start filing into the drab interior that perfectly reflect their bad attitudes, as they're scanned and searched by security guards with metal detectors to make sure that drugs, guns and other weapons aren't slipping into the building. Even with these daily searches, they still find their way in. Mya and Raven climb the long staircase to the third floor where the Academic Motivation Program is housed. They have to maintain at least a B-plus average to stay in the program, which is no problem for Raven, who has been an academic student her entire life. And Mya's parents spared no expense on private tutors to ensure that their daughter has the best chance at higher education.

Takia is in Cities and Schools, a program for kids with attendance and behavioral problems. She is a bright girl but doesn't have the same parental guidance and nurturing as Mya and Raven.

"Aw, look at these ninth-graders," Mya observes, looking at a group of rambunctious young teens pushing and shoving each other outside rooms 304, 305 and 306, the ninth-grade motivation sections. "Oh, just look at them. They get more out of control every year," Raven says over the immense noise that the ninth graders make.

"What's up, Raven," a squeaky voice yells. It was Raven's cute next-door neighbor, Tanisha.

"Hey, Nish, I forgot you were going to ninth grade," Raven says excitedly, embracing her young friend.

Tanisha is a cute tan-skinned girl with large lips. "Y'all got that shit on as usual," Tanisha says, looking wide-eyed at Raven and Mya's outfits.

"You look cute, Nish," Mya says, looking over Tanisha's fitted-blue Guess jean set.

Tanisha blushes. "Thank you, Mya. I know y'all gonna look out for me, right?"

"Of course, we got your back, Nish. We like family."

The other ninth-graders look impressed that Tanisha is cool with the fly seniors.

"All right, Nish. We'll catch you later." Raven and Mya head off to their new homeroom, 320. Mrs. Ashcroft, aka Mrs. Asscroft."

"Is that little Lil' Kim and Foxy Brown up in the building?" Ziggy Brown hollers as Mya and Raven step into the room. Ziggy is the resident class clown. Everyone loves his sense of humor. A tall, dark-skinned string bean of a boy, with Martin Lawrence comic skills.

"Shut up, Ziggy," Mya laughs, playfully shoving him. *Leave it up to Ziggy to get the jokes rolling on the first day of school,* she thinks, taking her usual seat in every class next to Raven. Row four. Perfect visible hiding space.

The class is filled with kids they've known for years, some as far back as elementary school. Some used to be friends. But times change, and people grow apart. With the social hierarchy that the girls entered at Overbrook High School, some form of associations with social suicide is better left behind.

Mya and Raven casually look through *Vibe Magazine* with rapper Mase on the cover, when Rasheeda Scott, a stout dark-skinned girl with tight microbraids, approached. "Hey y'all. How was y'all summer?"

Mya looks at Rasheeda with a frown, under her huge sunglasses. Mya suddenly dismisses her.

"This summer seemed so short," Raven throws off, in more small talk, knowing that Mya just played Rasheeda.

"So what you girls do all summer? I ran my babysitting business and stacked money all summer."

Mya sucks her teeth loudly, clearly ignoring her question. So Raven steps up,

"Girl, I went to Great Adventure with my boyfriend like ten times, and me, Mya and Takia saw *The Players Club* five times.

"All that sounds like a sweet, fun summer. Raven, you got a tattoo?" Rasheeda asks, pointing to Raven's arm with one long tail-blue press-on nail in a detective precision.

"Yeah," Raven says nonchalantly.

"Let me see."

Raven reveals her still-peeling love dedication.

"Oh Raven, you must really be in love with Mally. I feel the same way about my boyfriend, Brandon. But my mom would kill me if I got a tattoo. What did your parents say?"

"Girl, I got my parents in check," Raven says, knowing that her parents have no idea about her new tattoo.

At that moment, the classroom door slams shut. All the students jump to attention, rushing to their seats. Mrs. Ashcroft, the meanest twelfth-grade teacher at Overbrook, walks to the center of the room. She has an active reputation for breaking students down. A tall, robust brown-skinned woman with hawk eyes, and a close afro cut. She possesses an air of superiority around her. This is a woman not having it. Her long Afro-centric garb comes straight out of Erykah Badu's video. She gives the class an icily intimidating stare before walking over to the chalkboard and writing.

"Mya, you are so ignorant," Raven whispers, pulling a black-and-white composition book from her backpack.

Mya pops a stick of Winterfresh gum into her mouth. "I don't like that Jo-Jo-ass bitch. She's always trying to play the role of something she's not," Mya hisses at Raven. "Stacking money all summer, my ass. Raven, you're too nice to bitches. That's your problem."

"Stop talking please," Mrs. Ashcroft firmly puts down in a deeply nasal voice. "Read what I've written on the blackboard. Where will I be five years after I graduate?" She writes with a big exclamation point for all to see. "Get this question burned into your minds, people. You're seniors. After this coming June, you'll have to face the real world. Some of you will go off to prestigious universities, some of you will develop skills and crafts that will give you the tools to make a successful living. And the rest of you will become statistics. Jail and the welfare system will be waiting for some of you.

"I ain't gonna be on no welfare," someone hissed from the back of the room.

"And with all of the knowledge and guidance in me, I'm here to make sure that my students don't become statistics. Who can tell me where they will be in five years after graduation?"

Raheem Sampson quickly raises his hand, a cute, coffee-brown part-time rapper, most of the time wet head.

"Mr. Sampson?"

"Yo. In like five years, I'm gonna be signed with Bad Boy Records, driving a fat Benz and crazy ice like my man Puff Daddy."

The whole classroom bursts into out-of-control laughter.

"Nigga, you ain't even gettin' signed to Ripoff Records," a guy to the side of Mya yells.

"Quiet down, I want silence," Mrs. Ashcroft screams, grabbing a thick ruler from her desk. She bangs it forcefully on the dark oak desk. Only then does the class begin to settle down. "Mr. Sampson, thank you for your perfect fantasy life. Getting into the music business is one of the hardest things to accomplish. There are a million little snotty-nosed hip-hop kids thinking they can rap. What makes you so special?"

Raheem looks salty.

"Who else can give me a realistic view of where they will be in five years? Miss Scott?" Mrs. Ashcroft points to Lisa Scott, Miss Goody Two Shoes of Overbrook High School. She makes it her mission to be president and chairman of every committee that Overbrook has to offer. Honor Society president, Debate Team captain, Prom Committee chairwoman, and Yearbook editor. And Mya hates her guts. The girl has brains, but that's as far as it gets. An average-looking brown-skinned girl, tall and thin with no shape.

"Mrs. Ashcroft, in five years, I'll be a senior at Norfolk University studying pre-law with a minor in journalism, and hopefully I'll be interning at the Washington Post. I have my eye on politics."

Some students start making noises, annoyed with Lisa's very super-perfect grandstanding.

"Just the type of grade-A answer that I'm looking for. Now someone else give me an example." Mrs. Ashcroft scans the room and settles on Mya, now slumped in her seat, not paying the least bit of attention to anything being said, flipping through her magazine, her dark sunglasses still perched on her nose. "Excuse me, Miss Campbell, there's no sun in this room," Mrs. Ashcroft observes while approaching Mya's desk.

"So what," Mya snorts, rolling her neck.

"So, there's no sun in here, so remove your sunglasses now."

"Mrs. Ashcroft, these are four hundred dollar sunglasses. I *need* them on my face."

"I don't care how much they cost. I'm asking you one more time to remove them, or I'm writing up a pink lip for suspension."

Mya snatches her sunglasses from her face, revealing a hurricane brewing in her seething hazel eyes.

"Now, Miss Campbell, where do you see yourself in five years?" A sarcastic grin eagerly grows around Mya's mouth. She runs her hand through her hair seductively. The boys in the room are clearly having fantasies about her with that simple gesture.

"In five years, I hope," Mya lets out a giggle, "I hope I never become like *you* because you're miserable and bitter. And besides, from what I hear you teachers earn, it wouldn't fit in with my lifestyle."

At that moment, the next period bell rings. "Mrs. Ashcroft is salty," the students yell as they stampede out the door of what would surely be the most boring class of their senior year. Mya and Raven are the last to leave. She slides her shades back on and gives Mrs. Ashcroft the grisly face.

"Keep thinking you're cute, Miss Campbell," Mrs. Ashcroft says angrily, as Mya and Raven exit the classroom.

"I am cute, even Stevie Wonder can see that," Mya brags, turning around with the conceit and confidence of a ghetto beauty queen.

"Cute ain't gonna last forever. And with your nasty disposition and attitude, you're going to be in for a rude awakening," Mrs. Ashcroft pronounces before slamming the door shut.

"Girl, are you crazy? Don't start fucking with Mrs. Ashcroft on the first day of school. You need her class to graduate," Raven warns.

They disappear into the thick sea of students coming and going to their next classes.

"Raven, I hate that bitch! She thinks she's gonna shut me down. I'm gonna shut her down right back."

They head to the first floor, where their second-period health class is held. They spot Reggie, the best-dressed boy in Overbrook High School, a tall, cute dark-skinned boy with deep dimples. Whatever is new and hot fashion-wise, he rocks it first. He loves the girls' style, and they like his. People around school whisper about his sexuality. He is too well put together not to be gay. Reggie doesn't give a fuck, and the girls won't let anyone dog him out.

"Is that the divas I see?" Reggie screams at Mya and Raven. "No hugs?" he asks. "Let me see what you're wearing," making them turn like models on the runway. "All right now, you're doing the damn thing. I already see Miss Takia giving it up. Y'all whole squad be shittin' on these haters.

"Reggie, you look fly as always," the girls complement.

"Oh, thank you, ladies," Reggie says, popping the collar on his multicolored Moschino blazer.

The matching pants are a little loud, but loud is what Reggie is all about.

"Y'all know Kareema and them is hatin' already."

"Those bitches never stop," Mya huffs.

"Jealousy and envy is a bitch," Raven adds coolly.

"Y'all keep shittin' 'em. I gotta make this elementary functions class. Mr. Vogel be trippin'." Reggie gives the girls fake air kisses on the cheek before disappearing in the stairwell. The next two periods fly by. It is fourth-period lunch. Motivation program and health academy's joint lunch period. Half of the school cuts class to stay in lunch all day.

The Master Street and 55th and Vine project niggas gamble at tables. Craps and dice are the games of choice. If your mouth is louder than your pockets, someone is usually left bloody. The wanna-be rap niggas bang on the long brown lunch tables in the rear of the lunchroom, freestyling a bunch of gibberish that nobody wants to hear. The Jamaican kids have a section in the front right, reeking of weed, and overcooked beef patties. The Muslim kids have the windows, constantly trying to turn new converts even at that age. The Lansdowne Avenue crew of wild ghetto girls, who wore blue Dickies suits, are always looking for victims to roll on. Fighting is their addiction. All the brains, Lisa Scott, heads the pack of Overbrook's overachievers and snobs sit in the front center. That only leaves room for the ghetto-fabulous, who occupy the lunchroom's middle center, the building's most prized real estate. The nobodies scatter everywhere else.

Mya and Raven meet up with Takia, who has third-period lunch but cuts to be with her girlfriends. Once all three are together, it represents a triple threat as they strut into the lunchroom. *No Time* by Lil' Kim is blasting.

The whole room slightly pauses to take a look at the BCs, aka the baddest chicks. They sit at their favorite table, which everyone knows is off limits. The long wooden table is fresh with graffiti tags, reading, "59th Street Hustlers" and "MOB," Money Over Bitches, in either spray paint or permanent black marker.

"Mya, what's up with you and the boah Carmello Black?" Takia asks with a child's impatience.

Mya slyly grins. "Oh, that's my baby. We've been spending so much time together lately. I have a feeling he's the one, but there are so many bitches in the way."

"The way he's getting' money, you're going to have to deal with the bitches," Takia responds, popping a glazed donut stick in her mouth.

"If he's really feelin' you like that, he's gonna put them other bitches on the sideline," Raven adds, pulling out a bag of sour cream and onion potato chips from her book bag.

"Rav, it's different dealin' with hustlers, 'cause they have so many girls sweatin' them. You gotta step your game up to tame them," Mya sighs, frowning.

"Mya, look at Smokey and Rocky," Takia giggles, pointing at a group of four boys posted up against the wall near their table, all four in different-colored Coogi sweaters.

"Aww, Smokey looks cute," Mya observes, looking longingly in his direction.

Smokey had been Mya's first boyfriend, a tall, thin, dark-skinned boy, with curly hair and a chipped tooth like the rapper Nas. He was her first taste of the street life, far more mature than his seventeen years would suggest. He has potential to be big-time one day. He is the young boah of Frank from South Philly. He is getting a couple of dollars and drives a black Bonneville with tinted windows. He and Mya shared a steamy moment tenth-grade year; he took her virginity, so he continues to hold a special place in her heart. They shared many wildly horny nights in the back seat of his car. After a while, Mya got bored. The streets were calling her, and bigger boahs began to catch her attention. She was responsible for breaking his heart. But after seeing his sexy chocolate face staring her way, the warm memories readily came back to her mind.

She winks his way and right on cue, Smokey's right-hand man, Rocky, starts whispering in his ear. They both look Mya's way and burst out in laughter.

"I hate Rocky," Mya says, sucking her teeth. "Takia, I don't know how you ever fucked with him."

"Girl, don't remind me. He was the biggest mistake I've ever made, and I remember clearly, you were the one who talked me into messing with him." Takia shakes her head disbelievingly, contemptuously looking at her ex. A thickly built, light brown-skinned boy who's dick she rode harder than a bitch.

"Who are those cute light-skinned guys standing with them?" Mya asks of the two imposing boys in conversation with Smokey and Rocky.

"That's Ramier and Khalid Johnson. They're from The Bottom. They got kicked out of University and Bartram for fighting. They're cool with Mally's little brother Keith. They like Tyson with the hands, from what I hear. They cute boys," Mya says, admiring their rough good looks.

"Cute, but always in some shit. They've been locked up so many times," Raven interjects.

"What the fuck is that smell," Takia grunts, twisting her face up like Jim Carrey in *The Mask*.

"Somethin' do stink," Mya says, waving her well-manicured hand. They look to the end of the table to see a group of shabby juniors sitting there eating some foul-looking school lunch. Chicken nuggets, peas, and chocolate milk.

"No, they not eatin' those stinkin-ass freebie lunches at our table. I'm not havin' it," Takia demands with much attitude, standing aggressively.

"Get 'em, Ta," Mya and Raven playfully sing, edging Takia on.

"Um, excuse me," she addresses the four unattractive juniors with her grizzled face.

"Wassup?" One dark-skinned boy asks, smiling.

"Me and my girls down there are trying to breathe, and the smell of your food is blockin' our lungs. And you don't belong sittin' at this table anyway."

"It's the first day of school. The whole lunchroom is crowded. There's nowhere to sit," a chubby one in glasses, retorts, folding his arms. "We not movin'."

Takia's expression immediately turns vicious. "Yo, I'm tryin' to be nice to your punk-ass, but if you wanna pop off on some fly shit and make a scene, then we can do that," Takia says in a near-shout, drawing the attention of the rest of the lunchroom. She grabs one of their food-laden trays and dumps it in the trash can.

"Yo, we don't want any problems," the thinnest boy says with a look of defeat. His friends quickly follow his lead, moving two tables away.

15

Takia triumphantly sits back down with her friends, just one of the bad chicks wielding her power. Lunch lets out as teens rush from the big metal double doors. Everyone is smashed like sardines, passing through the small lunchroom hallway to the first-floor corridor.

"Walk me to the bathroom, girls," Raven yells over the noisy after-lunch crowd. The girls dip into the dreary, run-down girls' bathroom. Raven rushes into a stall.

"Rav, what you got the runs," Takia asks jokingly, pulling eyeshadow from her small Moschino tote bag.

"No, I gotta change my tampon."

"It always smells like fish in here," Mya hisses, standing next to Takia, applying her own lip gloss and spraying Versace Blue Jeans perfume around the bathroom.

"Takia, I really like the blonde hair on you.

"Thanks, boo!"

"You went to Hair Image?"

"No, girl, I had to stop goin' there. The shampoo girl was hatin' on me. I go to Platinum Shears now. Kenya do my hair now."

"You look like Mary J. Blige, girl."

"Aw, thanks."

They both retouch their makeup and survey themselves. The closest thing to ghetto-fabulous beauty perfection walking the streets.

The bathroom door swings open. In walks Kareema Thomas, aka the Mad Hater, with her cronies, TeTe, Amira, and Asia. At the sight of Mya and Takia, teeth sucking and eye rolling begin in full effect. The opposing group walks to the mirror on the other side of the room. Kareema eyeballs them through the mirror she occupies. Her black and blonde weave cuts into perfect layers. Kareema and her crew had always been second-

16

best to the BCs. They used to be frenemies until Mya pulled some dude from North Philly named Shariff that Kareema was hollering at. It had been full-fledged hate ever since.

Kareema is an average brown-skinned girl, not beautiful, but far from ugly. Her body remains her trump card, a nonexistent waist with hips, curves, and plenty of ass. Even women do a double take at her shape when she walks by.

That bitch look average, Mya thinks, watching Kareema, who is wearing a fitted black Dolce & Gabbana T, dark denim Guess jeans, and a pair of Dolce & Gabbana shoes that she was trying to preserve from last year. The number-one rule of the baddest chicks: Always switch up your footwear. Shoes are vital to a girl's reputation. Never be seen in shoes from last year. Raven walks out of the stall just as the cats are sharpening their claws. At the sight of Raven, TeTe tries to conceal her anger, balling her fist as if ready to strike.

Raven notices and rolls her eyes at TeTe. TeTe hates Raven over her boyfriend, Mally. She had been in love with him since they were in sixth grade at Shoemaker Middle School. It bordered on obsession. Mally never once looked in her direction and found her flirtations amusing. Raven did not see anything funny about it. When Mally and Raven became official, TeTe's heart was broken, and she had a vendetta ever since. Raven finds TeTe bitter and annoying, a tall, rail-thin tan-skinned girl with elf ears adjoined to a small peanut head. Her blue Moschino jeans are baggy, and her weaves are always matted. Amira and Asia are two low-budget whores who slept with half of the male student population. They tried to dress up cheap clothes. Average-looking brown-skinned girls. They are followers who do not actually have a reason not to like

Mya & Co., but the BCs overwhelming status makes most girls at Overbrook High jealous. "Bitches is so funny," TeTe says loudly, her lanky arms moving from left to right.

"Yea, I agree. Bitches is real funny," Kareema adds sarcastically. She and her cronies bust out like wild banshees, their laughter echoing off the bathroom walls.

"Funny, ha. I don't see no clowns in here," Takia addresses, facing off with the other squad.

"Takia, please, y'all always think someone's always pressed to talk about you lames," TeTe shouts, waving her lengthy arms through the air.

Takia takes a firm step toward TeTe. Before she gets any further, Mya catches her arm and begins speaking in a calm sarcastic tone.

"Takia, we can't go around entertaining low-lives. We're too pretty, our clothes are too expensive, and we just too fuckin' dimed-out," Mya adds, in a ready-to-drop-a-bitch stance.

Takia begins to get the joke. "Yea, you guys are right," she grins with a fake pout. "I forgot how haters do."

"Y'all bitches is nothin' to hate on," Amira screams, trying to make herself relevant.

Mya and the girls just laugh at her follower ass. They would not dare waste a breath on her.

"Mya, you should be the last one to talk shit, as much as I hear about you and your knees," Kareema says with building frustration.

Mya had been waiting for Kareema to come at her directly. "Kareema, maybe if you did what I do, your weight would be up. Or what's that shit Jigga say in *Imaginary Player*? Bitch, 'for the right price, I can even make yo shit tighter,' because those Gabbana sneakers on your feet are dogged."

Raven and Takia fall into vicious laughter. Mya had proven her point. Kareema now has the salty look of defeat across her face.

I'm done entertaining these whack-ass broads. Don't fuck with Mya! And that's that, she thinks while walking out of the bathroom like Mike Tyson after a TKO.

Takia and Raven follow, giving them the fuck-'em girl walk.

"Get your weight up, not your hate up," Takia hollers into the bathroom before slamming the door shut.

"I hate those bitches," Kareema growls, banging her fists hard against the tile wall. Her brown face turns blood-red.

"Man, fuck all them bitches! They gon' get theirs. That's my word," TeTe hisses, pulling out a freshly rolled blunt filled with weed from her back pocket. She lights it and takes a long toke.

School lets out at 2:45 p.m. It is a sunny September day, still eighty degree, with fall far and out of sight. Overbrook's notorious let out is popping. Hustlers and drug dealers in shiny Mercedes, BMWs, Navigators and other high-priced automobiles wait patiently for Brook's ample supply of young fly girls to get out of school. Kids from other high schools cut their last periods to make it up to Brook's last let out. Mya and the girls leave the building into the bright blinged world of ghetto-fabulous.

From one corner of 58th to 59th Street is packed with kids and young adults playing a role. Groups of girls stand next to well-known hustlers hoping to get picked. Expensive cars are parked everywhere. Guys driving motorcycles and Banshee four-wheelers do fast wheelies on the street with girls squeezing them for dear life, and their skirts fly up revealing colorful panties. The baddest chicks make their way through the crowded maze, pulling their hands away from guys they would never talk to.

"Yo, Pumpkin was supposed to be here at 2:45 p.m.," Takia sulks, pulling her black Nextel cell from her book bag, quickly dialing a number. "Yo, where you at? I'm in front of the Sugar Bowl. You around the corner? Hurry up!"

"Pumpkin is so corny," Mya observes while scanning the crowd.

"Yea, he might be corny, but that nigga breaks bread lovely."

"But his money don't make him cute," Raven comments, twisting a strand of her long hair around her left index finger.

"Raven, cute guys are played out. Ugly guys spend the most money on you, 'cause they're ugly, and they want a pretty girl with them, so they don't seem that ugly. And they'll pay to keep her around."

"Takia, what you just said makes not one ounce of sense," Raven argues.

"Well, that's my philosophy on ugly guys. Raven, and, I think I know a thing or two about ugly guys."

"I hope Mario is not with Pumpkin," Mya says, with distress on her face.

"Mya and Mario, sittin' in a tree, k-i-s-s-i-n-g," Raven and Takia sing teasingly.

I don't want to see this motherfucker at all, Mya thinks, ignoring her friends' antics.

Mario had been the first guy to break Mya's heart. He is a smooth-talking Black and Cuban pretty-boy hustler from The Bottom. And bitches love Mario. He gave Mya her first orgasm. He turned her out, eating her pussy every day until she came in his mouth multiple times. Yes, she was sprung on Mario in the summer of 1996. She stayed creepin' to 49th and Reno, his block.

His team is eatin', and he had no problem spending money on Mya. Sex, Neiman Marcus, eating at the Chart House, and Ruth's Chris every night... That was the best summer. Takia messed with Pumpkin, Mario's best friend, and trusted gun. They stayed over in New York at the Trump Plaza Hotel. The guys let Mya and Takia ravage through the Versace and Prada boutiques. Everything was gravy until some bad feminine itching prompted a visit to the gynecologist, where Mya was told that she had contracted crabs and a bad case of the clap. She had to swallow huge, disgusting-tasting pills, shave her pubic hair and take a big needle in her ass. When she confronted Mario, he denied it, angrily accusing her of cheating on him. Mya was so young and naïve; knowing that she hadn't slept with anyone else, she let Mario manipulate her into taking the blame for the mysterious STDs.

The next drama unfolded when some young girl from his neighborhood was telling anyone who would listen that she was pregnant by Mario. He denied it at first, but as the months dragged on and the baby was born as an exact replica of Mario, from his light coffee-brown complexion to his Afro-Hispanic features... is when the lies finally ran out, and Mya is shown pictures of the newborn from several of Mario's family members. He then admitted that he was the father.

She cried for a week straight and became a laughing-stock on the streets. She would not take her friends' advice and leave Mario for good. He was just too irresistible and sexually skilled. She forgave him for the pregnancy and hoped that with this third chance, Mario would change.

The last straw was on the night that she and Mario went to the Delaware Avenue movie theatre to see *Booty Call*. A group of girls confronted her over Mario, one claiming that she was his girlfriend who lived with her in an Upper Darby apartment. They tried to jump her. One of the girls threw a 64-ounce soda into her face while the others yanked her hair and pulled at her shirt. Even though Mario intervened, slapping a few of the bitches up, Mya was done. Her heart became an icebox, a naïve 16-year-old girl thinking that she could tame a grown-ass, conceited street nigga. She had been played. Mario tried in vain to get her back. She avoided his calls and dodged any attempt of his trying to worm his way back into her life. After Mario, she vowed never to let any man have her that open again. They had not seen each other in so long; being face to face with him made her nervous.

Mya is suddenly pulled from her thoughts by the crisp sound of *Street Dreams* by Nas being played loudly on the car stereo. Pumpkin's 1996 cherry-red 745 BMW pulls up to the curb. He jumps out of the driver's side, ugly as ever. He is a thin, dark-skinned guy with poppy eyes and buck teeth, a six-foot-two version of Flavor Flav of Public Enemy. He wears a red Polo Sport t-shirt and matching hat. The passenger-side door swings open, and out hops Mario, looking good as ever. He smiles very slyly at Mya. She steps back, as Takia nudges her with a sharp elbow.

If this bitch don't stop pushin' me, Mya thinks.

"What's up? Longtime no see," Mario says cheerfully as if nothing had happened between them while licking his kissable pinkish lips.

"I'm cool, Mario. How's your son doin'?" she responds coolly, stepping back from Mario's overtly sexual body language.

"He's cool, gettin' big, just had a big two-year-old birthday party for him at Chuck E. Cheese.

"Give me some money so I can get something to eat," Takia demands to Pumpkin, who has his bony hand firmly gripped on Takia's bubble ass. He digs into his baggy jeans and pulls out a thick wad of fifties and hundreds, handing her a crisp fifty.

"Give me something smaller. They don't change fifties at the Sugar Bowl.

"Look, I only carry Grants and Franklins. Mario, gimme a twenty," Pumpkin directs to Mario, who quickly passes it to Takia.

"Mya, you want somethin' to eat?"

"No, I'm cool."

Takia and Raven go into the Sugar Bowl. Pumpkin and Mario give each other a glance as Pumpkin follows the girls in.

"Yo, Raven, my man Nickel's still tryin' to holler at you," Pumpkin announces.

"So you been all right out here?

"I been straight." Mya's hazel eyes remain dark.

"You're a hard little woman to catch up with."

"When it's people you don't want catchin' up with you, you find ways to keep 'em away."

"Listen, I know I messed up, but I missed you baby girl," Mario smiles with an assured confidence in his brown eyes, adjusting the diamond bezel of his white gold Rolex.

Mya snaps her neck and looks Mario directly into his eyes.

"Mario, I put up with so much shit from you, and you have the nerve to smile up in my face like nothin' happened."

"You're right, I hurt you. But when you was with me, you didn't have to worry about nothin'."

"I know you ain't talkin' about that little money and gifts you bought. You know I ain't never been money hungry."

"Everybody knows you're a spoiled brat and your parents got deep pockets. You come from the best, but I bet that nigga Carmello Black showing you a real good time up north."

Mya looks at Mario wide-eyed. Her shocked demeanor gives him the confirmation that he needs. "Who told you about me and Black?"

"Come on, baby, you know the streets be talking. Everything gets back to me." Mario lets out a sly grin.

Takia probably been running her mouth, pillow talking with Pumpkin, Mya thinks furiously.

"I ain't mad, though. I know how the game goes. You onto the next nigga," Mario says, actively talking with his hands.

At that moment, a shiny black, wide-bodied 1997 S-Class Mercedes Benz sitting on immaculate chrome rims turns the corner at 59th Street. All conversation stops as all eyes focus on the high-powered machine in front of them, blasting *Can't Knock the Hustle* by Jay-Z and Mary J. Blige. The sleek Mercedes pulls up directly in front of Pumpkin's 745 BMW. The Benz window rolls down, revealing Carmello Black's dark rough-cut and handsome face. He is North Philly's notorious drug kingpin, with a widespread rep on the streets for being one of the smartest and deadliest hustlers. If anybody threatens his $30,000 per day strip, they find themselves dead, no questions asked. Carmello is the modern-day Meyer Lansky. He never gets his hands dirty, with a hood army of cold-hearted, trigger-happy thugs always ready to wet any nigga up. The sight of him jumping out of his S600 gets Mya's panties moist. His entire presence commands respect. He strolls so confidently, his chocolate skin flawless, his hair cut into a sharp Caesar, his muscular chest and arms protruding through his white Versace t-shirt. A giant iced-out Jesus piece hangs loosely from his neck, with baggy Iceberg jeans showing off his forest-green Polo Sport boxers and fresh, tan, double-soled two hundred dollar Timberland boots touch the ground for the first time; he buys them in sets of twenty.

He looks like Morris Chestnut, Mya thinks as Black approaches. *He's every girl's dream thug.*

"What's up, Black?" Mario asks nervously, extending his hand for Black to shake.

"Wassup homie?" Black responds in his deep husky voice giving Mario a half-handshake in a clear sign of disrespect.

"My nigga Black!" Pumpkin shouts, rushing over to Black, giving him a manly handshake.

Black responds as if he's never met Pumpkin a day in his life.

"What them things going for up north?" Pumpkin asks ecstatically in his reference to drugs.

Black gives him a nigga-don't-ask-me-any-questions stare. "Yo, I'm ready," Black says while pointing to Mya, turning his back on Pumpkin and Mario without saying a word.

Mya switches over to the passenger-side door of Black's Benz, turning to roll her eyes at Pumpkin and Mario one final time. *This revenge is the sweetest,* she thinks, eagerly sinking into the plush leather seat underneath her.

Pumpkin and Mario watch them speed off.

"Man, fuck that fake high sadiddy bitch. I put that bitch's name out on these streets and made her somebody," Mario foams.

"I know, dog," Pumpkin responds calmly. "Fuck that frontin' nigga Black. I heard that the Feds are on his ass as we speak."

"I only wanted some more of that good-ass pussy, anyway." They both chuckle viciously.

Black and Mya ride smoothly through his rough North Philly neighborhood like she is with the 'hood president. Cruising through this apparent war zone, guys young and old in expensive cars and squatters show Black the utmost respect, breaking their necks just so Black will wave his hand from that black tinted window in a sign of validation. The bitches, for their part, drool with excitement at the sight of Black's Mercedes. He pulls over for a few of them. The sight of a pretty, light-skinned wavy-haired Mya in the passenger seat evokes immediate jealousy and bitchiness, which Mya eagerly throws back.

Yeah, hoes, I'm with him, and what? Mya thinks, giving a few of the chicks a grisly face underneath her Chanel shades.

From 17th and Jefferson to Master and Diamond Streets, Black's Mercedes stops while collecting money from groups of young black teens and twenty-something-year-old guys dressed in the latest clothes and sneakers stand in front of abandoned houses on forlorn corners. They drive to 20th and Dauphin, where Black's right-hand man Faheem holds court with a group of young boahs, arguing over who is the best rapper, Biggie, Jay-Z or Nas.

"Yo, my nigga Biggie is the best that ever touched a mic!" One dark-skinned young boah in an oversized red hoodie yells as Black pulls up to the scene. Conversation hushes as Black hops out of the car. The group of young boahs scramble to shake Black's hand as if a famous rapper just fell into their presence.

Faheem, a tall, lanky guy with a basketball player's build watches her with intense hawk eyes; a full Sunnah beard covers his chin dressed in a black Coogi sweater and tan Tims, embraces Black like a brother. Mya watches everything with immense interest. They disappear into a run-down grocery store that Black owns as a front for his street business.

Five minutes later, Black and Faheem emerge. Black tucks a large paper bag under his arm. He walks to the passenger side door and opens it.

"Yo, I want you to meet my man Faheem."

Damn, don't put me on the spot like this, Mya thinks through a nervous smile as Black helps her out of the car.

Faheem puts on a cheesy smile, lusting over her with his stare. He definitely approves of what he sees. "Goddamn, Black, you got a pretty motherfucker!"

"Mya, this my main man Faheem. This my new young buck Mya," Black introduces.

"Hi," Mya says in her sweetest little girl voice.

"She everything you said she was and more," Faheem says while staring into Mya's hazel eyes and shaking her small soft hand. Even the young boahs gave approving glances, looking Mya over from her beautiful looks to expensive gear. A dime in all of their minds.

Black looks proud, flashing his perfectly straight white teeth.

"Shit, I'm about to roll up Overbrook and get me one like her."

"Naw, nigga, she one in a million. You're not gonna find one like this," Black chuckles, slipping his hands around Mya's waist.

She exhales softly. *Don't fall in love. Don't fall in love with him. You can't play yourself again. But he too damn sexy,* Mya thinks as Black's right-hand slips closer to her ass. After a few minutes of small talk, Black and Mya are back on the road headed for Black's secret Maplewood, NJ condo. Only the most selective few have entered.

"Let me talk to you on some real shit! Those niggas I see you talkin' to, I don't wanna see that again."

"Who, Pumpkin and Mario? Pumpkin mess with my girlfriend. I just knew them for a long time," Mya blatantly lies.

"Look, none of that shit matters to me. Them dudes are irrelevant clowns. You wit' me now, so who my girl associates with reflects back on me."

"Ahhh, you claimin' me now?"

"Naw, baby girl, I'm moldin' you. Your fly as shit, but you ain't reach your full potential. I'm the right nigga to mold you. Just play your part. Don't fuck up. And I'll give you the world on a platinum platter."

Mya finds herself speechless, searching her mind for the right snappy comeback, but remains a blank.

When they arrive at Black's complex, Mya notices a large number of top-of-the-line cars filling the oversized garage. Well-to-do white people in suits and ties arrive home from work. They take the elevator to the eighth floor. Once Black turns the key to 805, Mya is once again speechless, caught off guard by his condo's extravagance. A spotless black marble floor, futuristic black-and-white furniture, expensive paintings in brass frames line the walls. And a large bay window graces the skyline.

"Come into my bedroom." Black leads Mya by the hand down a long corridor into his immense master bedroom. He turns on his track lighting system by remote control and hops on his king-sized four-poster bed. "What you acting so shocked for?" Black teases slyly.

Mya slides off her Chanel sandals and climbs into bed with Black. His lambskin comforter feels tantalizing against her skin. *Damn, he smells so good,* Mya thinks, laying her head on his chest.

Two hours of small talk and watching hip-hop videos on his video jukebox later, Mya's stomach is full on Chinese take-out. After a bit too much shrimp lo mein, she and Black lay in bed watching *Goodfellas* on his huge television.

Should I give him some pussy? Should I? Bitch, just give it to him, Mya thinks, wrestling with her conscience. Her body shifts restlessly, her legs wrapped in Black's. He's dead into the movie, paying her no mind. She looks over his muscular build, a twinge of wetness seeping into her panties. She makes the first move, gently tilting her head to begin licking his ear. Black lets out a soft laugh, as her left-hand slides inside his boxers. She is stunned by the size of his dick. It has to be nine and a half inches, she guesses.

"Baby girl, we don't have to do this."

"I want to," Mya whispers.

"I know who you belong to. We got plenty of time for this."

Black's words send Mya into a tizzy. *Nigga, you gettin' this pussy,* she thinks while climbing on top of him. She pulls off her Versace halter, revealing a see-through black lace strapless bra, holding her full 36C breasts in place. She bends down and starts kissing Carmello passionately on the lips.

Black grabs the back of her neck and pulls her body close to him, sticking his tongue in her mouth, while rhythmically grinding against her. Mya lets out soft moans. She lifts up Black's undershirt, displaying his sculpted abs and muscular chest. She begins to lick his nipples.

Black bites his bottom lip, then turns Mya on her back and unbuttons her jeans, forcibly pulling them off. Her black lace panties are by now soaking wet. He spreads her legs apart and with his thick tongue, starts licking her pussy through those panties.

"Ahh," Mya moans in delight. Black moves her panties to the side and sticks his tongue deep inside of her. Her legs shake with pure pleasure. His full lips move from sucking on her clit to her thighs like the swift snake that he is. She rubs the back of his head as he eats her pussy like a prisoner getting his last meal.

"Damn, this feels good as shit," Mya screams vigorously as she comes with full force in Black's mouth. He does not leave a drop of her fluid un-swallowed. Mya gasps while closing her eyes.

"Don't go to sleep. You started something. We ain't done yet," Black says, pulling his boxers off, revealing his stunningly naked body with his large thick penis at full attention.

Girl, you in for it now, Mya thinks, unsnapping her bra. Black lays on top of her like some exotic Mandingo warrior. He slowly slips the head inside of her. She hollers, gritting her teeth and digging her nails into the side of his back. Once he loosens her insides, she feels the pleasure of his long, deep strokes. Her heart races. Black moves his body with the rhythm and precision of an experienced lover. He lets out deep groans as he drives her body, gripping her breasts.

"Carmello," Mya declares in the heat of their sweaty tangle. "Fuck me, fuck me, yes." Mya is at the heights as Black causes her hard orgasm again. He comes five minutes later. They then go two more rounds. By the time Black drops Mya off, she well knows that there is no denying it, she's in love. "I enjoyed myself tonight," she says softly, running her hands through her sweated-out hair.

"Me, too, things started off right. Yo, it's past one a.m. Ain't your peoples gonna be trippin' on you?"

"Hell no. My dad's cool. My mom be on some other shit."

"That's a badass house y'all livin' in," Black admires, gazing up at Mya's parents' large seven-bedroom house, the earth-colored Spanish-style home with large columns, well-kept lawn, and a two-car garage.

"Both of my parents are lawyers. My dad is the first black partner at his firm, and my mom's a junior partner in a corporate firm. So they did real good. My mom's extra hard about education.

"That's what's up. I got a little rich girl tryin' to play 'hood. Let me find out."

"Whatever, nigga," Mya laughs playfully, hitting Black on the arm as his cell phone rings loudly. He digs in his sweatpants, pulling a black Nextel flip-phone out.

"Speak," he demands. "That nigga did what?!" Black snaps, twisting his face into a grimace. "Yo I be down the way in fifteen minutes. I gotta handle some business. I gotta go."

"Alright," Mya pouts, just wanting to stay in his presence. "I'm gonna pick you up tomorrow," Mya leans over, kisses Black gently on the lips before sliding out of the car, feeling light as a feather from all the really good love that she and Black just made. All the house lights were off. She knows her parents had been asleep since the eleven o'clock news went off. She slowly opens the dark mahogany front door and creeps into the dim living room. She walks through the house, within the same rooms that scared her as a child. She now maneuvers through them with feline perfection, not knocking into one piece of her parents' expensive

31

furniture. She instinctively finds her way into the kitchen and switches on the light. She walks over to the large state-of-the-art stainless steel refrigerator. *There's never anything I want to eat in here,* she thinks while looking at the large bottles of spring water and green vegetables. She grabs a can of Pepsi and takes the back stairway to her large luxury bedroom. Mya's bedroom is every teenage girl's dream. She turns on the light, flings her book bag on the small pink loveseat lined against the perfect pale pink wallpaper that warmly engulfs the entire room. To say that Mya is obsessed with pink is a gross understatement. A large queen-size bed, perfectly made pink satin bedspread and an array of big, bright satin pillows in all shades of pink, from the darkest to the lightest. Her parents' Hispanic housekeeper Maria takes impeccable care of keeping Mya's sanctuary fit for a princess. God only knows the spoiled slob that she really is.

Mya may be spoiled on material things, but in her parents' quick dash up the ladder to success, they forgot to spend quality time with their own child, who used to crave horseplay with her daddy after his long days of work from his law firm, Mayer, Sachs & Campbell or baking cookies with mommy. As Mya grew, she became increasingly resentful. Her parents naturally began to feel guilty and, to pacify her, they gave her charge cards to major department stores and her own American Express platinum card. Her walk-in closet is the hood-fabulous version of Cher from *Clueless.*

Racks and racks of clothes in perfect alphabetical order, separated by the designer. Shoe racks hold stiletto-heeled pumps, knee and shoe boots, open-toe sandals by every designer in every style. Designer handbags possess their own action, carefully color-coordinated in separate bins. Mya's expensive passion of fashion is definitely her mother's doing, exposing her to a 'credit-card-is-a-girl's-best-friend' mentality. Even as their relationship had strained over the years, she continues to admire her mother's style and hard work ethic. But the battle lines between the two had long been drawn. Mya quietly scans her closet for the perfect outfit for her next day at school. It remains her nightly ritual since she was twelve years old. She could not sleep if her school outfit was not carefully picked out.

"Okay, let's see," Mya says, running her right palms through rack after rack of thousands of dollars of clothes. She singles in on a sky-blue cotton jersey, Jean-Paul Gaultier t-shirt dress with pineapples and bananas covering it, still with the three hundred and fifty dollar price tag attached. *And now for the shoes*, she thinks, swooning toward her immense shoe racks, scanning for the ultimate match. She picks up a pair of yellow Joan & David pumps, perfect to offset the colorful Gaultier dress. She also grabs a small yellow Prada clutch, the perfect icing for this sweet ensemble. This combination gives Mya sexual excitement. She has always been one with her clothes. With her school outfit now in place, she takes a hot shower, her body continuing to ache from the roughness of her and Carmello's lovemaking.

She enters her bedroom from her private bathroom. She turns on her Bose stereo system to the late-night slows jams on the *Power 99* station. Faith Evans *Soon As I get Home* calmly fills the room. She lotions her body with high-end Chanel N° 5 body lotion, and grabs her black cordless phone from her pink vanity table, before flopping on top of her soft, inviting bed.

Let me call Takia, she thinks as she dials her number quickly.

"Hello," Takia says groggily, waking from a dead sleep.

"Takia, wake up," Mya exclaims with excitement, sliding under her satin comforter.

"Wassup, Mya? It's one o'clock."

"Girl, guess what?"

"Girl, just say it," Takia sighs.

"Me and Black got it in. I gave him some tonight."

"What, bitch? Are you serious?" Takia asks, snapping out of her sleep. "Was it good?"

"Bitch, it was off the hook! He can fuck his ass off."

"Better than Mario?"

"Mario is a little boy compared to him."

"Girl, I'm glad you called. You played your part and stunted on that nigga Mario. He was salty as fuck."

Mya observes, flaring her nostrils. "But enough about his lame ass. I'm really feeling Black."

"I'm really happy for you. He looked good as shit. And you know, I don't do dark-skinned guys. Speaking of guys, Nickels came up soon as you left with Black. He got a shiny new expedition. You know he's okay, not cheap, not ugly."

"I think Nickels is cute in his own way," Mya agrees, stretching out as she feels sleep taking over.

"Yeah, I guess he's cute. Girl he was all over Raven today. He likes her so much. And I'm like, girl, he'll spend a couple dollars on you, but she's on that being a good girlfriend to Mally-type shit. I'm telling her, bitch, you better get on that nigga, so she ain't gotta keep working overtime at that little job of hers."

"Kia, I don't know what's wrong with Raven. When I saw that tattoo, I was convinced that she had a lot on her mind."

"Hold on real quick," Takia says, clicking on her other line.

Mya looks at her flawless French manicure while holding. Seconds later...

"Yo Mya, that's little Rell from South Philly. I need to holler at him."

"Alright girl, I'll see you at school tomorrow."

"Goodnight, Mrs. Carmello Black," Takia squeals before hanging up.

"Fuck you, bitch," Mya laughs while clicking off her phone. She turns her bedroom lights off by remote control. She stares into the still darkness of her bedroom and repeats several times, "Mrs. Carmello Black, Mrs. Carmello Black... I like the sound of that, she whispers. "I think I made the power move with this one." She rolls over on her side and drifts off to sleep.

Chapter 2

No Money, Mo' Problems

Raven Hightower, 17 years old, 5' 6½"

September 13, 1997

"Ladies and gentlemen, Marshalls, will be closing in the next fifteen minutes," the store announcer says over the intercom at the chain's Wynnewood, PA, location. Raven looks down at her small silver Gucci watch. 9:20 p.m. on the dot.

"Thank God," she says, straightening out racks of disorganized children's clothes where she worked at Marshalls department store.

"Miss, do you have any more of these in 4T?" A middle-aged redhead white woman asks, holding up a red OshKosh B'gosh corduroy jacket. Her two toddler sons pull a whole stack of sweaters off of the rack that she had just folded.

More shit I have to fix up, she thinks, rolling her eyes at the woman's unruly children. "Miss, whatever's out on the floor is what we have."

"Can't you check in the back?" the woman fires back.

Bitch, I'm tired and irritated, just trying to get the fuck out of here. "Ma'am, I'm sorry, we only have what's out on our floor," Raven answers while mustering a fake smile.

At 9:30 p.m., the store is closed. Raven and the rest of Marshalls' employees scramble to fix up and put away merchandise and turn in the contents of their correctly counted cash drawers. It was pay night, and all employees are in the typical rush. Once Raven finishes her count, she makes her way to the personnel office, where there is a nice-sized line of employees signing for their paychecks. As she waits in line, some of her coworkers carry on conversations surrounding her. Raven remains stone-faced and silent. Her long silky dark hair is pulled back into a ponytail. Raven has never associated with her coworkers. She has the reputation of being the stuck-up younger girl in the children's section.

Raven's philosophy: she was not there to make friends; rather, just to work for a paycheck, so she could shop to keep up her badass-chick image. She loves fashion, but her parents believe in giving their children the bare necessities in life. She has to make her own way. Her mother told her plenty of times, "If you want a pair of two hundred dollar jeans, then baby, you're going to have to work for them. Your father and I aren't spending that kind of money on jeans, sweetheart."

Her mother Maria Hightower's pearly white tooth bearing smile pops into her head. Because of her parents' reluctance to buy her designer clothing, Raven cannot bring herself to fucking drug dealers for money, even though Takia and Mya make it seem so sweet and easy. They always have the hottest gear before her and, most importantly, she just could not bring herself to cheat on her boyfriend of four years, Jamal, aka Mally.

Raven shares a special bond with him. They know each other like brother and sister. They can chill like homies and talk about anything, then fuck like crazy all night. He sells a little weed and works in his uncle's garage repairing cars. He is definitely not a full-blown street hustler, but he gives Raven as much as he can, even though sometimes it just is not enough. Raven does not mind working. She has had a job since fourteen, being a day-camp counselor, tutoring kids with special needs, a cashier at the Gap, shampooing at a hair salon, and a salesgirl at City Blue for a week. Whatever she had to do to make a dollar. The only place that she would not stoop to working was McDonald's or any other fast-food restaurant. She has to maintain some form of self-respect.

Once Raven turned in her drawer, and every penny was accounted for, she signed the payroll and was handed the white envelope containing what she worked fifty-six long hours for; her paycheck. Her body oozes with excitement. She turns in her blue and red Marshalls mock, just happy to be free. She happily puts on her blue denim Armani Exchange denim jacket, looking herself over in the women's bathroom mirror.

"Girl, you look like shit," she sighs, trying to straighten out her wrinkled blue Armani Exchange t-shirt. She takes the ponytail holder out of her hair, letting her silky dark trusses hang loosely around her shoulders. She glosses her lips with cherry-flavored MAC lip gloss.

"Let me look at this damn check. I have plans for this money," Raven says while puckering her glossed lips in the mirror's reflection. She digs into the back pocket of her skin-tight dark denim jeans, pulling out the folded white envelope and rips it open. Amount: Four hundred eighty-five dollars and sixty-five cents in bold black letters on her Mellon Bank-drawn check. Raven sighs and closes her eyes. Damn, all those overtime hours add up to shit. This ain't gettin' it," she sighs softly while walking out of the ladies room.

All of the store's employees are leaving, heading home or somewhere else. Raven stands alone in the parking lot. The cool September night air feels good against her bare face. Her hair blows gently in the wind. *Mally, you'd better hurry up. I'm not in the mood for this shit,* she thinks while watching cars leave the complex. The last few stores turn off their lights and pull down their gates. Raven stands stone-faced, arms crossed, waiting patiently. Twenty-five minutes pass before she hears the booming system and squeaky brakes of Mally's green 1989 Ford Taurus wagon. He pulls right in front of Marshalls, blasting *'Bout It 'Bout It* by Master P. She gets in and slams the door with a major attitude. Mally knows instantly that something is wrong. He turns down the stereo.

"What's up, baby? How was work?" Mally asks, flashing his light honey-brown colored eyes. Mally is handsome, not exactly a pretty boy, but is considered fine by many girls. His soft black wavy hair is always shaped up freshly. He has a stocky football player build. His smooth light caramel-brown skin and light-colored eyes make him very appealing to females. But he does not see other girls. Raven is his entire world, even if she breaks his pockets every chance that she gets. Raven sits screw-faced, ignoring him, her head against the car window. Mally drives down a packed City Line Avenue.

"Babe, what's wrong?"

"Nothing's wrong, Jamal." The alarm has rung. Whenever Raven has an attitude, she calls him Jamal.

"Come on, baby, what's the deal?" he asks, turning to her.

"I'm pouting because I wanted to go shopping this weekend, but with this little bullshit money I made, I'm not going to be able to buy much."

Mally does not open his mouth to say a word. Silence passes between them for the next five minutes. Raven stares out the window at the bright car lights passing them on the road.

"Yo, I should have a hundred dollars for you on Friday." His offer has the air of desperation, as this is not even money that he has yet made.

Raven sucks her teeth, thinking irritated, *What the fuck is a hundred dollars going to do?*

"Yo, I don't see why you keep breaking your neck to buy that high-priced shit."

"Because that's what I like to wear, Jamal," she snaps.

"No, that's what your stuck-up girlfriends like."

"No, my friends aren't stuck up, we just like the best. What's the problem with that?"

"Look, look, Raven, all I'm saying is that you don't need all that brand-name designer stuff to make you feel like you're a decent person. Mya's people got a couple dollars. She's spoiled as shit. And Takia is one of the biggest whores in West Philly," Mally hisses, turning roughly on 60th and Columbia.

"Yo, stop disrespectin' my friends. I told you about that shit before."

Mally pulls in front of Raven's parents' white and tan row house. "Why you always takin' up for them, followin' them and shit? Be your own person for once, Raven."

"First off, I don't follow nobody. We've all been best friends since sixth grade. We're more sisters than anything."

"I know, I've heard this shit a million times," his light-brown eyes flash with agitation. "Look, I'm not trying to keep arguing about this same shit." He leans over to Raven's side. Yo, my mom's working late tonight, so let's go to my house, put on the new R. Kelly [CD] and make up," he whispers.

Mally gently licks Raven on her earlobe. The moist wetness of Mally's lips sends a tingle to her private areas. She quickly snaps back to her paycheck disappointment and Mally's chronic lack of funds.

"Naw, I'm not in the mood right now, Jamal."

Mally balls up his face, scanning Raven's blank expression. "So you're mad about those little comments I made about your girlfriends?" he yells.

No, nigga, I just don't feel like fucking you tonight, Raven thinks while wanting to jump out of the car.

"Mally, I'm just not in the mood right now. I think I'm getting cramps and I have a headache."

"Alright then," Mally sighs. "I'll pick you up in the morning."

Raven nonchalantly opens the car door, when Mally grabs her left arm and pulls her close, aggressively sticking his tongue inside her mouth. She at first tries to pull away but is quickly entranced at Mally's deeply sensual French kiss. He stops, gently stroking her long soft hair. He always loves running his fingers through her hair. He stares deeply into her slanted, almost Asian-shaped eyes.

"Baby, I promise that you'll start getting more things from me once I finish automotive school and get my mechanic's license. I swear."

"Aw, Mally, I'm sorry. I don't mean to keep throwing money issues in your face. I love you." She playfully kisses Mally on the lips before sliding out of the car.

"I love you more, baby girl," Mally responds affectionately.

The September night air has turned brisk.

"How you doin' Raven?" Mrs. White, Raven's middle-aged neighbor from across the street, calls out to her, standing on her porch smoking a Newport. Raven searches her book bag for her house keys.

"Hi, Mrs. White! I'm doing fine, just getting in from work."

"That's good, baby. You always working hard, Raven. Keep it up."

"Thanks, Mrs. White, I sure will! See you later," Ravens calls back while turning her house key.

Damn, it's 9:30 p.m. and these little niggas are still at it, Raven thinks, entering her family's cozy living room. Her 14-year-old brother Ricky and his three best friends, Rysheed, Budda and Reese, hop up and down on her mother's black leather sectional couch, yelling at the 49-inch color TV set sitting in a freshly polished wall unit as they beat down on joysticks of Ricky's Super Nintendo video game system. Madden NFL 98 remains their favorite game.

"What's up, Raven?" Rysheed, Budda, and Reese greet her in squeaky adolescent voices. Their horny eyes watch her breasts and ass in her fitted jeans and top.

She walks by the TV and brushes them off quickly.

I'm not feelin' you, little dudes, tonight.

She walks through the spacious dining room filled with family portraits. The long shiny wooden table, a large crystal vase centerpiece with artificial red roses and a stack of unopened mail. She walks into the kitchen, where her parents are watching *Nightline.* Her father, Big Ricky, a Septa driver, is still quite attractive for a man in his late-forties. His light olive complexion and slanted eyes that Raven inherited look half dazed at the small kitchen television. He has a nice solid build, wears his head bald, a well-trimmed salt-and-pepper goatee the only indication of his age. Her mother, Maria Hightower, sits silently, her pretty almond-shaped eyes glued to *Nightline*'s report on the nation's crisis on credit card fraud. Maria, a highly educated sixth-grade English teacher, with a master's and soon-to-be doctorate under her impressive belt. She has the same dark mocha skin complexion as her youngest daughter. Her dark shoulder-length hair is pulled back in a tight bun. Maria, the daughter of Black and Dominican parents, is strikingly beautiful at age forty. She still possesses a quiet youthfulness. After giving birth to three children, her figure is still intact underneath the gray knee-length sweater dress that she wears.

"Hey mom, hey dad," Raven says cheerfully, bending down to kiss her father on his cheek.

"Hey baby," Big Ricky says embracing his daughter.

"Hey, Rave, how was school today?" Maria chimes in.

"Same old. New roster, new homeroom. I have advanced Spanish, biology and advanced calculus."

"Good, baby," Maria says sipping a lukewarm coffee.

"Well you know, Kelly had advanced calculus in the eleventh grade," Big Ricky says eating a piece of pound cake.

Here we go with the Kelly does everything better than Raven routine. She is Raven's older sister by twelve months and eleven days. Kelly is Mr. and Mrs. Hightower's pride and joy. The perfect daughter. Perfect student. She even picks perfect boyfriends. Whatever Raven excels in, Kelly has already done twenty times better. If Raven gets an A on a test, Kelly had gotten an A plus. The Hightowers have compared their daughters since they were toddlers and this resulted in a stiffly competitive nature between the sisters that carries through to this day. Since Kelly graduated from Girls High School with a 4.0 GPA and then accepted to the University of Pennsylvania with damn-near a full scholarship. The pressure is on Raven to do as good or even better. Her parents never approved of her going to Overbrook, the ghetto neighborhood high school. She had other choices, having been accepted to Central, FLC, and her sister's precious Girls High, but fought hard to attend Overbrook to stay close to her best friends, easily being accepted into their scholars' magnet program. She could not imagine her high school years without Mya and Takia. They define who she is to a large extent.

"I'm getting ready to go to bed. Budda and them are about to get their loud asses outta my house," Mr. Hightower says while standing up from the kitchen table. "You coming up, dear?" he affectionately asks his wife.

"I'll be up in a little while, honey," Maria says, looking up at her handsome husband, both clearly still very much in love after twenty-two years of marriage.

Raven has always admired her parents' relationship and hopes to be as lucky in a long marriage.

"Okay, guys, y'all ain't got to go home, buy y'all get your asses outta here," Mr. Hightower says loudly, walking into his living room filled with teenage boys.

"Aw Mr. Hightower, just twenty more minutes. We almost done. Come on, dad," Little Ricky pleads.

"No, that's it. You guys have been sittin' in here playing these damn video games all day. Good night fellas."

Maria scans her daughter's face, which is like looking into a mirror. The only distinctive difference between their features is Raven's Asian-slanted eyes that she took after her father instead of her mother's almond-shaped ones. She knows her child well enough to know when something is wrong.

"Raven, what's wrong, baby?"

Raven pouts like an aggravated child. "I was trying to go shopping this weekend, mom. My paycheck was garbage. You think you can give me some money?"

"Raven, didn't your father and I just give you back-to-school shopping money?"

"Yeah, but four hundred dollars until spring ain't nothing, mom. It barely bought two bags of clothes," Raven huffs.

"Well, baby, if you spend money sensibly instead of buying two hundred dollar pants and shoes, you'd have more to show, darling. Kelly has always been able to manage money so well."

"Mom, Kelly and I have totally different tastes." *Well, why does Kelly have to be brought into every conversation concerning me?* Raven thinks, biting the inside of her mouth.

"I know you two have different tastes. I birthed both of you, didn't I?"

"Yes, mom," Raven says rolling her eyes.

"Baby, the bottom line is that you like to buy expensive things. That's your choice. We let you have a job for you to make your own money, as long as you keep your grades up. Your father and I work hard to maintain a comfortable lifestyle for you, your brother and sister. And before I give you three hundred dollars for jeans, you should think about the prices of books and dorm fees for your first semester next year. Now that's money worth spending. Your education will last you when the clothes on your back are old and faded."

Mrs. Hightower is always giving Raven long intellectual empowerment speeches.

"Mom, you're right," Raven admits.

"You need to open up a bank account and start saving some money. The real world is right around the corner, baby." Mrs. Hightower stands from the table. "And with you and Kelly both in college at the same time, thank God your father, and I have been saving for both of your education. And Little Ricky is going to zoom through high school before you know it. That's where we choose to put our money."

She gently strokes Raven's hair. "Baby, don't stay up too late. Summer's over, and you know how you hate getting up early in the morning."

"I'm goin' to bed soon, mom."

"Alright, goodnight."

Maria picks up her tan Coach pocketbook and heads through the dark living room and up the stairs.

Raven ponders her mother's words over a bowl of Breyers Cookies & Cream. "11:30 p.m.," Raven says, looking at the time flashing on the microwave on the clean kitchen counter. She washes out her bowl and cuts off the kitchen light. The living-room television is left on. Raven smiles looking at her little brother spread out on the butter-soft leather sectional. He is becoming more handsome every day, with their father's olive complexion and a full head of soft curly black hair. Soft freckles adorn his face. The girls in his eighth-grade class and cute girls from around the neighborhood have big crushes on him.

My little brother is a dime piece for real. Raven cuts the television off and sluggishly climbs the stairs to her small middle bedroom. She does not bother to turn her light on, stripping out of her clothes and throwing herself into her soft full-size bed. Wrapping herself in the soft cotton blanket comforts her tense body. "Things gotta get better. Tomorrow, I need a come up," she whispers before drifting to sleep.

Clang. Clang. Clang. Raven's alarm clock sounds off loudly. "Ohh," she moans, rolling out of her sleep. She reaches over to her small nightstand with her eyes closed and shuts off her alarm clock. 7:30 a.m., the clock blinks in insistent red color. She wipes the cold from her eyes and sits up, the sun seeping into her bedroom through pale blue mini blinds. Raven throws herself back into her fluffy pillows.

Bitch, wake up, she tells herself. After five minutes of tossing and turning, she gets her day started. She drags herself to the bathroom and starts a hot steam shower. The hot water hitting her body at rapid speed wakes her up immediately. She brushes her teeth, blow dries her hair, rubbing her body down with cocoa butter skin lotion. After ten more minutes of wrestling with what outfit to wear, she settles on a hot-pink Isaac Mizrahi logo sweatshirt, a pair of Mizrahi jeans and her favorite black-and-white Joan & David sneakers. She brushes her hair loosely around her shoulders, topping her outfit off with a Chanel double-C necklace that she spent a whole paycheck on. She looks herself over in her dresser mirror, pleased with her look and very excited because Mya and Takia had never seen this outfit before. She found her entire outfit at a bargain price at Loehmann's Department Store in Media. Raven is the world's best bargain shopper. She has a knack for finding top-of-the-line designer brands for cheap. She even switches a few price tags here and there. She might not have Mya's money or Takia's line of balling drug dealers, but she keeps up with her friends just fine. She has such a knack for making nothing look like something. Mya and Takia never know exactly what Raven spends on her clothes. They just assume her clothes are as pricey as theirs.

SALEEM ROBERTS

"Shit, 8:27a.m., Mally's gonna be here any minute." Raven grabs her clear patent-leather Bebe book bag and runs down the stairs. The house is empty and still. Mr. Hightower starts his Septa shift at 6:30 a.m. and Mrs. Hightower and little Ricky leave at 7:15 a.m. every morning. Raven does not have to be at Overbrook until 8:45 a.m. as a senior. She gruffs down a bacon egg and cheese Hot Pocket and a glass of Tropicana orange juice before Mally beeps his horn like a madman outside.

"Damn, nigga, here I come!" She leaves the front door, locking it behind her. It is a nice, sunny September morning. Mally looks sexy to Raven as she gets in the Taurus wagon. Was it the goatee he is growing or the fresh Polo button-up shirt he has on? He begins to drive, face forward, without acknowledging Raven's presence. His handsome face is tense.

"Mally, you mad at me about last night?"

He continues driving up Lansdowne Avenue, remaining silent.

"You don't hear me talkin' to you?" Raven asks playfully, tickling him on his right side. He lets out a light laugh, pushing her hand away.

"Yo, stop touching me."

"Are you mad I didn't come to your house last night?"

He throws Raven a sarcastic glance. "That was the icing on the cake of the shit I've been mad about with you lately. Yo, all we do is argue over money, and it's gettin' on my nerves for real."

"I know I've been stressin' you out lately, baby. I appreciate everything you do for me. You're my best friend, for real."

"Whatever. I thought Mya and Takia were your best friends."

"Baby, it's two completely different things. You're my special best friend. The things we do I could never do with them." She leans in closer to Mally, sticking her tongue out and begins kissing his neck while her left-hand slips to his dick, tightly pressed against his Guess jeans. She begins to rub in a circular motion. He is instantly rock hard. The tint on his car windows comes in very handy.

"Girl, you better stop before you start something you can't finish this morning," Mally says in a deep groan as he pulls in front of Overbrook High School.

"There goes Takia and Mya," Raven squeals, diverting her attention from Mally to the image of her friends in front of the school through the tinted windows.

"Fuckin' figures," Mally hisses with a frown.

"Don't worry, I'll take good care of you later." She wets her lips, pulling Mally close. Their lips lock in a deep French kiss as he runs his fingers through her silky hair. "That's enough for now," Raven teases as she opens the side door.

"Have a good day, Boo," Mally says wiping the saliva from his mouth.

"I'll have a special treat for you later."

"Aight"

She closes the passenger door and watches him speed off, blasting *Firm Biz* by The Firm. She watches him turn the corner before walking over to join Mya and Takia. A group of junior girls whisper and comment on Raven's outfit as she passes by.

"Hey girlfriends!" she shouts in an exaggerated high-pitched ghetto-girl voice. Raven, Mya and Takia squeal in delight, those two happy with their sister's arrival.

"I see y'all bitches getting' started early in the morning," Raven chuckles, pointing to the large white

Styrofoam platters Takia and Mya have in their hands from Ace's Diner.

"Girl, I was hungry as shit," Takia giggles, smacking her lips.

"Bitch, you're always hungry," Mya chimes. "Rav... Why you didn't call my cell phone this morning? I woulda ordered you a platter," she continues, taking a sip of a small apple juice.

"I ain't feel like talkin' to nobody. Me and Mally was goin' through it last night."

"Over what?" Mya and Takia say together, moving closer to Raven with overwhelming interest.

Raven chokes up a bit. She hates putting her friends between her relationship business with Mally. He does not care for them and he damn sure was not on Takia's and Mya's favorite list. "We started arguing over him giving me a couple dollars."

"See? That's bullshit, Raven. That nigga should be passin' off," Takia snaps.

"Yeah, Rav, you can do so much better. You're such a pretty girl. Guys with money are always askin' about you," Mya adds.

Damn, why I get these bitches started, Raven thinks while observing Mya's and Takia's wardrobe.

Mya is top-notch as always in brown-fitted Fendi logo printed pants and a light-brown Fendi top with the double Fs in the corner of the t-shirt, her soft hair slick in a ponytail with giant black-and-white Fendi shades resting atop her head. These are the same ones that Mary J. Blige wore on her *Share My World* album cover. Mya is the poster child of ghetto-fabulous, and Takia is the glorified hustler's chick in a fitted multicolor Versace mini dress, with Versace written all over it in red, blue and green cursive, and pointy-toed black Via Spiga knee boots and a big red-leather Prada bag. Her honey-blonde wave is freshly layered in soft curls. Raven immediately feels underdressed and corny, not to the rest of the world, but to her two over-the-top "friends." In her mind, she remains the underdog.

"Rav, I'm diggin' the Isaac Mizrahi," Takia says, walking with the thick urban teenage student body into Overbrook.

"Yeah, bitches don't even be hip to Mizrahi, and I'm still in love with your Joan & David sneakers, Rav," Mya says as they enter the graffiti-plastered doors.

"I swear they say shit out of pity sometimes," Raven thinks, passing through the large blue metal detectors. School is loud and rowdy as usual. Raven seems to float through Mrs. Ashcroft's first period. Raven is present physically, but mentally she is not. The next two periods are a dream. Even the 'hood circus called *lunch* moves in slow motion. Mya and Takia carry on about the latest 'hood gossip, but it is as if she heard not a word they said. The only thing on her mind is her relationship with Mally. She loves him dearly but seeing how easy life is for her girlfriends continues to tempt her to mess with fast-money niggas. By the time the last-period bell rings, Raven becomes ecstatic. She has enough advanced Spanish, biology, and calculus homework to keep her busy for the next few days. The school let out does not have its usual excitement. After fifteen minutes of standing around, Carmello Black picks Mya up in his shiny black Benz. He nods, speaking to Raven and Takia who remain together.

Takia waits for Little Rell from South Philly, a cute tan-skinned boah with a thin build and sexy lips. He is twenty and getting a lot of money in his 'hood. That is all that Takia needs to know, like a spider drawn to prey. He drives a white Mercedes E-class wagon. Takia brags to Raven how big Rell's dick gets.

I don't care about this skinny nigga's dick, Raven thinks while she listens to Takia's testimony about how cute Rell is; if she did not know any better, she almost feels that Takia is after more than just Rell's money. Once he shows up, Takia offers Raven a ride home, but she is a girl on a mission, a top-secret shopping mission. She takes the three-hour ride to Franklin Mills Outlet Mall, sure to find a bargain in the Saks Fifth Avenue OFF 5th and Neiman Marcus Last Call outlet stores for the small amount of money she has to work with as the El train runs smoothly through Center city Philadelphia toward the Greater Northeast. She daydreams out the window as the train stops at Bridge and Pratt, the end of the line, where Raven has to take another bus to Franklin Mills. With four hundred eighty-five dollars, Raven is well prepared to spend hours ravishing through racks of marked-down designer clothes for the perfect finds.

After the hour-long ride on the forty-three bus, "Last stop, Franklin Mills," the driver announces. Raven stretches, awakening from the long nap that she enjoyed. The multicultural crowd files off of the bus. Franklin Mills is a giant jack-in-the-box mall with over three hundred outlet stores like Nordstrom, Guess, Spiegel, Gap and Old Navy, and her personal favorites, Saks Fifth Avenue OFF 5th and Neiman Marcus Last Call. The mall bulges with people in a rush, carrying colorful plastic bags from various stores. After a brief walk, she finds her first destination: Saks Fifth Avenue OFF 5th outlet store, where the all-powerful department-store chain sends its last-season leftovers at a much-reduced price. Her blood rushes as she starts hunting through the racks of high-end leftovers. Well-dressed white and Asian women tear through the racks alongside ghetto-fabulous drug dealer baby-mom-type chicks, all looking for low-priced couture. Raven's eyes scan the newest racks. She comes across a few finds. Her slanted eyes narrow at the sight of a fuchsia-pink Iceberg cardigan with Daisy Duck embroidered on its back and Iceberg written in the left corner. She grabs the price tag. Ninety-five dollars. *Shit.* Raven looks the sweater over once more before deciding that it is definitely an investment. After twenty minutes of searching, Raven finds an Escada name belt enclosed in tan patent leather with Escada spelled out in big gold letters. Seventy-five dollars. *Not bad, all.* "This one is also a keeper," she whispers, before moving on to a rack of slacks, where she finds a cute pair of marked-down Armani finely tailored pants, one hundred dollars. *The only reason that I'm getting these are because the metal Armani sign is smack-dab visible on the butt. Now onto shoes.*

Raven scans the racks of size 8½ shoes. Three young blonde white girls, well-dressed, maybe a few years older than Raven, are mauling through the shoeboxes like typical madwomen. Raven spots a pair of black leather ankle boots with a pointy stiletto heel, made by Adrienne Vittadini. Raven fears to look at the price. One hundred seventy dollars. *I'm about to be broke,* she thinks while walking around the store in her boots, loving the fit and style. "But I have to have them," she says aloud, admiring them in the mirror, she lets out a sigh, realizing that this will consume the rest of her money. She makes her way to the registers.

"Ma'am, your total is four hundred sixty-five dollars."

Damn, that's my whole paycheck. Raven is clearly brokenhearted emptying the crisp twenties and fifties from her wallet, reluctantly handing the money to the quirky Asian saleswoman, who hands her two shiny black plastic shopping bags. After twenty more minutes of window-shopping, Raven buys two logo Bebe t-shirts at fifty percent off and eats some Taco Bell in the food court. Her pockets are drained. She starts the long bus ride home, dead tired when she finally arrives home. She sits her shopping bags on the living-room floor. The house is pretty quiet, the living-room television off, with only a dimly lit wall-unit lamp. Raven nonchalantly walks in the dining room toward the kitchen, hearing her parents' voices uncontrollably laughing. Raven hears a familiar husky female voice that she knows all too well. She stops in mid-motion. Her older sister Kelly's voice, who always has to be the center of attention. Kelly, who would twist any situation that Raven was accomplishing. A goal of her own selfish benefit. The two had never been close, completely opposite in every aspect of life. Their whole relationship is based on one beating the other at any and everything. Raven steps into the kitchen. She and Kelly's eyes meet.

Raven sees taunting in Kelly's eyes and knows that competition is still in the air.

"Hey, little sister," Kelly addresses her sister in her deep voice, flashing a pretty smile on her light, coffee-brown-skinned face. She is a mixture of both her parents' skin complexions: Maria's dark-rich mocha and their father's light olive. She possesses long, soft curly hair like Raven's and their mother's bright almond-shaped eyes. *She is surely a beautiful snake*, Raven thinks watching Kelly sitting bright and perky in a red-and-blue preppy U of Penn sweatshirt.

"Hey Kelly," Raven greets her sister, with a fake smile on her face. "Hey mom, hey dad," Raven kisses her parents on their cheeks as usual.

"Hey baby," her parents cheerfully respond, still giggling from whatever funny joke that Kelly had told.

She always has such a knack for making their parents laugh.

"Where's Little Ricky?" Raven randomly asks her parents.

"He's over at Budda's house playin' that damn video game. For once, we have some peace and quiet around here. Kelly has driven from campus to have dinner with us," Mr. Hightower says affectionately, beaming at his older daughter.

Oh, like I could forget about the brand-new car that you guys cosigned for Miss Perfect after she graduated from high school last year. Raven's mind races as she sits down at one of the kitchen table chairs.

"There's some fried chicken and mashed potatoes in the oven."

"Mom, I'm not hungry. I ate at the mall."

"So how's school, Raven?" Kelly asks inquisitively.

"Well, it's only the sixth day of the school year. Calculus and biology are cool. Advanced Spanish is boring."

"I'm surprised that Overbrook offers advanced anything," Kelly observes smugly.

No, this bitch didn't! "Overbrook's magnet programs are some of the best in the city. How's UPenn, Kelly?"

"Wonderful. I'm so happy. I'm passing every exam. All of my grades have been A, and I can't wait to pledge a sorority next year."

"Raven, have you narrowed down where you're going to apply for college?" Mr. Hightower asks while sipping a cup of hot coffee."

Dad, don't put me on the spot like this in front of Kelly. 'I've done a lot of thinking. It's between Temple, Hampton and the University of Maryland Eastern Shore. They all have really great psychology programs," Raven answers with a proud smile.

55

"Raven, Hampton is getting really ghetto, and Temple has been losing prestige for years. Why don't you apply to UPenn? *If* you can get in." Kelly smiles sarcastically, throwing salt in the game.

"Yeah, baby, maybe you should apply to UPenn," her father chimes in, staring at Raven. *Here we go again. Alright, dad, I'll apply there.*

"Isaac Mizrahi," Kelly strains to announce the high-end designer printed across Raven's chest. "Isn't that one of those designers those ghetto rappers are always shouting out on their records?" she asks with an air of superiority. "I can't stand those ghetto rappers. I'm into *No Doubt*, Alanis Morissette, and Fiona Apple. That's *real* music."

"It's pronounced Isaac Mizrahi, and he's a top American couture designer."

"That top probably costs one hundred dollars or more," Kelly responds, looking from one parent to the other.

"Well Raven's always been into that name-brand stuff," Mrs. Hightower observes, facing Kelly. "She's always had a job to support the way she shops, and has maintained her grades," she concludes, defending her younger daughter.

"I just don't understand how spending one hundred dollars or more on a piece of clothing is sensible," Kelly continues, raising an arched eyebrow Raven's way.

"I feel what I do with my money is my business. It's not my fault. I take pride in my appearance, instead of walking around looking like an unkempt, non fashion-coordinated mess all the time." Raven speaks with aggression, looking directly at Kelly.

"I guess that spending your last on clothes is what makes you proud. That's such a ghetto way of thinking. Just my opinion."

"Look, I have homework to do." Raven rolls her eyes, rising from the table, heading out from the kitchen. "Every time she comes here, she has to start some shit with me," Raven hisses while grabbing her shopping bags, walking up the hardwood staircase. She enters her bedroom, wearily tossing her bags on the floor of her overcrowded closet, then pouncing down on her soft bed, when her Panasonic cordless phone starts ringing. Raven had her own phone line since she was fourteen and maintains the monthly cost on her own.

"Hello?"

"Rav!" Mya and Takia say in unison, bursting into girlish laughter.

"Wassup, y'all?" Raven answers in a sad, whiny voice.

"Raven, what's wrong? Today in school you seemed depressed," Mya asks out of concern.

"You did seem upset," Takia adds.

"I was just tired from work and arguing with Mally. That's all."

"Oh," Mya and Takia both suck their teeth. That was the exact cue they needed to express their feelings about Raven and Mally's relationship.

So Raven quickly changes the subject. "I already wasn't in the mood for some bullshit. I come home, and Kelly's in here with my peoples nitpicking with me. I swear I be ready to beat her ass."

"Rav, why Kelly always be drawling on you? She's so jealous, Mya snaps. "Kelly just needs some good dick," Takia says as they burst into loud laughter.

Raven stretches out on her bed. "I'm not worried about that girl at all y'all. She's a Scorpio. They're vindictive."

"Anyway, onto some better shit. Guess where we're going on Sunday?"

"Where?" Raven asks excitedly, a broad smile finally breaking from her saddened expression.

"Club Gotham Teen Night," Mya yells.

"For real, we goin'?"

"Yes, bitch, and my mom is giving me the keys to the Benz."

"We gonna shit on everybody," Takia answers, with a mouthful of food loudly chewing.

Club Gotham is the exclusive playground of Philly's ghetto-fabulous. Moët & Cristal flows. Biggie Smalls, Lil' Kim, Foxy Brown and Jay-Z all have performed shows there. The biggest ballers and baddest bitches twenty-one and older all come to party. But every Sunday is teen night. You have to be sixteen to nineteen to enter. The most fly teens from high schools around the city throw on their hottest gear and descend upon the club to get a small glimpse of the fast life, their older brothers, sisters, and cousins live.

"Yo, we have to be stuntin' hard," Raven squeals.

"Girl, you know we have to do it like we're doin' it for TV," Takia giggles.

All three girls burst into boisterous laughter.

"Yo, I gotta get this biology and calculus homework done. I'll holla at y'all tomorrow."

Raven pulls her big textbooks from her book bag.

"Damn, I forgot about that calculus homework, and I'm goin' to the movies with Carmello tonight, Mya expresses. "Rav, I'll scan your paper tomorrow in homeroom, aight?"

Raven hangs up her cordless phone, opening her biology textbook to chapter four.

Club Night: Sunday, September 20, 1997

I guess this looks aight, Raven observes her chosen outfit of the night, her favorite, most-valued pair of black stretch Versace jeans, pale pink ostrich-skin cowgirl boots, and a black tube top underneath a pale pink leather jacket. Her smooth, dark complexion is shiny from cocoa butter, her long hair pulled into a ponytail. She has light-smoke eyeshadow and with the scent of Versace Blue Jeans clinging to her body. She feels as ready for tonight as she can be.

"Raven, your friends are outside beeping the horn for you," Mr. Hightower yells up the stairs.

She grabs her black-and-white Moschino clutch, makes sure her house keys and three crisp twenty dollar bills are inside that she practically had to beg Mally for.

"Bye dad, bye little brother," Raven calls in a rush to her father and brother occupying the couch watching a Sixers versus LA Lakers game.

She closes the front door behind her. Her heart pumps fast at the sight of Mya's mother's new Mercedes E-Class in the middle of the street. *Queen Bitch* by Lil' Kim plays loudly. Young boahs from the corner walk down the block to get a closer look. Raven climbs into the back seat, sinking into the soft butter leather.

"Wassup, bitch?" Mya asks over the loud stereo system while hitting the gas speeding off like *Speed Racer.*

"Is y'all ready for Club Gotham?" Raven replies, fixing her ponytail.

Mya turns down the car stereo as Raven notices the iced out black mother of pearl dial Rolex hanging on her small wrist.

Should I compliment now or later? I'll wait, Raven thinks, noticing Takia wearing a platinum-blonde Lil' Kim-style wig. It's long and straight, looking striking against her caramel skin. Raven cannot figure out if she approves of the color or not.

"We gonna have a good-ass time, y'all. I still can't believe your mean-ass mom came up off the Benz keys," Takia says, applying lip gloss in the front passenger-side rearview mirror.

"I know, Mya, how'd you do it?" Raven chimes in.

Mya sucks her teeth, entering the crowded Schuylkill Expressway.

"Why? I'm daddy's little girl," Mya responds in an overly dramatic squeaky voice. "I told my dad some sob-ass story and threw a bitch-fit. You know, he can't stand to see me cry. He always eats it up like candy. He asked what would make me happy, and I said to borrow mom's car to hang out with my friends." She bats the most innocent eyes as if there were anything innocent left about Mya Campbell. "He got in my mom's ass, so she passed over the car keys. And here we are." A conniving smile crossed her lovely face.

They gossip about all of the latest drama in school. When they pull up in front of Club Gotham, it is packed, with the line winding around the corner. Fly cars are double parked and constantly circling the block. Mya pulls into the parking lot. Guys peer into the car trying to get a better look at the chicks inside the white E-Class.

"Oh, he's cute as shit," Takia hollers with a child's delight at a thick-built brown-skinned boy in a royal blue and orange Coogi sweater. After a hectic search, they come across a parking spot. Once they exit the car, they all look each other over approvingly. Takia is a sight for sore eyes in her blonde wig, pink Coogi halter-top, matching miniskirt, and dark blue Dolce & Gabbana pumps. She looks like an extra from Lil' Kim's *Crush on You* music video. Mya wears her Moschino Cloud set, tight light-blue Moschino pants with white clouds covering them and the matching sheer top with a white Victoria's Secret strapless bra and a new quilted white Chanel bag, with her Rolex shining. She is dressed without even trying very hard, as usual.

Takia and Mya make a big fuss over what Raven considers a simple outfit compared to theirs. There are two lines, one for girls and one for guys. The opposite sexes check each other out heading through large black steel doors. The girls are searched by two large female security guards. They open their handbags and even search their hair, looking for mace, razor blades, and other weapons. They enter the dimly lit club. The huge dance floor is packed. Bodies move to the late Notorious B.I.G.'s hit *Nasty Boy*. The log bar area is filled with people posted up in their finest Sunday couture, sipping on ginger ale and Pepsi in champagne glasses. Because this is teen night, the club does not serve alcohol. As the girls make their way through the crowd, they catch the hard stares from guys from North and South Philly, who readily drool at the sight of these three fly pretty young things that they have never seen before.

Other girls peep that their gear is official and begin throwing hateful glances, whispering, "They them chicks from Overbrook that niggas is always sayin' is fly as shit."

Raven is somewhat nervous from being the center of attention. They find an empty corner by the bar and set up shop. Young niggas start hollering in abundance. The other girls trying to be cute dancing around the bar area filled with rage at the male population's attention on the three baddest chicks. Raven, Mya and Takia brim with confidence and conceit. When *Get Money* by Junior Mafia spins by the DJ, Takia and Mya throw their hands in the air and begin moving their bodies to the strong bass line, rapping each lyric along with Biggie and Lil' Kim. Raven rocks to the music, laughing at her girlfriend's hyper energy when a tall, light-skinned boy with curly hair, wearing a black-and-white Iceberg t-shirt and jeans grabs her hand. She stares in his face. *He is sexy and has nice hair and lips,* Raven eagerly thinks as he starts dancing close, grinding against her.

"Yo, what's your name, shorty?" he asks over the blaring music, pressing his soft lips against her ear.

"Raven."

"I'm Nadir, and I'm checkin' for you."

Raven releases a faint giggle.

"You got a man?" Nadir asks, eyeing her from head to toe.

Damn, this nigga's turning me on. She struggles to keep her composure.

"Yep, a good one at that."

"Oh, word?" Nadir answers with a sexy smirk. "You got pretty hands." He lifts Raven's delicate hands in his strong grip.

"Your man needs to put some diamonds on your hand."

Before Raven could think of a comeback, she glances down at Nadir's wrist and is blinded by the diamond face of his Rolex and huge pinkie ring. The rock is huge!

"Yo Nadir, come on," one of his homies hollers at him.

"Aight, hold up," he nods. He reaches into his back pocket, pulling out a black cell phone. "Yo, what's your number?"

"I don't give my number out. I told you, I have a boyfriend."

"Nadir gives Raven one last pretty-boy smile, licks his lips in a sexually suggestive manner.

"Aight then," he pulls a pen out of his jeans pocket, grabs a napkin from the bar and jots down his number. "Hit me when you want some baguettes on those soft hands. He purposefully places the napkin in Raven's hand before disappearing into the thick crowd.

"Yo Rav, who was that? That nigga is a dime, Takia says dancing up to Raven. "Where's he from?" Before Raven can answer, a thick-built dark-skinned guy in a white and black Moschino t-shirt and Yankees fitted hat starts rubbing on Takia's ass.

Takia is about to snap on him, when she realizes that it is Tyree from North Philly, one of Takia's long list of get-money niggas. Tyree starts whispering in her ear while his hand slips down to her ass. Raven looks for Mya, who has been in deep conversation with a tall, dark-skinned basketball-player-type build, wearing a dark-green Polo Sport sweatsuit. So Raven chills as the DJ begins spinning *Put Your Hands Where My Eyes Could See* by Busta Rhymes. The clubs lets out at 1 a.m. The parking lot is packed. Everyone posts up on the sidewalk next to their cars.

"I had mad fun, tonight, y'all," Mya says, walking beside Takia and Raven arm in arm, pulling away from guys trying to holler.

"Yea, it was definitely poppin'. I can't wait until we're twenty-one and go to clubs every night of the week," Raven interjects.

The cool September air nips at the back of their necks.

"Me, either, but yo, why was Tyree tryin' to get me to roll out with him?"

"For real?" Mya asks inquisitively, adjusting her stunning diamond-encrusted Rolex. "Niggas think because they spend a couple dollars, they horny asses

63

entitled to pussy whenever they want it. Naw, homie, it don't work like that," Takia snorts.

"I told you them nut-ass bitches was in there," a high-pitched female voice yells out. Raven turns her head to see Kareema, Asia and Amira standing with two other short brown-skinned girls who she has never seen before. They are walking fast up to them. Raven knows by their body language that it is about to go down. Raven's heartbeat quickens. Whatever is about to happen, she knows that she has to stick with her girls. Bitches talk real tough during school hours. This time, Kareema's deeply raspy voice rings out clearly. Raven, Takia, and Mya stop and stand their ground, facing off with the group of vicious bitches. They look like a devious bum-bitch army.

"Aw, hell naw. Y'all bitches know better than to play tough out here," Takia screams, a look of savagery in her pretty brown eyes. When it comes to tussling with girls, Takia definitely has heart and is respected for knocking chicks out. Raven stands silently, watching everything play out. A big crowd begins to gather around, waiting for something to jump off. Mya slowly pulls the Chanel sunglasses off of her face and slides them in her pocketbook. The one gesture let Raven know silently that there would be no running tonight.

"Yo, yo fuck all this arguing shit. Kareema, steal that bitch," the short, dark-skinned girl whom Raven has never before seen, yells out.

Raven also notices that Kareema and her squad are wearing sneakers and sweatpants, their hair pulled back.

Was this shit planned? These hoes came ready to fight, Raven thinks, nonchalantly taking out her earrings.

"Kareema, hit this bitch now," TeTe growls, edging her girlfriend on. Kareema clinches her fist, charging at Mya like a carjacker fleeing the law.

Mya drops her Chanel pocketbook, throwing her hands up. As soon as Kareema gets close, she swings a jab at Mya.

"You nut-ass bitch, you had this ass-whippin' comin' for a long time," Kareema yells, hitting Mya hard in the shoulder.

Mya throws a wild haymaker to Kareema's face. They both collide. The crowd rushes in close to see the two girls pulling each other's hair. Mya and Kareema try equally to kill one another. Then Kareema pushes Mya with all her strength. Mya is quickly knocked off balance and stumbles to the ground. Kareema then punches Mya in the jaw.

"Fuck that bitch up. Get that bitch," Kareema's friends taunt.

Takia can no longer stand by. She runs up to the fight, grabs Kareema by the hair and cold-cocks her in the right eye. Kareema lets out a loud cry and instantly releases her grip on Mya's hair. This action ignites an immediate brawl.

Amira, Asia, and their two unknown recruits rush Takia and Mya like rabies-infested Pit Bulls. As Raven raises her left fist to swing on one of the girls, she feels a hard blow to the back of her head. She elbows whoever is attacking her in the gut. Her tender hair is yanked as if to be pulled out by the roots.

Raven pulsates with rage. She gives her attacker a sharp jab to her stomach and pushes her back. She turns to see TeTe, who punches her dead in the mouth. "You are fuckin' dead, TeTe." Raven goes from zero to a hundred real quick, rushing TeTe with a scorching fire.

She grabs TeTe by her shirt collar with one hand and uppercuts her several times with punishing accuracy.

TeTe becomes scared. She stops swinging and tries in vain to get Raven off of her. Raven digs her hands deep into TeTe's weave, swings her off balance, slamming her body hard into the concrete.

Raven begins stomping her, kicking her repeatedly in the stomach. She hears the crowd screaming, but finds herself altogether out of control.

Amira and the two unknown chicks corner Takia. All of them swing wildly at her. They pull her wig off, but she refuses to back down from any of them. She has one of the short newcomers by the hair with one hand, punching the other two with her free hand. Mya has Kareema and Asia on her, pulling her hair and hitting her in the head. She cannot properly protect herself. Raven has only a split second to decide which friend to help. Takia can hold them off a little longer, but they are getting the best of Mya.

Raven makes her decision, running up on Asia and grabbing her by the back of her shirt with the force of Mike Tyson and drills her in the jaw, then begins yanking all of the glued-in weave tracks from her head. With her free leg, she gives Kareema a brutal face kick, knocking her off of Mya. Blood instantly rushes from her nose.

Mya hops up with feline-like reflexes. Ripped up shirt and hair all over the place, she leaps on top of Kareema with cannibal-like hunger, while Raven and Asia square off.

I'm not waiting for another bitch to swing on me first, Raven thinks, throwing a heavy left-handed punch to Asia's face, choking her with her free right hand.

Raven digs her sharp fingernails into Asia's face so deeply that they literally sink into her flesh. *This bitch can't fight,* Raven observes.

Asia attempts to attack her by swinging her arms in a wild windmill style without coordination. Raven knees her in the stomach, forcing an asthma attack. Asia stops struggling and begins wheezing, falling to her knees, crying and throwing up her arms in defeat.

"I have asthma, stop! I have asthma!" Asia pulls an inhaler from the pocket of the hoodie she wears. Raven knows that Asia wants no more damage. Mya and Kareema go at it like Holyfield and Tyson. Raven quickly pulls off her cowboy boots, now concerned with helping Takia. The crowd had grown louder and larger. Raven runs barefoot, pushing people out of her way to get to Takia. A group of guys from the club break up the fight.

"Get the fuck off me, nigga," Amira hollers as two guys hold her in their strong grasp. Two husky security guard try to force Takia's locked hand from the short brown-skinned girl's head, whom she is fighting. Takia's halter-top is ripped, exposing her large round breasts. Some of the guys gawk as if they had never seen tits before.

"I'm gonna fuck you up, Takia," Amira screams, trying to break out of the guy's grasp. Without hesitation, Raven runs up and starts attacking Amira like a human punching bag.

"Let me go! Let me go," Amira screams, kicking relentlessly in the air.

"Slow down, Tyson," a guy says, grabbing Raven from behind.

"Get the fuck off me!" She struggles against the large arms that hold her.

Raven stomps on his foot, breaking out of the hold. She turns around, ready to take a nigga on too. She looks up to see Nadir's handsome face smiling at her.

"Wow, shorty, I don't want no problems," he chuckles with both hands open wide as if she were the police. The sounds of sirens fill the parking lot, flashing red and blue lights of two Philadelphia police paddy wagons come flying to the center of the parking lot. Everyone starts running, and the fight is officially over for now, but far from finished. Raven and the girls are bloody, scratched up and with hair pulled every which way, but they had stuck together. That remains the most important thing. Mya pushes ninety on the Schuylkill, wiping the scathing scratches on her sensitive and smooth light-skinned face and neck.

Takia sits silently in the passenger seat, stone-faced. "We gonna get them bitches if it kills us."

"Yeah, we gonna stomp them out," Mya hisses with foaming passion behind her hazel eyes. "Raven you were like Wonder Woman tonight. You was comin' at them hatin' ass hoes," Mya laughs.

"You definitely rocked the shit outta Amira," Takia giggles, her mood finally lifting.

"Rave, you represented tonight. I didn't know you had it in you, girl," Mya says, getting off at the Girard Avenue exit.

"Me either. Once TeTe hit me, I just snapped. I was probably imaginin' I was beatin' Kelly's ass." They break into much-needed laughter.

Although their mood had changed, underneath it all, Raven knew that she would have to use her fists again a lot sooner than she knew.

Chapter 3

DIAMOND CLUSTER HUSTLER

Takia Williams, 17 years old, 5' 8"

September 21, 1997

12:30 a.m. flashes across Takia's Sony VCR on the bottom of the forty-six inch box television that Pumpkin bought her last Christmas. Takia's large back room is dark. She lays spread on her stomach atop her comfortable queen-sized bed, underneath a warm satin-and-wool blanket, one shapely caramel thigh hanging out. Takia begins slipping into a deep sleep that is interrupted by the loud sound of her cordless phone on the nightstand next to her bed. She rolls over with her eyes still closed, picking up the receiver.

"Hello," Takia answers, her voice groggy.

"Yo wassup?"

"Who's this?"

"Hakim."

"Who?" Takia asks, clearing her throat.

"I got your number on South Street the other day when you was comin' outta Platinum. I was in the black Lexus jeep, dark-skinned boah, with a Sunnah beard."

Takia sits up on her bed, wiping cold from her eye. "Oh, I remember now."

"So wassup, what you doin'?"

"Nigga, it's almost one o'clock in the morning."

"Damn, girl, you don't play no games. Yo, I'm tryin' to see you tonight."

"Oh, that's what's up. I hope you know I need compensation for my time."

"Shorty, I know you about a couple dollars."

"Alright then, I live at 5527 North Vine Street."

"Alright, I'll be there in a half."

Takia hops out of bed, turning her light on. Takia's bedroom is surprisingly neat and organized. She has two mint-green onyx dressers, a multicolored floor rug, state-of-the-art stereo and television, all paid for by the many street niggas who admired her assets. Takia is a natural-born hustler. She learned at a very early age that life isn't fair and she had to use what God gave her to get ahead.

"Street niggas" is a game Takia has mastered. There isn't a nigga getting money in the city of Philadelphia that Takia did not know or deal with directly. Power and money are what turns her on. If Raven or Mya knew half of the shit that Takia has done in her life for money, they would be totally shocked. She tells her best friends enough, but a girl has to keep some secrets to herself. Takia opens her narrow closet, packed to capacity with her most prized possessions, loads of designer clothes, bags and shoes that she worked very hard to attain. Takia's obsession with expensive clothes is her therapeutic way of dealing with years of being called "the dirty little girl," whose hair was never combed, whose sneakers were always worn and dogged, and whose clothes sometimes smelled like mildew. She was always the girl in elementary and middle school, whose

70

mom had always forgot to pack a lunch or pay for a class trip. As soon as Takia was old enough, older guys started noticing her voluptuous body and pretty face and began eagerly spending money on her. The allure of holding crisp hundred-dollar bills in her hand sends carnivore-like hunger through her. She made a promise to herself by any means necessary that she would never be broke, or that dirty, sad little girl again. Thank God for Raven and Mya, who were all Takia had in those dark, sad days. Mya would give her tons of unworn clothes with tags still attached, and Mr. and Mrs. Hightower treated her as a second daughter, letting her go on family vacations and sending Raven with an extra school lunch just for her. How she so envied her friends' lives back then. They came from amazing, loving families, but today is a new day.

Takia is reborn, creating an image of herself as a fly-sexy, slick-talking bad bitch who knows how to talk to niggas and making them part ways with their cash was a bigger turn-on than sex itself. Takia grabs a fresh bottle of Summer's Eve feminine wash, a bar of Dove soap and a big, fluffy white towel. She only wears a pair of black lace panties. She opens her bedroom door, stepping onto the frosty hardwood floor of the row house that she shares with her dysfunctional alcoholic mother. Michelle, who has been a constant disappointment in Takia's life, putting one abusive boyfriend after another in front of her only daughter. Some of whom would wait until Michelle was knocked out in a drunken stupor, and would creep into Takia's bedroom and fondle her young budding body. And if she dared even to mention it to Michelle, she would be called a lying little bitch and slapped and punched repeatedly. Michelle's drinking made her verbally and physically abusive beyond measure. Takia took the brunt of her mother's rage until she was old and strong enough to fight back. Michelle grew resentful of her daughter's beauty that she inherited from her handsome father that she only knew by the name of Eugene Thomas from one faded picture that she kept in a shoebox under her bed. Takia was his twin. She has his caramel skin, soft jawline, and small button nose. She used to pray at night that he would come and save her, but that dream quickly faded when she lost her virginity at thirteen to one of her older brother's friends. Her naïve innocence was lost entirely.

All that Michelle would tell her of her father was that he was a no-good son of a bitch who ran off and deserted them for another woman and had a whole family that he loved and took care of in Atlanta, Georgia. And how she looked just like him, and that is why Michelle could not stand the sight of her some days.

Her two older brothers, Malik and Amir, had different fathers from Takia, but both adored their little sister. They did as much as they could to take up the slack for their negligent mother. Malik, the oldest, had pressure on him from the day he was born. Michelle gave birth to him at 14 years old. She was a baby with a baby. Michelle and Malik share a special bond. He is the favorite of her three children. They kind of grew up together and would fight almost like brother and sister, not mother and son. That is because grandmother Florence, Michelle's mother, held the family together until her death when Takia was two years old. Malik was eleven and Amir was eight. Michelle was unable to cope with the demands of life. Her mother, a strong, proud and devout Baptist woman who worked in the Office of Deeds and Records at City Hall for forty-five years, had sheltered her and her children by giving them a home, structure and hot meals. This gave

Michelle plenty of free time to party, indulge in drugs and have affairs with many men, never having to fully take on the responsibility of motherhood. After grandmother Florence died of a stroke, Michelle had a complete mental breakdown. In a two-year period, she ran through the large pension and Social Security that her mother had worked so tirelessly for decades to make sure that her only daughter and grandchildren would have something to live on after she left the earth.

This is the point when her alcoholism began. She would sit in bars for hours wearing flashy clothes and bragging about how much money her mother had left her. This attracted the attention of sleazy hustlers, petty gamblers, and 'hood fortune hunters. Michelle was so fragile and insecure that all a man had to do was say, "I love you" and she would open her checkbook. Once the money was gone, so were most of her admirers, and she was stuck in debt with three children. But back then all Takia had was Malik and Amir. They took turns walking her to and from school, made sure that she did her homework and made sure that she ate dinner, even if it was only a dollar shrimp roll and their splitting three fried chicken wings from the Chinese corner store. And both showed her genuine love. She remembers both of their handsome, dark-skinned faces as though it were yesterday. Big, bright and expressive brown eyes that they all inherited from their mother. As a seven-year-old child, Takia thought that her older brothers were ten feet tall, Malik being ten years older and Amir seven years older. As with most boys who had no hope in the world, they both turned to the streets and began hustling for a local drug crew called the West Philly Hustlers. Both quickly established a rep. Malik was smart and business savvy, and knew how to cook product so potent that the crackheads would sell their mother for a hit. And Amir was the muscle, with a sharp arm for boxing. Built thick and sturdy, there were not too many people who could handle him in a street fight. And he was also quick with the trigger and had no problem putting two bullets through any nigga's head.

Once the cash started pouring in, Michelle, like the grown-up child she was, turned a blind eye to what her sons were involved with. Her bills were paid. They bought a new black leather furniture set, 50-inch television, a new Black & Decker refrigerator, and stove, and gave her enough petty cash for her to get her hair done and indulge in some retail therapy. Life with Takia was even a little sunnier. She had new Reebok sneakers in every color, Sergio Tacchini sweatsuits, Guess jeans and plenty of fresh New York & Co. clothing. Amir even threw out one of their mom's asshole boyfriends by force. He and Malik were now the men of the house. And between him and Malik, there was a cluster of fly chicken heads in and out of their house. Girls certainly had a thing for her brother. She admired their big hair and bone chains, gold figure-eight earrings, asymmetrical-like Salt-N-Pepa hairstyles and big Gucci bags. And they all loved Takia. They would say, "Aw, look at Malik and Amir's little sister. She's so cute." A few of them even took her to get her hair styled at Hair Image, a popular West Philadelphia hair salon that all of the drug-dealers' girlfriends went to get their hair done.

Life was on the bright side until December 31, 1992. Six days after Christmas. Malik was fatally shot in the head by a rival drug dealer whose girlfriend he was creeping with. Takia's world was in shambles. This sad time was one of the few that she could remember in her life when she and Michelle embraced in genuine love. They both hugged each other, crying in Michelle's bed, shedding tears for their strong, beautiful Malik, whose big brown eyes would never open again.

Takia lost her older brother. Michelle lost her first-born and best friend. After the funeral, Amir began a savage rampage, high on a mixture of marijuana, cocaine, and syrup from 30th and Jefferson Street. He found out where his brother's killer's mother lived, did a home invasion and avenged Malik by taking out his killer with four headshots. His mother and two younger siblings were killed in the process. Eight days after Malik's funeral, Amir was arrested for multiple homicides, tried and convicted, and is currently serving two consecutive life sentences in Graterford State Prison. He still writes to Takia occasionally and never forgets to send her a handmade birthday card every year. But in her mind, both of her brothers are dead. She is a young woman alone in the world. After these incidents, she and Michelle never speak of Malik and Amir again, as if they never existed.

Michelle's drinking grew worse, beating Takia for even sneezing the wrong way. But the things with her brothers were well in the past. She tries her best to block these things from her mind. The hot water from the rusted bathroom showerhead hit her naked body. She scrubs the white Ivory soap foam with a pink washcloth between her legs. She always takes extra precaution with her hygiene. Guys did not hate anything more than stink pussy. She would never let herself be caught out there with niggas saying that her pussy was sour.

Takia turned off the leaky showerhead. "Damn, this shit needs to get fixed," she says as the water from the shower continues to drip down into the rusted white tub. "I'm not paying for shit to get fixed in this house. I've already put enough of my money into bills around here anyway." She shivers, stepping onto the cold scraped black tiled floor, quickly wrapping the fluffy white towel around her body. As water from her wet body drips onto the floor, she opens the bathroom door feeling the cold hallway on every crevice of her still-wet body. She dashes to her room, slamming the door while plugging up her large space heater. She dries off, applying Victoria's Secret cinnamon-apple lotion to her skin. Once done moisturizing, she stands up, walks butt-naked to her closet, where she caught a glimpse of her oiled-up naked body. Takia puts on a conceited smile, looking intensely into the mirror, attempting to get the perfect Playboy playmate look together. She squeezes her perfectly round, 34D breasts before letting her hands glide across her washboard-flat stomach, where a small butterfly tattoo is drawn right underneath her navel. She wiggles her thick full hip and juicy thighs. Her body has no stretch marks, not even a sign of one blemish. Her body is flawlessly one color, and an ass round like a basketball.

Takia admires her body—her meal ticket. Niggas lusted and wanted to feel and taste it, and would pay the highest price to get inside of Takia's world.

"Fuck it," I'm not getting' cute for this nigga," she hisses, searching through her closet. She pulls out an orange Limited-brand sweatsuit. She slips on a pair of black lace thong panties and matching bra, puts some on Secret powder-fresh deodorant and slips on the soft, comfortable cotton sweatsuit. After dressing, she stands in front of her closet mirror, placing two pairs of small gold Chanel stud earrings in her ears, while applying MAC lip gloss to her full lips, when her cordless phone starts ringing. She leaps onto the bed and grabs the phone.

"Hello?"

"Yo, I'm outside your crib."

"Aight, I'll be out in one second."

She sprays herself down with her bottle of Versace Blue Jeans perfume, snatches a stick of Doublemint chewing gum from her red Prada bag and makes sure that one hundred dollars in cash is tucked inside. Because one thing her mother told her that did make sense was never to go out with a man with no money in your pocket, in case you two get into an argument, and he gets mad and leaves your ass stranded somewhere.

Takia cuts off her bedroom light, closes her door, and pulls a heavy keychain from her Prada bag with ten different sets of keys. She twists one into the lock that she had installed after Michelle had stolen three hundred in cash and several pairs of designer shoes that turned up missing. She double checks to make sure that her door is locked up tight before running down the squeaky hardwood steps. As Takia passes the living room, *The Late Show with David Letterman* is blasting on the brand new 40-inch television that Takia bought for Michelle's forty-third birthday, after the 50-inch that Malik had bought years ago died out. Takia never even got a thank you. She grabs the remote control, muting the volume, taking a final disgusted look at Michelle passed out on the beat-up black leather sofa. An empty bottle of Hennessy lay next to her.

Takia opens the heavy metal front storm door, stepping into the chilly night. She again goes locking up doors like a prison warden. Hakim waits patiently in his black Lexus jeep double parked in the middle of the street. The stench of trash fills Takia's nose as she skips over a clogged-up sewage drain overflowing with garbage. She opens the passenger-side door and slides into the warm, cozy Lexus. *Cupid* by 112 is quietly playing on the car stereo. The heat from the car vents is relaxing and sensual.

"Wassup?" Hakim asks in a nasal voice.

Takia looks him over silently. He is cuter than he remembers, dark chocolate with slanted eyes, a full Sunnah beard, fresh bald head and a solid build. *Not bad, but not anything to get excited over either*, she thinks, observing Hakim's silver-toned Movado watch. *He was probably about twenty-six or twenty-seven, easily*, she thinks, scanning his skin for a sign of age.

"Wassup, cat got your tongue, shorty?" Hakim asks, snapping Takia out of her daze.

"Nah, I'm just tired. You woke me up outta my sleep. It better be worth my while," she jokes with a hint of seriousness.

"Don't worry, I'll give you whatever you want. You had my dick brick since I saw your sexy ass on South Street."

Hakim slides his left hand up and down Takia's thighs.

Hakim, we gonna get this money straight before I take anything off, Takia thinks, giving him a sexy porn-star look that she knows will make his dick even harder than it already is. After a twenty minute ride and small-talk about bullshit, they arrive at Hakim's Mt. Airy apartment, a nice, cozy two-bedroom apartment with wall-to-wall carpet and dark burgundy leather couch, big-screen television and pictures of Hakim with his boys on trips to Vegas, Miami and Cancun hung all over the apartment walls. He was holding stacks of money and dressed in fly Versace at the Mike Tyson fight in Vegas.

Takia is somewhat impressed, but nothing major.

"Here you go," Hakim says, handing Takia a glass of chilled Moët champagne.

"Thank you," she responds politely, sitting the glass of Moët on the shiny glass living-room table.

Takia has a rule. She does not drink with guys on their first sexual encounter. She needs to keep focused on the business at hand.

Hakim pulls off the red and black Marc Buchanan jacket that he wears, and red Polo Sport-fleece hoodie, revealing broad shoulders, a firm chest, and a small potbelly. Takia finds Hakim sexy in an odd, goofy sort of way.

I hope his breath don't stink, Takia thinks, as Hakim sits down next to her. He slides his hand under Takia's sweatshirt and starts to fondle her breasts. She faces Hakim, biting down on her moist bottom lip.

"Yo, let's get down to business before we go any further," she whispers in his ear, making sure that her wet lips and tongue hit his skin at just the right moment. Hakim begins sweating and stuttering immediately.

"Alright, alright," Hakim stutters, dashing to her bedroom.

I got this nigga, Takia thinks, admiring her skill of driving men crazy.

Hakim emerges from his bedroom wearing only a pair of black boxing shorts and a smile. He has a fistful of money, and stands in front of Takia and lays a hundred-dollar bill on the living-room table.

This motherfucker must think I'm a smoker or something. Takia frowns her face up in disgust. Hakim knows immediately what the problem is, and puts two more hundred-dollar bills on the table. Takia puts a smirk on her face, shaking her head no at his increased offer.

Hakim sucks his teeth and lets out a huge sigh, as his chest moves up and down like an asthma patient. He throws down two more hundred-dollar bills, making it an even five hundred dollars.

"Hmmm, five hundred dollars? A pretty good score, but I know I can get more."

"Baby, that's half a stick out there," Hakim pleads, grabbing his dick through his boxers.

He's begging, I got this motherfucker. She digs through her pocketbook, pulling out her cell phone, pretending to dial a number. This should do the trick. She stands up off the couch, stretching the arch in her back, sticking her ass out at just the right angle.

"Yeah, Yellow Cab, I need a cab ASAP." Takia lets her free hand drop to the brim of her sweatpants in a sexually suggestive manner, and Hakim is hooked. He throws the remaining hundred-dollar bills, he held gripped in his hand on the table. Eight hundred dollars was laying ready for Takia's taking.

Jackpot! The sight of all those green Benjamin's makes Takia horny, and she is now ready to fuck. She slowly stands up and pulls off her orange Polo sweatshirt, revealing her big, firm 34D breasts.

Hakim's mouth waters, knowing that he was about to finally get that sweet young pussy that he paid for and craved. Takia slides her sweatpants down. Her sexy caramel-colored thighs and ass look edible to Hakim. She kicks off her sneakers and switches over to Hakim like a thoroughbred.

"Damn, girl," Hakim says, wrapping his hand around her soft ass. Takia begins rubbing his chest. *He has an average-sized dick,* Takia thinks, and Hakim grinds his penis against her. *Let me put the flip on this nigger.* Takia slowly drops to her knees and pulls that average sized dick out of his boxers, and starts sucking it with the intensity of a malnourished lioness.

"Oh, shit. Oh, shit," Hakim moans as his eyes roll to the back of his head, running his hands through her weave while moving his dick back and forth within her mouth.

Takia slips, spits and smacks, moving her tongue like a snake, up and down Hakim's dick, stroking it with her hands with the wetness of her fists. Takia is a pro and does not let out a moan or a groan.

"Goddamn, shorty, let's take this to my bedroom." Hakim pulls her to her feet.

"Hold up," Takia says, scooping up the eight hundred-dollar bills and quickly puts them inside her Prada bag, which she then places underneath the couch, just in case Hakim decides to change his mind afterward.

Hakim is on the bed completely naked, with a candle lit on the nightstand. It is the only thing illuminated in the dark room. Takia unfastens her bra and lets her panties drop to the floor.

I hope this motherfucker comes quick. She crawls onto the bed in between Hakim's legs and starts licking and sucking his balls. Hakim starts moaning like a little bitch. She puts her wet mouth back to his dick, sucking on it with rapid speed. After ten minutes of getting an awesome blowjob, she climbs on top of him, feeling that he is ready to explode.

"Baby, you're worth every penny of that money," Hakim groans as Takia grinds against his dick. She becomes turned on every second thinking about how she will spend the eight hundred dollars.

"Yo, let me stick it in," Hakim moans, lifting Takia up and turning her on her back.

"Hold up, Hakim, get a fucking condom first."

"My bad, baby, you got me so horny that I want to melt in your pussy raw. You on the pill, right?"

81

"Yeah, I'm on the pill, but I don't play that raw shit."

Hakim can feel her body become tense underneath him. "Alright, girl, it's cool." Hakim bends over to his nightstand drawer and pulls out three LifeStyles condoms.

Hopefully, your ass will be a four-stroke creep, Takia thinks, watching Hakim slide on one of the condoms. He mounts her, putting her legs over his shoulders, sliding into her moist pussy.

"Fuck, damn girl, your pussy's good as shit." Hakim groans, stroking at a slow pace, taking in every heated sensation inside of Takia's warm walls. She finally lets out a genuine moan of pleasure. Hakim's strokes were starting to feel good to her.

Fuck it. I might as well get a nut out of the deal. Takia starts twisting her hips and squeezing her vaginal muscles against Hakim's dick. Her movements drive him crazy.

"Yeah, girl, gimme that pussy. Give it to me." Hakim starts thrusting like a madman inside her. "Oh, shit, I'm about to come," Hakim screams in heat. As he comes, filling up the condom, sweat drips from his body onto Takia.

Damn, that was easy, Takia thinks, wiping Hakim's sweat from her chest. He pulls out, collapsing next to her on the bed.

Good, my pussy put this nigga to sleep. She quietly slips out of Hakim's bed, picking up her bra and begins to fasten it.

"Yo, don't even think about putting that shit back on, ma. We ain't done yet. I just started to get my money's worth outta that pussy."

Takia stands staring at Hakim with disgust in the darkened, candlelit room. She snatches her bra off and lies back down limp on the bed, waiting for Hakim to take what more he wanted from her body. Hakim is back up within five minutes, making sure that he got his money's worth out of her; hitting her doggie-style from the back, smacking her ass roughly with his hands, then knocking her down sideways. After three more long nuts, Hakim finds himself all tapped out, falling to sleep easily like a tired child as Takia takes a long shower, trying to scrub off Hakim's scent and touch. She lays down next to him in a ball and goes to sleep.

At 8:30 a.m., she wakes Hakim and makes him take her home. Hakim is trying to be all lovey, dovey with her, calling her baby and wanting to take her to IHop for breakfast, but she is irritated with him and just wants to be out of his presence.

"Alright, young buck. Hit me up later, and we can grab something to eat," Hakim says with a pussy-whipped grin on his face. He pulls in front of Takia's house.

"I'll meet up with you later," she says nonchalantly as she quickly closes the car door before Hakim could get another word out of his wet-ass mouth. "Nigga, the only time I want to hear from you is when I'm trying to get some paper outta your nut ass," Takia whispers, pulling her house keys from her Prada bag. She opens the front door and walks in toward the hardwood staircase. She longs to be comfortable in her bed when a deep scratchy voice from years of chain smoking stops her instantly.

"Where the fuck have you been, out whoring with one of your niggas?" her mother Michelle asks sarcastically from her permanent bed on the couch. Takia could have ignored her and went straight to bed, but she could not resist cursing her mother out every chance she got.

"First of all, don't worry about where I been. Mind your business."

"Girl, don't forget, your fast ass is still livin' up in my house."

"Last time I checked, this is my grandmother's house. You never owned a fuckin' house. The only reason bills get paid and things get fixed in this house is because of the money I bring in," Takia hollers, entering the cluttered living room where Michelle sits on the black leather couch, a faded scarf wrapped around her head and wickedly mean expression on her aging dark-brown face. Mother and daughter look nothing alike. Where Takia's features are soft and pretty, Michelle's are harsh. Even in her youth, Michelle was never considered a pretty woman. With constant drinking, she aged rapidly. Michelle is a tall, dark-skinned woman with indented circles under her eyes and a wide pig nose, always flaring her nostrils being ugly and her daughter being blessed with beauty caused a deep-seated jealousy from the day that Takia was born. Empty Chinese takeout containers were cluttered on the table, while Heineken bottles lay on the floor.

"Michelle, you are triflin'. It stinks in here," Takia crunches up her face as her nose picks up the scent of something foul.

"Fuck you, you little bitch! You swear you're hot shit 'cause you're fuckin' all those little-ass drug dealers. Sure, you're young and pretty now, but that ain't gonna last forever."

Takia lets out a vicious laugh. "You're such a hater. As long as I've got it, I'm gonna keep workin' it." She puts her hands on her hips and twists her neck.

"You ain't nothin' but a whore who ain't gonna be shit."

"I might be a whore, but I'm a paid whore. Michelle, as many men I seen you bring in this house..."

Michelle's eyes grow wide with hatred. "Well, little miss paid whore, the gas bill just came in the mail. We behind five months and they gonna cut us off." Michelle sits up and crosses her arms.

"Fuckin' figures," Takia says, rolling her eyes. She digs into her Prada bag and pulls out three of the new hundred-dollar bills and throws them onto the table in front of Michelle. "Make sure this shit gets paid. I can't wait to move the fuck outta this bitch," Takia yells, storming up to her bedroom. She collapses onto her bed. "Fuck school today. I'm too tired." She pulls off her clothes and falls fast asleep. It was past five that afternoon when she is awakened by the ringing of her cordless phone.

"Hello," she whimpers.

"Yo, can I get a lick, nigga?"

"Who is this?" Takia says clearing her throat.

"It's Rell."

"Little Rell?" Takia asks in a girlish squeal. Rell is just the guy to put a smile on Takia's face. He is twenty-one but has the laid-back maturity of an old-head. He is from South Philly's notorious Seventh Street, a crew known for getting money. Rell and Takia have played a lot of phone tag and have played a lot of sexual games in various hotel rooms. She has different feelings for Rell that she had for other guys. He makes her insides erupt whenever she is around him.

"Rell, what you doin'?" Takia asks, rubbing the inside of her sore thighs, becoming horny from the sound of Rell's voice.

"Nothing, just chillin'."

Takia could hear guys talking loudly in the background. "Rell, where you at, a crap game?"

"Yeah, just catching these dudes' money. You know how I do it."

"What are you doin' after you done playin' with the boys?"

"I ain't got nothin' lined up. Why? What you got in mind?"

Takia's anticipation is building. "I wanna see you tonight."

"Well, we can do that. I'll be at your crib by midnight."

"Okay, I'll be ready."

"Yo, you better be ready. You always takin' long as shit, Takia."

"I'll be ready, I promise."

They both bust out laughing.

"Yo, let me get back to these dudes. I'll hit you up when I'm outside your crib tonight."

Takia hangs up the phone and falls back wistfully onto her bed, gently caressing her nipples, her eyes closed as she daydreams about Rell. "Um, hum, Rell, if I was your girlfriend, the things I'd do for you."

Takia suddenly opens her eyes. "Rell, maybe I should be your girlfriend. He is certainly fine as hell and has plenty of money. But I'll think about all that when I wake up," Takia says while yawning herself back to sleep.

Takia is awakened by the loud sound of the phone beside her bed. "Hello," she says groggily.

"This is Rell. I'm on the E-way. You ready?" Rell's voice comes through over loud music.

Takia jumps out of bed as 11:20 p.m. jumps out across her clock in red. "Yeah, I'm doin' my hair now. Call me when you get outside," Takia blurts out, lying with ease. She turns on two large crystal lamps, rummaging for the perfect outfit to wear for Rell.

Through her years of dating hustlers, Takia had accumulated a large batch of clothes, so much that she was running out of space. "Hmmm, I haven't worn this yet," Takia says while pulling a brown French Connection dress from her closet. "Yes, this will be sexy with my dark brown Nine West knee boots." Takia lays her outfit on her bed, grabs a fresh bar of Dove soap, a pink towel and a bottle of Summer's Eve. Fifteen minutes later she is applying lip gloss to her shiny, full lips. Her long blonde weave bumped to perfection. The French Connection dress clings to every part of her body. She sprays herself down with Gucci Envy perfume when the cordless phone starts ringing loudly again.

"Yo, I'm outside," Rell says.

"Aight, I'll be right out."

Takia looks herself over once more in the mirror, winks seductively pleased with her reflection. She grabs her tan Prada bag and hurries down the stairs. "Rell, you're gonna get it tonight," Takia says as she quickly walks out of the front door.

Rell's silver E-class wagon sits in the street, a chariot fit for a dope boy. Takia locks up the house and switches slowly to Rell's car. She feels the nip of the cool night air under her dress. She opens the passenger side door. *Kissing You* by Total fills her ear. Rell grins at her from the driver's side, his cool tan skin and perfect white teeth make him quite appealing to most girls. He looks younger than his twenty-one years. He can easily pass for seventeen. He possesses a handsome baby face, thin muscular build and sleepy bedroom eyes like Nas the rapper. The red Iceberg sweater that he wears fits him well.

"What's up, Caramel?" Rell says whipping his car through the wild West Philly streets.

"I been chillin', just goin' to school," Takia replies, trying to sound innocent.

"Man, get the fuck outta here. You been out on the streets."

"Rell, come on, I got a few friends, but I ain't got no rings on my finger," Takia giggles, dangling her well-manicured hands across Rell's face.

He smirks. "Yo, if you stop jugglin' so many niggas, I'll put a boulder on your finger."

Takia falls silent.

"Yeah, that shut you up. I'd love to make you my girl."

"But it's hard for me to trust men. I don't think I'm the wifey type."

"Why you say that, Takia? You bad as shit. You're gorgeous, always got good shit on and when we're in the bedroom together," Rell says biting his lower lip, "well, you already know."

Before Takia has time to think of a snappy comeback, Rell pulls his Mercedes wagon into the parking lot of the Center City Marriott Hotel.

"Just imagine your life with me," Rell says sincerely, pulling Takia by the neck and giving her a deep wet French kiss.

I'm gonna be your girl, and you're gonna be my man, Takia thinks while moving her tongue back and forth within his mouth.

Rell moves his fingers, gently stroking Takia's breasts.

"Oh Rell, I love you. I'm about to be wifed up."

Chapter 4

YOU'RE MY LITTLE SECRET

Saturday, October 15, 1997

"Yo wake up sleepy head, Carmello Black says teasingly, hurling a pillow at Mya's head.

"Stop," she says, half asleep. Her naked body twists in the soft lambskin blanket atop her bed. The smell of bacon and eggs fills Mya's nose. Her growling stomach finally forces her from her slumber.

"Here we go, baby girl," Black says, placing a silver tray filled with turkey bacon, scrambled eggs, toast, and orange juice on Mya's lap.

She smiles gleefully, thankful for the blessing that this is her man. Her wonderful, strong man. Carmello's dark skin glistens in the early-morning sunlight. He wears only a pair of Polo boxer briefs, his muscular chest protrudes from a fresh set of pushups. Mya takes a sip of the chilled orange juice. Black bends down and gives her a juicy peck on the lips.

"Girl, even your morning breath tastes good," Black chuckles, lying beside Mya. She and Black had not left each other's side since they met, and everybody on the street knows that she is his girl. The more she is around Black, the more knowledge she gains. He taught her how to win the code of the streets. His power turns her on just as much as his unlimited supply of stacks that he passes off one high-powered shopping spree after another. Mya knows that she is his main girl, but she is certainly not a fool. She knows that he has other chicks lined up to fuck and fuck dry. But both hoes know their place and know not to even stare at Mya the wrong way. She was Black's baby girl. She loved his intellect. She is safe whenever she is with him. Black's cell phone rings constantly, always fucking up the mood. Mya finds out on more than a few occasions. This sunny morning was no exception. As Black's fingers start making their way inside of Mya's vagina, his cell phone begins ringing loudly. He jumps up and picks up on the second ring.

Yo, I wish that cell phone would fucking disappear, she thinks, watching Black's smooth chocolate face ball up into a disturbing grimace. His body becomes stiff. Mya is alert by his change of body language.

"I ain't give them orders. Shit. Lil Heem is in critical condition," Black's voice falls almost to a whisper. "Yo, man, we gotta cut this phone shit out. I'm on my way up there."

"Baby, what happened?" Mya asks, almost stuttering.

"My young boah, Khalid, hit Lil Heem from Huntington Park three times with a TEC-9 at Broad Street Eddie's last night. I told that little nigga not to do nothing until I gave the order. These fools been beefin' over some little whore from 21st and Diamond that been ran through by damn near the whole North Philly. This shit could start a war," Black screams. "We don't need this kind of heat from the law," he seethes with anger.

Mya jumps back in fear. Black sees that he frightened her and quickly calms his rage.

"I'm sorry, babe," he says while gently stroking her hair. "It's a lot going on right now. I didn't mean for you to see that side of me." Black gently kisses her forehead. He pulls her out of bed by the hand.

What the hell just happened? Mya thinks as hot water from Black's marble and gold glass shower hit her body. Once Mya and Black shower and dress quickly, they head to Philly at a rapid speed on the New Jersey Turnpike. Black sits stone-faced, grabbing the steering wheel as though wanting to rip it off. A gray Prada skullcap sits on the side of his head. Mya watches him from the corner of her eye, wanting desperately to break the silence. But every time she got the courage to speak, nothing would come out of her mouth.

Black's cell phone rings every two seconds; one of his crew giving him up-to-the-minute info on the situation. Mya sits silently, soaking up the situation and putting the pieces of the puzzle together.

"Is that hot-head ass nigga dead? Could have us going to war with them Richard Allen project niggas. Lamar been itchin' to try to start some shit with us. Yo, if my money counts get fucked up, I'm gonna break Khalid's legs," Black hisses through clenched teeth, pulling in front of the Who Styles You hair salon on 56th and Market Street in West Philly. Who Styles You is a ghetto-fabulous salon where fly girls and hustlers' baby moms get their hair done. Boosters sell TVs, DVDs, and Prada bags—some imitation and some authentic—all in that same order. Mya had been a regular customer since she was thirteen. The salon's owner, Cocoa, is the only person that Mya trusts with her long, flowing locks. Black reaches into his pocket and pulls out a wad of money, handing Mya five crisp new hundred dollar bills.

"Alright, baby," Carmello says as Mya opens the passenger door.

"Don't worry about picking me up. I'll call my mom," Mya responds with a look of complete concern.

91

"Aww, my baby worrying about me?" Black chuckles. "I'm sorry you gotta get exposed to this kinda shit." Black's eyes look tired and slanted.

Aww, my boo looks tired and stressed, but I got just the right medicine for him later.

They exchange a quick peck on the lips. Mya flings her big, tan Gucci bag over her shoulder, adjusts the diamond bezel of the Rolex on her left wrist. She closes the passenger door and watches Carmello race off.

She makes her way into the gaudy, black-and-white, leather-clad furniture salon. Mya could feel the stares and hear the hushed whispering. She knows the chicks in the waiting area are talking about her. She ignores them, signing her name on the client sign-in sheet at the reception desk.

"Hey, girl," Nikki, the bubbly receptionist, greeted. She is a cute brown-skinned girl with a wide gap in between her two front teeth.

"Hey, Nikki," Mya says, swinging her gold and tan Bebe sweat jacket.

"Girl, Coco got three in front of you. There was all kinds of drama in here earlier. You know little Shonte from Southwest."

"Yeah," Mya says, looking at Nikki with widened eyes.

Nikki was known for keeping the gossip going on in the shop. Anything happening in the streets, Nikki knows about it. She caught a couple of beatdowns running her big mouth, but that did not seem to stop her.

"Child, let me tell you. Her baby father, Meathead, from 60th Street, came up in here today like the Tasmanian Devil. Shonte been fuckin' with Cortez from Jay Street up North. Well, Meathead found out about their little affair and commenced to whippin' her ass all over the shop. She was bleedin' all over the place. He was threatenin' to kill her and everything. We had to call the cops. It was like the nigga was possessed."

"Damn," was all Mya could muster.

"Mya, I'm ready for you," Kiki, Coco's young shampoo girl, says in a high-pitched voice.

"Okay," Mya responds, quickly walking away from Nikki.

I'm so glad. I'll never tell that chick my business, Mya thinks.

"Hey girl, how you doin'? Lookin' good as always," Mya was greeted pleasantly by stylists and other patrons with whom she is familiar.

The salon is crowded as usual on this Saturday afternoon. She sits down at the sink so that Kiki can wash her hair. She catches two tanned-skinned girls getting their hair blow-dried across from her, rolling their eyes at her, then falling out in laughter.

What the fuck y'all laughin' at? Mya thinks as Kiki washes and conditions her mane. Mya relaxes. Getting her hair washed always relieves built-up stress. She lies comfortably under the washbowl with her eyes closed tight, the warm water hitting her head as visions of her and Carmello's lovemaking fills her mind.

"What are we getting done to this hair today?"

Mya's wet dream is interrupted by the loud, boastful voice of Coco, her over-the-top hair stylist. Coco stands in front of her grinning. Coco is a petite, heavyset, chocolate-brown woman with dark close-set eyes. She changes hairstyles like she changes clothes.

"I want somethin' soft and curly," Mya says sulking, putting out her lips.

"Okay, girl, I'm gonna give you somethin' productive. I'm gonna give you that Aaliyah Swoop look with pretty spiral curls flowin' in the back," Coco announces, putting her long, hot-pink colored fingernail in the air.

"Co, do whatever you want, as long as I come out lookin' good."

Mya was placed under the hair dryer's intense heat. Fifteen minutes later, she is shampooed, conditioned, blow dried, and ready to be styled. She sits in Coco's chair. Coco takes her sheet irons and starts pressing out Mya's beautiful hair. She then starts severing and curling. As Mya turns her head to the right, the two tan-skinned girls who were giggling at her earlier are whispering like Latoya. Toya was an older, troublemaking stylist who never cared for Mya. She had always been jealous of Mya's age and the abundance of designer and material possessions that she had.

I know these bitches aren't thinkin' shit, Mya thinks, frowning, looking at them up and down. One was wearing a yellow, body-fitting Express sweatsuit with Express written in pink across the chest. The other was thin-built with an average face, a shoulder-length wrap, with the latest Guess jeans and a red and black Moschino t-shirt. Toya keeps cutting her eyes at Mya and whispering to the thin girl sitting in her chair. Toya is twenty-five but acts more like fifteen. She is angry all the time because she has three children by three different men. One was murdered, and the other two are in jail serving football numbers. She keeps the drama going in the salon, and Coco is always threatening to fire her. And since Mya had started dating Black, Kiki the wash girl had told her everything. Things like that she was not his girlfriend, just his young side dish, that Black was going to play and how he was going to drop her when he was finished running through her young, fast-ass pussy. And that Mya is nothing more than a fast-ass little girl who is too grown.

"Look, I see what's going on. I will deal with Toya's ass later on," Coco whispers lightly in Mya's ear. Her nose is filled with the strong scent of Coco's V/S Versace perfume.

"Girl, ignore them haters. They messin' with a boss bitch. Hate and jealousy come with the territory. Chicks who never knew your name are now seeking you out. They all wanna know who's that girl. Baby, you a superstar now." Coco's words ring out in Mya's ear. Coco finishes up Mya's hair as she spins Mya around to face the mirror.

Mya, even with all of her conceit, is taken aback by her own beauty. She looks like an exotic video girl. Long shiny black hair crowns her head. Coco gives her that Aaliyah swoop look, revealing one hazel eye with layers of soft curls down her back.

Oh, I'm such a bad young chick, Mya smiles at her reflection, basking in the moment of her own youthful perfection. *Let me show these bitches something real quick.* Mya's confidence level soars. She digs into her Gucci bag and hands Coco two fresh hundred-dollar bills, then tips Kiki twenty-five dollars. Mya throws her bag over on her shoulder, getting in her diva stance, swinging her flowing hair, and starts switching through the salon. When she gets in front of Latoya's basin, Mya smirks sarcastically, rolling her eyes at the haters and begins running her fingers through her hair before turning on her heels with a dip in her hips and strutting away.

"Oh no she didn't," one of the chicks retorts angrily.

"Oh yes, she did," Mya giggles out load, turning her head in Coco's direction. Coco winks one of her dark close-set eyes at Mya, who once again has all eyes on her as she walks confidently out of the salon.

"Mom, I need you to pick me up from the salon," Mya says into her cell phone. The smell of weed and greasy Chinese food pollute the air.

"Oh yes, young lady, I'm on my way. We need to talk immediately," Latanya snarls into the phone and abruptly hangs up.

"Mom, mom," Mya shouts into her cell phone receiver, but Latanya had already hung up.

"What the fuck is she talking about?" Mya whispers, her heart racing. Guys with cars keep pulling over to talk with her. She dismisses them one after the other. Guys walking by the salon smoking blunts try to come at her with their best game.

"Yo Shorty, wassup? Lemme take you on a nice date."

Mya simply ignores them in silence. Mya stands vagrantly while Latanya seems to appear from nowhere, pulling up in front of the salon. The fall sunlight jumps off the fresh wash job on Latanya's E-Class. Lataya does not play when it comes to her baby. Sometimes it seems as though she cares more about her car than her own daughter.

Mya slides cautiously into the passenger seat. She can tell by her mother's blank expression and heavy foot on the gas that drama is brewing.

What the fuck is she trippin' about now? Mya thinks. She was covering her tracks with Carmello by telling her parents that she had been spending the weekends and late nights at Raven's house.

"Mya, can you please explain why you told your father and I you were staying the weekends over at Raven Hightower's house for the past three weekends straight, filling out college applications for Howard, Spelman and Penn State?" Latanya demands in a calm, condescending voice, adjusting the band on her silver Tiffany & Co. watch.

"I had an intuition this morning, so I called the Hightowers. And do you know what Mrs. Hightower told me?" Latanya raises her voice, facing Mya, her hazel eyes wired with rage.

Oh shit, she knows! Mya's stomach becomes queasy.

"Mrs. Hightower had no idea what the hell I was talking about. She had not seen you at her house for weeks!" Latanya screams.

"Mom, let me explain." Before Mya can say another word, her mother reaches over and backslaps her hard across the face. The forceful sting sends a shock through Mya's body. Her mother had not struck her since she was a child, and by reflex, Mya takes her left hand and slaps her mother back with force.

"You little bitch," Latanya seethes. She slams on the brakes with such force that she and Mya both slam into the dashboard. She pulls the car over to the side of the busy Haverford Avenue intersection and places the car in park.

"Mom, I'm sorry for hitting you," Mya pleads. Latanya stares at Mya with icy disbelief. A look of scornful disgust is in her eyes. Without warning, she starts punching and pulling Mya's hair.

"Mom, stop, get the fuck off me," Mya cries, trying to block Latanya's attack.

"Mom, you want to fight me like a bitch in the street!" Mya screams. "Fuck it then. She grabs Latanya's hair and starts choking her. This only makes her mother act wilder.

"You little bitch!" She digs her nails deeply into Mya's face until blood begins to run while yanking her hair as if to pull it from the roots.

People begin pulling over in their cars watching the scene. After five minutes of tussling, punching, and hair-pulling, Mya and Latanya sit in silence, tears falling from both of their bloody and bruised faces. Latanya finally puts the key in the Mercedes ignition and drives off. As they pull into the driveway of their perfect house in their perfect neighborhood, they both give one another one last icy stare, silently saying *Daddy doesn't need to know about this.* Half a lifetime of resentment and frustration have just exploded in a few minutes of fury.

Once inside their lavish house, mother and daughter retreat to their bedrooms, each deep in thought about the other.

I can't believe I just had to fight my mom, Mya thinks while using a hot washcloth to wipe the blood from her face. "Look at my fucking face," she says, grimacing at her reflection in the large heart-shaped bathroom mirror that confronts her. Her freshly done hair is ruined. She checks the bald spots in the mirror, feeling the tenderness of her scalp. She pulls her clothes off and lies restlessly across her bed, finally nodding off to sleep. Her cordless phone begins ringing beside her.

"I don't feel like talkin' to nobody," she hisses. "Hello," she shouts, putting her teeth into the receiver.

"What's up, bitch?" Takia's loud voice says happily in Mya's ear.

"Takia, I'm goin' through some real shit right now. I don't feel like talkin'." Mya tries her best not to sound aggravated with Takia.

"Yo, what is wrong?

Just as Mya opens her mouth to speak, Latanya opens her bedroom door, dressed in a pink silk bathrobe, holding a frozen ice pack to her forehead.

"Let me call you back," Mya quickly says while hanging up the phone.

"Young lady, this incident is not to be discussed with your father. He does not need to be upset with this nonsense. He's working on several very important cases for the firm. This is a distraction that he does not need."

"You just don't want daddy to know because you are dead wrong."

Latanya's hazel eyes widen with anger. "Mya, I will not feed into your bullshit. You are not to leave this house. I know you've been having sex with some filthy lowlife, like some common street whore. I didn't work hard my whole life for my daughter to become a selfish, self-centered, egotistical little bitch."

Mya's mouth drops. Even in their worst arguments, Mya's mother had never spoken to her in such a way. Tears again begin to fill Latanya's eyes, while emotions overtake her. She looks as if she wants to grab Mya and embrace her, but something is holding her back.

"When I was pregnant with you, your father and I were struggling. He was working his way through law school, and we were living in this little one-bedroom apartment in the most filthy part of South Philly. That winter I was about eight months pregnant. We had no heat and were just barely getting enough to eat."

Latanya hesitantly walks over and sits on the edge of Mya's satin-covered bed. She senses her mother's reluctance yet comes closer, intrigued; she had never heard much talk about her parents' past or anything about them being poor. She did not even know who her family was. This provokes intense interest in Mya.

"Mya, times were hard back then. I was taking business administration classes at Philadelphia Community College, working double shifts at night at the Broad Street Diner, waitressing on my feet for ten hours at a time until sometimes my toes would bleed, busting my ass for some lousy two dollar tips."

"Mom, I thought you went to Temple," Mya says while putting a shaking hand on her mother's shoulder. She was not used to showing her mother intimate affection.

"Community College was way before Temple University and Penn Law. Mya, there's so much I've tried to forget about my past. And in trying to do so, I've caused you pain. What a fool I've been..."

Latanya turns and looks Mya in the eyes, those self-same eyes that she possesses, with almost identical features, her younger twin. She places Mya's hands in hers. "Sweetheart, I had a very difficult life when I was your age. I grew up in that hard section of Philadelphia called 'The Bottom' on the corner of 37th and Wallace Street."

"Hold up, mom—you from 'The Bottom'?" Mya asks, looking at her mother with what seem like brand new eyes.

"Yes, yes, I grew up in The Bottom with my mother Carolyn and my granny Olivia, who took care of me."

"Your mother's name is Carolyn?"

"My mother's name *was* Carolyn," Latanya answers, her voice dropping ever slightly. "Carolyn Moore was her name, and she was fine, tall, light-skinned, and regal. She had sandy blonde hair and great big emerald-green eyes. Granny Olivia was half white, her father a poor Irishman and her mother, Dorothy was Haitian. That's why we have a fair complexion and fine hair."

Latanya gently runs her fingers through Mya's disheveled locks. "My mother had me when she was fifteen. I never knew who my father was, only that he made his living as a musician, and much older than my mother."

I always knew that I was a mix of something, but could never put my finger on it. A black and Irish girl, that's me, Mya thinks, quietly and intensely listening to Latanya's story.

"Granny Olivia always said that Haitian mixed with Irish blood made us strong but also crazy as hell, which was very much the case with my mother. She was a free spirit, and her beauty attracted many men. She had a new man all the time. She loved to drink, she loved to party and could dress her behind off. She stayed sharp and had the foulest mouth. God, that woman loved to cuss," Latanya chuckles, a grin appearing on her face. "You have so much of her in you that it scares me sometimes. When I was about six or seven, she started leaving for weeks on end. My grandmother was strong, she was a maid in a wealthy white woman's house up here on the mainline until she became sick with cancer and had to have her left leg amputated. This was in the late '60's, medical technology was not as advanced as it is now. My granny had to stop work and get on welfare, and the pennies they gave us were barely enough to get by. The older I got, the more resentful I grew toward my mother who would pop up every five months with some new hustler lowlife and a shiny Cadillac dressed to kill. Bearing gifts and a bright, beautiful smile, she made me kiss these men on the cheek and call them uncle such and such; Uncle Frank, Uncle Tom, Uncle Phil; after a while, I couldn't even keep up with them all. I can still smell their stinking cologne and cigarettes. As I grew older, I started seeing the lust for me in their eyes. Granny Olivia would always scare these men and put them in their place. She and my mother would argue; their arguments would be terrible. Then my mother would leave, promising to come back for me. I'd cry and wait by the door for days, praying that she would come back for me, but she never did." Mya's eyes began to water.

"I became a bitter, reclusive girl. Thank God for school, learning and education became my addiction. I was a straight-A student from sixth to twelfth grade. I didn't have many friends; I was teased because I only had three dresses to wear and one pair of shoes; that's how poor we were. I made a vow to myself that I would work my ass off to get out of that stinking ghetto and give my children the life I never had. When I met your father, he was a sophomore at the University of Penn, I was a senior at Bartram Motivation. I can still remember the first day we met like yesterday. He was so ambitious, strong and he was beyond fine." LaTanya and Mya both chuckle.

"My dad was a jawn, huh?"

"Honey was he?!" LaTanya says, twisting her full pink lips in a conceited smile. "Your father was something else. A lot of girls were after him, but I got him." LaTanya glows with confidence. "We both struggled and sacrificed for a better life. When we found out I was pregnant with you, it fueled us even more. We had so many plans for you. And girl when you kicked me, you were ready for the world, even in my womb. The night you were born it rained so badly, but as soon as you were delivered, the sky cleared up and the sun came out. A little angel is what Granny Olivia called you. She was there the night you were born, I remember how happy she was to hold you. That was one of the last things she did."

"What happened to her?" Mya asked alarmed.

"She died of a heart attack three days after you were born. It was the most painful time of my life. After Granny's death, I became obsessed with success, obtaining wealth and material things. When your father and I bought this house here on the mainline, where my grandmother was once a maid, I felt I vindicated her.

"When your father became a partner at Sachs & Mayer; the first black man ever and myself, a junior partner at Goldwyn & Goldstein, I became blind. The more money we obtained, the more I pulled away from you. I barely knew what you ate for dinner at night. That was the housekeeper's job in my book. There was always some fundraiser, country club appearance, and charity ball to attend. I thought the money made up for my absence, now I don't even know who my daughter is anymore." LaTanya chokes up with tears.

"No mom, it wasn't your fault. You did the best you could." They embrace each other in the first hug they've shared in years. Mya feels her heart beat against her own. "Oh mom, I'm sorry for all the times I disrespected you."

"No baby, I'm sorry for all the time we missed. I'm so sorry Mya."

They hold on to each other so tight as if trying to fuse into one body. They finally found their way back to each other after so much lost time. But how long do sweet reunions last?

Chapter 5

RAVEN: I CAN'T FUCK WITH YOU

November 13, 1997

"Oh God! Where the fuck is Jamal?" Raven says shivering, the brisk November air blowing against her body.

Wearing a thick navy blue united color Benetton ski jacket and warm lime green Gap hat and scarf set covering her head and neck, she still felt the cold breeze. Long johns underneath her dark blue Express jeans did not make her any warmer. The darkened stores of the Wynnewood Shopping Center are silent. She had been off from Marshalls for over an hour. All of her co-workers and employees from other stores are gone. The parking lot is empty except for a few miscellaneous cars; Raven is completely alone. Raven cell phone begins ringing inside her small Fendi tote bag. She pulls off one black leather glove from her right hand.

"Shit it's cold!" She shouts digging through her small black leather bag. Jamal's number flashes across her Nokia cell phone screen.

"Hello!" She snaps.

"Yo Raven, the engine went on the Taurus. I'm tryna get my moms car to pick you up."

"So when did you know your car broke down Jamal?" Raven says, holding her arms together shivering.

"I'm stuck out here. This shit just happened. I tried to start the car, and it was dead. I'm looking under the 'hood now to see what's wrong."

"Save the bullshit, Jamal!" Raven screams, her dark mocha face flushed red. "Jamal, I'm fucking freezing my ass off!"

"Look, Raven, I'm sorry, I'll be there as soon as I can. It's not like I planned this shit."

"You know what Mally? Fuck you. I'm gonna catch the bus." Raven hits the end button on her cell phone, not wanting to hear another excuse from Jamal.

Fuck him. She thinks, sprinting across the dark parking lot toward the 108 bus stop, the only bus that runs out of the shopping center after 10:00 p.m. It ran every hour.

"11:10 p.m." Raven sighs, checking her small Gucci watch. "I just missed one. The next one doesn't come until midnight." She lets out a frustrated scream.

Mally blows up her cell phone calling back to back. She simply cuts off her ringer ignoring him. *There's nothing this nigga has to say to me.* She thinks, reaching the bus stop. She's completely alone, nothing but darkness in sight. She starts to feel a little nervous observing her surroundings. She faintly hears *Crush On You* by Lil' Kim in the distance. The music becomes clearer and clearer. Raven looks over her shoulder to see the blinding lights of an SUV approaching. The trucks blasting stereo system was cutting her ears. *I hope this is not a fucking rapist.* She thinks, her heartbeat quickens.

The dark green Tahoe pulls up beside Raven. Dark tinted windows roll down revealing a familiar smiling face. Nickels, one of Pumpkin's homies from 39th and Reno Street has been pursuing Raven for two years, and for two years she has been fleeing him. How ironic it is that here in the freezing cold, not a soul anywhere; their paths cross? Nickels is a dark-skinned, thick built chubby guy with deep dimples, average at best in Raven's mind. He's smiling at Raven underneath an orange Polo Sport skull hat.

"You need a ride, pretty lady?"

"What's up Nickels? I'm cool, just waiting for the bus. It should be here in a minute."

"Girl you freezing your ass off. Let me take you home."

The inside of Nickels truck did look warm and inviting, and the next 108 wouldn't come for another thirty-five minutes. *Fuck it, he's only taking me home.* Raven runs to the passenger side and hops in. The blasting heat hits her immediately. She pulls off her leather gloves, rubbing her small hands together.

"What you doin' out here this time of night?" Nickels ask while undressing Raven with his eyes as he floors the gas.

"I work at Marshalls, my boyfriend was supposed to pick me up, but something happened with his car."

"You still mess with the lil' dude that fixes cars huh?" Nickels laughs loudly.

"Yes, I do. He's out here working, making money the legit way." Raven answers defensively rolling her eyes.

"Slow down lil' mama, I'm just playing. I believe in working smart, not hard."

"What are you doin' out here? That's a better question."

"I have an apartment up the street on 75th and Brockton Road. I was trying to swing by RadioShack to get a new remote for my system." Nickels points his finger to the neon blue, thousand watts, high-priced car stereo system that's installed in the dashboard of his Tahoe.

Raven only sees systems like this in get-money dude's vehicles like Carmello Black, Pumpkin, or any number of Takia and Mya's male friends. As Raven observes Nickels, she begins to find him to be adorable. Smooth chocolate skin, long eyelashes; she finds his conversation to be cocky and entertaining, bundled up in a big tan Woolrich coat, driving wildly with one hand barely touching the steering wheel. She can't fight being just a bit intrigued by him.

"You hungry? I feel like getting somethin' to eat." He asked, turning on Wynnfield Avenue.

Should I just be a little spontaneous? It's not like it's a planned date or anything. No, just get home. Raven's mind wrestles with herself.

"No, I ate at work, and I have an early morning with school tomorrow." Nickels looks disappointed, his face goes blank."

"Look, Raven, I'm gonna stop playing the fuck around with you," Nickels says, pulling his truck over on the corner of 55th and Lancaster Avenue. I've had my eye on you for a long time, you fine as a motherfucker. I know you got your lil' boyfriend or whatever, but I just want us to be friends. Raven sits silently, listening to Nickels little speech.

"We are cool." She says in an uncomfortable whisper.

"Girl, I mean special friends." Nickels has lust in his eyes. His chubby hand slowly reaches over, massaging the back of Raven's neck. Her heart says stop him, but her mind is inviting him.

"We'll have to see," Raven says gently, moving Nickels arm away from her neck.

"Yeah man, stop fucking playing with me. If you be my friend, I'll put plenty of this in your hands." Nickels smirks, digging in his coat pocket, revealing a thick wad of money.

It's more money than Raven had ever seen at one time. Her eyes grew big, but she maintains her cool. *That must be $10,000 easily?* She thinks. Nickels peels off three hundred dollars in crisp Benjamins, placing them in Raven's hand. She stares at the money, more money than she'd made that week at Marshalls, and definitely more money than Jamal had given her in months. *Was it really this easy to get money from guys? Is this what I've been missing out on? No, give it back, nothing this good comes your way this easy. There's always a price to pay.*

"If you be my friend, I'll look out for you. You too bad not to be spoiled." Nickels is grinning ear to ear, knowing he just scored major cool points.

After ten more minutes of small talk, Nickels pulls in front of Raven's house. She continued having second thoughts of giving him the money back, but couldn't. The three hundred dollars was burning through her pocket, just waiting to be spent.

"I'm gonna be at Brook let out tomorrow." Nickels yells out the driver side window. "I'm takin' you to lunch, and I'm not takin' no for an answer." He yells, speeding off.

"Raven, what are you doing?" She asked herself, walking up the steps, digging through her Fendi bag for her house keys.

The inside of the Hightower's house is pitch black. It's almost 1:00 a.m. Her parents and Little Ricky had long been asleep. Raven turns the living room lamp on, takes off her coat, hat and scarf sinking deep into the comfortable living room sofa. She lets out a sigh of relief. Even the familiar scents of her home are refreshing to her. She reaches over to her jacket, pulling out the fresh hundred dollar bills, staring at them as if it was the first time seeing money. She runs her fingers, feeling the smooth texture.

"I can go shopping tomorrow." She says.

Raven had been itching to go to the Toby Learner boutique on 16th and Samson. They sold exclusive couture pieces from the top European designers. Mya and Takia always shopped there, Raven only window shopped and occasionally bought a marked down sale item. Her paychecks never quite cut it, but Nickels gesture of friendship was going to give her, her first official Toby Learner shopping experience where she didn't have to worry about a price. *I see why Takia and Mya only fucked with hustlers. You get everything you want quick.* Raven's deep thoughts are interrupted by the annoying ring of her cell phone. Jamal's number flashes across the screen.

"Leave me the hell alone, Mally you getting on my last nerve. I need a change, some excitement in my life. Hmm, maybe I should get rid of you?" She feels sleep overtaking her body. She kicks off her Nine West shoe boots, stretches out on the couch, falling into a deep sleep, knowing heartbreaking decisions could be ahead of her.

Chapter 6

RAVEN: THE DRAMA

8:00 a.m. Wednesday Morning

Ah, I'm so tired. Raven thinks, looking herself over in the bedroom mirror. She tossed and turned the night before, finally sleepwalking to her cozy bed at 5:30 a.m., sleeping soundly for an hour and a half. Her parents and brother had already left for the day; silence once again engulfs Raven's world. She studies herself, just the same as she did every other day, but today, something seems different. She gently brushes her long black hair back into a perfect ponytail. The deep brown of her flawless mocha skin tone shined from baby lotion, her slanted Asian eyes looked soft like a doe. She smiles at her reflection, in love with herself. One thing is for certain, she is an exotic pretty chocolate girl. Raven looks sleek and simple, dressed in a mint green Gap turtleneck, skin-tight dark denim pencil pocket Guess jeans, with her gold-plated Escada logo belt and black leather Via Spiga knee boots. Brand new gold hoop earring gives her ensemble a retro vibe.

Raven moistens her lips, applying bronze lip gloss and eyeshadow when her cell phone starts ringing loudly from her nightstand, disrupting her peaceful silence. She knew exactly who it was. She rolls her eyes lowering her head.

"Jamal, I don't want to deal with you today." She hesitantly answers.

"Yo, I'm outside," Mally says with an attitude. She hangs up without a word.

She throws on her black wool peacoat, grabs her black patent leather Bebe book bag and house keys, slowly walking down the shiny dark hardwood stairs, wishing she could avoid what was waiting for her on the other side of the door. Jamal sits stone-faced in the driver seat of his mother's 1995 white Honda Civic. It's a sunny Wednesday, November morning.

"Good morning Raven." Mrs. Jones, a friendly neighbor, calls as she gets into her car for work.

"Hey, Mrs. Jones."

"Tell your mother I said hello."

"I sure will." They both smile and wave at each other.

Raven feels the tension as soon as she gets into the car. Jamal is tight-lipped, his handsome face in a deep frown; his wavy hair is wild and curly as if he needed a haircut wearing a wrinkled oversized t-shirt and forest green Dickies pants. He shifts the gear out of park, cutting his honey light brown colored eyes; they almost seemed to glow in the dense sunlight. Raven could see the anger in them. Jamal was never good at hiding his emotions, whatever he was feeling was written all over his face. Raven sits still, twiddling her fingers together. *I know he about to start his shit.*

"Raven, what was all that about last night?" He asked calmly, breaking the silence. "My car was down, shit was out of my hands. I did everything I could in my power to pick you up. My mom gave me her car, I hauled ass up to your job, you nowhere to be found.

Then I call your phone and you acting like an ungrateful bitch. What was I supposed to do? Fly up there like Aladdin on a magic carpet? Raven, you been actin' real funny lately. Tell me what the fuckin' problem is?" The veins in Jamal's neck, his handsome face turning red, his honey brown eyes deep like a man searching for answers.

Raven takes a deep breath, staring out the car window at the different color row houses. Passing by kids who were walking to Brook. Jamal turns on 59th and Lansdowne.

"Mally, I don't know how to say this, but we ain't workin' no more. We goin' in two different directions."

"Yo, what the fuck is you sayin'? You breakin' up with me?" Mally yells.

"I don't know Mally. I don't know what the fuck I want right now." Raven cries tears building in her eyes.

"I can't believe you sayin' this shit right now. After all the shit we been through; I don't know who the fuck you are right now."

"I'll tell you who I am. I'm a girl growing up, and the boy I've been in love with since I was fourteen is still in the same place."

"I ain't tryna hear the shit. It's another nigga ain't it? Them girlfriend of yours done got in your head, I know it; I know it's them bitches." Jamal says choked up, pulling in front of Brook.

"Jamal, here we go again. My friends don't have shit to do with how my heart is feelin'. I'm my own woman, maybe you really don't know who I am anymore." Raven opens the car door jumping out.

"Raven we not done talkin'," Jamal shouts as Raven slams the car door.

The crowd of urban teenagers is filing into the building. Raven looks back at Mally who's staring at her lost; his honey brown eyes have tears in them. *Oh, Mally, I'm sorry; so sorry.* Raven thinks, pushing her way through the crowd.

"Hey, Raven. What's up girl?" Was heard from guys and girls making their way through the school. Her mind is so gone, she barely acknowledges any of them. Once she'd been scanned by the gray metal detectors, Raven rushes to the first-floor girls bathroom. The smell of fish and cheap perfume fills her nose. Raven enters one of the small stalls, pulls off her book bag, sits down on the toilet and tears start rushing down her face uncontrollably. Her heart starts pounding as if it's going to burst from her chest. She pulls at her hair as if she wanted to pull it out by the root. Snot runs from her nose; Raven cries like someone just died, but something had died; a five-year love that Raven had put all of her faith and dreams into. She knew that last look she and Jamal gave each other, meant that it was over. Five years of Valentine's Day, first kiss, first time making love are all gone just like that. Falling in love was fast, but falling out of it was even faster.

"Girl, get yourself together." She wipes the tears from her eyes, crossing her legs rocking back and forth sobbing for the love she was losing for Jamal, and especially for herself.

Was she really making the right decision? Raven sat silently in the small gray stall through the entire first period, emerging at the beginning of the second period. The drab graffiti walls looked especially gloomy. Raven wanders in a daze into her second period English literature class.

"You're five minutes late Ms. Hightower." Mr. Riley, the middle-aged, overweight Caucasian teacher says, meeting Raven with a frozen glare. "Ms. Hightower, so happy that you decided to grace us with your presence."

Mr. Riley says condescendingly in his snotty high-pitched voice.

All eyes were on her since Mr. Riley had put her on blast. The boys give her sexually seductive look overs while the girls, as usual, checked her gear from head to toe. As she makes her way through the rows of the desk, she finds her sixth-row seat next to Mya who looks baffled to see her.

"Raven, you never miss Mrs. Ashcroft first period class, I needed to see your homework from last night." Mya hisses with an attitude. "Rav, you don't hear me talkin' to you." Mya hisses louder, rolling her eyes.

"What?" Raven says, shaking her head as if she was snapping out of a trance.

"Raven, what's wrong with you?"

She looked at Mya for the first time since she sat down next to her. She finds her best friend particularly stunning. Mya has her long wavy hair pulled back in a long French braid, a yellow and pink Dolce & Gabbana headband that enhanced her hazel eyes, and hot pin and black Dolce & Gabbana fitted tracksuit with D&G written up the sleeves and pants leg. She looked ghetto-fabulous to the extreme.

"Rav, is you cool?"

"Me and Mally broke up this morning."

"For real?" Mya's eyes light up with interest. "What happened? He was trippin' wasn't he?"

"Excuse me, Ms. Hightower, and Ms. Campbell I'm trying to teach my class. Shakespeare's classic play Hamlet is far more important than any meager conversation you two are having; or do one of you think that you can teach this class better than, I?"

"Aye Mr. Riley, with the dough you gettin', you couldn't pay me to teach shit." The entire class burst into roaring laughter. Mya flashes a dazzling smile; she was in full-blown diva mode.

"Ms. Campbell you're right, I believe being an ass is your life's calling. Now get out of my classroom this instance." A few students laugh loudly. Mya quickly scans the room, gritting on anybody who dared laugh at her.

"Come on Raven, let's get out of this corny ass class." They both get up, get their book bags and with heads held high, switched out the room giving their fuck 'em girl walk. Mya turns to Mr. Riley, rolling her eyes with force before slamming the classroom door. "Girl I can't stand Mr. Riley," Mya says, strolling down the quiet third-floor hallway. Walking on the polished dark green floor past the rows of tan lockers. "So Raven, what happened?" Mya whispers, putting her arm around Raven's shoulder in a comforting way.

"At this point, it is what it is. We fight all the time, we barely have anything in common anymore. He can barely do anything for me. It just boiled over; last night Nickels drove me home."

"Nickels?" Mya says surprised.

"Yeah, Nickels." Raven almost blushes. "Me and Mally are growing apart."

"Rav, I know I said a lot of negative stuff about Mally, but he is a good guy. Do what you feel is best for you, not because of what me and Takia say."

"Girl you know I got a mind of my own," Raven says hesitantly, secretly knowing that her friends were a factor in her decision to break up with Mally. *I am a follower; a fucking follower without a mind of my own.* Raven thinks as she and Mya walk to the third-floor girls' bathroom, only to find Kareema, TeTe, and Asia in an in-depth conversation about a boy from 58th and Malcolm Street. Once they lay eyes on the baddest

115

chicks, all conversation ceases. The two groups of girls face off with each other. If looks could kill of few of them would be dead.

Things had cooled off since the big free fall at Club Gotham, but bad blood never stops running. Raven looked TeTe up and down, she looks corny as usual rocking a red Limited logo sweat suit and black Ked sneakers. Her black weave looked dry. Since their fight, TeTe didn't look Raven's way. *The way I feel right now, I will body her boney ass.* Raven thinks, checking herself out in the mirror. Kareema is eyeing Mya, checking her out like a tigress. Mya smirks, watching her through the dull mirror, applying pink MAC lip gloss to her lips.

"I love being me. When you're a bad bitch, they always try to throw dirt on your name." Mya boldly says, adjusting the headband on her head.

Raven turns, looking the three haters in the face. *I wish y'all bitches would make a move.* She thinks as she and Kareema lock eyes. The frown on her face made her less attractive than usual.

"Come on y'all, I don't have time for these delusional haters." Kareema snarls, switching her huge ass out of the bathroom with TeTe and Asia following behind her.

"Bum bitches," Mya says, facing Raven.

"Mya, girl what am I gonna do? I don't know anymore." Tears start swelling in Raven's eyes.

"Oh Raven, don't worry. I'll help you get through this, I'll be your shoulder." Mya says, embracing Raven. At that moment, they became more than girlfriends; sisters linked by the heart.

Fourth-period lunch is packed to capacity. It felt like the whole school was cramming into the overly crowded lunch room. Rows of boys in blue and tan Dickies suits lined the walls outside the lunch room. They are the tough Master Street Boys, small-time hustlers who had boxing skills like professionals. They winked their eyes and flirt as Mya and Raven sashayed by.

"What's up Mar, Dre, Tone, and Mook?" Mya smiled, speaking to a few of them. They would never holler at the Master Street Boys, but they had an official allure about their squad.

Raven and Mya are greeted like celebrities by the groups of fly and not so fly teens, seated at various assigned seating locations in the crowded urban jungle called lunch.

"Where y'all been?" Takia's voice hollers over the loud talking crowd around them as Missy Elliot's *I Can't Stand The Rain* played over the stereo system.

Raven and Mya turned to see their other best friend approaching. She glows with big blonde layers of curls flowing down her shoulders, bright red Versace logo sweater and black stretch Versace jeans hugging every one of her dangerous curves. Ever since Takia had become Little Rell's girlfriend, she seemed happier than Raven had ever seen her. She had cut off all of her male friends and became a one-man girl. Her whole world had become about Rell, and for the first time, Raven saw a guy who really loved Takia for more than just her body. Even in the midst of her relationship drama, Raven was more than happy for her friend.

"Yo Ta, Raven, and Mally broke up," Mya whispers in Takia's ear.

"Good, Raven I been told you to drop Mally's broke ass."

"Can y'all move so we can sit down?" Mya yells at a group of special ed kids who quickly get up from the BC's favorite table; even though it was not any of their lunch periods.

"Rav, you did the right thing," Takia says.

"Damn Takia, you could be a little more sensitive. Raven and Mally have been together forever; he's her first real love. You know a bitch be feeling sick leavin' a nigga like that."

"You right Mya, I'm sorry Raven."

You should be sorry. Raven thought, giving Takia the silent treatment.

"Raven, I've always told you never settle for less. Sometimes people outgrow each other in relationships."

"I know," Raven says, irritated from the lecturing, running her hand over her smooth forehead.

"But Takia, guess who she talking to?" Mya says mischievously.

"Shut up Mya," Raven says, trying to cover Mya's mouth with her hands.

"Bitch who?!" Takia squeals.

"Nickels!" Mya blurts out, smacking Raven's hand away.

Why did she tell Takia? I'm never gonna hear the end of this.

"Raven, I always told you Nickels liked you. What brought about these changes in you? This can't be my best friend since I've known since the sixth grade." Takia says, shaking her head, widening her eyes as if Raven was an alien sitting in front of her.

"For the record you two, I'm not messing with Nickels. He gave me a ride home, and I found out he's a cool guy. Plus Mally and I been having problems."

"But anyway, Rell is taking me to Jersey to the Feather's Nest Hotel for the weekend. We staying in the Jungle Room, they have hot tubs in every room."

"Girl, I heard the Feather's Nest was the shit," Mya says, admiring the platinum princess cut diamond ring on her left ring finger.

"Yo, look at Smokey, Rocky and them twins. They look like they about to get at somebody." Raven says pointing to the group of four boys moving quickly through the lunch room all dressed in black Dickies suits.

"Something about to pop off. Smokey arguing with Mar from 59th Street." Takia screamed, standing up on the lunchroom table to get a better view of the scene. The sight of a fight about to break out always caused a huge commotion. Kids were screaming, jumping on top of tables, pushing and shoving each other to get a better view of the violence.

"Oh shit! Smoke just sucker punched Mar in the face," Takia screams at the top of her lungs. Raven and Mya quickly join her on top of the table.

Smokey, Rocky, and the twins Ramier, and Khalid Johnson go into a bloody war like free fall with the boys from 59th and Master Street; fist flying everywhere. Smokey's four-man crew were up against seven of Master Street's roughest but held their own.

"Damn, Smokey fucking Mar up!" Mya shouted as Smoke caught Mar, a thin built light-skinned boy. Smoke hit him with four accurate uppercuts to the jaw.

The twins can fuckin' rumble. Raven thinks, and Ramier and Khalid slammed and boxed the heads off four of the 59th Street Boys at one time.

"Tone givin' Rocky that work. Get his punk ass!" Takia hollers. Tone, a short, stocky brown-skinned boy who was known to have major box game, was certainly beating Rocky senselessly, jab after jab to Rocky's face. Rocky was trying unsuccessfully to land some punches but was getting his ass kicked.

The teens are screaming like they're watching a Tyson versus Holyfield fight on HBO. Just as things are getting bloody, five blue uniformed school security officers rushed through the dark gray metal cafeteria doors jumping into the mix, breaking up Smoke and Jamar, slamming them on a long brown lunch table, handcuffing each of them. Two officers grabbed the twins, who each had three Master Street Boys on them. The crowd of teens is in an uncontrollable frenzy. Five more security guards rush in, pushing and shoving kids out the way.

"Get back! Get back!" They yell, trying to regain control.

"Yo, fuck y'all flashlight cops! Y'all ain't no real cops." Students scream, throwing food and open juice containers at the school security officers.

After five minutes of tussling, school police had the guys under control, each on being taken out in handcuffs. The NTAs and lunch aids started getting the crowds to fade out.

"Go to class people, go to class!" They shout timidly. Most of the NTAs and lunch aids are terrified of the students.

"Yo, them niggas was getting it in, Smokey got hands. My old boo made me proud today." Mya says playfully as they file out of the crowded lunchroom into the sea of kids changing classes trying to get into the next lunch period.

The next period is pretty much the same, one fight after another. A domino effect had taken place. Raven was restless with everything around her. When the last period bell rang she felt relief, there was nothing she wanted more than out of the stinky building. Students were rushing to get outside and what a sight it was. Overbrook's infamous let out is packed and more out of control. Half of University High School is up at Brook for a basketball game. University High had a long-standing rivalry with Overbrook. *Which school was more fly? Who had the best girls? Whose basketball team was the best?* It had been a heated topic of debate for years; *Which high school was the most fly, Overbrook or Uni.?* It was kind of like what came first, the chicken or the egg; and whenever two school's basketball teams played each other, it was certainly an Easter Day fashion show; both school's rocking their Sunday best.

"I forgot it was a game today," Raven says, scanning through the large crowd.

"Look at these University hoes," Takia says, popping gum in her mouth, looking in the direction of the girls standing in front of the Sugar Bowl dressed in Moschino, Armani Exchange, and Versace.

They were certainly staring too, fascinated by Overbrook's fly girls and University did not lack in the fly guy department. Groups of cuties from down 'The Bottom,' dressed in Coogi, Iceberg, and Polo Sport, and fresh Guess jeans were definitely liking the eye candy Overbrook had to offer. And right on cue like a scene in a Biggie video, Nickels' shiny Tahoe turns the corner, blasting *Can't Nobody Hold Me Down* by Puff Daddy and Mase. He pulls right in front of the large crowd in front of the Sugar Bowl, rolling his window down; his chubby cheeks grinning underneath a red and blue Sixers fitted hat.

"I see Nickels came to pick you up Rav," Mya says, nudging her shoulder.

A rush of adrenaline overcomes Raven, the sight of Nickels shiny SUV sitting on glistening rims. The fact that all of the girls were eyeing lustfully after Nickels is a turn on. Seconds later Little Rell turns the corner, his Benz wagon freshly washed and wax. He pulls up right behind Nickels' Tahoe, hopping out like a ghetto superstar. Fresh orange Iceberg History t-shirt with

Snoopy on the front, and a big iced out Jesus piece hanging around his neck.

Chapter 7

Takia: Mafia Land

December 2, 1997

"Oh my God, the test said positive!" Takia screams,
holding the E.P.T. home pregnancy test showing off the
pink plus sign in the air for Mya and Raven to see.

"Takia, let me see that!" Mya bogarts, snatching the
test out of Takia's hand. "It really is positive. Takia,
you're really knocked up!" An eerie silence follows
Mya's statement. Through all their years of being
sexually active with guys, pregnancy was always the
girls' biggest fear. Not only will their parents kill them,
but bad chicks didn't have babies. Sure, they knew
plenty of their classmates and girls from the
neighborhood who were teenage moms, or had
abortions, but never had any of their immediate circle
dealt with the infamous "P" word until today. If Takia
was bothered by her newfound circumstances, she
concealed it very well.

"What are you gonna do Takia?" Raven asked laying
across Mya's huge bed, her body tight in the fetal
position. They all had been holding up at Mya's house
waiting for the results. Takia looks lost, her face and
eyes blank.

"What am I gonna do?" She sighs. That's a question she never dared to ask herself.

"I mean, I'm ready for a baby. I'll be eighteen in less than a month, but is Rell ready for a baby? Now that's an answer I don't know, and that scares me the most."

"Ta, if you want me to go to Planned Parenthood with you, I will," Mya says while trying on a pair of black suede Mary Jane pumps, sitting at her large vanity.

"You're only a few weeks at the most. An abortion is only like four hundred dollars. Tell Rell to give you the money for shopping, but you know what it's really for." She says so nonchalantly as if she's been in the situation herself.

Mya looks startled at the way Takia and Raven were staring at her. Blood rushed to her cheeks making a pretty blush.

"Well, that's what my cousin Regina told me her girlfriend Tia did when she found out she got pregnant. Why are y'all staring at me like that?" Mya shouts defensively.

Raven quickly diverts her eyes, but Takia grins sarcastically.

Bitch, you really make me wonder about you sometimes. She thinks. "I know one thing is for sure, I'm not killing my baby. I'm gonna keep it real with Rell, and if he loves me like he says he does, he'll stick by my side."

"Takia, you're way off. Of all the females, you should know that messing with a street dude is one thing, but having a baby by one is a whole different story because nothing is guaranteed with them." Raven says, sitting up on Mya's bed fixing the silver and white Moschino belly shirt she wore. Since Raven had been with Nickels, her wardrobe had increased tremendously. She had way more confidence as well, but she was still as judgmental as ever.

"Raven, how would you know how street guys are? You just started messing with one, what... like a week ago?" Takia says flatly, a grimace on her face, slowly running her fingers through her eighteen-inch blonde weave ponytail lounging on Mya's pink leather loveseat.

"What Takia?" Raven says, rolling her small slanted eyes. "I learned the game fast, that's all I'm saying."

"Raven girl please, you the last one to be giving anybody advice on street niggas. Girl, you can't tell me nothin'. You just getting' a little taste."

"Before you two whores start drawling on each other," Mya says, smacking her lips. "Puff Daddy and The Family's concert tickets go on sale Friday, and we need to be in that motherfucker."

"The tickets go on sale for real? We got to be in that shit!" Raven squeals, jumping up and down on Mya's bed.

"Yo, what are we gonna wear is the question?" Takia says. Her pretty brown eyes are wide with anticipation.

"What y'all mean? We comin' through the concert in fox and mink coats like Big Mamma Queen Bee." Mya announces standing switching through her bedroom like Tyra Banks on the runway.

This was a much-needed distraction. For the next ten minutes, the worries of teen pregnancy were far from their minds. The world of fashion and ghetto-fabulous hip-hop filled their minds.

"Hello, babe," Takia says sweetly into her cell phone. "You outside? Okay, I'm on my way out."

"That's Rell." Takia has a look of fear and distress on her face as she buttons her lavender Donna Karan peacoat.

"Look, Ta, I'm sorry for what I said earlier. Just be strong, and if he trips, your sisters got your back. And we'll get through this like we do everything else." Raven says as she and Mya embrace Takia in a loving three-way hug.

"Stop, stop, y'all about to make me start crying."

"You better not. Remember, whatever you choose to do, we got your back. We love you Takia. Now go see if that man really loves you." Mya playfully smacks Takia on her butt.

"You two are the best friends any girl could have wished for." With one last look, Takia dashes down the winding mahogany staircase of Mya's parents home, exiting into the calm black night where Rell's Benz wagon was waiting.

"What's up baby?" Rell says, smiling sideways popping a CD into the six-disc changer. Jay-Z's *In My Lifetime Vol. 1* begins playing low in the background.

He'd begun letting his mustache and goatee grow in. He was starting to look more like a grown man, than a baby face. Since the day Takia became his girl, her whole life had been so much better. Her body belonged to one man, not a dozen hustlers who she hated touching her most private parts. She cut every single one off. Once she became Rell's girl, even Pumpkin, who she definitely had a long-term love for had no place in her life any longer. She was not just Takia the whore, gold digger, mistress, or sideline hoe; she was Rell's wifey. His main girl. He overlooked all of her past indiscretions, bad reputation, and her days of straight up wildin' in the streets. But would a baby mess up her perfect world? In Rell, she found strength and love so strong. From all the great disappointments in her life, she finally found someone she could lean on.

"Why you so quiet?" Rell asked, driving through Fairmount Park to the expressway.

"Nothing, I'm just tired."

"I noticed you been restless for the past few nights. What's on your mind Takia?"

"Nothing." She whispers, running her hands up and down the sleeves of her peacoat.

"Listen, you know you can talk to me about anything." Rell reaches over and affectionately massages Takia's neck with his strong right hand.

"You're too damn good to me. I don't wanna lose you. Lord, somebody, tell me what should I do." Her mind races staring out the passenger side window at oncoming traffic, bright headlights zooming by.

"Why are people always in a rush to go nowhere?" Rell says nonchalantly. "Lately, all we've been doing is rushing to go nowhere."

Once they arrive at Rell's Penrose duplex, directly behind the Northeast Philadelphia Airport, one of the several rental properties he owned, they both collapse on the soft queen size bed tired from a long day of running to nowhere. Takia lays her head on Rell's chest, her eyes closed, but her body wide awake.

"Rell, you up?"

"Yeah." He yawns.

"I have something important to tell you."

"What's that babe?" He's clearly in and out of sleep, his hand tight around her waist.

"Rell, I'm pregnant."

"You what?" He jumps up, fully conscious.

"I swear I didn't do it on purpose to trap you." Takia cries. "Rell don't be mad at me."

"Shhh." Rell put his index finger to Takia's lips. He sits beside her, his sleepy brown eyes studying her from top to bottom. Takia lays on her back wearing only a

127

strapless pink bra and matching panties. She had never felt more vulnerable and inferior then at this very moment.

"You having my baby?" Takia slowly shakes her head yes. "Why would you ever think I'd be mad at you? We created something out of love." Rell pulls Takia up, and they embrace tightly.

"Oh Rell, I didn't know how you was gonna feel. I want this baby so bad."

"And we gonna have him. I'm with you every step of the way."

"Hold up. Him? How you know, it's a him and not a her?"

"Because, in my family, we only make boys."

"That might change with this one buddy." They both laugh joyously. The tension was finally broken.

Rell put his head on Takia's stomach and kissed it gently and laid there until he went to sleep. She rubbed his head tenderly, looking down at him, thanking God over and over again for the joy that was coming into her life. With that, for the first time in weeks, Takia was able to get a good night's rest. The next few weeks flew by. These were the best times of her life. She was doing better in school, attending regularly and maintaining a steady C plus average. She was never dumb, just never applied herself or had anyone who cared. Between Rell and Raven, both of them helped her tremendously with her homework and projects. She hadn't felt this motivated about school since she was in the seventh grade. Rell had been taking her to all of her prenatal appointments.

The doctors guaranteed everything was fine. Takia and the baby were perfectly healthy. Even morning sickness was not so bad. Rell had announced to everyone in his family that Takia was pregnant. His two older sisters, two dozen aunts, first cousins, and most of all his mother were ecstatic. Takia finally had a place and a family where she belonged. Rell even surprised her with a small birthday dinner at the Chart House on Delaware Avenue on her eighteenth birthday on the twentieth of December. Mya, Carmello Black, Raven and Nickels and a few of Rell's family members were all in attendance. The only person Takia managed to keep her pregnancy announcement away from was Michelle. She didn't want her mother's evil misery or scornful words putting a damper on her joy, and the less Michelle knew of her business, the better.

The first time she felt her baby kick inside of her, she was in love. But a whole different kind of love that she never imagined existed. No amount of money or jewelry could ever compare to the love that was growing inside of her.

Chapter 8

TAKIA: THE BAD BOY SHOW

January 5, 1998

For weeks, all anyone at Overbrook, or Philadelphia for that matter talked about was the Puff Daddy and The Family concert. Anybody who was somebody or fly was gonna be there. Mya was lucky to score third-row seats for her crew on her mom's American Express card. This was more than a concert, this was the defining moment of the ghetto-fabulous era. *Power 99 FM* radio station advertised the concert every five seconds. Takia got excited every time she heard *It's All About the Benjamins* blasting through her stereo system.

"What the blood clot?! Wanna bumble with the Bee huh? Bzzz, throw a hex on the whole family. (yeah, yeah yeah) Dressed in all black like "The Omen," have your friends singin' this is for my homie, and you know me, from makin' niggas so sick..." Takia would scream at the top of her lungs doing her best Lil' Kim impersonation.

The biggest hip-hop stars of the era were going to be live on stage. Puffy, Mase, The Lox, Busta Rhymes, Jay-Z, 112, The Firm, Foxy Brown, Usher, and of course Takia's idol, Lil' Kim, and Junior M.A.F.I.A. Kim's *Hardcore* album helped Takia gain confidence and an edge on how to talk slick and play niggas like dummies. She would recite Lil' Kim's lyrics to *Big Mamma Thang* and *Queen Bitch* while getting ready for school. She thought of herself as Princess Bee. The first time she got some lame nigga from up 57th and Lansdowne Avenue to buy her DKNY sneakers, sweatshirt, and a Nautica ski jacket from down on Market Street for six hundred dollars her freshman year. She stared at her Lil' Kim's poster of her squatting, legs open looking powerful and glamorous and knew her imaginary big sister would be proud.

Every fly teen at Overbrook who was lucky enough to get their blinged out hands on one of the precious tickets, boasted like it was one of Willy Wonka's famous golden tickets. But the biggest question on everyone's mind; *what are you wearing?* This became a greeting of some sort. Bragging had taken on new heights, between crap games, guys boasted about having custom Rolexes and exclusive Versace and Gucci sneakers that hadn't hit the stores. Girls talked about Gucci knee boots and sheer Fendi catsuits. But of course, everybody was looking to see the baddest chicks.

What will the flyest girls in school be wearing? Inquiring minds definitely wanted to know. Whether friend or foe, hater or dick eater, they all asked Takia, Mya, and Raven constantly. They all smirked concededly replying...

"Just wait until the night of the show, you'll see us. You won't be able to miss us the way we'll be stunting." The girls definitely felt the pressure.

"Slow down Mya." Takia giggles from the backseat of Carmello's brand new dark silver Lincoln Navigator truck.

It was barely two weeks old, and the fresh car smell of leather was potent. Raven sat in the front passenger seat browsing through *Vogue* and *Elle* magazines like a crazed couture demon.

"I need the perfect look. The show is in two weeks, and all I have is a pair of black Gucci pumps. I have no outfit." Raven pouts like a child tossing her long dark ponytail to one side of her shoulder.

"Girl once we get to New York, they got every store you could dream of on Madison and Fifth Avenue," Takia says, chewing on a stick of Doublemint gum.

Mya focuses behind the steering wheel, her wavy, curly hair wild all over her head, her hazel eyes look tired from a long night with Carmello.

"Nickels gave me a stack. I should be cool right?" Raven asked, unbuttoning her green, yellow and pink Coogi cardigan sweater.

"Yeah, a stack should be cool," Takia answers, not wanting to burst Raven's bubble. But on Madison Avenue, a thousand dollars wasn't shit. Mya throws Takia a wide-eyed glance through the driver side visor mirror silently telling Takia she was thinking the same thing.

"Hey Rav, put in my Total's [CD], I wanna hear *Kissing You*," Takia says, digging through her Moschino book bag.

"Yeah, put Total in." Mya chimes in, entering the Holland Tunnel, emerging a few minutes later in New York City, 'The Big City of Dreams' as Snoop Dogg would call it. As he famously crushed the large skyscrapers in his music video during the height of the East Coast versus West Coast rap beef.

Takia rolls the window down and breathes in. The air in New York City felt different. The legions of yellow cabs racing from one street to the next. People rushing at a rapid pace gave New York City a pulse that Philly

132

could never have. She laughs at Mya driving wildly as any New Yorker, dipping in and out of traffic.

"Fuck out the way!" She screamed while beeping the SUV's horn. Mya and Takia had become New York City experts, learning their way around the city when they were dating Pumpkin and Mario.

"Make a right on Broadway," Takia says, noticing Mya's hesitation to turn in the middle of a busy intersection. Thanks to Takia's photographic memory, a few traffic lights later they were in fashion heaven.

"Oh, my fuckin' God! I can't believe this." Raven squeals, jumping around in the front seat like a child on their first trip to Great Adventure.

"This is every 'hood girl's dream," Mya whispers, her face covered in large black Chanel frames.

The sun shined brightly on the beautiful boutiques on both sides of Madison Avenue. Once the girls found parking, they were like three hungry lionesses with an appetite that only shopping could fulfill.

"Where should we start?" Raven says, spinning around gleefully.

"Let's start at Versace," Takia suggests, not knowing where she should start herself.

They whipped through Versace like a hurricane. Prada, Chanel, Donna Karan, Dolce & Gabbana, Gucci, Moschino, Jean Paul Gaultier, Escada, Fendi, Iceberg, and Christian Lacroix soon followed. They literally shopped until they dropped. Raven learned quickly that a thousand dollars only went so far. Her shopping spree stopped at Gucci. She wasn't thrilled about it either. Rell sent Takia well prepared with three stacks, but Mya is limitless with her resources. Between Carmello's four thousand dollars in cold hard cash, and her Platinum Visa card that her parents paid staggering charges every month. Two pairs of six hundred fifty dollar Chanel sandals and a five hundred dollar bodysuit were nothing. Plus two pairs of Fendi sneakers at four hundred fifty dollars a pop, eight hundred dollar Gucci knee boots and a whopping one thousand three hundred pair of Christian Lacroix white leather Swarovski crystal trimmed thigh high boots were priceless. Mya was showing and proving that she was the definition of a material girl.

Takia did pretty well herself. The seven hundred dollar pair of brown mink trimmed leather Versace sandals, and five hundred dollar tan Escada mini dress will go perfectly with the full-length mink swing coat that Rell had let her put on hold at Diane Furs. She loaded up on several pairs of Dolce & Gabbana stretch jeans and matching logo t-shirts. Plus shades from Gucci, Chanel, and DKNY catsuits and colorful Iceberg tights.

The long ride to New York had been worth it. The baddest chicks found the couture goodies to stunt on friends and foe alike. For a split second, Takia felt like Jay-Z's song, *Can't Knock The Hustle.* She felt like standing up in the Navigator and, "Screaming through the sunroof, money ain't a thang." It was past midnight when they arrived back in Philly.

"Wake up Takia!" Mya yelled, tapping her hard on the shoulder.

"Damn, I'm tired." She thought yawning, gathering up her shopping bags.

"Aight, see you bitches in school on Monday," Takia says in a low groggy voice.

The weight of the shopping bags was heavy against her arm. The night wind whipped against her body. The thin pale blue and yellow Iceberg sweater felt like nothing was covering her body. She shivered looking through her Moschino bag for her house keys. Once she opened the door, Mya beeped the horn, then sped off. She rushes through the door to escape the cold, throws her shopping bags on the floor, turns on the living room lamp and starts pulling things out of her bag admiring her designer delights. But she is suddenly startled when she hears Rell's voice loud and aggressive from the bedroom. He's arguing with someone. Takia slowly walks to the bedroom, presses her ear against the door and begins eavesdropping.

"Man fuck that!" Rell yells. "That nigga gotta give me more time to come up with the money. Ninety thousand dollars ain't no chump change. Nino, tell Anthony I need another week or two, I thought Ra'Quan was stable. I never thought he would fuck up three keys." "Man, I know I brought him to the table, but y'all been fronting me shit since I was sixteen. Y'all gave me my start." "Nino, I know business is business."

Takia feels a sharp chill move through her body. She opens the door, Rell is sitting on the edge of the bed wearing a pair of black Polo Sport boxers. His bedroom eyes looked watery. When he sees Takia standing in the doorway, he jumps to his feet.

"Yo, when did you get back?" He demands. She stands silent, staring at him, her soft brown eyes alert with fear. "Yo Nino I gotta call you back, my girl just got here. I'll hit you later."

"You don't hear me fuckin' talkin' to you, Takia?" Rell asks aggressively walking toward her.

"Rell, what is going on? I heard your conversation. Who do you owe money to?"

"What? You listenin' to my phone conversations now?" He screams, raising his fist in a way Takia thought he was about to punch her. Takia steps back in fear. "Oh, baby I'm so sorry. Come here." Rell says calmly, realizing he's taking his anger out on Takia unfairly. "I'm in some deep shit right now.

"What is it?" Takia asked, beginning to cry.

"My man Ra'Quan from Fifth Street, a nigga I've known my whole life asked me for my coke connect with the Italian mob from South Philly, so he could get started taking over Williamsport, PA. It's a lot of fiends out there. The deal was that I was gonna get broken off thirty percent, and the mafia guys would get forty percent interest for fronting him the work. But the nigga done disappeared without a trace. Now they're after me to pay the debt."

"But that's not your fault." Takia cries.

"Listen, I've been dealing with these dudes since I was about sixteen. They run Philadelphia, Jersey, even up to New York. Italians are different from us, they take that family loyalty shit very serious. They fronted him the keys on the strength of me, and because I brought him to the table, the payment for the keys is now my responsibility. They want almost one hundred thousand dollars by this Friday or..."

"Or what? They gonna kill you?"

Rell's face goes blank. "That's a major possibility."

"All these clothes and jewelry we got in here. Sell all this shit!"

Takia starts pulling clothes wildly out of the closet and drawers, emptying a jewelry box filled with diamond rings, gold Rolex watches, and other precious gems. Rell grabs her from behind, closing his arms tightly around her.

"Listen Takia, I'm gonna handle this. We ain't never gonna have to sell shit. I wanted to keep all of this from you. You're pregnant Takia, you don't need this kind of stress. We're gonna be just fine, but listen to me carefully." Rell said facing her, grabbing her gently by the face. "Don't talk to anybody about this. None of your friends, nobody. Do you hear me Takia?" She slowly shook her head yes. "Come on, let's go to bed."

Rell turned the lights and television off as Takia slipped her clothes off, slipping into bed, laying on her man's chest as he gently strokes her hair. Her hand falls to her stomach feeling her baby kick inside her. She let out a deep breath wanting to wake Rell but didn't dare. A new life was just beginning safe inside her, but she was sick and worried about the old one lying beside her.

Chapter 9

TAKIA: I'M A FLY GIRL

The night of the Puffy show had come quickly, and though this should have been one of the most joyful times in Takia's life, she smiled on the outside but secretly was crying a river on the inside. Raven and Mya said she had been acting strange since they had come back from New York. She blamed it on her growing pregnancy, but if they truly knew what she was dealing with, they would be frightened to the core.

Let's get this show on the road. She thought while applying pale plum MAC lipstick sitting in Mya's huge vanity mirror.

The girls decided to get dressed at Mya's house for the concert. Takia looked stunning, her pregnancy-enhanced her beauty giving her skin an extra glow. The breast milk flowing in her bosom made them bigger and fuller. Fresh from Platinum Shears hair salon, twenty-inches of honey blonde European hair straight flowed down her back. Eyeshadow and blush was cover girl perfect, and the Escada tan satin mini dress fits every curve. She slips on her mink Versace sandals. Accessories were last. Her silver-toned diamond encrusted Movado watch, and the princess cut diamond ring Rell bought for their six-month anniversary is placed on the same hand as her watch. Takia rose to take a better look at herself in Mya's full-length mirror.

"Bitch, you look fucking hot," Mya says, walking into her bedroom holding a bottle of Moët and three champagne glasses looking fabulous wearing white Gucci stretch pants with an enormous gold Gucci double-G logo belt.

Mya's pants were tucked into the five-inch white Christian Lacroix thigh boots, and her breasts were almost popping out of the white Gucci printed bra top with small silver G's all over it. Her hair was pulled back in a long ponytail off of her beautiful face. Takia was in awe. She had never seen Mya look more beautiful. Her hazel eyes seemed to twinkle. The diamond Rolex watch, bracelet, and bangle earrings gleamed. She was wearing so much ice, she could have rocked the mic on stage next to Lil' Kim and Foxy Brown.

"Let's put our coats on." Mya giggled, grabbing the black garment bag containing her six thousand dollar full-length white fox coat that she fell in love with at Zinman Furs, begging Carmello for weeks to buy it for her.

Takia pulled her dark chestnut brown mink swing coat from its own garment bag, and they slip on their expensive furs. Takia slides her hand up and down the soft mink.

"It's the softest thing I've ever felt in my life," Takia says. "I think I'm beginning to fall in love with fur."

They both start spinning around in their coats, striking a pose when Raven opens the bathroom door looking like a gorgeous vision of 'hood loveliness, *dressed in all black like The Omen*. Black strappy open toe Gucci pumps with black patent leather Versace pants that look painted on and a sheer black-and-white Versace shirt with a black satin strapless bra revealing her firm breasts underneath. Her hair was bone straight with a part in the middle. Huge black and gold Versace glasses cover her small delicate face. Nickels large gold Jesus piece medallion hangs around her neck. Full soft pink pouty lips were all that was seen of her face and topped off with a tapered waist length black fox coat.

"Look at us," Takia says, pulling Raven and Mya close to her in the full-length mirror.

The three of them were left basking in amazement at each other's reflection. *Have there ever been young chicks from any 'hood that were this official?* They had surpassed chicks twice their age. The embodiment of the teenage 'hood dream. Everything they ever hoped for, all their material wishes was theirs, and if their status weren't known, by the end of the night, they would be ghetto-fabulous legends.

Mya gives a dramatic teeth-baring smile. "I think this calls for a toast." She pops the Moët open and fills the glasses, handing Raven and Takia a chilled glass. "Let's go fuck this concert up!" She declares.

They quickly gulp down the Moët and take one final look of their own perfect youthful immortality dressed in fur and diamonds. This was the moment they have been waiting for their entire high school lives. Takia tried to enjoy the moment, but an eerie feeling crept over her. The First Union Spectrum was filled to capacity. It was 8:45 p.m. the first opening act Usher had just left the stage. There appeared to be a million young adults out to get the chance to see The Bad Boy Family perform in all its blinged out glory.

Takia had been to plenty of concerts, every Powerhouse since she was about 12 years old, but the excitement and energy of this night were unlike anything she has ever experienced. It was electric. Ticket scalpers were selling tickets for two hundred dollars, groups of desperate well-dressed people were flashing crisp Benjamin's at the scalpers. None of them knowing if the tickets were real or not. They just wanted the chance to be a part of the action. Takia knew how dimed-out her squad was when they made their way to the front of the line. Guys and girls looked mesmerized by the three fur-clad beauties.

"Yo, that's what I'm talking about right there. Them three shorties bad as shit," A handsome dark-skinned guy dressed in a black mink said to one of his homies. And the baddest chicks were not the only ones who came out of the house fly.

Takia never saw so many fur coats in her life. Iced out watches, chains and rings were all around her. Guys were looking good. The real big balling niggas were out, and for a split second, Takia's mind was off of worrying about Rell, truly enjoying herself. The old Takia was even re-emerging as a tall sexy light-skinned guy in his early twenties wearing a gray fox bomber jacket, and a head full of wavy hair rubbed up against her. Their eyes locked.

"What's up shorty? Where you from?"

"West Philly."

"I'm from 58th and Malcolm, Southwest. My name is Zykee, slide with me after the show. I got a room at the Doubletree on Broad Street and a bag full of money." He whispers in her ear.

Takia was definitely turned on and contemplated for a second, but quickly remembered that she was in a monogamous relationship with Rell. "Well look, if it's meant to be, we'll catch each other after the show." She turns her back on him and quickly follows behind Raven. Zykee grabs her hand, but she pulls away.

Once in the center of the First Union Spectrum, Takia was blown away by the extreme flossing. She could tell people spent their last dime on outfits, maybe even their rent and car note money for one night at the ghetto-fabulous ball. She knew it was more than a few Cinderella's in the mix. Mya leads the way like the queen of the pack with Takia and Raven in perfect formation behind her. Niggas heads were snapping doing double takes. Groups of girls looked lost. The fur, the gear, and the swag had them sick.

"Yo, that's them fly little bitches from up Overbrook." A guy yells from the crowd.

Takia smirks at the sight of Kareema, TeTe, and Asia up ahead of them. *Stunting on the haters is the ultimate payback.* She thought tapping Mya on the shoulder.

"I see them bitches." Mya starts twirling her fingers through her hair while switching extra hard. Takia and Raven followed, not missing a beat.

Takia throws Kareema a taunting grin while silently peeping their gear. Sales rack Iceberg and Moschino that the baddest chicks would wear as pajamas, not to the hottest concert of the year. Their enemies look like scared deer in headlights. Envy and jealousy flowed out of their pores, but what else was new. Just as Takia was soaking up the limelight, the intro of Foxy Brown's *Get Me Home* started blaring over the arena speakers. The large crowd rushed from the hall to see the 'Ill Na Na' rock the stage in a baby blue mink bikini.

For the next hour, Philadelphia's finest watched, danced and sang along to the artist who defined their generation. Jay- Z performed *Ain't No Nigga*, *Dead Presidents,* and *Where I'm From* in a black bulletproof vest. Busta Rhymes was larger than life with *Put Ya Hands Where My Eyes Could See.* 112 sang *Cupid* so sweetly, and Nas, AZ, and Foxy rocked the stage as The Firm. Puffy and Mase shined brighter than the platinum color in their shiny suits, rocking *Can't Nobody Hold Me Down, Feel So Good,* and *Mo Money Mo Problems.*

They even brought Biggie back to life with larger than life images of the late king of New York doing some of his greatest hits like *Warning, Juicy,* and *Big Poppa.* His tragic death was still an open wound to many fans in the urban black community, but Takia's defining moment of the night came when the house lights dimmed.

"Y'all ready Philly?" Lil' Kim's voice yelled through the mic in the darkness.

The people let out a gigantic roar. Lil' Kim's *Big Mamma Thang* started playing. The Queen Bee emerges on a gigantic bed in all her queen bitch glory, wild blonde wig, and red lingerie. Takia, Raven, and Mya were standing on their seats spitting every lyric with Kim.

"I used to be scared of the dick, now I throw lips to the shit, handle it like a real bitch. Heather Hunter, Janet Jacme, take it in the buns, yeah, yeah, what?"

Kim then ripped into her classic hits *Queen Bitch, No Time, Crush on You* with Lil' Cease and her classic verses from Junior M.A.F.I.A.'s *Get Money* and *Players Anthem.* The show came to a climatic end with Puffy, The Lox, Lil' Kim and Biggie doing a roaring version of *It's All About The Benjamins.* Takia had never seen a more dynamic show in her life where the audience and artist were all connected for two hours. The Bad Boy family was the universe that the 'hood superstars of Philadelphia lived in.

The concert let out was like the Grammy Awards. People were everywhere. It was freezing, but the mink covering Takia's body kept her warm enough. Guys were flirting in abundance, pulling over in Benzs, Range

Rovers, and Lexus trucks drooling, ready from some fresh young pussy.

"Yo, me and my man got four stacks. Takia, what's up with you and your girlfriends? We tryin' to go to Atlantic City." A cute thin, light-skinned boy named Kareem says, hanging out the passenger side of his friend's money green Lexus LX 450.

"Kareem boy, if you don't go 'head. I'm a married woman now."

"Word? I did hear you was going with Lil Rell."

"That's right," Takia says proudly.

"Takia, let's go," Mya says impatiently, a frown on her pretty face.

"Mya if you don't go 'head with your conceited ass. Always mad about something. I remember when you was my homie Smoke's girl. You was always drawling about somethin'."

"Fuck you, Kareem. First of all, don't be bringing up that old ass shit with Smoke. That shit was like twenty years ago."

"Man, whatever with you Mya, pretty Raven always been my favorite anyway." Kareem snickers getting out the car. "What's up Raven? You wanna go to Atlantic City? You can have all these stacks." Kareem pulls out a big wad of money wrapped in rubber bands.

"Nigga please, I wipe my ass with that little bit of money you holding."

"That's right, tell his ass Rav." Takia and Mya laugh extra animated.

"I got ten more where that came from." The Lexus driver reveals himself.

Takia senses something familiar about him, but can't place where from. He was fine as hell. Tall, light-skinned, big brown eyes with full lips. He wore a fresh black Marc Buchanan leather jacket, black Guess jeans and a pair of tan suede double sole Timberland boots. Plus he was pushing the new Lexus LX 450, so Takia was very interested in who this nigga was.

"Raven, I guess you don't know how to call nobody, huh?" The handsome boy says, strolling in front of her.

She blushes. "Where I know you from?"

"Pretty little Raven. Girl, you don't remember me?" The guy folds his arms against his chest. Takia watches Raven search her memory for a clue of the guy who is definitely unforgettable. "I'll break it down for you, Club Gotham, almost a month back. You and your girl's right here was rumblin' some broads in the parking lot, and you was playing Mike Tyson." He laughs throwing his hands up in a boxing stance.

"Nadir." Raven squeals.

"Bingo! Took you long enough." He laughed. Takia could tell by Raven's body language, she was feeling Nadir. "I been waitin' for your call. Look at you looking like something to eat." Nadir starts rubbing his fingers up and down Raven's fox jacket. At that exact moment, Nickels pulls up in his Tahoe.

"Raven, what the fuck you doin'?" He hollers, hopping out the driver side. He looks mean, his hand tucked inside the orange Coogi sweat suit jacket he wore as if he has a gun tucked. "Who the fuck is this nigga?" Nickels snaps, stepping in front of Raven like he was about to smack her.

"My name Nadir homie."

"Nigga, I'm talking to her."

"Nickels, we just cool." Raven stutters looking petrified.

Takia didn't like this scene one bit. "Nickels, back out my girlfriend face like that," Takia says, moving in front of Raven.

"This that drawling shit I be tellin' you about. Man get yo ass in the car!" Nickels hisses, getting back in the driver seat. Raven hesitates before opening the passenger door.

"Raven, you don't gotta go nowhere with him if you don't want to," Mya says, approaching Nickels' Tahoe.

"I'm fine, just go 'head, I'll call y'all tomorrow."

Takia could tell by Raven's demeanor, she was secretly crying out for help. Before Takia could say another word to convince Raven not to leave with Nickels, he sped off. The last thing they saw was his truck brake lights. The magical night was officially coming to an end. Kareem tried to convince Takia and Mya to chill with him and Nadir, but that was not happening. Bad chick rule number one, never mess with anybody that your girlfriend has feelings for. Some niggas were community property, and others were completely off limits. Nadir was cute. The old Takia would have jumped at the stacks he was holding, and Mya never let Kareem touch any part of her body. But Takia could tell Raven's feelings for Nadir were running deep so she would put him in the off-limits category.

Both she and Mya were both too young to get into the twenty-one and over after party at Gotham. Their fake IDs had been confiscated months ago at Pegasus Nightclub in West Philly. Takia was feeling sleepy, and her feet were starting to swell in her Versace sandals. Mya was over it too, wanting to get to Carmello who she had been sweet-talking with on her cell phone the entire time she was driving Takia home to Rell's duplex.

"Baby, I'm in front of Takia's door, let me call you right back." "Of course, when I get there, the only thing I'm gonna be wearing is my fur coat." Mya giggles in a seductive voice before hanging up. "Girl we shitted on them bitches tonight," Mya says sleepily.

"Girl when I saw Kareema and 'em, I knew they was mad. Girl, you know we gonna be the talk of Brook on Monday."

"Did you see how good Mase looked?"

"No, Puffy was the sexy one."

"No, Nas!" They both burst out in laughter.

"Lil' Kim was my favorite," Takia says, trying to find her house keys in her Fendi bag.

"I was feeling Foxy's outfit better, I'm sorry."

"You always trying to say Foxy is better than Lil' Kim."

"I just feel Foxy's style more sometimes." Mya retorts.

"Whatever girl. What Lil' Kim say? "I used to wear Moschino, but every bitch got it, now I rock colorful minks because my pockets stay knotted." Takia says, emulating Lil' Kim's dance moves from the *No Time* video.

"Girl, anyway, I'm not about to go back and forth with you over Lil' Kim and Foxy Brown tonight. Did you see how Nickels was acting a fool talking to Raven like she wasn't shit?"

"I know, and Raven acted like a nut. Almost as if she was scared of Nickels or something. Do you think he beating on her?" Takia asked Mya wide-eyed like a revelation ran through her mind.

"He better not. We'll jump his fat ass!"

"Either jump him, or that fine ass Nadir is gonna take her from him," Takia says opening the door. "If I wasn't with Rell and he wasn't on Raven, I'd fuck with his fine ass."

"Girl who you telling? Raven better jump on Nadir. Nickels Chubb Rock looking ass is getting played out." Mya laughs hysterically. "Call me tomorrow Takia."

"Alright." Takia quickly runs up the duplex steps, keys in hand.

She couldn't wait to take her sandals off and lay in the bed next to Rell. She opens the apartment door, locks it tight. The room is pitch black. She reaches for the living room lamp when a strong hand grabs her in the darkness.

"Rell, what are you doing?" She chillingly discovers it wasn't Rell when a second pair of hands grabs her by the throat. She's violent slammed to the ground. Frozen in fear she begins to sob.

"Don't make a sound or I'll kill you right now bitch." A man with a distinct Italian accent whispers in the dark.

Suddenly the living room light is turned on. She looks up to see two dark-tanned Italian men with slicked back black hair, dressed in finely tailored gray suits with devious dark expressions on their faces.

What the fuck is going on? Please don't let them kill me and my baby. Her mind races.

"Tyrell, this must be the pretty little girlfriend I heard so much about."

Takia is lifted by two men in suits and thrown on the sofa. What she saw next makes a river of tears flow. The chances of her and her baby surviving until morning became slim to none. A smug looking Italian man with a long scar down his face and dark beady eyes has a black Glock pointed at the side of Rell's head. Blood is dripping down his face and mouth; he's very badly beaten.

"Anthony, leave her alone. She don't know nothing. Let her go."

"Tyrell, she's a pretty little black bitch. Wonder what that brown pussy feels like. Right, Frankie and Paul?" The two goons holding Takia let out dry evil laughter.

She had been violated by men before, if it would take her body to save Rell and her baby's life, then so be it.

"Don't fucking touch her!" Rell cries. "No Takia, don't!" Rell is instantly slapped across the head with the Glock. Blood squirts everywhere.

"Leave him the fuck alone!" Takia jumps up, trying in vain to attack the mafia men.

"Bitch, sit the fuck down!" Takia is slapped with great force by Paul across the face. The sting was agonizing.

God, please don't let me die tonight. She silently prayed.

"Say goodbye to your girlfriend, Tyrell."

"I'll do anything, please don't kill him." Takia pleads, pulling her dress off, revealing her bare naked breasts. Life or death, by any means necessary. Anthony put on a malicious smile.

"Tyrell, your girlfriend is offering her sweet little pussy in exchange for your life. That's some real Romeo and Juliet shit. Frankie, Paul, fuck that little black bitch!" Anthony commands.

The two henchmen started ripping off her panties and manhandling her body like vultures. Takia looks up at Rell, the tears, and helplessness on his face.

"I'm sorry baby." He whispers.

"Tyrell this isn't just for Ra'Quan. We know you've been stealing for years. Taking money, thinking we wouldn't notice. We know everything. That's why in the old country, they say never do business with niggers." Anthony then pulls the trigger on the Glock.

Takia watches Rell's head explode, and his brains splatter across the room. Takia let out a scream the came from a place that only the depths of her soul could conceive. Rell's body falls to the floor, shaking violently in convulsions.

"Rell, Rell, no God, please no!" Takia tries to run to Rell before being hit over the head with a gun by Anthony. Everything around her went dark. The last words she remembered was Anthony's evil chuckle.

"We're gonna have so much fun with this black bitch. We're gonna take turns in her cunt all night."

"Umm, where am I?" Takia moaned when a sharp stabbing pain in her head hit like a ratchet.

Every inch of her body seemed to be sore. *What happened to me?* Rell's head exploding was all that filled her mind. She saw blood. Rell's blood was all she saw. She began to scream at the top of her lungs, opening her eyes from the blood filled darkness.

"She's waking up! Takia it's alright, it's alright!" She distinctly heard Mya's and Raven's voices.

"Little girl, you better not die on me. Your brother was enough." Michelle's deep raspy voice sent an energy shock through Takia's being. She frantically pulled at the IVs in her arm.

"Takia, it's alright, nobody's gonna hurt you." Mya cried, trying to calm her best friend.

Two Caucasian nurses dressed in blue scrubs rushed into the room. "Hold her arms so she can't harm herself."

"Where is Rell?" Takia cries, struggling with the nurses. "Get the fuck off me bitch!" She hisses with a crazed look in her light brown eyes.

"Ma'am we're gonna have to sedate your daughter." One of the nurses says to Michelle who just shakes her head yes. Her frail body rocking back and forth.

"She's still in shock from the rape and miscarriage."

"Miscarriage? My baby is dead?" Takia screams, "They killed my baby!" Takia grabs one of the nurses by the neck.

Mya and Raven struggle to get Takia's iron-tight hold off the nurse, while the other pulls out a syringe filled with a clear liquid and without hesitation, sticks it in Takia's arm. Seconds later she falls back with a dazed blank expression.

"My baby. My poor baby. I was gonna love you. Rell was the only one who loved me." Takia slurs before passing out.

Mya and Raven cry in each other's arms, tears for their lost sister. How did their ghetto-fabulous materialistic life come to this? And if this could happen to strong, street-smart, tough Takia, what the hell did the streets have in store for the both of them?

Chapter 10

MYA: WHAT ABOUT YOUR FRIENDS

"Baby you hardly touched any of your food," Carmello says to Mya while tossing a large shrimp in his mouth.

They sit in a large booth at the swanky upscale Chart House restaurant, where people pay a hefty price for the best seafood and champagne that money can buy. Any other night Mya would be laughing and grinning, but lately, Mya Campbell hadn't been smiling at all. Since Takia's mental breakdown, she had a heavy load on her mind.

"With everything going on with Takia, and the terrible stuff that happened to her, I wish I could've done more to help her." Mya twirls her fork through the large plate of shrimp alfredo placed in front of her. Wearing a simple black Iceberg sweater dress, her long wavy hair loose flowing down her back, as she sits in silent mourning of her best friend.

"Babe, I keep telling you there's nothing you or anybody else could have done to prevent this from happening. Rell got in over his head. A lot of money got fucked up. Doing street business with Italians can be tricky. Rell didn't know how to play the game. You're lucky you ain't get caught up in that shit. I'd be lighting

South Philly up right now if something had happened to you." Carmello reaches across the fine white linen-clad table, placing Mya's hand in his, staring with his dark brown eyes full of compassion.

The brown and black Fendi logo sweater and large platinum and diamond cross hanging around his neck make Carmello look sophisticated. He'd been spending more time with Mya since Takia's tragedy. Deep in Mya's heart, she thought Takia would be strong enough to bounce back from her rape and miscarriage, but no such luck. Takia was mentally and physically gone. The loss of her baby and Rell's death caused her to have post-traumatic stress disorder. She was on Prozac, Ritalin, and all types of medication. She had no clue where she was; screaming gibberish constantly asking where Rell and her baby were; fighting hospital staff like a wild woman. Ms. Michelle had signed the papers for Takia to be placed in Belmont Behavioral Health Hospital. Mya and Raven tried to visit her, but she didn't even recognize her best friends. Her hair was wild all over the place, and she had a crazed look in her honey brown eyes. It was too painful for Mya to bear; she ran out of the visiting room. How could she look at her sister; her pride and her strength at such a low point? A piece of Mya was dying. She knew nothing would ever be the same. She starts tearing up at the dinner table thinking about poor Takia.

"Babe, you alright?"

"No, I just wanna go home," Mya whispers.

"That's cool." Carmello waves down their waiter. He pays the two hundred fifty dollar tab and leaves a one hundred dollar tip on the table.

"Boo, it's been almost three months since that shit happened," Black says, pulling his black Navigator truck in front of Mya's house. "You can't stop living your life baby girl." Carmello gently runs his hand through Mya's hair. "I know your prom is coming up next month, and then your graduation. That's a lot to celebrate."

Mya starts grinning, Black has such a great way of cheering her up.

"You're right. I'm graduating from high school. This should be the best time of my life. But to see one of my best friends hurt and there's nothing I can do about it is the hardest pill I've ever had to swallow; and that baby, that poor baby. Takia wanted that baby so bad."

"You don't need to be alone right now, stay the night with me."

"I would love to, but me and my mom got an understanding now. I have to follow the rules, but I promise, I'll spend all day with you tomorrow after school." Mya says, leaning over kissing Carmello deeply on the lips.

"Okay, I'm gonna hold you to that promise." As that sweet, intimate moment plays out, Black's cell phone begins ringing. He sucks his teeth agitated. "Yo." He says flatly. "Faheem, why the fuck you call me about this petty shit?" "Nigga, you can't handle the spot I put you in dog?" "I understand all that." "Aight then." "I swear, you my man a hundred grand, but don't ever in your life call me about no bullshit like this again. You hear me nigga?"

I'm not in the mood for this shit right now. Mya thinks, slowly opening the passenger door.

"Yo, I'll call you tomorrow," Black says, covering the cell phone as he speaks.

She simply rolls her eyes, sliding out of the huge Navigator truck. Carmello quickly pulls off.

Business is always calling him. Mya thinks, feeling the early May winds against her legs. Spring was definitely in Philadelphia.

Overbrook was buzzing with gossip about Takia. Rumors were rampant. People were saying somebody slipped her a mickey, or even that she killed Rell for the insurance policy money. But none of their nosey asses knew the truth. With Takia gone, Mya felt half empty. Her last days of high school had become some bizarre dark dream. She and Raven were still the baddest chicks, but the trio was now a duet. And these days the two were singing the wrong key. Raven had become withdrawn. She never wanted to talk about Takia. The more Mya pressed the issue, the further Raven ran away. She never felt more alone in her life.

As she made her way down the crowded third-floor hallway, exiting her fourth-period advanced Spanish class; her hair pulled into a slick ponytail, black Fendi stretch jeans covers her ass; a brown Fendi logo cardigan sweater held snug around her waist while a huge brown Fendi bag hung off her left shoulder. A blank expression was on her pretty face. Mya had long become accustomed to the whispering and eyeballing by the nosy Overbrook High students. But since Takia's situation, she felt trapped under a microscope. Their eyes scanned her suspiciously as she makes her way into her fifth-period world history class. Mya makes her way to her seat, she could feel the eyes of her haters upon her. TeTe and Asia whisper and cackle, but she ignores them.

"So class, Alexander the Great died in the year 323 B.C. leaving the world's greatest empire to be split amongst its comrades." Mrs. Pearson, the middle-aged pleasant dark-skinned history teacher, said smiling brightly.

Mya starts taking down notes for Friday's history quiz when Raven walks into the classroom ten minutes before it was over. She looks uneasy. Her long hair was wild and uncombed, and black Gucci sunglasses covered her face. A blue denim skirt revealed her legs, red snakeskin cowboy boots, and a white Iceberg Snoopy t-shirt completed her outfit. It all looked thrown together and wrinkled.

"Ms. Hightower, your lateness and absentees are getting out of control." Mrs. Pearson said calmly. Raven does not respond and quickly slides into the seat next to Mya.

What the fuck is going on with you Rav? Mya thinks, staring Raven up and down.

Raven sits stone-faced as if in a daze. Once the six-period bell rings, kids start rushing out of Mrs. Pearson's class.

"Raven, we need to talk now," Mya says, grabbing Raven's arm before she could disappear.

Raven simply shakes her head yes. They head to the third-floor girls' bathroom where three plainly dress sophomore girls were chatting away about junior and senior boys they thought were cute. As Mya and Raven walk in, their conversation ceases, eyes wide in amazement.

"Yo, y'all three out," Mya says smugly, pointing her well-manicured finger at the rusty bathroom door.

"No problem." They quickly filed out immediately. "Yo, they fly as shit. That's gonna be us in a few years." The cutest of the three girls whispers.

Mya makes sure no one is eavesdropping. "Yo Rav, what's up with you? You been acting so funny lately. You don't answer my phone calls. You don't wanna talk about Takia. What's the problem?" Mya's face becomes red with anger.

Raven slowly removes her sunglasses revealing a large fresh black eye. Mya's mouth drops and eyes began to water.

"Oh, Raven. Nickels did this to you?" She shakes her head yes. "That bitch ass nigga! Raven, Black will get that nigga murked."

"No!" Raven yells. "Don't say nothing to nobody; that will make it worse."

"Raven don't no man got the right to beat on you."

"Mya you don't understand." Raven cried, tears rolling down her face.

"Raven how long he been hittin' you?" Mya begins choking up with tears.

"The entire time we been together. Only when I make him mad."

"Make his fat ass mad?" Mya shouts.

"Listen, everybody can't have the perfect life like you. You always had everything you wanted. Now I'm finally getting mine!" Raven screams bitterly.

"Girl, no amount of money or material shit is worth a nigga's fist." Mya retorts, gently trying to console Raven who was pushing her away.

"You and Takia always bragging about hustlers and niggas getting money. That's all you two ever talked about. Now, look where that shit got Takia." Raven begins pacing back and forth in the damp bathroom.

"Raven so you're blaming me and Takia for what Nickels is doing to you?"

"Y'all definitely had a part to play. Y'all hated Mally so bad because he wasn't a hustler. You put a ton of pressure on me, so I left the guy who loved me unconditionally and became what y'all wanted; a fuck toy for a lunatic. I have clothes, jewelry, and pocketbooks for days. But I feel empty inside like I sold my soul to the devil and I hate you and Takia for it."

Mya looks as if someone knocked the wind out of her. "Raven, how could you say you hate me? All I ever did was love you. You're my sister. I never put a gun to your head and made you talk to Nickels. Raven, you made your own choice. All I can do now is try to help you get away from his abusive ass." Mya tries to embrace Raven in a sisterly hug.

"Don't fucking touch me!" Raven yells, her face twisted in tears. She pushes Mya so forcibly she falls to the tiled floor.

"Mya, you're such a fucking hypocrite! You're selfish, vain, judgmental and always looking down on people. All you care about is your parents and boyfriend's money. I'm so sick of you and your conceited bullshit. And you know what? Takia got what was coming to her. Mya just stay far the fuck away from me." Raven put her Gucci sunglasses back on and walks out of the bathroom.

Mya can hear the click-clacking of Raven's heels against the hallway floor. *God, why is this happening to me? Why am I losing my friends one by one?* Mya whispers laid across the filthy bathroom floor holding herself. "Raven I just wanted the best for you. For both of you. Oh Takia, I need you more than ever right now." She speaks softly as she sobs uncontrollably.

Chapter 11

RAVEN: BROKEN HEARTED

"Whose pussy is this? Whose pussy is this?" Nickels moans, thrusting in and out of Raven like an animal, sweat beating down his chubby face.

Oh, just hurry up and finish. Raven thinks in disgust, mustering up the strength to finish yet another round of faking an orgasm for Nickels.

"Fuck me harder baby. It's your pussy. Fuck me!" Raven moans at the top of her lungs, sunk deep in the mattress of their dark Center City Hilton hotel room.

Nickels was only the second guy that Raven had been intimate with, and this experience was the complete opposite of Jamal who was soft and tender, taking his time in every way to please her. Nickels was rough, forceful and lacked true compassion with his lovemaking skills. But he made up the difference with cold hard cash. Raven had become used to Nickels hard pounding.

Thank God it's over. Raven thought as Nickels ejaculated inside her. She was on the pill. They had long stopped using condoms.

"Damn Rav. Girl, you got some good ass pussy." Nickels said out of breath, rolling over on his side, his fat belly and man breasts shaking.

He had been gaining more than his fair share of weight over the past few months. Along with his shorter temper, fits of verbal and physical rage had long turned Raven off, but she was too petrified to leave. Nickels had a short fuse due to his own insecurities. The more angry and violent he became, the more money attached to lavish gifts he threw at Raven. The pattern of black eye to new Prada bag was starting to wear her down. She lived a double life. It was becoming a huge headache hiding expensive clothes and handbags from her mother, and sneaking in and out of the house all hours of the night wearing pounds of makeup to hide the bruises Nickels left on her fragile body.

Her grades had constantly been slipping, her A-plus grade average had slipped to a low B-minus. Raven used to go above and beyond with her school work, now she only did enough to get by. Everyone began noticing the change in her. The once sweet demeanor was now aloof, cold, almost downright mean. She avoided Mya and stopped going to visit Takia at the hospital. Her life was moving so fast. Who she was before 1998 seemed like a distant memory. She cried for a week straight after her huge blowup with Mya, but shallow pride would not bring her to apologize. When she saw Mya some days at school, the wonderful sweet days of their friendship would fill her mind and emotions would make her want to grab and hug her ex-best friend. Then feelings of resentment would fill her mind.

She argued with her parents constantly, disobeying their rules purposely.

Raven, now do you have everything you ever wanted? Raven asked herself staring deeply at her reflection in the mirror.

The once sweet innocence in her soft brown eyes is gone, her long silky black hair soaking wet down her shoulders.

"They always say, be careful what you wish for." She whispers.

"Yo, hurry up. I'm hungry as shit!" Nickels yells, banging forcibly on the bathroom door.

Raven sighs, lowering her head. "Okay babe, here I come," Raven says in the sweetest voice she could muster while a stream of tears roll down her face.

Thirty minutes later, she and Nickels are sitting at a booth in Bookbinder's, a five-star restaurant located at 15th and Walnut. They meet up with one of Nickels business associates named Wink and his girlfriend KiKi, a short brown-skinned girl with bow legs and an enormous ass. She has an annoying squeaky voice that irritated Raven. She was outfitted in the latest Gucci riding boots, double G belt, and shoulder bag in brown suede and leather. Raven wasn't feeling this chick at all. They sip white Zinfandel while the guys small talk. Raven caught Wink, a tall very dark-skinned guy with a big mole on his face undressing her with his eyes. His iced out Presidential Rolex and red short sleeve Coogi sweater were official. But he's definitely not Raven's type.

I can't wait until this is over. She thinks as waiters place expensive entrees in front of them.

Nickels gets repeated phone calls from his workers, he refers to as his 'pack boys.' The plan of action was he and Wink would be driving to DC to meet a new connect. They speak in hush voices. They would both put up the front money for the new product, joining forces and a new partnership. If things go according to plan, Benjamin's by the pile would be for the taking.

Raven and KiKi sit silently while the guys talked for the next two hours. She felt a few bitchy stares coming from KiKi's direction. Raven simply ignored her ass. It was nearly 12:30 a.m. when Nickels dropped her off.

"Baby this shit I got lined up this weekend could set us up for a long time. I'll have more than enough money to buy you a car when you graduate and set you up with your own apartment. Either Korman Suites, or Barclay Square out Upper Darby. Fuck working hard for that scholarship bullshit, I got it."

Raven simply nods her head in agreement. Nickels leans over, planting a sloppy French kiss on Raven before she could escape out the passenger door. Nickels speeds off, and Raven finds her house keys deep within her black patent leather Prada knapsack, slowly opening the front door attempting to tiptoe into the house. She turns the living room lamp on and to her great surprise, her parents are both sitting on the couch in their night clothes. Her mother's head is full of rollers, a cold look of anger on her chocolate face.

"I'm so glad you decided to come home past your curfew again." Mrs. Hightower hisses standing to her feet. Mr. Hightower just shakes his head in disbelief. "I went through your room today. What is all of this?" Mrs. Hightower yells, emptying a trash bag full of clothes, shoes, handbags and designer sunglasses. "Raven, this stuff costs a small fortune and you ain't been working nowhere."

"Look, Raven, we know what's been going on." Mr. Hightower interjects. Mrs. Hightower has a look of fury in her almond-shaped eyes.

I thought I'd hidden everything good. Raven thinks, looking dumbfounded.

"Raven you've been sneaking around for months, lying. Don't think I can't see the bruises." Mrs. Hightower cries.

"Who is this thug you've been seeing? I'm gonna break his face." Mr. Hightower says coolly, a long day of work shown on his handsome olive toned face.

"You are forbidden to leave this house. Do you hear me?"

"Yes mom, the whole neighborhood can hear you." Raven is beyond irritated.

"I don't like your attitude young lady."

"I don't like you going through my personal stuff either mom," Raven yells defiantly.

"Raven, as long as you're under this roof, you will follow our rules." Mrs. Hightower fires back.

"Maybe I won't stay the fuck under your roof then."

Before Raven could blink, Mrs. Hightower slaps her across the face with a stinging impact knocking Raven against the wall. Raven was stunned. Her mother hadn't struck her since she was a small child. It was enough that Nickels had hit her. Now her mother? It was too much for her to register. She opens the front door, running off into the night. Mr. and Mrs. Hightower chase after her in slippers and pajamas, pleading for their daughter to come back. Raven runs and runs with no destination. She wanted away from her parents, Nickels, and her problems with Mya and Takia. She was running away from her dreary existence. She ran five blocks to 58th and Nassau Road, into the middle of the street without looking and was almost struck by a car. The quick-thinking driver swerved, barely missing her. The loud screeching of loud brakes made Raven sprint to the other side of the street.

The driver gets out his car. "Yo what the fuck is wrong with you shorty?" She takes a closer look, it's

Nadir. "What you doing running through the streets like this?"

"I'm going through a lot right now. I'm stressed, I just needed some fresh air."

"Let me take you home. It's too late for you to be out here by yourself."

"I'm alright." She protests.

"I can see you're not alright and I'm not leaving until you get in my car. I'm stubborn and persistent, I never take no for an answer." He smiles. A sneaky ladykiller grin forms on his face.

Raven couldn't resist his charm. At this very moment, Nadir was her saving grace. She got into the passenger side of his Lexus and an immediate sense of security flooded through her.

"Raven where you live at? I'm gonna take you home."

"No, me and my parents are going through some deep shit right now. I can't go home."

"Raven talk to me. What's going on?" Nadir leans over and squeezes her hand.

She attempts to play it cool, but the frustrating pain building inside of her finally burst. She began crying a hard deafening cry. A river of tears stream down her face. Nadir embraces her protectively, it reminded her of how Jamal once held her.

"Do you want to go back to my place for the night?" Nadir asks innocently.

Raven shakes her head yes. He speeds off, driving through Wynnfield, hitting Kelly Drive to his apartment in the Art Museum area where wealthy college students and yuppies lived. He had a quaint two bedroom apartment, expensive cream leather sectional furniture, large television and expensive crystal tables lined the living room. All the trappings of a certified hustler surrounded Raven, But what surprised her the most is the display of finely crafted African art, showcasing beautifully dressed African people in headdresses and Kente cloth with dark-skinned African women carrying baskets on their heads in the middle of magnificent villages. These scenes of African life pleased Raven.

"I know there's more to black women than being hood-rats, whores, and bitches."

"Wow, this is black womanhood in its purest form."

"You thirsty or hungry? There's a 24-hour pizza store down the street."

"No, I'm fine. I just need some peace and quiet."

"So what's really going on with you pretty? I don't like seeing you upset like this." Nadir says concerned, taking off his black and red Avirex leather bomber jacket.

"Where do I start? I lost my two best friends. I lied and deceived my parents; I lost all of their respect. I'm stuck in a relationship with a guy who thinks using his fist and beating me is love, and I've accepted that it's normal. Nadir I lost myself, my identity." Raven cries, placing her hands over her pain stricken face.

Nadir instantly engulfs her in his strong, comforting arms. "Shh, Raven you just got sidetracked. When you live in the fast lane, this happens sometimes." Raven rests her head against his firm chest. "You just gotta dust yourself off and try again. We all get blinded by material shit, so much sometimes we lose track of our worth. Raven, you're worth something. A lot. I knew that when I first saw you at Club Gotham. I can look in your eyes and tell you ain't the average gold digger out here trying to get a come up off a nigga. I saw the intelligence in your eyes." He tenderly wipes the tears from her cheeks. "And any man that would put his hands on a woman is a bitch-ass coward. I knew that fat nigga you was fucking with was a bitch. I could see it in his eyes that night in the parking lot after the Puffy show. He don't deserve you. Raven I gotta keep it real with you baby girl, I been dreaming of the moment when we would be together. I see you going through so much turmoil right now, and it makes me emotional. And I'm not an emotional kind of dude. If you was with me, I would never make you cry, I would never take you for granted. I'd build you up instead of tearing you down. I'd keep you laced too. But there's more to a relationship than that. Sex and money is only temporary. I learned that lesson the hard way."

Raven looked up at Nadir, a tremendous feeling of love for him took hold of her. She sits up and kisses him, her lips quivering ever so slightly. He returned her tender show of affection, covering her mouth with a flurry of wet kisses. She moans lightly. Nadir's kisses were unlike anything she's ever felt before, not aggressive and crass like Nickels, or soft and unsure like Mally. His kiss was passionate and confident. He simply took her breath away. She wanted him, she wanted to be with him in every way; to give her body to. With the passion as, she wants to escape Nickels' cruelty.

"Hold up Raven," Nadir says, pulling away from her.

"What's wrong?" She whimpers.

"Yo, we don't need to do this right now. You going through too much."

"I want to." She says assuring. She takes his hand, looking deeply into Nadir's handsome face that is almost on the verge of being pretty.

He pecks her on the lips. "Only if you sure."

"This is the only thing I've been sure of in a while."

He leads her into his bedroom. They lay down in his comfortable queen size bed. He gets on top of her, licking her ears and neck, teasing her with his tongue. Raven's eyes roll in her head.

"Oh, Nadir don't stop." She moans, but this was the real deal, no faking.

He unbuttons her jeans, a lustful hunger flashes in his soft brown eyes, covered by long curling lashes. They both strip. Raven is turned on by his sculpted and well-defined body, ripped abs, strong biceps, and a tight chest were hers for the taking. She never realized how well built he was because Nadir was always covered by baggy clothes.

So this is what's been hiding under those clothes. Raven thinks observing Nadir in his full nakedness.

His eight-inch curved penis full and erect. She almost forgot what a hard male body looked like in the months she has spent underneath Nickels out of shape body. Nadir was about to give her the medicine she had been craving. He spread her legs, burying his face in her throbbing pussy locking his full lips around her clit, gently biting and pulling at it with his teeth.

"Oh my God!" She squeals.

Nadir slips two fingers inside of her, slipping and sliding out of her wetness sending a jolt of sensation through Raven's body which she never experienced with Mally or Nickels. Her legs began to quiver as he licked and sucked all of her sweet juices. He rolls her over on her stomach, his tongue begins exploring her editable ass, slipping his tongue in between her cheeks, sucking and licking between her pussy and asshole. Raven bites down on her lower lip in ecstasy. He mounts her, grinding his penis against her ass while massaging her back. His hands making their way through the never-ending wonderland that was Raven's body. He bites the back of her neck before entering her pussy from behind. She bites the pillow as Nadir begins moving his thick penis in and out of her tight walls.

"Goddamn Nadir!" She moans.

He grips her waist becoming one with her. He lays the full weight of his body, tucking his arms underneath her belly, leaning his forehead against her back. Raven echoes with pleasure feeling the storm of a powerful orgasm erupting deep inside.

"Nadir I'm gonna cum! I'm gonna cum!" She yells, her toes curling back.

The tingling bursts from her insides like a leaking faucet. Ten minutes later Nadir followed. What she had been doing with Mally was child's play. Nickels attempt at intimacy was a bad joke. But Nadir had just made love to her. Anybody can fuck. Brainless animals in the wild can do that. Nadir had unleashed the art of lovemaking on Raven. She was his happy student. He continued his lessons, each one taking Raven to sexual heights she never knew existed. Raven was through dealing with boys. Nadir is a man, who separated himself from the boys in every way possible. She watched him sleep soundly, no snoring, slobber or drool. He was perfect. His square jawline, thick eyebrows, perfectly shaped pinch of a nose made him resemble a beautiful angel in slumber. An angel whom she needed desperately. She watches the sunrise through Nadir's black mini blinds. Her cell phone starts ringing from the back pocket of her jeans on the floor. She slid out of bed, the room temperature was pleasing to her body. Nickels number flashes across the Motorola cell phone; she cracks a half smile.

Goodbye Nickels. I'm through playing with chump change. She thinks, walking to the kitchen throwing Nickels shackles off, tossing the cell phone in the trash can.

Nadir had woken her from the daze she was in. A psychiatrist of *sexual healing 101*. Never again would Raven allow herself to be a victim. She was a girl who learned in one night how to become a woman.

Chapter 12

RAVEN: I HATE YOU SO MUCH RIGHT NOW

"I'm in the clear." Raven sighs in relief, walking out of the front doors of Overbrook High School.

It is clear May afternoon, only a few weeks from graduation and her eighteenth birthday; June 10th to be exact. She's almost a grown woman, and her adult decision to cut all ties with Nickels had saved her life. She told her parents the truth and broke down in her mother's arms. Her father swore he would kill Nickels for all of the abuse his daughter suffered. A gigantic boulder of guilt is lifted off her shoulders.

Nickels, on the other hand, did not take Raven dumping him too kindly. He stalks her at school and in her neighborhood; left threatening voice messages promising to knock her fucking head off for embarrassing him in the streets. He vows she will never get away from him, and that she will be dead before he lets her go. Somewhere in the darkest corner of her mind, she knew that Nickels was capable of killing her. It sent a cold chill through her. Every time she saw a dark green Tahoe, she darted like a deer in terror. She's become a master of walking through alleyways and backstreets. Always looking over her shoulder with fear for Nickels. His chubby brown face twisted with rage, his fist clenched to beat her back into being his bitch or sex slave; forced to give him head until her mouth became numb and swallowing every drop of his cum.

The sick twisted sex acts Nickels harassed Raven into performing were grotesque. She tried to erase the demeaning violence of her body out of her mind by throwing herself back into her studies. She certainly had more than enough back reports, and homework assignments to keep her busy for a while. And her teachers were more than happy that their bright academic star pupil was back to performing at her best. Her grades turned around quickly; Ds and Fs soon became As and Bs. She had taken her SATs scoring a perfect score of one thousand six hundred. College is still in her sights, she was getting her mind right, and Nadir was definitely a good influence.

They both agreed to take things slowly. Raven tries to hold back her growing feelings for Nadir, but he is just too fine for her to ignore. He is unlike any guy she has ever met before; street smart, a born leader, got to a dollar faster than a MAC machine, deeply intellectual, and a devout Muslim. He even convinced Raven to give up pork; something she struggled with; pork bacon and links breakfast sausage were her favorites.

It also didn't hurt that Nadir was the portrait of a pretty thug. His clear light skin, full lips made for kissing, and a head of thick wavy hair made him very easy on the eyes. And when he entered her with his large pulsating dick, he always made her pussy throb and gush like a river bed giving her orgasm after orgasm until she couldn't endure it anymore. He conquered her body and her heart.

Besides her father, Nadir was a grown ass man. He opened doors for her, made sure she got in the house safe; she felt safe in his presence. She kept Nickels stalking and threats from him. Raven knew Nadir had several guns and a squad of homies from Germantown and Logan that were definitely ready to ride at his beckon call. He vowed several times to blow Nickels head off if he ever came near her again. She knew Nadir would go to war over her. But what if Nickels kills Nadir? It was a thought that Raven could not bear.

Raven bides her time laying low, hoping the whole thing will blow over. Nickels has enough street money to buy twenty pretty young girls lined up for sex and Neiman Marcus shopping sprees. Nickels will get over her when the right new girl with a tight wet pussy comes along.

How long can Nickels be obsessed with me? Raven's thinks, crossing 59th and Colombia toward the Sugar Bowl. She had been craving a cheese pretzel and hot beef sausage all day long.

She is dressed casually, wearing a black-and-white Versace t-shirt and white Versace jeans; her hair in a messy ponytail. She paid for her food and began her walk home. Since quitting her job at Marshalls and getting back on track at school, her parents kept her on a tight leash. She had to report in with them before and after school and be in the house by 3:30 p.m. And not a minute late. Her parents' home had become somewhat of a prison, but she didn't mind; as long as she could sneak out for a refill of Nadir's all you can eat sexual buffet. That is all she craved. She outwardly smirks at a mental image of her naked on top of Nadir, riding him like a porn star. Her daydream is cut short by the sounds of *(Always Be My) Sunshine* by Jay-Z and Foxy Brown on the clear stereo system. The thought that it is Nickels pulling up beside her is terrifying.

"Yo Raven, come here."

She casually turns to see that it is Pumpkin. She breathes a sigh of relief. His red Lexus is shining from a fresh waxing, a wide grin on his ugly face covered by huge Versace sunglasses.

"Hey Pumpkin. What's up?"

"Yo, I been trying to find out what's up with Takia. I felt bad when I heard about Lil Rell getting murked by them filthy ass Italian motherfuckers. I went past her mom crib a few times. She told me about the rape and miscarriage and Takia losing it mentally; it fucked me up real bad. Raven, you know how close me and Takia was. That was my lil' shorty for real." Pumpkin says, while pulling off his shades, she saw a genuine look of concern on his face.

"She's still in the hospital Pumpkin. She was hurt really bad, Ms. Michelle doesn't want anybody visiting her. She has daily sessions with a psychiatrist; Ms. Michelle keeps me updated on all her progress."

Pumpkin shakes his head. "She already had a fucked up life living with Ms. Michelle's drunk ass, Now this. I'm gonna go past with some money in an envelope, but I'm gonna make sure she gets it. I know not to trust Ms. Michelle with shit. You don't live far from here. You want a ride to the crib?"

"Naw, I'm cool Pumpkin. I'll make sure I tell Takia to get in contact with you."

"I'm going that way, Raven. Damn girl, I don't bite." Pumpkin chuckles.

Don't get in the car with this nigga. She thinks, but against her better judgment, she opens the passenger door.

He puts the new Ginuwine [CD] on, speeding off. Pumpkin parks in an empty space on Raven's street; they engage in a twenty-minute conversation about Takia and her tragedy. Pumpkin goes on and on saying

173

if Takia had stayed with him and been his girl, he would have protected her and that Lil' Rell was in too deep. He tried to warn her not to fuck with him.

"I heard about you and Nickels breaking up." Pumpkin says, popping a piece of Big Red gum into his mouth; he needs it. Raven had been smelling his stale breath the entire ride.

"Yeah, it wasn't working out. I don't have any hard feeling toward Nickels." Raven says, pinching her right arm feeling uncomfortable talking about her and Nickels situation.

"You ain't gotta bullshit me, Raven, me and Nickels been homies for years. I know that nigga got a problem putting his hands on women. I tried to talk some sense into him. He put one girl in the hospital with broken ribs and a dislocated shoulder, but usually guys that have insecurity issues like to beat on women to make themselves feel big. You know? That Ike Turner shit. You seen the movie *What's Love Got to Do with It?*

"Pumpkin, it's almost 4:00 p.m., I gotta go," Raven says, looking at her silver Gucci watch.

"Before you go, I gotta tell you a little secret."

"Oh, what's that?"

Pumpkin narrows his dark beady eyes on Raven. "I've always wanted to know what the inside of that chocolate pussy feels like." Pumpkin slides his hand over and squeezes Raven's thigh.

I set myself up for this one. She thinks, repulsed by Pumpkin.

"Raven I'm no stingy dude. I'm very generous, name your price. I've been wanting you for years."

"Pumpkin no thanks. I don't mess with none of my girlfriends' exes."

174

"I was never Takia's boyfriend, we were friends with benefits. Benefits that can now go to you." Pumpkin strokes Raven's hair; that made her skin crawl.

I'm getting the fuck out of here! She thinks. "Pumpkin I have to go." She stutters, practically jumping out of his Lexus.

"Remember what I said. All you gotta do is name your price." Raven slams the car door before he could get another word out.

"Pumpkin you don't have a chance in hell of ever touching me. Not even for twenty thousand dollars." Raven hisses, rushing into the comfort of her parents' home.

Once she locks the door behind her, she breathes deeply. She can still feel Pumpkin's clammy boney hands on her.

"Raven is that you?" Mrs. Hightower calls from the kitchen.

"Yes, mom."

"You're late."

"I know, I'm sorry. I got held up in my last period class." Raven whimpers, walking into the kitchen. The fresh scent of garlic and basil hit her nose from the pot of pasta cooking on the stove.

"We need to go over your Temple application after dinner."

"Okay, mom," Raven says, dashing up to her bedroom.

She shuts the door collapsing on her bed, closing her eyes. Thoughts of Nadir crept back into her mind. He became her lover and the rock she could depend on. They have grown beyond close in the two months they have been seeing each other. He was helping her heal the wounds Nickels had scarred her with. He had the talents of a motivational speaker, so much more than the average street nigga. The layers to him were endless. Raven loved discovering a new layer of him every chance she got. She was in love, and it was blooming more and more every second. The ringing of her new Nextel cell phone snapped her out of her inner thoughts. Nadir's number flashed wide on the screen. Her mocha-brown face brightens.

"Hello, baby." She answers in a kittenish tone.

"How was your day boo?" Nadir's deep voice asked on the other end.

"It was fine. Trigonometry quiz, world history test, and computer science class. But it's even better now that I'm hearing from you."

"Is that so?"

"Yes, it is. Because I have a ton of social studies homework that's due tomorrow. And I have to pass to graduate."

"Well get to it. I was just checking on you. I don't like not hearing my baby's voice all day. And only being able to see you a few hours on the weekend ain't enough."

"That's all gonna change. I'll be eighteen June tenth and a high school graduate. I'll be able to make my own decisions, and I promise you'll have me all to yourself."

"That's a promise you better keep." Nadir chuckles.

"Yo, what's up Na?" A raspy male voice says in the background.

"Aye Rav, I just ran into my man Khaleef. I gotta talk to him real quick. I'll hit you back tonight."

"Okay, love you." She says gleefully, ending their call; tucking the cell phone deep in the pocket of her Bebe book bag.

Her cell phone was a big secret from her parents. They confiscated a lot of her high-end items that Nickels had bought for her. She kept the things she could not live without. She was under constant supervision.

Raven hates lying to her parents, but her communication and budding relationship with Nadir is the only thing keeping her going. Her parents would not understand at all. They viewed him as another low life thug drug dealer; he'd never get their approval. He is too vital to her life to give a fuck about her parents' opinions.

She laid out on her neatly made bed, exhaled, rolling over on her belly; turning on her small Sony stereo. *Release Some Tension*, SWV's latest album began playing. Raven certainly has more than enough tension to release. She skips to track seven, *Rain*; the soothing melodic track has become her and Nadir's lovemaking theme. When they spent long damp, rainy days making love in his apartment, this song was constantly on repeat. She closes her eyes and begins caressing her breasts. Visions of Nadir on top of her, holding her legs over her head, pushing his throbbing dick with speed inside her walls. Raven's panties instantly become wet.

"Mmm hmmm." She moans as the images of her fantasy becomes all too real.

Just as she was slipping two fingers inside herself, stroking her wetness...

"Raven! Mom and dad said get your butt downstairs for dinner. Now!" Little Ricky hollers with a loud bang on her bedroom door.

Raven jerks out of bed with her heart pounding, beaming with the embarrassment of almost being caught masturbating.

"I'll be down in a minute, don't be banging on my door like that little boy. Like you the cops or something."

"Kill the message, not the messenger."

"I'll kick your butt. Stop getting smart."

After changing into some comfortable gap sweats and her favorite pink fuzzy house slippers, she prepares herself for the lion's den awaiting her. Wednesday night's Kelly always comes over from UPenn for dinner with the family. Mrs. Hightower is an excellent cook, but with Kelly around throwing insults about her slipping grades and the grief her parents were facing because of Raven's behavior made any meal with her vicious older sister hard to swallow. It hurt Raven that her own flesh and blood was so set against her. That she couldn't even confide in her own sister about all of the beatings and abuse Nickels had put her through. She should be able to cry on her shoulder and be comforted by her only older sister, but instead, Kelly views her as a rival. All Raven gets is sarcasm and a cynical glance from her, but Raven is reaching her boiling point with Kelly.

She nonchalantly walks into the dining room; all eyes on her like Tupac's hit. Mr. Hightower's face turns blank chewing the fork full of pasta he just stuffed inside his mouth. She sits next to Ricky, directly across from Kelly. Her pretty brown eyes fixed on Raven who glares at her coldly lowering her gaze, quickly devouring the delicious plate of pasta in front of her. She hadn't realized how hungry she was. With all the twists and turns in her life, her appetite had dropped dramatically.

"Kelly, have you decided on a sorority yet?"

"I think I'm gonna pledge AKA dad."

"That's great honey, I was a Delta myself." Mrs. Hightower chimes in, sipping a glass of white wine.

"Raven, have you figured out where you're going in the fall?" Kelly asks snidely; Mr. and Mrs. Hightower give each annoyed glances from across the table.

Raven puts her fork down ready to face off with Kelly. "I'm thinking Temple."

"Temple?" Kelly chuckles sarcastically, a snotty grin on her face.

"Yes, Philadelphia's prestigious Temple University. What's so funny about that?"

"Nothing really, except your horrible grades. Not even with your lucky SAT score will you get in. You'll barely be able to get into community college." She snickers.

"Kelly, what is your problem? You're always worried about me. You're in this invisible competition by yourself."

"Competition? Raven, don't flatter yourself. You couldn't touch my academic abilities if you were leaning on my shoulder. I think it's sad all the stress you're putting on mom and dad."

"Kelly you don't know a damn thing about what's been going on with me. Who do you think you are to pass judgment on me? Keep your Ms. Perfect ass on UPenn's campus."

"This is a family dinner, no fighting at my table!" Mr. Hightower yells, banging his fist on the dining room table.

"No daddy, somebody needs to talk some sense into her selfish, materialistic ass," Kelly says defiantly; a grimace on her pretty olive complexion face. "You run the streets with drug dealing trash, whoring like a female dog, and your friends are sluts. Look at what happened to Takia. She was raped, left for dead, and became mentally unstable. She's still locked up in the psych ward. Isn't she? The poster child for the next lifetime welfare recipient." Kelly's words sliced through Raven like a razor.

"You hateful bitch!" Raven hollers, lunging at Kelly with speed.

She punches her in the face before placing an iron grip on her throat. Kelly gets a strong grip on Raven's hair; they both tussle wildly falling onto the dining room table, knocking it over.

"Stop this! Stop this right now!" Mrs. Hightower cries, pulling Raven by the shoulders.

She and Kelly both have an iron grip on each other's hair. Raven choking Kelly by the neck.

"Cut this shit out!" Mr. Hightower growls, picking Raven up off her feet, throwing her on the living room sofa. Raven jumps up, attempting to go after Kelly again. "Sit your ass down!" Mr. Hightower demands, shoving her with brute force.

"You see how ghetto she is? She attacked me for trying to talk some sense into her. Raven, are you smoking crack? It's clear that she must be on drugs."

"Kelly shut up!" Mrs. Hightower shouts with her dark-skinned face tense.

"What?" Kelly says outraged, rubbing a big knot on her forehead. "Your deranged daughter just assaulted me, mom."

"I sat back for years watching you viciously torment your sister and tonight it boiled over. I should have put a stop to this nonsense years ago. I will not have my children trying to kill each other."

"I can't believe you're defending her." Kelly defiantly yells.

"I'm sick of your bullying and nitpicking. Your sister could be dead right now. And you could care less as long as you score higher than her on some goddamn test." Mrs. Hightower roars; the entire family looks on in disbelief.

Never had they seen her raise her voice in such a way. Her normally sweet passive nature was transformed into an aggressive militant mother on a warpath.

"Maria, calm down." Mr. Hightower says, grabbing her shoulders.

"Take your damn hands off me, I'm talking to my daughter." She foams, violently breaking out of her husband's grasp.

Mr. Hightower steps back, his olive colored face flushed red. He never saw his wife so upset during their twenty-five years of marriage. Her Dominican and black blood was boiling.

"Mom, you are overacting. Why are you defending Raven?" Kelly whimpers on the verge of tears.

"Your sister was being beaten to a bloody pulp by some thug; hiding black eyes and limping around with bruised bones." Mrs. Hightower begins wailing tears.

"Mom it's okay, it's okay," Raven says embracing her mother who's trembling.

"You are supposed to love your sister, not destroy her. And if you can't comprehend that, then you need to leave this house and don't come back until you've learned how to treat your blood."

Kelly looks flustered, her bewildered eyes look to her father for help; her co-conspirator and champion in her years of attacks on Raven. His eyes are cast down in defeat; there would be no rescue. Tonight he's silently siding with his wife at the expense of his eldest and most beloved child. He turns his back on the women in his life, walking over to comfort his namesake and only son Ricky Jr. who is sobbing in the corner of the dining room. Witnessing his sisters fight and his mother's outburst was too much for his young thirteen year old mind to comprehend. Mr. Hightower puts his arm around his son and guides him upstairs.

"Fine mom, I don't have to come here anymore," Kelly says, grabbing her belongings and rushing out the door, slamming it with force behind her.

"Mom, are you okay?" Raven asks, holding her from the back in a tight hug.

"Yes, baby I'm fine." Mrs. Hightower sighs. "Raven, forgive your sister, love her even when she doesn't love you. Never be like her. Holding on to hate and grudges will destroy the soul. Pray for your sister, she's tarnishing her heart." Mrs. Hightower faces Raven, tears welling in her dark almond eyes. She kisses Raven on the cheek. "I'm going to bed, I have a pounding headache."

"Good night mom," Raven says in a saddened tone.

Mrs. Hightower climbs the stairs. A bond as thick and hard as cement has been forged between she and her youngest daughter. The connection Raven felt was lacking all her young life had come full circle in such an unexpected manner. Raven is overwhelmed, she had never felt more love and affection for her mother since she was a very small girl. And surely her damaged heart could use a little love.

The next few weeks flew by in a barrage of tests, college prep courses and putting back the pieces of Raven's life. Prom fever is all over Overbrook. Raven is sick of hearing girls in her classes chatter on and on about prom dresses and their hairstyles. Flipping through *Hype Hair* magazines with popular R&B artists, Faith Evan, Changing Faces, Monica, and Toni Braxton on the cover. Raven decided to skip the senior prom. She and Mally attended the junior prom, the large 8x10 photo of her and Mally wearing matching royal blue and cream hangs on the mantle of her parents' home. After a year of hell, graduating and getting the hell out of

Overbrook High School was the only agenda that concerened Raven.

She has never been more focused in her life. She was scoring an A-plus on nearly every test and quiz she took. She has become a distant loner. The once outgoing, friendly girl was now standoffish and distant, barely speaking to anyone; sitting in the back of classrooms, skipping lunch and hiding behind large Chanel, Gucci and Versace sunglasses.

She and Mya become masters of avoiding each other. The once inseparable sisters now coldly pass each other. The entire student body gossiped about it regularly. The lyrics to Nas' song *The Message* hit Raven hard.

"A thug changes and love changes; and best friends become strangers."

She missed Mya terribly, but her pride was enormous. She would not bend and be the bigger woman of the two. And today was no different. She slows her step a bit, walking down the crowded third-floor hallway. Loud restless teenagers change classes; the slamming of lockers as lustful teenage boys muster their best macking skills, kicking game to shapely young girls of their desire.

The sixth-period bell rings; Raven mentally prepares herself for her biology test ahead. It was Friday, the perfect spring weekend ahead. She could not wait to creep to Nadir's house on Sunday to give him a taste of her red light special. It's been a week and a half since she was able to lay up under his fine ass. She could feel his tongue in the crack of her ass already. She opens the third-floor girls' bathroom; she and Mya nearly collide into each other.

"Excuse me," Mya says flatly, hazel eyes diverting from Raven; the neon pink and yellow Gianfranco Ferré logo t-shirt she wore looked snug.

Has Mya been gaining weight? Raven thought, observing her through her dark tinted Chanel glasses. "My bad." She replied dryly as they pass each other.

She feels an empty sense of longing for her old friend, she watches Mya walk down the hallway, her tan Gucci logo shoulder bag bouncing against her. She thinks for a split second to call her name, but pride is a powerful detractor. Raven enters the foul smelling bathroom, the strong odor of fish and urine overtake her sensitive nose.

"Do they ever clean these stinking ass bathrooms?" She yells, entering a stall. "Trifling ass bitches." She says, frowning at the sight of an unflushed tampon floating in the toilet.

She lifts her right leg, using her foot to flush the toilet; refusing to touch the handle. She quickly unbuttons her Dolce & Gabbana blue denim jeans, releasing her pounding bladder.

"I hate these trifling ass bathrooms." She exits the stalls, walks over to one of the rusted sinks and washes her hands.

"Raven, girl what's going on with you and Mya?"

Raven turns to see Tanisha, her young freshman neighbor looking quite grown up wearing a form-fitting, V neck black and silver Versace Jeans t-shirt, revealing too much ample cleavage. Her cute tanned baby face covered in too much makeup and a long full weave with a swoop bangs and a size too small pair of black Guess jeans. She looked much older than her fourteen years. Raven hadn't noticed Tanisha's transformations; she'd been too caught up in her own drama to notice little Nish' was moving a little too fast.

"Nish', nothing is going on with me and Mya." Raven acts confused.

"Come on Raven, even Stevie Wonder can see there's drama going on with you two. Y'all don't speak to each other. Y'all don't even sit together during lunch. This is like TLC or SWV breaking up or something. You not speaking and whatever happened with Takia; y'all are the talk of the entire school."

"Is that so? Nish', people need to mind their business. And you need to worry about passing and doing your school work instead of Overbrook High School gossip and rumors."

"I know Raven. It's just so fucked up to me because I look up to y'all. You Mya and Takia are my role models."

"Don't say shit like that." Raven hisses, grabbing Tanisha sternly by the shoulders. "You don't want to be like us, Nish'. It looks fly and glamorous from the outside looking in, but run away from it as fast as you can. Stay away from them hustlers. I had a nigga hurt me really bad; I could be dead right now Tanisha. I've cried so many nights, more than you would ever think. Do you hear what I'm saying to you?"

"Yes I hear you Raven. You're hurting my arms."

"I'm sorry." Raven releases her iron grip. Tanisha starts backing away from Raven as if she's insane. "Nish', the fast money is not worth it. I don't want to see you end up like me, or even worst; like Takia. Stay focused on your education. Them streets out there don't love nobody." Raven pats Tanisha gently on her head; her slanted brown eyes swollen with tears.

Tanisha shakes her head yes, abruptly leaving the bathroom. Raven darts into a stall, locking the door. She would not let Nish' see a single tear fall, but now alone she erupts in emotion. It was enough that her life was a disaster. But all this time had she Mya and Takia been influencing young girls to be turned out in the streets? The thought was unbearable.

Chapter 13

TAKIA: SHE HAS ARISEN

"Where am I?" Takia groans, the first words she'd spoken in months, her mouth is dry and lips cracked.

She rolls her head from left to right, running her hands through the twisted tumbleweed of locks wild over her head from neglect and lack of hair care. Her mind races with thoughts and images of Rell. His head being blown off, her vicious rape, and the sorrow from her miscarriage. Grief erupts in her gut. She lets out a deafening cry. She sits up in her hospital bed, she was awake and fully conscious. Takia is awakening. Her mind was returning. She was stepping out of the dream world like state she had been living in, the harsh reality she blocked out had returned. A switch clicked on in her mind.

"My baby! Where's my baby? Those motherfuckers killed my baby!" She hollers at the female nurses sprinting into her room, shocked expressions on their wrinkled middle-aged faces.

"Takia, calm down honey." They plead as she claws and pushes at them, jumping off of the bed like an agile tigress.

"I want to go home. Let me out of here." She cries pushing one nurse to the floor with sheer force. The

other nurses back out of the room with fear. Takia bolts
behind them barefoot and disoriented.

"I have to get the fuck out of here!" Her mind raced,
running down a winding corridor of the Belmont
Hospital mental ward.

An elevator on the tenth floor was in sight. Takia
could feel freedom in her grasp but is quickly seized by
two large male orderlies who grab her arms, lifting her
off her feet. She goes wild, kicking and spitting at them
with all of her strength.

"Get the fuck off me!" She spat. Her honey brown eyes
were ablaze with a mad woman's fire. A nurse appears
with a loaded syringe, jabbing it into her left shoulder.
After a continuous struggle, Takia's vision slowly
becomes cloudy. "My baby, why my baby..." She slurs,
collapsing into a deep sleep.

"Takia, baby, mommy is right here. I know I haven't
done right by you. I've failed you and your brothers. God
has been punishing me for my evil deeds. I started going
to church and got saved right on the altar. With God's
mercy, that demon alcohol will be out of my life. I'm
going to the welfare work program, and I'm taking up
data entry classes. I made a deal with God, if he gives my
beautiful daughter a second chance, I will give my all to
being the mother I never was to either of my three
precious children. I lost my sons to the sin of greed. And
you Takia, I lost you to these streets. Instead of
protecting you, I let you give away your precious body, a
woman's greatest gift. I've been such a Goddamn fool."

"Michelle." Takia groans, slowly awakening.

Takia opened her eyes upon a smiling Michelle. She is
neatly dressed, wearing an ivory silk blouse, and navy
blue trousers. Her once unkempt wild hair and
headscarf were styled in soft curls. Her usual cruel,

bitter face is smiling a joyous grin. Michelle cries, wrapping Takia in her arms tightly.

"Baby I'm taking you home. This place is killing you. I'm signing you out immediately."

Takia holds on to Michelle for dear life, crying her heart out, leaning on her mother's strength. A miracle had truly come down to this family.

"I just wanna go home, Mom. Take me home." That was the first time Takia had referred to Michelle as Mom in many years.

Michelle signs Takia out of Belmont Psychiatric Hospital against doctors' orders. Her short reply was, "My child needs Jesus and not crazy people medicine."

Takia breathed in the fresh air as if inhaling for the first time, staring aimlessly at the sun from the taxi window, the fresh spring air gently caressing her face; Michelle's arms wrapped tightly around her.

"Mom, how long had I been unconscious in that hospital?" She asks hesitantly. "What happened to me? Why was Rell killed?" Her bottom lip quivering.

"Baby you were in there for almost five months. You've been laying lifeless in that place. I prayed to The Lord every day for him to bring you back to me. And today my faith has been justified. Baby Rell was a good boy, he loved you, truly loved you. He got involved with some bad men; Rell got in over his head and then... and then they..." Michelle began choking up in tears. "They killed him, and raped you causing you to have a miscarriage. Them some evil, heartless bastards. They gonna pay for what they've done. In this life or the next."

The cab turned onto Vine Street. The little row house Takia lived in all her life was before her. Memories came racing back to her mind. All the suffering hit her like a boulder. Both of her brother's handsome faces popped into her mind. Michelle paid the cab driver and helped Takia out of the car. Neighbors stood watching from their porches. Mrs. Thelma, Melva, and Francine, a few older ladies from the block walk over and embrace her with love. It felt good to know that they cared. She saw the genuine love and concern in their eyes as they kiss her cheek and rub her back. Michelle opened the front door of the house.

"Surprise, surprise! Welcome home Takia!" Raven and Mya yell.

Pink and white balloons fill the impeccably clean living room. Once filthy and in disarray, was now neat and spotless with new drapes, carpet and a dark burgundy sofa and loveseat. Takia was stunned. She couldn't be standing in the same house that was once so dark, now warm and inviting. Mya and Raven throw their arms around her in an unbreakable embrace. Their love for her is boundless. The three girls begin to cry. Their sisterhood is once again complete.

"Takia I love you. You are my sister." Mya cries, covering her forehead with kisses.

"I prayed every day for you to come back to us," Raven says through muffled tears.

"God took Rell and my baby away from me, but he left me you two. That's a blessing in itself. I can start over and get back to living my life. You two know my stubborn ass ain't giving up."

That broke the ice. The three of them laughed and kept on laughing. It had been so long since Takia laughed and it was about time.

"Girls, I made us a nice lunch," Michelle says, walking out of the kitchen carrying a large tray of delicious smelling fried chicken, collard greens, baked macaroni and cheese and cornbread; all Takia's favorites which she devoured. She lost quite a bit of weight having been tube fed and many hunger strikes. Mya and Raven brought gifts. Mya gave Takia a bottle of Chanel N°5 perfume and a red and white silk Fendi scarf. Raven gave her a basket filled with all the latest CDs from Brandy, Xscape, Monica, Mya, Total, Jay-Z, Mase, DMX, and Dru Hill. This was perfect since she has been so out of touch with the latest music. They sat and talked about all the latest 'hood gossip. Takia had been long out the loop and had no clue as to what Raven and Mya were talking about. But she could definitely sense a change in the two of them. She could not quite put her finger on it, but she felt a silent tension between her two friends. They had both been through some drama and were saving face not wanting to rain on her homecoming parade.

After another hour of small talk and pleasantries, Takia was tired and wanted to lay down. She is overwhelmed and needed to get back to the discipline of having a daily routine. She had been confined to a mental ward for months. Mya and Raven understood and left at 4:00 p.m. vowing to visit every day. Although appreciative of her surprise visit from her besties, Takia was happy to see them leave. She wanted to be alone.

After tight hugs and sweet goodbyes, she retired to her bedroom which was like entering a time capsule. Everything was like she left it before she moved in with Rell. Her queen sized bed covered in pink sheets and matching satin blanket. Her black stereo system and racks and racks of CDs just as she had left it. She hit power on the stereo remote, *Share My World* from Mary J. Blige's latest album began to play at just the right volume. She skipped to track number nine, *Missing You*, a deep soulful ballad about lost; missing a loved one terribly. She turned the volume up, the queen of hip-hop soul's husky emotional voice fills the room.

She opened her closet, there were all the neatly hung clothes on hangers in dry cleaner plastic bags. The items she left and disregarded when she moved in with Rell. All designer names she worshiped and idolized, sold her body for, lied, cheated and stole for now looked as worthless as a penny. Rage was pouring out of her. She bit down on her bottom lip and started grabbing the clothes from the hangers, flinging them around the room ripping shirts and dresses in half. Shoes and boots were tossed from the boxes and onto the floor.

"I fucking hate all this shit. I hate it!" Takia cries before tearing into her black and mint green onyx dresser drawer pulling out her bras and panties. Dumping them all over the floor when she stumbles upon a picture of her and Rell taken on a trip to Atlantic City's famed boardwalk at a picture booth on the pier.

She holds a white teddy bear he won for her, Rell's handsome face gleaming and her sleepy eyes were staring back at her. The exact day and memory came rushing back to her.

"Damn Takia, you ate three cotton candies and two hot dogs. You greedy as shit!" Rell's low voice fills her mind with his relentless laughter.

Yes, she could feel his presence as she lay across her bed, folding her body into the fetal position staring at the photo of the life she used to live. Her first true love snatched away. Rell taught Takia how to love. He gave himself to her unconditionally because he wanted more than just her body.

"Why was he gone so soon? It's not fair. It's so many evil cut throat niggas that's walking the streets that should've got killed, not Rell. I guess the good ones die young; that's what the old-heads always say. These streets are cold as a motherfucker, and we paid the ultimate price, Rell." She cries choking up, touching the picture transfixed with Rell's image.

Her hand slips down to her flat, barren belly where her baby once kicked, moving inside her. She wanted her baby so much because it was Rell's baby. She wanted a piece of him to hold on to. Someone that didn't need anything from her but love. Maybe God was punishing her for all the dirt she had done. Every single man she cared about was snatched away from her. First her father, then her two brothers, and finally Rell. Any man she cared about vanished from her life, blown in the wind. But the low life freaks, pervert niggas that tricked on her were around like wolves chasing sheep. She wasn't going back to being a sex toy for dope boys. It had to be more to life for a black girl lost.

"Why me God? My happiness is always snatched away. It's like a motherfucker put roots on me or something. Everything I love crumbles up and dies." She yells, opening the new Brandy *Never Say Never* [CD] Raven had brought for her. She skips to the track, *Have You Ever* and turns the volume to the max.

"Have you ever been in love? Been in love so bad, you'd do anything to make them understand. Have you ever had someone steal your heart away? You'd give anything to make them feel the same. Have you ever searched for words to get you in their heart? But you don't know what to say, and you don't know where to start."

Tears began to swell in her eyes, Brandy's lyrics set off a new wave of emotions. She went all her life with being cold and unfulfilled, never trusting or being able to love, and now, she was 18 years old. Takia had taken a gamble, rolled the dice and given Rell a chance. In return, he built her up like a skyscraper and gave her security. He was her family.

Was it all a dream? Like Biggie would say, she questions herself.

Rell was now the early spring breeze blowing against her window. She walks over to her closet again, looking with an eye of disgust and then began destroying Versace blouses and ripping Dolce & Gabbana shirts like they were useless because now they meant nothing. No material possession she owned would bring Rell back to her, and the realization that she would go on and live her life while his had ended was too much for Takia to bear. She laid down on her bed with the photo of Rell held tightly against her chest rocking herself to sleep.

"Have you ever needed something so bad you just can't sleep at night? Oh, Rell... oh, Rell. My Rell." She sighs until sleep overcomes her. His face would soon appear in her dreams.

Chapter 14

MYA: BONNIE AND CLYDE

"Mya that looks lovely on you," LaTanya exclaims as she exited the fitting room at the L'Impasse boutique on 8th Street in New York's trendy West Village shopping district.

Mya is twirling in a lavender silk satin Valentino gown. LaTanya had picked out the low-cut gown with a deep V bust line. LaTanya's choice was spot on, the color looked striking on Mya's pale skin.

The split would have to be altered higher. Mya thinks, looking at her ass in the snug gown.

"You look fabulous," LaTanya says, walking up behind Mya.

LaTanya looked pretty fabulous herself wearing a black and cream tweed Chanel blazer, flowing black pants, and Chanel ballerina flats; her hair in a tight bun pulled off of her beautiful face.

"Here are more of the latest gowns from Paris: Oscar de la Renta, Chanel, and Carolina Herrera." A bubbly strawberry blonde headed saleswoman wearing too much makeup says, approaching carrying several couture gowns in her arms.

Mya's mind is made up on the Valentino. L'Impasse has a reputation for high-end clientele. Pop stars and

R&B royalty drop heavy cash to be red carpet perfect, and for Mya's senior prom, her last true moment of stunting as Overbrook's resident queen of fashion, no small detail could be left to chance. The other female students were bragging about custom made dresses they were getting made that cost a stack by popular tailors like Rodeo Kids Designer Fabrics on Philadelphia's legendary fabric row. But Mya Campbell's standards and taste levels are too high. Only a prom dress fit for a princess will do.

Once Mya's absolutely satisfied, LaTanya hands the saleswoman her American Express. The dress costs a small fortune. But the fact that Mya and her mother mended their relationship; it was money well spent. After Mya's measurements are taken for alterations, the saleswoman assures the dress will be shipped to their Bala Cynwyd home within a week. They get into LaTanya's Mercedes, which is freshly waxed. The late May air is muggy. LaTanya drives sternly through New York City's congested traffic. She knows her way away around New York well, having traveled back and forth for many litigation and settlement hearings for her extensive list of corporate clients. She heads uptown toward 5th Avenue. She and Mya are on the hunt for prom shoes and whatever else catches their eyes.

Once they find a space in an overcrowded parking lot, they cross the intersection and enters Sak's Fifth Avenue's immense department store. Mother and daughter descend on the first-floor perfume counters, racking up designer fragrances by Escada, Calvin Klein, Versace, Armani, Jean Paul Gaultier and of course Chanel No 5. True shopping savages, they spent an hour in the women's ready to wear department on the third floor. LaTanya picked out several casual spring looks by St. John, Donna Karan, and Yves Saint Laurent. Mya's retail sixth sense goes wild at the sight of a black nylon Prada knapsack and waist pouch. She couldn't make up her mind.

Why not get both? She thinks, handing them along with two leather Gucci belts, one black, one red with large silver double G's on the front; two pairs of bright colored neon pink and yellow Dolce & Gabbana stretch jeans, and several flashy tops by Versace to the smiling attractive dark saleswoman who was counting her large commission in her mind.

Next stop, the sixth floor for women shoes, or as Mya referred to it simply as heaven for girls. Rows upon rows of the spring 1998 shoe collections on dazzling displays. A candy shop for women who spent a little cash on their shoes. Awaiting salespeople with perfect white teeth, dressed impeccably greet LaTanya and Mya, ready to help them rack a hefty credit card bill. Chilled apple cider is served as more than a dozen shoe boxes are spread out before them.

"I want us to stop by Takia's house and check on her first thing next week. I pray for the girl. I knew her mother had a bad drinking problem, both her brothers got caught up in the streets; that girl sure had a rough start in life." LaTanya grimaces taking a sip of chilled champagne that a sales associated had just handed her.

Mya fashions a strappy black sequined Salvatore Ferragamo sandal, ignoring her mother's statements. What happened to Takia broke Mya's heart. Not sharing each other's personal or intimate secrets were torture, but Mya had no more tears to cry. Carmello was making a solider out of her. She could hear his deep baritone voice in her ear at that very moment.

"It's a cold world out here baby girl. When you in the game, somebody gotta lose.   Emotions are for the weak, and we cut from a different cloth." Black would often say.

"How's my second daughter Raven doing? She hasn't been at the house in forever."

"Mom, it's crunch time before graduation. We'll both be eighteen in a few weeks, and then it's the real world like you said to me back in September on the first day of school. Plus, we're in high school mom. What's a friend anyway?" Mya says coolly.

LaTanya's hazel eyes go wide. "Raven and Takia are your real friends. And that's hard to come by in life. You're so dismissive of them. I remember you cried and begged for me to let Takia stay with us for two weeks because her mother's heat was cut off during the big blizzard in 1994. You made me buy you Raven and Takia matching Express jean sets when you guys were in the eighth grade. Do you know how many sleepovers you hosted for those two? I'd peak in your room and see you three snuggled up in bed closer than sisters. You, three girls, are a trinity Mya, never forget my words. Get your sisterhood back on track."

"Mom, you're talking about stuff that happened a million years ago. It's a new day. We're going from girls to women. Those three little girls you're referring to from back in the day ain't the same anymore."

"Baby, some friendships are worth fighting for."

"You're drawlin' mom, I don't want to talk about them anymore," Mya shouts, her cheeks turning red. Two women trying on shoes next to Mya looks startled.

"Fine, Mya I'm not trying to argue with you. Case closed." LaTanya retorts, flagging the flamboyantly dressed thin, dark-skinned salesman, who quickly comes over to her.

The ride home was quiet. LaTanya heads to the New Jersey Turnpike back to Philadelphia. LaTanya was playing Anita Baker's *Rapture* album loudly, singing off key with every song. Mya lays her head against the window as relentless rain begins pouring, thinking about her lost sisterhood. She had to admit, she had not felt more alone in her life. She had Black, but his immense presence could not fill the empty void Raven, and Takia left. Girls can be mean, petty and vindictive. So when you find a woman who completely understands you, loves you even on your worst days; she's more than a friend. Sister is more appropriate.

I've lost both my sisters. She thinks as a single tear falls down her left cheek before drifting off to sleep.

Mya was exhausted. It's past 9 p.m. when they arrive home. Mya and LaTanya lugged their couture cargo inside, practically collapsing on their beds. 1:30 a.m. Mya was awakened from her sound sleep by her Nextel cell phone ringing beside her. She cracks a smile because she's been missing him all day.

"Hello." She says, clearing her throat.

"Sup with you? How was prom dress shopping?"

"Long and drawn out. I tried on fifty dresses before I found the best one. You still have to get fitted for your suit."

"I'm gonna run down Boyds and take care of that this week."

"My dress is lavender."

"Okay, I'm gonna grab some lavender gators to match."

"Omg! We gonna crush the prom, I can't wait!" Mya exclaims. "When am I seeing you?"

"Throw on some clothes, I'm parked in your back driveway right now."

Mya jumps out of bed wearing only a pair of green lace panties. She slides on a pink tube top, and a pair of black Jean Paul Gaultier stretch jeans. She runs to the bathroom, gargles with Scope and puckers her lips applying Maybelline dark plum lipstick. She opens her bedroom door, disappearing in the house down the back stairs leading into the kitchen. Once out the side door leading to the driveway entrance, past her father's beige Jaguar and mother's Mercedes, Carmello sits in his S500 Mercedes with the headlights turned off. The early morning summer breeze is tantalizing to her entering the passenger side.

"Hey baby, I missed you so much." Mya coos, leaning over giving Carmello a deep wet kiss.

He wears only a black Polo wife beater, with biceps like steel, he squeezes her tight around her waist.

"I need to show you something, come take this ride with me real quick."

"Okay," Mya whispers, wondering where or what was so urgent he had to show her at two in the morning.

They cruised down Lincoln Drive listening to Aaliyah's *One in a Million* album. *4 Page Letter* was one of Mya's favorite songs. Secretly she knew Carmello had a crush on young R&B diva Aaliyah. It was cool, Aaliyah was bad, but in Mya's world, Aaliyah couldn't fuck with her on her best day. She watches Carmello from the side of her eye, focused on the road. His perfect, even dark skin, freshly faded shape up, and new gold Rolex watch with the iced-out face on his wrist as he turned the steering wheel. She was beyond infatuated with him. She felt powerful in his presence. She could never fuck with the help and small-time cats now that she was the boss' girl.

They get off at the Broad Street and Allegheny exit. After turning and winding down one rough ran down looking street after another, Black pulls in front of an abandoned building, parking at the rear. He dials a number on his gray Nextel phone.

"Yo, I'm 'bout to come in. Let's go." Black says to Mya, exiting the driver side.

She looks around the dark secluded area. It looked like all kinds of evil was lurking in the gloom. A twinge of fear passes through her, but she quickly composes herself, remembering who her man was. Her heart turns hard leaping out the passenger side, ready for whatever was waiting in the darkness. Carmello knocks three times on a rusted graffiti door, a slit at the top opens revealing two dark, creepy eyes. Mya glances up noticing a black security camera with a blinking red light.

Where the fuck are we? She thinks nervously.

The door swings open. They enter a well-lit warehouse, Mya instantly recognizes Black's right-hand man Faheem, his second in command; Black's number one street soldier known for executing all Black's deadly bidding. He greets Black with a silent handshake and a brotherly hug. Looking over Black's shoulder, Mya catches him winking at her, smiling seductively.

"What's up Mya?"

"Hey." She responds dryly, rolling her hazel eyes.

They move through another dimly lit room. Mya is startled by the ferocious barking of half a dozen large Pit Bulls chained to several large workout benches with hundred pound weights attached to them. Barbells and free weights the size of Mya's body sit on the floor.

"Oh my fucking God!" She shrieks back in fear.

The pits bark, struggling against their chains, razor-sharp teeth ready to rip flesh from human bodies. Black and Faheem burst into uncontrollable laughter at Mya's fright.

"Babe, it's okay." Black chuckles still laughing, waiting for Mya to come to him. "Shut the fuck up!" Black snarls at the barking Pit Bulls. Instantly they are quiet and as tamed as puppies panting excitedly as Black pets each one of their heads. "Come on boo, they won't bite."

Mya hesitantly takes Black's hand, he ushers her past his trained killers as he refers to them. He leads her into the main room of the warehouse. Mya gasps, trying to comprehend what her eyes are viewing. The entire room is filled with two dozen men, and women stripped down to their undergarments wearing surgical masks, filling an endless supply of small clear bottles with crack. The filled vials were then placed in rubber bins, which were then emptied into large clear dumpsters.

"It must be hundreds, no thousands of vials." Mya thought as her eyes drift to four stone-faced dark-brown skinned guys holding semi-automatic weapons. Keeping watch over the group of workers with cold, uncaring eyes.

There wasn't a chance in hell of anyone stealing one vial of precious crack. Black's presence in the room, causes a pause, eyes staring at him and Mya with interest before returning to their endless robotic task. They enter an office with black leather furniture, a clear glass desk, and a giant size Scarface movie poster hanging on the wall. A small dark-skinned woman sits at the round glass desk wearing a Kente cloth, putting large piles of money in front of her through an electric counting machine.

"Aunt Tameeka, what's up?" Black warmly greets. "This my mom's younger sister. She's been down with me since I flipped my first eight ball."

"Nice to meet you." Mya greets.

The woman glances up at her, eyes blank and expressionless. She returns to her counting, jotting down numbers, and figures on a white notepad.

"She's an accountant." Carmello brags, flopping down on the fresh black leather couch. "Sit down," Black tells Mya, who quickly sits beside him.

Black narrows his eyes on Faheem who silently gets the message, leaving the office quickly.

"$90,000 profit minus $10,000 for payroll and $5,000 for re-up supplies for next week. Your net pay my dear nephew for this week is $75,000 thousand." Aunt Tameeka says proudly, handing Carmello two manila envelopes stuffed with cash.

"Good shit Aunt Tameeka." He says. "Aunt Tameeka, you took a little extra out for yourself right?"

"No nephew. You're doing more than enough helping me pay for your cousin Malik's college tuition at Cheyney. You do more than enough for our whole family."

"Oh, Aunt Tameeka this is Mya, my girl."

Mya quickly got the feeling Aunt Tameeka was not feeling her. She gave her a stern stare, her dark-skinned face unreadable.

"So you the little light-skinned heffa that got my nephew sprung huh?"

"No, the fuck she didn't!" Mya thought, fighting with herself to hold her tongue. Her screw face facial expression said it all.

Aunt Tameeka chuckles loudly. "Nephew I think this little girl got some heart. If looks could kill, I'd be laid out. I was just testing you sweetheart. Whoever my nephew loves, I love. But I gotta get home. I have to drop your cousin Shareff at Engineering and Science High School at seven in the morning." Aunt Tameeka kisses Carmello on the cheek and gives Mya a kind smile before leaving the office.

It's past 4:00 a.m. when Black drops her off.

"You know why I brought you to the underworld?" Carmello asks turning the Benz off. Mya shakes her head no. "The underworld is the heart of my empire. It's the hive, and those workers you saw is my busy bees makin' the honey that goes on the streets. I needed you to see my operation in the raw. Remember, I said I was moldin' you?"

"Yeah."

"I want you to be with me long term, but I gotta be able to trust you with everything. Even my life if it comes down to it." Black was staring straight into Mya's eyes with a serious intensity she never saw before. She listened to every word carefully. "I got another two to three years on top of this drug game. I'm gonna take what I learned from my old-head Enrique, God rest his soul. Realest nigga I ever met. He schooled me to the game early and gave me my first pack when I was fourteen. He was Spanish, Colombian and flashy, always had fly cars and jewels. I was in the streets running wild. My pops was dead, and my mom suffered from a lot of mental issues. So I had to step up and become the man of the house. Enrique owned a chop shop. He taught me how to drive and let me park the cars. Even had me making little deliveries for $200 or $300 here and there. He even got me my first piece of pussy; bad lil' bitch named Maria. I still remember her."

Mya throws Black a jealous frown.

"When I was sixteen he taught me how to cook potent product. A certain recipe and the ingredients are mapped out in my mind. Enrique would always say, "Never teach another motherfucker how to cook product because if they learn the key to how you cooking money, they don't need you no more." I'm like a cash cow. I keep everybody around me eatin', so they need me. Even if they hate me, they need me. Enrique got killed summer of '95. The king was dead, and the vultures swooped down. I remember I was just a lil' nigga with a lot of heart. Me and Faheem go back to the block. We been friends since high school. It would be just me and Fa gettin' rolled on by six or seven niggas. But as long as we was standin' back to back, just us two was all we needed. So when it came time for war after Enrique passed, we recruited the grimmest dudes from our 'hood and went to war. When the smoke cleared, I was a young king. But one thing Enrique said to me that will always be stuck in my head is, "Ain't no hustlers retirement fund. Old drug dealers become young niggas' targets." That shit made me paranoid. So I'm planning five years ahead from now. I got my real-estate business, Aunt Tameeka handles all of my paperwork, federal and state taxes. I own ten row houses throughout the city, four duplexes, and three triplex units. I wanna start building a solid foundation for us."

"For us?" Mya says, tears building in her eyes.

"Yes for us. I figure you graduate, then off to college next fall. After four years you'll have your degree, this legit money should be moving perfectly, and I'll buy us a plush crib with a white picket fence out in Jersey. We'll get married, have us a couple gorgeous dark-skinned babies and live out our happily ever after." "Mya, why you cryin'?"

"You really want to be with me? You're talking about marrying me?"

"Yes, Mya you was never no fling to me. The first day I pulled up on you I felt something different. And I been with lots of girls, but my heart I can say belongs to you. It's gonna be me and you ole girl, out here rollin' until death do us part. And when I propose, the rock gonna be as big as a boulder weighing your hand down."

They both laugh. "I don't like nothing average and ain't a damn thing average about you. I been hard and distrusting of hoes all my life, but you changed me."

Mya knew Carmello loved her, but never in her wildest dreams did she think he would want to marry her. Black had shown his hand, all aces. Yes, Mya Campbell had certainly played her cards right and was holding the king of diamonds. She kissed him good night, returning to her bed, her head overflowing with dreams of her and Black's new life as husband and wife wrapped in each other's arms making love continuously. Mya's future's is looking so bright, she'll have to wear Fendi shades.

The next morning is total slow motion. Mya had less than four hours of sleep. It reflected in the deep yawning and puffy circles forming underneath her eyes she observes brushing her mane straight down her back in her bathroom mirror. Full pink lips glossed and kissable, she switches out of her private bathroom, admiring her teenage perfection in her full-length mirror in the center of her luxurious bedroom.

"You are the 'hood teenage dream Mya Campbell. You took it to levels bitches only dreamt of." She tells herself, adjusting the giant black and gold patent leather double C belt, snatching her small waist in, even more, a black tube top holding her perfect firm 36C breast in an upright position, and black satin Versace pants looked painted on.

Since she and Black started fucking nonstop, her ass was spreading, getting fatter by the day. Her thighs were also getting thick as molasses. The black and red high heeled Chanel sneakers that Lil' Kim and Foxy Brown were rocking in *Vibe Magazine* were $700.00 a pop with tax. She got the last pair at Bloomingdales. They were on hold for Mary J Blige, but Mya convinced the salespeople to give them to her. That's what a $300.00 tip will get you. They felt tight against her size seven and a half feet.

"I really need to start breaking my shoes in early." She thought, strutting around her bedroom when her Nextel began ringing from the vanity table filled with dozens of designer perfume bottles.

"Mya come on, I have a 9:30 a.m. conference meeting with my Japanese clients." LaTanya snaps in her ear.

"Okay mom, here I come." She sighs, slamming the flip phone closed.

She grabs her new cat eye Chanel shades with Chanel in gold on the handles and black quilted Chanel Caviar shoulder bag. She takes one final look at her image, smirks confidently.

"If there was a badder young chick killing shit like Mya Campbell on the verge of eighteen, I'd love to meet her," Mya says blowing a kiss at her reflection before hurrying out of her bedroom.

LaTanya huffs impatiently as Mya hops in the passenger seat. She puts the Mercedes in drive, speeding off, her cell phone glued to her ear giving her secretary instructions.

"Leslie, have coffee, tea, and croissants set up in boardroom B14. I'm dropping Mya off at school, I'll be arriving shortly." "Countdown to prom, are you super excited?" LaTanya asks grinning. The gleaming of her freshly painted crimson manicured nails on her petite hands spinning the Mercedes steering wheel.

Mya perks up. "I am mom. I have my hair and makeup appointment booked and then it's lights, camera, action."

"Your father and I can't wait to meet your date," LaTanya asks inquisitively.

"Mom, he's real laid back and chill."

"Oh really? What's his name?"

"Carmello."

"Oh... Carmello, interesting name. How old is he?"

"Twenty-three." Mya almost whispers.

LaTanya cuts her eyes at Mya. "Twenty-three is a little old for you."

"Mom please, I'll be eighteen in less than seven days, don't start drawlin'. I'm way too mature to mess with high school boys."

"Mya listen to me, most older guys are only after what's between your legs."

"Carmello's not most guys," Mya says curtly, with a slight frown on her face. *I can't-do this shit with her today.* Mya thinks.

"You're seventeen, I'm forty-two. I think I have more authority on men and their intentions. You're a beautiful girl Mya. What men say and what they do when it comes to a beautiful woman are two different things."

Blah, blah, blah. Mya thinks, turning up the volume on the radio. Dru Hill's *Sleeping in My Bed* begins playing.

"Your aunts Renée and Lisa and your cousins are all coming to see you off on your prom day. I have to prepare myself for this little visit. Your father's overbearing older sisters have never thought I was good enough for him and made their disapproval known on more than one occasion." LaTanya says, turning the stereo down.

"I love Omar, Ebony and Kyree, my only first cousins. Whatever Aunt Renée and Aunt Lisa start yapping about is irrelevant." Mya says sarcastically.

LaTanya pulls in front of Overbrook. "Have a good day, Mya."

"You too mom." She slides out of the passenger side.

The late May weather is filled with traces of the hot summer to come. The near ending school year makes urban teenagers restless. Groups of weed-heads smoke blunts in front of the building. The smell of marijuana fills her nose as she passes by. Overbrook had once been her kingdom that she ruled over with an iced out hand. The large looming, brick building in front of her used to be the first and last thought in her mind. Today it doesn't hold the same allure, or maybe Mya Campbell has just grown up.

As she walked into school, it was the same as any other day. The Joe Familiar fans smiled, waving, and breaking their necks to speak. Mya walks head held high, emotionless and unfazed by the admiration she receives.

"Omg! Bitch you got the new Chanel sneakers." Overbrook's resident fashion queen Reggie squeals with sheer delight.

His floral print Versace shirt matches the powder pink hush puppies he wore perfectly. His brown face wide with delight, he instantly put Mya in a better mood. They've grown closer since she and Raven's relationship had deteriorated. Takia was being homeschooled, so Reggie had become her partner in crime.

"Well you know me, I gotta keep shit that's new." Mya brags, putting her right hand on her hip.

"Yes Ms. Mya, you definitely have the best-dressed spot in the yearbook on lock."

"The female spot that is, cause you're the best-dressed boy in Overbrook period."

Reggie chuckles. "I'll take that award."

"Excuse me," Kareema says dryly, pushing past Mya, bumping roughly into her.

"What you need to do is watch where the fuck you going!" Mya shouts.

"Reggie you better get your girlfriend before I trash her again."

Kareema faces off with Mya, a mean, devious look upon her plain brown face. The pale yellow Jean Paul Gaultier top and matching pants made her huge ass and hips look enormous like a wicked bumble bee.

"What bitch? You ain't trash shit. I rocked your jaw back." Mya hands Reggie her Chanel bag. *"Yo, let's end this rivalry once and for all."* Mya thought, stepping in front of Reggie, her hazel eyes cold.

"Mya, you don't want it with me." Kareema spat with spit flying out of her mouth.

Reggie grabs Mya by the arm, pulling her down the hallway. "Mya come on, she's not worth it," he says as a large crowd was gathering, thirsty to see a fight.

The two most popular girls in school, squaring up ready to kill each other. Their beef and dislike of one another was more than well known. The big fight at Gotham was at the top of all gossip. This was about to be an Overbrook showdown that the class of 1998 would never forget.

"That's enough. We're not having any fighting this morning. Get to class people." Rick and Rhonda the two large school police officers holler with authority walking up to the scene.

They had a reputation of cracking the heads of violent and unruly students.

"Look at you two girls, y'all look too nice to be fighting this early in the morning." Rick, a 6'4" giant of a man with full cheeks on his large brown-skinned face and a wide gap in his mouth chuckles.

"Mya, let's go! Kareema is mad she's wearing that discounted Gaultier outfit. You fresh to death in Chanel." Reggie says, grabbing Mya by the hand.

"Reggie, what your punk ass just say?"

This is not over. I'm gonna put hands on that bitch by the end of the day. Mya thinks, entering the first-floor stairwell, silently plotting her next move walking onto the third-floor pissed beyond words.

"Hey Mya, you're looking fly. Love your Chanel sneakers." Two well-dressed light-skinned sophomore girls greet, bubbly as she passes them, both wearing matching Versace t-shirts.

She ignores their compliments, face balled up underneath her Chanel frames. She walks into Mrs. Ashcroft first period ready to explode. Ziggy Brown, the resident class clown, couldn't cheer her up with his vulgar sense of humor. Raheem Samson and Nasir Smith go on loudly about conspiracies behind the deaths of Tupac and Notorious B.I.G. Lisa Scott brags about the enormous amount of scholarship money she received, passing her acceptance letters from Howard, Spelman, Drexel, and NYU around as if they were Oscar or Grammy Awards.

Raven walks into the classroom three seconds before the bell rings, head down, and her hair in wild curls. Mya saw the black-and-white newspaper printed Moschino cotton jersey dress that read "extra, extra Moschino all about it" written in bold letters across the front. The dress came from Toby Lerner, an upscale boutique. It fit Raven's slender body perfectly. Her large Jackie Onassis inspired Gucci shades cover her face as usual. She rushes to the back row of desks, disappearing into her silent exile. Mya wants to grab Raven by the shoulders, look her in the eyes, and tell her how sorry she was for the part she played in encouraging her to date hustlers. To tell Raven, she cried a thousand times imagining the beatings and bruises she endured at Nickels' hands; how she had to live with the guilt every day knowing she wasn't there to protect her sister; either of them, Raven or Takia. Tears formed underneath her Chanel shades.

"I know your high school graduation is a few weeks away, but until you receive your diploma in your hand, every one of you is still a student at Overbrook High School. There are no sunglasses allowed in my classroom. Ms. Campbell, Ms. Hightower, do you hear me?" Mrs. Ashcroft screams, a deep grimace on her unattractive face.

Mya slowly takes her shades off. *I can't wait until I never have to set eyes on this miserable bitch* thinks, rolling her eyes with tremendous force at Mrs. Ashcroft.

She turns her head looking Raven directly in the eye. Mya sees the longing in her eyes. Raven was silently sending a message, she misses her as much as Mya does. She smiles broadly knowing her best friends frost bitten heart was melting. The entire class was staring, including Mrs. Ashcroft. Their falling out was of the top most importance to students and staff alike. They were at the center of life at Overbrook.

The next periods fly by. World history and English literature was Mya's favorite classes. She excels at creative writing, but is always too caught up with boys and fashion to develop her talents. The hallways were muggy from the rising summer humidity. Mya's sensitive nose catches the foul odor of funk.

Somebody skipped the damn deodorant this morning. She thinks, covering her nose with her left hand.

The first floor corridor is crowded with students changing classes. The opposite sex flirted with each other. The hotter the temperature rose outside, the hornier the student population rose. Mya catches the usual lusty stares and glances from freshman and senior boys alike, admiring her exposed shoulders, firm breasts and perfect sized bottom. They often whispered that Mya's proportions were just right. They also recognized the Chanel belt and sneakers. She was the most official girl of the class of 1998. She projected the definition of flawless with the simplest of movements.

Mya and Reggie had taken to eating lunch together. Raven had stopped entering the lunch room all together. She waited to enter the rusted lunch room doors when she catches the taunting conniving eyes of Kareema, TeTe and Asia gritting on her hard.

"Oh these bitches are plotting, ain't shit sweet. If it's me against all these nut ass bitches, so be it."

TeTe breezes by, a vindictive grin on her thin brown skin face. She slightly bumps into Mya with her shoulder. Asia follows, slightly stepping on one of her Chanel sneakers, then laughs viciously. Mya's blood is turning to lava. Kareema deliberately steps in front of Mya. Their eyes meet, this was the showdown that had been brewing for the last three years. The climatic ending would happen today. Kareema takes a deep swallow with and without warning hawk spits in Mya's face. A gulp of slippery mucus filled spit clings to Mya cheek and chin.

"Fucking bitch!" Mya hollers like a war cry, punching Kareema brutally in the face.

The 'hood world war three commences. The screams and yells are deafening. The entire school had been waiting for something to jump off since the infamous brawl at club Gotham some months back, but today, live and in living color, the two flyest girls in school dressed in European couture were trying to kill each other. This was really beef, the kind Biggie talks about in *Life After*

Death Volume 1. Kareema grabs Mya's hair, yanking it back violently. Mya digs her nails into Kareema's face while landing several brutal punches to her chest. They fall over onto a long graffiti covered lunch table. The students surrounding them were a bloodthirsty mob, standing on top of the lunch tables screaming and shouting, loving the out of control violence.

"Bitch I hate you!" Mya hisses, bending her knees.

She hops on top of Kareema giving her all face shots. The princess cut diamond ring on her hand cutting Kareema's face. Blood begins leaking. Mya felt herself overtaking Kareema by sheer determination.

"Get off my girlfriend bitch!" TeTe hollers, punching Mya hard in the back as Asia locks onto her hair, yanking her back.

Kareema lands a hang maker busting Mya's lip, blood gushes instantly.

"They gonna have to kill me." Mya's mind races while being attacked by all three girls like a wolf pack.

She maintains an iron grip on Kareema's hair. Asia and TeTe severely kick and punch Mya in her back. The roar of the crowd rose louder. Suddenly Asia and TeTe stops attacking her. She could feel a commotion going on, bodies are falling into her. Suddenly, the strong arms of the school's security guards were pulling her and Kareema apart. Mya is lifted off her feet. She's whipped through the air and is stunned by what her eyes land on. Asia is laid out in the center of the floor, Raven has TeTe against the wall, beating the brakes off her boney ass. TeTe's head bangs against the dark blue tile lunch room wall before more school security guards force them apart. Each of the girls is placed in handcuffs and taken to the first floor disciplinarian office.

Mr. Ford, the hawk eyed no nonsense gray haired school disciplinarian meets them with a hostile frown on his coffee brown skin face; still handsome for a man in his fifties. His arms were folded against his chest, the cream dress shirt and burgundy tie he wears are pressed to perfection.

"These two in room one, the other three in room two." He instructs the school's security officers handling them. "You young ladies are not only facing suspension, you're seniors there's a big chance you can forget about prom or participating in graduation all for being stupid. Your parents are going to be mighty pissed off at you. I'm calling every one of them in a minute. It's the last weeks of your high school life and you're gonna end it being dummies." He shakes his head, walking into his office, slamming the door loudly.

Mya and Raven are ushered into a tiny room which resembled a police interrogation room. They sit on small orange plastic chairs, both of their heads in disarray. After they're un-handcuffed, Mya pulls a small Chanel compact out of her bag, observing the scratches on her face and blood soaked lip. Another day in battle for the couture woman warrior. Mortal combat was becoming a regular occurrence for Mya.

"Them ugly ass bitches really tried to go to work on my face." She laughs, trying to break the ice between she and Raven.

They hadn't really said a single word to each other in months, putting on a fake façade in Takia's and Ms. Michelle's presence and today out of the blue Raven runs to her rescue. She doesn't quite know how to take the situation.

"Raven, thanks for having my back today." Mya says softly, her face flushed with emotion.

"I saw Reggie in the hall, he told me Kareema and them was plotting on you. I felt something strange in my gut and I ran to find you."

"Look Raven, I know I played a big part in your decision to fuck with Nickels. I had no idea that motherfucker was abusive. When I think about the shit you've been going through with him, it breaks my heart." Mya begins crying.

Raven quickly embraces her in a silent hug. "I miss you so much Mya."

"I miss you Raven." They both begin sobbing. "Raven you're the sister I never had. If I did anything to ever hurt you, I'm sorry. I'm so fucking sorry." Mya cries, large amounts of tears bursting down her face.

"Mya it's okay. I was wrong for lashing out of you too. When I was drowning in my pain I was so down and fucked up. I need you to forgive me too." A damaged sisterhood is on its way to mending. Two broken hearts find a first aid kit. All it took was a wild all bitch brawl to bring back two of the baddest chicks to each other's life.

Chapter 15

MYA: PROM NIGHT 1998

Mya sits at the heart-shaped vanity in the center of her bedroom, draped in a dark purple rose as Tiffany, the twenty-something-year-old MAC cosmetic makeup artist Mya hired does her face perfectly. She left nothing to chance. This was the most defining moment of her life thus far. Every detail would be remembered, gossiped, and analyzed by Joe dick-eaters and haters alike solidifying her reign at Overbrook High School as the baddest chick once and for all.

"Girl, your face is goddamn beautiful!" Tiffany praises, applying the final coat of blush to her cheeks. "Look at you, the black teenage dream."

Mya turns her head, pleasantly stunned by the sight of her hazel eyes, hooded in dark smoky eyeshadow. Soft pink blush brings out her perfect bone structure, moist lips, the color of the ripest red cherry. CoCo had outdone herself. Mya's hair is pulled back in a sleek ponytail, soft waterfall curls crown her face. She could be the *Jet* beauty of the week or Miss Teen USA easily.

"Baby you ready? It's almost show time." LaTanya says, entering the bedroom. "Aw Mya, you look like the most beautiful princess." LaTanya gushes holding a glass of red wine in her hand.

The pale green satin blouse she wore looks striking on her. She has a sleepy look in her hazel eyes from long nights of working on her heavy caseload. Her reputation as one of the best corporate lawyers is a title that didn't come without dedication.

"Your aunts and cousins are growing restless waiting for you. This is my second glass of wine. I need a little buzz to tune out Lisa and Renée's shady remarks. The catty criticism began as soon as they walked in the door. They're downstairs kissing your father's ass like he's the Holy Messiah," LaTanya comments in a condescending manner. "But enough about those miserable heffas, I have something special that adds the perfect finishing touch for tonight." She hands Mya a small Tiffany's jewelry box.

"Mom, you didn't." Mya squeals with childish delight opening the jewelry box, finding two large shiny diamond earrings.

"Goddamn those rocks are big!" Tiffany says, eyes wide open, she stops beating Mya's face to get a clear look at the gleaming gems.

"Mom, you didn't have to go all out like this."

"Mya you're my daughter, my only child. I waited twelve years to see you off on your prom night. Nothing's too much." LaTanya embraces her. They hold each other tightly and LaTanya lands a flurry of kisses on Mya's face.

"Mom stop! You're gonna ruin my makeup."

"I'm sorry, let me get myself together, I'm getting so emotional." LaTanya rushes out of Mya's bedroom.

Tiffany stays to help her get dressed. The lavender Valentino gown is altered with a deep plunging neckline, her breasts are held together by a nude strapless bra. The split is cut high rising up the thigh. Her milky legs are bronzed to perfection. Silver open toe Gucci stiletto sandals fit like a glove. She twirls several times, the Tiffany diamond studs blinged beautifully matching the diamond tennis bracelet, and platinum princess cut diamond ring on her engagement finger. She could stand next to Halle Berry on the Oscar's red carpet and not feel intimidated. She had never felt more regal or beautiful in all of her life.

The senior class was arriving at the Adam's Mark Hotel on 4000 City Avenue where her subjects were waiting patiently for their royal highness to arrive. All the queen needed was her king by her side. At the moment, Mya's thoughts are interrupted by a loud knock on her bedroom door.

"Is my favorite niece dressed and ready for her senior prom?" Mya instantly recognizes the loud booming voice of her Aunt Renée.

"Yes I am auntie, come on in!"

"My Lord, look at my little niece all grown up!" Aunt Renée hollers, walking over to Mya with a wide grin on her chubby light-brown skinned face, a mouth full of pearly white teeth with a large gap in the front.

She's a thick, full-figured woman with a no-nonsense attitude. She was a Septa bus driver who had no problem saying anything that was on her mind. Her two sons Omar and Kyree are the apples of her eye. She's her father's youngest sister. Even though her mother didn't get along with her aunts, she was very fond of them, and loved her cousins dearly. They were the little brothers, she never had.

"You better go girl!" Aunt Renée says doing her best Martin Lawrence impersonation snapping several pictures on her small Kodak throw-away camera. Mya poses. "Baby you look super-duper fly like that song by that hip-hop artist... the fat girl in the trash bag..."

"Missy Elliot."

"Yeah, that's her. Baby you looking fine, But that fine ass chocolate man who just walked in the door looking like a fresh Hershey bar ready to be eaten. Girl he is scrumptious."

"Carmello's downstairs?" She whispers.

"Yup, and he's talking to your father. And if you ask me, your mother has had one too many drinks." Aunt Renée says, rolling her eyes.

The subliminal jab at her mother went completely over her head. Her mind was set on getting to Carmello. She takes one last look at her reflection before darting out of her bedroom, heartbeat quickening as she descends the winding, freshly waxed dark mahogany staircase. She was met with a frenzy of flashing cameras.

"Yes Mya!" Her mother, father, aunts, and cousins yell as she reaches the bottom of the staircase.

Carmello stands behind them grinning like the young don he is, dressed in a dark gray custom double-breasted suit from Boyd's, a gray and lavender Versace dress shirt, and a matching tie. His haircut is sharp as a tack and the lavender gators with gold buckles on his feet cost a small fortune. The diamond face of the platinum Rolex on his right wrist is immaculate. All she could see in the room is him. Their eyes meet, locked on each other in absolute love.

Is this a preview of how our wedding day will be? Her concentration was broken by her father's voice.

Vincent Campbell is beaming with pride at the sight of his beautiful daughter. He looks at her with only the love a father can feel for a daughter. He takes her in his arms. Vincent is a tall, 6'1" well-built man with thick waves of salt and pepper hair, deep dimples, and smooth chestnut-brown skin. For a man in his late forties, he was extremely well preserved and handsome. Mya his only child, seeing her delight was worth all of the struggle. The sacrifice of working like a slave putting himself through law school, and navigating his way through the rough Richard Allen housing projects of North Philadelphia. Vowing that his children would have a better life than the one his parents gave him. He had more than fulfilled that vow. Mya had never wanted for anything in life. She never knew what 'struggling to pay the bills' meant. She never went one day with her stomach growling from hunger, or sleeping bundled up in a house with no heat. She had been shielded from the hardships and pain that life could bring. But by giving Mya her every material wish, both her parents are guilty of blindly ruining her mentally and spiritually.

"My daughter has never looked lovelier. I'm so proud of you baby." Vincent says, smiling proudly down at her.

"Thank you daddy." Mya says choking up. They embrace warmly.

"Carmello, I'm trusting you with my most prized possession, my baby girl." Mr. Campbell jokes, as he addresses Carmello.

"Mr. Campbell, sir she will be in the best possible care. I assure you." Carmello says with the most charming grin on his chocolate face.

After ten more minutes of posing for pictures with the Campbell family, everyone gathers in the driveway to watch Mya and Carmello drive off. Just as Mya was about to sit in the passenger seat, her name was called out.

"Mya! Mya, wait!"

She turns her head to see Raven driving toward them.

"I made it just in time. You look all that." Raven says out of breath, her black hair in a wild ponytail.

"Raven I'm so happy you made it to see me off." Mya says proudly, putting her arms around Raven.

"My second daughter is here." LaTanya coos, embracing the girls.

"I couldn't have lived with myself if I didn't come see you off." Raven whispers in Mya's ear.

For a few seconds Mya and Raven are lost in the translations of sisterhood. Mya and Carmello pull out of her parents' driveway in his freshly waxed drop-top Mercedes SL500. Raven and Mya's family waved goodbye. Black drives calmly down City Line Avenue toward the Adam's Mark Hotel. Mya checks her flawless makeup in the passenger seat overhead mirror, a hint of conceited confidence in her eyes.

"Babe we here." Black says, snapping out of her gaze, obsessed with her own perfection.

Mya looks up to see the grand Adam's Mark Hotel and the view lit up immensely. Traffic was at a standstill, limousines, rented sedans, and luxury cars are all waiting to enter the hotel's main entrance. Mya pulsates with energy, butterflies fill her stomach. Twelve years of school, making it her mission to be the most fly. All the planning, shopping, and dressing to the nines had all come down to this very moment. She takes a deep breath and exhales as Black drives slowly toward the front of the hotel. He turns to Mya with a cocky smile.

"You ready to shut this whole shit down?"

She bites down on her bottom lip, cuts one smoky hazel eye at Black who hits the bottom of the six-disc CD player, *Ain't No Nigga* by Jay-Z and Foxy Brown blast with a boom through the expensive car stereo system.

Mya sings along with the lyrics, "I keep it fresher than the next bitch, no need...for you to ever sweat the bitch. With speed I make the best bitch see the exit, indeed. You gotta know you thoroughly respected, by me. You get the keys to the Lexus, with no driver. You gotcha your own '96 somethin'...the ride. And keep your ass tighter than Versace, that's why you gotta watch your friends, you got to watch me, they connive and shit."

Black floors the gas, pulling the Benz wildly up to the curb at the hotel entrance. He jumps out of the driver side strolling with the confidence of a mack. His pinkie ring with a diamond the size of a golf ball glistens as it reflects the lights from other cars. He gives the car keys to a smiling red-headed parking attendant in his early twenties who was even more thrilled when Black pulls out his gold money clip filled with fresh Benjamins. He peels off a hundred dollar bill, handing it to the dorky valet who stutters...

"Thank you sir. Thank you sir." Black ignores him, pulling open the passenger door.

This is it! Mya thinks, remembering not to hop out, but gently slide out, looking like a knockout.

She conjured the images of actress Halle Berry, or supermodel Naomi Campbell as she reveals one bronze curvy thigh, six inch Gucci platform sandals, and a perfectly polished pedicure the exact glossy color of her lavender Valentino gown. She surveys the spectacle around her, all eyes were glued to her and Carmello. A large crowd of students, family, and friends lined the outside entrance of the hotel yelling, "Sharp as shit! Killed them dead! That girl dress is bad!" Older women hollered as they entered the crowded lobby filled with prom-goers dressed in bright colored and animal print gowns with cutouts on the side. Many girls in sexy two-piece dresses with halter tops, French rolls, and spiral curl hairstyles. Guys looked dapper in suits of various color linen, Versace shirts, gator and ostrich skin shoes, fresh Bigen-dyed haircuts; some so dark that beards didn't match their natural skin color. Mya and Black's presence is felt in the room immediately. The word traveled fast, everyone knew the most popular girl at Overbrook High School and the king of North Philly were in the building.

Mya hands vice principal Lawrence Chambers her prom ticket, and they enter the ballroom. Black and gold balloons fill the room with a banner reading Overbrook Prom 1998. The DJ is playing *A Party Ain't a Party* by Queen Pen. The dance floor is filled, girls were bent over grinding, backing their asses up on their overly excited male partners. Mya was greeted by a barrage of compliments, Girls she's known since middle school drooled over her Gucci sandals, and she is begged to take photo after photo. Black stands backlighting her shine. They stand in the picture line, Mya immediately spots Kareema and TeTe; both in dresses that Mya could tell were locally tailor-made. TeTe's hair actually looks salon done for once and to Mya's great surprise, TeTe's prom date is Mally.

Mally is a real lame ass nigga. How he go from a dime like Raven, to a dollar food stamp bitch like TeTe?

Mya sizes up Kareema, she wearing a strapless tangerine colored gown, the back was low cut. She looks presentable, but is still ten steps behind Mya. Her date had on a matching blazer, white linen pants and tangerine colored ostrich loafers; tall and well built, light caramel skin, handsome just enough. Mya had never seen him before.

"That's the bitches right there I was rumbling with at Gotham and school. They been hatin' on me for years." Mya whispers in Black's ear, he focuses in on them.

"Them funny lookin' chicks right there? They not fly at all." He chuckles viciously. "Hold up, that's my young boah Rasoul with them. Haha, watch this..." Black grabs Mya's hand pulling her directly to the front of the line.

Kareema and Mya's eyes lock. *Bitch you can't touch this!* She thought rolling her eyes at TeTe and Mally.

As soon as Rasoul sees Black, he practically leaps to shake his hand. "What up B? You up in Brook prom repping North Philly style."

"I had to hold my shorty down." Black retorts with a hand gesture toward Mya.

"Girl you look like a bag of money." Rasoul jokes, shaking Mya's hand.

Kareema lets out a loud sigh, clearly aggravated, her raging anger building at the sight of her prom date being Joe with her sworn enemy.

"Rasoul we going ahead of y'all, I hate waiting." Black grins.

"Cool, anything for you Black." Rasoul again shakes Black's hand like he's President Bill Clinton himself.

"Oh hell no! How you gon' let them go in front of us like we ain't been standing in this fucking line for like a half an hour?" Kareema growls, her arched eyebrows raise give Mya and Black the grizzle face.

Black's face hardens into an icy frown that could send a chill through anybody his eyes landed on.

"Rasoul, I don't play that disrespectful shit. Keep this bitch in check because she wit' you the problem gon' fall back on you. Feel me? Now get her out of my presence before she ends up missing." He says with extra bass in his voice.

"Hold up dude. Who you calling a bitch?"

Mya steps in front of Black about to back slap Kareema. Before she can react Rasoul has Kareema gripped by both her arms, pushing and lifting her with brute force off of her feet, shoving her away from the picture line.

"Shut the fuck up! Keep your disrespectful mouth closed. Do you know who the fuck that man is? Both of us could wind up dead because of you. I will lay you the fuck out in here!" Rasoul says sternly to Kareema who's protesting in vain, tears filling her eyes.

TeTe chases after them, Mally stands facing Mya and Carmello giving Mya a disdainful stare.

"Mally, what the fuck your punk ass looking at, with that cheap ass rented tuxedo on?" Mya hisses.

"Nothin'. Nothin' at all." Mally says, shaking his head before disappearing into the crowd.

Carmello and Mya pose like bosses, smiling victoriously in the black and gold backdrop as the photographer snaps away; standing behind her, with his hands holding her waist. A power couple in the making. After they take the perfect prom photo, they head back in with an aura like they owned the place. Everywhere Mya turned, she received another compliment on how gorgeous she looked. And not just from students, but teachers and faculty members are just as taken aback with her elegant attire. The DJ begins playing Montell Jordan's hit *This Is How We Do It* and she wants to dance. Mya faces Carmello, swaying her hips and tossing her hair to the beat. Carmello pulls her close, turns out he's an excellent dancer. They get caught up in the song, a small crowd gathers cheering them on chanting...

"Go Mya! Go Mya! Go Mya!"

As the song comes to an end, the DJ yells out, "Yo, class of '98, we about to slow things down."

R. Kelly's *It Seems Like You're Ready* fills the room. Black slyly grins at Mya, pulling her close to him, wrapping his arms around her waist. She rests her head on his shoulder, the scent of his Versace Blue Jeans cologne fills her nose; her hands slowly travel up and down his sturdy back. This was a moment that she wanted to savor, as R. Kelly's lyrics fill her ears. "Girl are you ready? To go all the way?" and she is. She had never felt closer to Carmello. There were no other niggas like him. The way he protected her, showered her with love, and taught her the rules of the streets; he was everything to her; her lover, teacher, and best friend. And maybe even one day, her baby father. Even though she was young, in Mya's mind, she could spend the rest of her life with Carmello Black. As the song comes to an end, a silence fell over the ballroom breaking Mya's thoughts.

"Hello class of 1998. You all look like bright stars tonight." Yolanda Jones, the school's principal says from the school's stage in the center of the room; her petite figure covered in a bright red pantsuit. "The time has come to announce the prom king and queen of the class of 1998. When I call the nominees for prom king and queen, please join me on the stage. We're going to start with the king. As chosen and voted, by your peers, the nominees for prom king are; Ziggy Brown, Raheem Samson, and Reggie Lawson."

The guys are cheered for loudly as they stroll onto the stage; Ziggy in a black tuxedo and black gators. The tuxedo fits his slender body perfectly, his dark skin face glowing and handsome, swaying his arms back and forth dancing like Puff Daddy himself in the *Been Around the World* video. His antics caused a deafening of laughter. Mya had to contain herself from crying laughing so her makeup wouldn't run. Raheem Samson looked high as a Wu-Tang Clan member, his light-skinned face flushed and red, eyes hanging low; his red and white suit disheveled. He just waves, geeking like a fool. Reggie looked like he'd been dipped in platinum, wearing a shiny metallic silver suit, an exact replica of Mase's attire in his *Feel So Good* video. He places his hand on his hips and spins around in a circle like Madonna voguing.

"Go Reggie! Go Reggie!" All the girls holler.

"Again, let's give a round of applause for these fine young men." Mrs. Jones proclaims. "This is so exciting." Mrs. Jones rips open the small white envelope in her hands. "The 1998 Overbrook prom is king is...Ziggy Brown!"

Ziggy takes center stage doing the Bankhead Bounce as Mrs. Jones places a gold crown on his head. Reggie rolls his eyes and storms off of the stage in disgust. Ziggy snatches the microphone from Mrs. Jones.

"I just wanna say, y'all made the best choice, and all y'all who got the screw face on, y'all just mad. Go 'head with y'all PHDs; player hater degrees. I'm the only king up in here. Thank you. Thank you. Y'all far too kind." Ziggy takes a bow to an enormous applause.

"Congratulations to you Mr. Brown." Mrs. Jones counters, regaining control of the microphone. "Now onto to our prom queen. The beautiful nominees for prom queen of Overbrook's 1998 senior prom are... Lisa Scott, Kareema Thomas, and Mya Campbell."

The screams are beyond deafening. Mya kisses Carmello on the lips before walking through the crowd of her peers and onto the stage next to Lisa Scott who looked corny and matronly in a black satin gown, covered up to the neck; and her hair pulled back in a stiff French roll. The split on her gown was only to the knee.

God, my mother wouldn't even wear that dress. Mya thinks staring her up and down, her only saving grace were her beautiful doe eyes.

She was known as the smart girl in school. But as a fashionista? Not at all. Kareema cringes at the sight of Mya, her nostrils flared still visibly upset by her ejection at the picture line. Mya just grins at her.

Not only did my man check the shit out of you, but I'm about to snatch prom queen away from your lame ass.

"Give it up for these lovely young ladies."

Mya closes her eyes and exhales, her final moment to triumph over her two biggest enemies of her entire four years of high school. Kareema and Lisa Scott had been hateful thorns in her side; tonight she would have her revenge.

"And the prom queen of the class of 1998 is... Mya Campbell!"

She opens her eyes to the loving admiration of her peers. Mrs. Jones places a gemstone tiara on her head. She winks her left eye at Lisa Scott and Kareema before Mrs. Jones hands her the microphone.

"I just want to thank all of you guys that voted for me. It was too many choices to make for prom queen, I understand that, but you made the right choice. I made it my duty my entire four years at Overbrook to be the flyest and most official girl; and tonight I'm vindicated. Now let's get back to partying!"

The ballroom erupts. She and Ziggy pose for photos before dancing the official prom king and queen dance to Gina Thompson featuring Missy Elliot *The Things That You Do(*Bad Boy Remix*)*.

"Mya! Mya! You the flyest." They chanted as she and Ziggy two-stepped, challenging each other.

She caught Black beaming with pride at her from the crowd. Senior prom had been every magical dream Mya imagined and so much more. But the after prom got even juicier. Black had checked them into a honeymoon suite at the Inn of the Dove hotel in Jersey.

"Yes daddy! Yes daddy!" Mya yells in ecstasy as she bounces up and down on Carmello's thick dick, riding him ferociously wearing only her tiara.

"Yes, ride daddy's dick," Black moans, gripping Mya's ass! Her creamy breasts bouncing like melons as he guzzles Moët champagne out of the bottle.

She flips around, her ass facing him as she grips his ankles, sweat dripping out of every pore of her body. He slaps her ass with several aggressive slaps that made her yell out in pleasurable pain. The sex was intense and fulfilling. Mya's juices flowed all over Black who was covered in her wetness as he whines his waist driving deeper and deeper into her, hitting her G-spot.

"I'm about to nut!" She screams.

"Me too!" Black grunts.

They both erupt in strong orgasms. She collapses on his chest, the bed soaked in sweat. He slowly strokes her tangled hair.

After they cool down and lay motionless for a moment, Black whispers, "You sleep?" The bathroom light lit the dim room.

"Naw." She whispers.

"I need to talk to you about something very important. I gotta make a big run to Miami in a few weeks to grab some major work from my Colombian connect. He got the purest cocaine in the states. I been doing business with him for a long time. He don't deal with a lot of people and don't really deal with blacks either. But because of my relationship with Enrique, he's always showed me love."

"Why you not taking Faheem?" Mya asks, half sleep.

"Fah is my man, a hundred grand, but this move I'm about to make is gonna change our operation completely. Fah likes the money we making the way it is right now. Yeah we living good, but on some real shit, Mya I'm getting tired of this life. Everybody don't always see my vision, so I'm making an executive decision to make this shit happen on my own. I'm about to set myself up to go legit. I got a bigger picture, but the only person I can trust to help me with this is you. You know I would never put you in danger, right?"

"Yeah." Mya's now in full attention, sitting up in the bed; her eyes focused on Black.

"Listen, I have plans for us. For the long haul. After this run, I'll be counting millions. I know you're people got money, but I'm gonna set it up so we'll have our own. I'm gonna pay for your whole college tuition, buy us a plush ass crib out in Jersey built from the ground up, and after you graduate college we'll get married."

"You wanna marry me Black?"

"Of course! Why you think I made you my girl? When I first saw you I knew you had all the potential in the world. You're beautiful, book smart, polished, and wise beyond your years. Why you think I been molding you all this time? So you can be prepared for this moment right here."

"I don't know Black. I mean what if something goes wrong? My parents would kill me. You know they're both lawyers."

"Look, are you with me or not ma? This is chess, not checkers, and I need my queen with me on this run. This gon' set us up for life. It's gonna be me and you ole girl. I'm gonna buy you an engagement ring the size of an ice cube. And in five years, when we sitting back in our seven-bedroom mansion with the four-car garage, his and her Benz's and Range Rovers, we gon' be laughing about this very moment; with our three or four cute little chocolate babies running around with good hair."

"Three or four? Two at the max, I gotta keep this size six body tight." Mya chuckles. "So it's just this one run. Right?"

"Yeah, then I'm out the game. I'm going legit and open up my real estate business like I told you. Do you trust me?" Black leans closer to Mya, gathering her up in his arms staring at her in the darkness. His lips so close she could taste his breath. "Come on Bonnie, hold your Clyde down." He begins tickling her on her side.

"Stop!" She hollers, trying to wiggle out of his grasp. "Okay, I'm down."

"That's what I like to hear; and it's a plus. It's gonna be your first trip to Miami. You gonna love South Beach. Me and you on the beach, sipping piña coladas, and five-star hotels. I can't wait to see you in a little bikini."

"Okay Black." She says excitedly.

"You sure you down? Cause I need you to be on point and ready."

"I'm ready Black. I see the bigger picture. You just made me realize, ain't no other niggas like you. The way you put this whole plan together just showed me the difference between you and the rest. I wanna thank you for coming into my life. I feel so bad for second-guessing you."

"That's understandable. What I'm asking you to do is a lot for even chicks twice your age, but I know you can handle it. I built you up to be a soldier."

"So Miami, here we come." Mya says, laying back in Carmello's arms, her heart pounding quickly in the dark; her mind racing with reservations about making a run with Black, but it was too late, she'd given her word. She was trapped inside the devil's triangle. She knew it was more to being the boss' girl besides shopping sprees and glamorous living. And this would be her first test.

"We gon' bust this last move and say goodbye to the game." Black speaks softly in her ear before they both drift off to sleep.

Chapter 16

RAVEN: MURDER WAS THE CASE

The last period bell rang, signaling the end of another long tedious school week. The closer it got to summer, and the temperature steadily rising; the more restless and unruly the masses of urban teenagers became. Rushing out of the metal doors like inmates committing a prison break. The bright clear seventy-five-degree weather is refreshing. Overbrook's infamous let out is popping. Mercedes, BMW's, Lexus', and Range Rovers in an array of colors with shiny rims waxed to perfection are parked in front. Young hustlers post up in their finest spring couture parlayed beside their high priced sedans, seducing the young girls as they walked passed. Guys on dirt bikes and motorcycles zoomed up and down the street. Raven looks at the spectacle as she exits the building. She was once at the center of that crowd and ruled the ghetto-fabulous stage with her best friends. She takes a final glance at the scene; it's bittersweet.

She begins her walk down her back-alley route that she takes day in and day out. She passes a group of Jamaican teens arguing in patois; their dreadlocked heads bobbing up and down. All conversation stops at the sight of Raven in her rainbow-colored Coogi mini dress. Their eyes lust after her ample body. Once she's out of eyesight they went right back to arguing loudly. She paid them the least bit of attention. She walks down one driveway after another. She turns down 61st and Turner Street, as a familiar car pulls up beside her.

"Oh no!" She huffs.

It's Mally's green Taurus wagon at the intersection directly in front of her. The light turns green; she would have to walk past his car. They hadn't been this close to each other since their breakup. She only spotted his car riding past Overbrook let out, but avoided him at all cost. She couldn't take looking him in the eyes. As she walks closer her heart races, she feels awkward.

Don't fuckin' look in his direction! She pleads with herself, stepping down off the pavement.

Curiosity takes hold of her. In a frantic hurry, she turns her head glaring inside of Mally's car. His light brown eyes meet hers, shock, and surprise on his handsome face that quickly fades into a mean grimace of utter disdain. Her heart sinks to her ankles as her gaze drifts over to the passenger seat. Her eyes lock with a smirking TeTe who's staring her down in a taunting manner.

No the fuck he is not with this boney skeleton looking bitch?! Raven thinks, her temper boiling into jealousy.

She always knew Mally would move on to another girl, but TeTe was an underhanded sneaky choice. She was one of Raven's sworn enemies. Mally couldn't stand TeTe and knew firsthand about their beef. She was a total downgrade; nowhere near Raven's level in terms of beauty, style, or intellect. Raven had known how obsessed TeTe was with Mally since they were in junior high school. Writing him love letters, buying him Valentine's Day gifts, and stalking him on the playground at recess. As soon as their breakup was public knowledge TeTe couldn't wait to throw herself at him like a wet dog in heat. Raven was aware of TeTe's motives. But what was Mally's motive? He was so attractive, and he had access to way badder chicks. *Was it the easy pussy score, or was it the ultimate revenge against her?* Raven pondered. Either way the sting was felt. Raven assumed she wouldn't give two shits about who Mally was messing with, but she was sadly mistaken. She is totally in love with Nadir, but the sight of TeTe in Mally's passenger seat; the seat that once belonged to her for so long, remorse overcomes her.

She takes her black Gucci shades off for a split second. She and Mally lock eyes, his tender honey brown eyes go from hard to sad. They silently communicate; it was still there. It will always be love between them. A car behind Mally beeps their horn loudly, snapping them out of their stare down. Mally hits the gas speeding off. TeTe throws Raven one last ice grill rolling her eyes, lips poked out in a jealous frown.

"Fucking corny ass bitch!"Raven yells locking eyes with TeTe as the drive off.

Raven becomes so caught up in the moment with Mally, that she gives reckless abandon to her surroundings. Hardly paying any attention to the gold Acura Legend coupe with tinted windows, driving at very slow speed a few feet behind her.

Mally you think you getting at me by fucking with TeTe? Sorry buddy, but you played yourself with that one. Raven thinks, whipping her hair off of her face.

"Did you think I was gonna let you get away from me bitch?" A familiar voice growls from closely behind her.

She can feel his breath on the nip of her neck. Her knees buckle, she jerks her body around; with great horror she's face to face with Nickels! His face twisted like a monster, nostrils flaring. His chubby hands quickly wrap around her neck. A stinging open hand smack lands across her face and agonizing pain quickly shoots throughout her body. She screams out in traumatizing fear.

"Help me! Help me! Somebody please!" She yells at the top of her lungs.

She struggles to break out of Nickels strong grasp. He reaches into the back of his Guess jeans pulling out a black .38 revolver pointing it roughly at the center of Raven's chest.

"Shut the fuck up bitch before I kill you right here!"

Raven looks into Nickels' eyes, she doesn't see a soul. She internally hushes herself and becomes still. She knows Nickels will not hesitate to blow her brains out where she stood.

"Get the fuck in the car right now!"

"Are you okay sweetheart?" An elderly woman with light-gray hair calls out to Raven from the doorway of her house.

Yell out, tell her to call the police. Raven thinks before forcing back tears. "I'm okay ma'am, thank you." She and Nickels quickly get into the Acura. *This motherfucker switched up cars to throw me off.* She thinks as he angrily turns the corner.

An icy chill runs through Raven's body, thoughts of jumping out the passenger side door to make an escape speeds through her mind. Nickels slams down on the gas as he continues to make wild turns.

"What the fuck is wrong with you Raven?" Nickels aggressively asks, smacking her upside the head like an outraged father. "You think you just gonna up and leave me like I'm some kind of nut ass nigga? You got me fucked up. I bought and paid for you. I own your ass!" He proclaims, spit flying out of his mouth. "You can't play me. When I met you, you was catching the bus, busting your ass at Marshalls, fuckin' with that broke ass young boah Jamal. Bitch I made you! Gave you more money than you ever seen."

Raven felt the rage boiling inside her, like Tina Turner's climactic scene in *What's Love Got to Do with It.*

"Fuck you and your money Nickels! I don't want nothing to do with your fat ass!" Raven yells, mustering her courage.

"Fuck you just say to me?" Nickels slams down on the brakes at the corner of 57th and Spruce Street, his brown-skinned face cold and unforgiving.

Raven hit a major blow to his fragile ego. He punches her with supreme force to the left side of her head causing her right side to bang against the car window. Her left ear begins ringing and her jaw is in excruciating pain. Her eyes begin watering, but that does not prevent her anger from boiling over.

"Pussy you not gon' be beating on me!" She screams, unleashing punches with all of her might, striking Nickels in his eyes and face.

"Bitch is you crazy?!" Nickels hollers trying to get a grasp on Raven's wrist. But she has gone wild, breaking free, digging her sharp manicured nails into his face and neck like a cat fighting for its life. Blood begins seeping from his wounds.

"I'm gonna break your neck!" Nickels yells out in a painful roar.

He grabs Raven's hair with one hand and with the other hand, he smacks her in the back of her head with his gun.

"Now calm your ass down before I pull the trigger!" The fight goes out of Raven.

"Nickels let me go. Please, just let me go." Raven cries out with barely enough energy to muster at her wit's end.

She covers her face with her hands rocking back and forth. Nickels ignores her pleas, starts the engine, driving off again. A few moments later they arrive at Nickels stash house on 62nd and Catherine Street. Nickels orders her out of the car. They enter the ran down row house with chipping white paint. A strong haze of marijuana hits Raven's nose, she begins coughing. Nickels two young boahs, Makil and Nafis are sitting on the dented up blue cloth sofa having a weed session with two dingy brown-skinned girls with long micro braids similar to the singer Brandy.

"Yo, y'all gotta clear this the fuck out now!" Nickels orders.

"Damn Nickels, we just rolled up dog." Nafis, a thin light-skinned boy with big brown bloodshot eyes and dark full lips from smoking one too many blunts says.

"I don't give a fuck what you just rolled up! Get the fuck out and don't come back until I tell y'all to!"

Nafis and Makil both take a good look at Nickels bruised face and Raven's disheveled appearances, immediately knowing it was a domestic dispute.

"Yo we out." Makil, an attractive medium-brown skinned boy with hair braided in fresh cornrows says to their female company who grabbed their containers of fresh Chinese food and quickly file out of the rusty front door.

Nickels turns the deadbolt, even placing on the chain lock. He then immediately directs his attention to Raven, not wasting a second. Drops of red blood stained the white Dolce & Gabbana t-shirt he wore, his pot belly protruding underneath.

"We gonna get some shit straight. You leaving me is not happening. I'll kill you first. Do you hear me Raven? Now get the fuck upstairs," he orders, roughly shoving her up the squeaking staircase.

He pulls a set of keys out of his jean pocket and unlocked the deadbolt lock on the back room door. Raven surveys her familiar surroundings. A pile of fishscale cocaine atop the dresser, large bundles of weed on a flat black coffee table, and small crack vials with red and blue caps ready to be served to the awaiting fiends and smokers. Raven had spent many nights bagging up nick and dime bags of weeds, filling crack vials, and counting all of Nickels money, making sure his workers weren't cheating him. He might have been a drug dealer, but mathematics was not one of his strongest points.

He locks the door, walks over to the small closet where a medium sized gray safe was on the floor. Nickels turns the combination, revealing several large stacks of money wrapped in rubber bands. He pulls out two large wads of money from his front pocket, easily twelve grand, throwing it into the safe.

"Nickels my parents are expecting me home. They'll call the cops if I'm not in the house soon." Raven pleads feeling trapped.

"Fuck your parents and the cops. You not going nowhere until you understand you my bitch. Bought and paid for. All the money I spent and fancy shit I brought you was the down payment. I own that pussy!" Raven begins crying again standing in the back corner of the room. "Yo, that crying shit don't move me. I'm a man first. You don't just pick up and cut me off. What the fuck is wrong with you?"

"Nickels I'm not happy. You keep beating on me."

"Because your dumb ass keep making me beat you. You don't listen Raven, that's your fucking problem." His beady brown eyes narrowing with rage. "And as a matter of fact, let me show you I own you." Nickels charges toward her, ripping her Coogi dress completely off of her.

"Stop! What the fuck are you doing?" She sobs, swinging, and shoving against him.

She is no match for Nickels' two hundred and forty pound overweight frame. He pushes her down on the filthy soiled full-size mattress in the center of the room and starts ripping off the remainder of her dress.

"No Nickels! Stop! Don't do this!" She screams, kicking, and twisting her body away from him.

"Stop fucking kicking!" Nickels orders with a swift blow to her right kidney.

"Ah!" She cries out in agonizing pain.

He stands to his feet, face covered in sweat as he unbuttons his pants; with a devious grin of sadistic pleasure. His Nextel flip phone starts ringing.

"Yo." He answers out of breath. "What you mean nigga? That ain't what we agreed on homie." "Yo, I done fronted y'all niggas too much work!" "What you mean shit is slow? I need my paper asap. That slow shit don't got nothin' to do with me!" "Where you at right now?" "The projects at 55th and Vine Street?" "I'm on my way up there right now! Don't get lost Aamir."

"I gotta handle some business, I'll be right back. I'ma give your stubborn ass some time to think and for it to sink in that you belong to me." Nickels leaves the room.

She hears the sound of the key locking the door and then hears his heavy feet descending the stairs. Raven leaps to her feet, looking for a way out. The door was locked tight; she pulls and twists the knob in vain.

The windows! Her mind raced.

She tries to open the two dusty back room windows behind black curtains. Her heart sank in terror. They were nailed shut in case of a home invasion. She is totally trapped.

"I'm not gonna make it out this room alive," she whispers. *My phone!* She grabs her pink and black Moschino book bag, dumping everything onto the floor.

Her small black Nextel cell phone Nadir bought her fell onto the filthy mattress. Her last saving grace. She quickly dials Nadir.

"Nadir help me! Help me please!"

"Calm down. What the fuck is going on?"

"Nickels kidnapped me at gunpoint. He beat me up and tried to rape me!"

"I'm gonna kill that motherfucker. Where you at?"

"He got me locked up in the back room of his stash house on the corner of 62nd and Catharine Street. 6202 is the address. Please hurry!"

"Sit tight baby, I'm on my way right now! This situation with Nickels ends today." Nadir's tone means by any means necessary.

Raven looks around the room and finds a dirty white t-shirt to cover her bare breasts. She sits on the floor Indian style, rocking herself back and forth, praying to God for her life.

"Lord if you're listening, please let me make it out of this situation alive. I've worshipped money and material things, and if by your grace I make it out of this room unharmed, I will change my life. I swear on everything."

The seconds and minutes seemed to turn into hours.

What if Nickels kills Nadir? That thought entered her mind before. But the reality was that both men could collide and only one would make it out of the house with a pulse.

Sweat drips down every crevice of her body; the room is stifling hot with no ventilation. She hears footsteps on the squeaky stairs, footsteps that grew louder. She jumps up, backing into a corner. A violent thunderous barrage of bangs against the door; it flings open! Nadir enters like a smoking gun wearing a white Polo shirt and holding a black 9mm caliber handgun. His gorgeous face hard, ready for war.

"Nadir you came for me!" Raven cries, jumping into his arms.

"I promised you I was coming for you." He holds her tight as she sobs on his chest.

"Nadir don't ever let me go. Please." She cries, tears run uncontrollably down her face.

"I gotta get you safe now, Come on let's get the fuck out of here! No man is gonna ever hurt you again. I put that on everything."

They head toward the stairway when the sound of an elephant stampede is heard. It's Nickels with Nafis behind him; with a crazed deranged look in his eyes. In a panic, Raven knows she and Nadir will not leave the house alive. One of Nickels crackhead lookouts on the block must have tipped him off that Nadir had broken into the stash house. Nadir quickly pushes Raven behind him.

"Oh, this the pretty motherfucker you been creeping with, you stank ass whore?!" Nickels yells through clenched teeth, pointing his .38 caliber pistol at Nadir who responds lifting the 9mm.

"Listen homie, we ain't gotta do this. Let me take Raven out of here. Nobody gotta get hurt."

"I remember your face clearly now, and your Lexus truck outside. You was the nigga talking tough the night of the Puffy show. You was lusting over Raven that night. I might smoke a lot of weed, but I got a good ass memory. Raven you been taking my dough and spending it on the next nigga!" Nickels hollers with sheer embarrassment.

Raven cowers behind Nadir's back.

"Yeah, that's me. All the beatings and using this girl for a punching bag; all that shit stops today nigga. Either you let us walk out of here, or somebody's gonna be laid the fuck out. Your choice."

Nickels begins to sweat profusely, pure savagery in his eyes.

"Your brains about to be splattered all over this fucking room." Without hesitation he pulls the trigger.

Nadir flings Raven back against the wall, He's been hit in the shoulder. He immediately returns fire with a flurry of bullets. Raven hits the floor, putting her hands over her ears as the loud sound of gunshots ring out around her. Nadir hits Nickels with a fatal shot to the head. He collapses immediately, blood begins pouring from the large hole open in the center of his face. Nadir falls on his back, blood pouring from his shoulder and leg.

"You killed my fucking old-head!" Nafis screams, leaping on Nadir like an ape on steroids, fighting over the gun.

"Get off him!" Raven yells, punching Nafis in the face with all of her strength.

"I'm gonna kill you too bitch!" Nafis growls, hitting her in the stomach, knocking the wind out of her; she falls over in pain. "Pussy, you gonna have a closed casket with I'm done with you!" Nafis says, punching Nadir several times with rapid speed in the face.

Nadir is fighting with all of his might to hold on to the gun. Nafis is straddling him. Raven leaps to her feet knowing this was the fight of her life.

"Get the fuck off him!" She uses the full force of her right leg, giving Nafis several horse-like kicks to the face, knocking him off of Nadir.

She grabs the gun from Nadir's hand, pointing it at Nafis who was back on his feet, nose bloody and swollen.

"You ain't built for catching no bodies bitch. Gimme the fucking gun!" He taunts, sizing her up. The gun weighs a ton in her small hands. "Gimme the gun. I'ma fuck you before I kill you, so I can see why Nickels was so sprung over you. You and your boyfriend gon' die!"

Nafis becomes still as a statue before charging her. She pulls the trigger with hesitation, the power of the gun knocking her off of her feet. Nadir groans out in anguish, his cries brings Raven back to her senses.

"Nadir! Baby get up." She cries, trying to lift his heavy one hundred and eighty pound body.

"I think my kneecap is shattered." Nadir slurs in agony, leaning on Raven; blood soaking through his shirt and pants.

"They step over Nickels' and Nafis' lifeless bodies." Nafis took three shots to the chest.

They slowly make their way down the stairs.

"Where are your car keys?"

"My back pocket," Nadir whispers as they walk out of the front door.

A small group of smokers and nosey neighbors congregate in front of the house.

"Get the fuck out the way!" She orders with authority.

The sight of Raven and Nadir covered in blood sent shock and fear through the small crowd. Raven sees Nadir's Lexus jeep double parked on the sidewalk. She unlocks the door and helps him into the passenger side seat.

"Somebody call the cops! Nickels and Nafis is in there dead!" A frail male crackhead screams running out of the house.

Raven climbs into the driver seat, starts the engine, and speeds off. She's an excellent driver. Mally taught her how to drive back when he had his first car.

"Hold on Nadir, I'm gonna get you to a hospital. You hear me baby?" She looks over at him drifting in and out of consciousness. Nadir's head is slumped against the window. Raven floors the gas.

"Nadir Khalid Aameen, don't you dare die on me! You hold on. In the name of Allah, Jesus, and whoever else is up there; my heart can't take losing him. Not this one. He came back for me." Raven professes running red lights.

A few seconds later she pulls into the emergency room section of Presbyterian Hospital on 40th and Powelton Avenue.

"Help me! Somebody help me please! My boyfriend's been shot!"

Minutes later an emergency unit of nurses and doctors rush Nadir onto a stretcher through the trauma unit. Raven collapses in a chair in the waiting area covered in blood.

"I can't lose you Nadir. I can't. I need you now more than ever. How can I live without you? You're my everything. I know that now. I had to go through it with Mally and Nickels to know that you're my one and only true love," she cries.

Chapter 17

TAKIA: SHAKE YA ASS

"Takia, are you finished the math assignments yet? Your homeschool instructor will be here tomorrow to grade your work. Did you finish? Takia girl, do you hear me talking to you?!" Michelle yells from the screen door of their front porch.

Leave me the hell alone! Takia thinks, sitting in a dark green plastic lawn chair. The sun is blaring down on the busy 54th and Vine Street. Cars blasting loud music speed from one corner to the next and groups of guys are talking shit loudly in front of Chinese stores on the corners. West Philadelphia was alive with the sounds of early summer. Takia sits, taking it all in and clothed in pink Gap sweatpants and a matching tank top. Her once flowing shoulder-length hair is gone, replaced with a short close Toni Braxton haircut, dyed black. The contrast looks striking against her lovely caramel face. Without the proper hair care, all of the long months she spent in the hospital, damaged her hair, so it had to be cut.

In the wake of all the tragedy that has befallen her, Takia's beauty has not suffered. She has never been more beautiful, but broken still, in a million tiny pieces. Her weekly therapy sessions with psychiatrist Eva

Miller had some light breakthroughs. But late at night in the quietest moment of darkness, Rell's face would stalk her dreams. The images of the strong man in her life; smiling his gorgeous smile, his arms around her protectively. But when she reached out to hug him she would awaken with arms stretched out in the dark. Tears filling her eyes when reality struck that it was all a dream. The Seroquel and Prozac left her lifeless and dragging like a zombie. She slowly started taking them every three days, instead of every day as doctor Miller prescribed. Takia developed a new addiction that filled her with a high escape, weed; nick bags, and dime bags by the pile. Horace, the old-head Jamaican guy who fronted the corner store on the corner of her block as the neighborhood grocery store had the strongest marijuana in West Philly. He had a thing for Takia. He gave her twenty bags as gifts and in return, every so often she let him eat her pussy in the storage room of the store. Even at her lowest point Takia could still charm a snake hustler around her little finger. And the hustlers hadn't abandoned her. Pumpkin and Omar from North Philly, Kyrie from Southwest Philly, Tyrese from G-Town, light-skinned Wayne from Chester, and another long list of players that had the time of their life on that wild rollercoaster ride called, Takia Williams came back out to play. Her home and cell phone were disconnected. They showed up at her front door trying to sweet talk Michelle. She flared her nostrils like a raging bull. She chased their pussy hungry asses off with a heavy roar. Takia was thankful for her mother's protection. She was still too fragile to play mind games with conniving street niggas.

Mya and Raven both stopped by to visit her frequently, both filling her in on the comings and goings of their lives. Raven was in deep trouble about the situation that happened with Nickels. She was petrified that the police were going to charge her for the murder of Nickels and Nafis. Queen Mya could not stop bragging about her and Carmello getting married. And living in a house on the hill. Takia could care less listening to them babble on and on about their issues when she was still coping with the fresh loss of her child and the first man she ever loved. Not play love; she and Rell had that real love. That kind of love Method Man and Mary J. Blige sing about on *You're All I Need*.

I took one look at you, and it was plain to see, you were my destiny...and my destiny went up in smoke. Takia thinks, rolling up her next blunt. She had become a roll up expert. She could roll a tight Phillies Blunt with her eyes closed. She sparked it up, sniffing the sweet smell of weed wrapped inside when the sound of *Hypnotize* by Notorious B.I.G. booms in her ear. A money-green Saab pulls in front of her house. She is relieved when a female driver hops out.

"Little Takia? Is that you girl?"

Takia squints her light brown eyes and realizes that the girl walking up to her is Bianca, aka Buttercup. Her neighbor who is five years older than Takia. She was always considered a dime. An average height girl who had the brown-skinned complexion of the inside of a Reese's Peanut Butter Cup. That's how she inherited her nickname Buttercup. Buttercup is bowlegged with a Coca-Cola body, beautiful wide Diana Ross eyes, and juicy full lips. She had a hot two-year affair with Takia's brother Malik. She always had the latest handbag; a true fly girl. She started dating a big-time drug dealer from Chester who put her in a white 3 series BMW coupe. He moved her into a two-bedroom condo in King of Prussia; she made it big time. Her mother and grandmother still lived in the corner house at the bottom of the block. Buttercup would roll through to visit, boss bitch style. When Takia's brother Malik got killed and she fell on hard times; hair not done, barely anything to eat, and wrinkled dirty clothes; Buttercup would roll up in her BMW and call out to her. Takia would run over to the passenger side, Buttercup would dig through her Gucci bag, and hand her a crisp hundred-dollar bill. Then, she would tell her to get something to eat and go get her hair done smelling like fresh Camay and baby powder. She wore a big diamond clustered ring shining on her well-manicured hand. Young Takia would watch her drive off and dream of living a ghetto-fabulous life. Buttercup was the blueprint for who Takia would become. It had almost been two years since they've last seen each other, and as Takia admires her, it seems that nothing has changed but the year. The convertible Saab looked perfect. Buttercup's perfect body looked amazing fitting a sensual black catsuit with Iceberg written up the leg in silver lettering. A honey-blonde bob wig crowns her face; a blinged out tennis bracelet shown lovely on her wrist, and the black Chanel sneakers on her feet looked as if they never touched the ground. Her facial expression exudes her delight to see Takia.

"Hey boo! How you been?" Buttercup squeals as they embrace warmly.

"Hey Buttercup! You looking fly as always girl."

"I been meaning to check on you. My mom told me what happened to you and your boyfriend." Buttercup looks genuinely filled with concern. "I know how painful and fucked up you feel when you lose a nigga you in love with. When I found out your brother Malik was murdered, I swear on everything I cried for five days straight. I kept asking God, why...but I had to pick myself up and carry on. And that's what you have to do

Takia. We women living in a cold hustlers' world. We gotta try and make the best life we can in this hell we living in. The type of men girls like us choose to date ain't no doctors and lawyers. Feel me?" Takia shakes her head in agreement. "They some ghetto boys out in these streets, fighting every day to stay alive and get at a dollar. We the women that hold them down. It's stressful. And we gotta hope and pray every night that they make it back to us. The only thing guaranteed to a drug dealer is a bullet and doing football numbers in the Feds. And us women are left out here to pick up the pieces; stuck with babies on some welfare mom shit or moving back with mommy because dude serving ten to twenty and a bitch ain't save a dollar when the money was flowing like water. Can't pawn them bags and shoes! Hoes don't think about saving a dollar for a rainy day. The reason I'm kicking this knowledge to you baby girl is because you got too much potential to waste Takia. You a bad little chick. Your shape is banging, your face is flawless, and you already know how to work these niggas. I've kept an eye on you from afar. I know you hurting right now, but your man is gone. As sad as it is, you still gotta make a way out here. My last nigga got sentenced to thirty years to life. I was about to lose everything; stressed, crying every day. The stash he left me was running out. I was literally down to my last stack with two thousand dollars a month rent, car note, insurance, and my day to day bills. It was looking real fucked up for me until I looked in the mirror and told myself, *bitch you gotta stand up on your own two!* I put on my big girl panties and took responsibility for my life. I'm getting real money now; real money on my own. And you can do the same."

"What kind of work you doing Buttercup?" Takia asks, taking in all of Buttercup's words.

"Let's just say, I used all of the assets God gave me to get what I want. And you got plenty of what's needed to get this cash." Buttercup playful slaps Takia on her thick ass. "You see my car? I paid cash, straight out. The ice on my wrist? Ain't no nigga put a dime to it. All me." Buttercup grins victoriously, dangling her diamond bracelet in the air. As she is bragging a horn begins to blow.

"Yo come on! You holding up traffic." A man's low baritone voice screams from a black Volvo station wagon behind Buttercup's Saab. A white Honda was behind him, beeping his horn loudly.

"Hold the fuck up!" Buttercup snaps, switching over to the driver side. She quickly wrote her number down on a white piece of paper. "Hit my jack when you ready to pick yourself up and start stacking some paper." Buttercup says, handing the paper before putting her foot on the gas, disappearing as fast as she arrived.

Takia stares at the paper, 215-424-9531. She returns to her plastic lawn chair on the porch, sparking a blunt; her mind pondering on Buttercup's speech.

The next two weeks flew by. The June heat began to make her restless, the mundane nature of her day to day routine was boring the hell out of her. Homeschooling five days a week, weekly sessions with doctor Miller three days a week, and Michelle's constant overbearing monitoring of her every move; she was feeling suffocated. After her talk with Buttercup, the old Takia was slowly returning. Her pockets were empty. She hadn't been so broke since her early teens. In the midst of her endless grief, she forgot the power of the all mighty dollar. The more she got her mind back, the more the old lust for Benjamins returned. She still had her stockpile of designer clothes, but it was nothing like the feeling of counting fresh Benjamins in her hand.

Mya stopped by bragging about her and Carmello's upcoming trip to Miami and all the shopping she had been doing at the shops in Bal Harbour, Miami's exclusive luxury mall. Takia would stare blankly off into space, blocking out her best friend. She was delighted for Raven and her newfound love with Nadir, she still couldn't believe Nadir had killed Nickels. She knew he was a piece of shit and had abused Raven, but kidnapping her at gunpoint? When it was all said and done, Takia was happy Nadir blew Nickels head off, so Raven could finally find some peace. She deserved it. Raven was innocent until she and Mya pressured her into the streets. They both had her wildin' and got her turned out. Nadir was a thorough dude and from what Takia could tell, he loved Raven. Not to mention that he was fine as fuck. Mally's broke ass or Nickels dead ass couldn't hope to be half the man Nadir is. *Raven has found herself a keeper.* Takia thought, laying on her bed flipping through a *Source Magazine* with the late, great Tupac on the front cover as Mariah Carey's *Honey* video plays on mute on channel sixty-five on the video jukebox.

"I'm bored as fuck." She groans, twisting, and turning on her soft queen size bed; a pair of black cotton panties was all that covered her curvy caramel body. "I want out this damn house." She pulls Buttercup's number out of her small pink D&G wallet, picks up her mother's black cordless house phone dialing quickly.

"Hello." Buttercup answers in her cute high pitch voice.

"Buttercup, what's up girl? This Takia."

"Hey Takia. What it do?"

"Nothing. In this house, losing my mind. I thought about what you said. I need some cheddar, I'm trying to get on."

"That's what I'm talking about baby. I see you came to your senses about getting your bread up."

"What I gotta do?"

"I'm gonna pick you up tonight around midnight. Wear a short tight skirt that shows off your hips and ass. Do your makeup real nice. You got a wig right?"

"Yeah, a whole collection." Takia chuckles.

"Alright, put on a nice blonde one."

Takia slowly puffs her freshly rolled blunt listening to Usher's *My Way* album, patiently waiting for Buttercup to arrive. 12:25 a.m. flashes across the alarm clock on her nightstand.

"Buttercup, where you at?" Takia says, pacing back and forth, losing her heart to go through with Buttercup's offer; wrestling with her inner thoughts. *Maybe I should just chill? Bitch you might be moving too fast!* She tells herself taking a long drag of the rich marijuana flowing out of the blunt when the cordless phone rings, startling her out of her restlessness. "Hello, hello?" She stutters into the receiver.

"I'm coming down the block, come outside. Girl, I got caught up with this lame ass nigga from Delaware trying to play mind games with me over a petty ass $1,500." Buttercup sucks her teeth.

"Okay, here I come." Takia takes one last look at herself in the full-length mirror; her makeup looks flawless. Dark smoky eyeshadow and mascara cover her light brown eyes. She looks at least four years older. Dark plum lipstick made her more lips succulent, the dark-honey blonde wig frames her face perfectly; the tight black spandex she wears with two slits up the leg-revealing her creamy thighs, a heart-shaped tattoo with Rell's name in the center is shown from the baby oil she used to moisturizes her body. She grabs her black Prada handbag that contains her house keys and her last $50;

all the money she had to her name. "Bitch, here goes nothing." She whispers to her reflection before dashing out of her room, and down the stairs past Michelle who was on the sofa watching Jay Leno. Her big eyes were alert as Takia rushes through the living room.

"Takia, where you going this time of night?" She hollers, jumping to her feet. "Girl you hear me talking to you?!" She hisses, on Takia's heels.

"Mom please, I'm going out with my girlfriend. Chill, I'll be back in a little while." Takia yells at Michelle, climbing into the passenger seat of Buttercup's Saab. "Hurry up Buttercup, pull off." She hits the gas as Michelle approaches the passenger door. "My mom be drawlin'. She acts like I'm five years old. I'm not a little ass girl anymore."

"Give Ms. Michelle a break, she means well." Buttercup giggles.

Takia looks her over, Buttercup traded her blonde wig in for a short deep auburn red one with low bangs, almost covering her eyes. A red tube top was tightly squeezing her breast. She oozes sex appeal. She turned her car roughly through the vast West Philly maze of a neighborhood. Missy Elliot's *The Rain* plays lightly through the car.

"You ready to get this money?" Buttercup asks slightly.

"You never told me where we were going or what I had to do."

"You'll see in a minute. Here, take a shot of this Henny to loosen you up." Buttercup digs through her oversized Louis Vuitton shoulder bag and hands Takia a dark brown bottle of Hennessy.

"Buttercup, I don't know about this. Maybe this is a bad idea."

"Yo Takia, I ain't come all the way down West Philly for you to be acting like a scary ass rookie. I'm your fucking old-head. I'm never gonna have you in a fucked up situation. You trust me, don't you?" Buttercup asks sternly, her big eyes wide and alert. Takia shook her head yes. "I got you." Buttercup whispers, turning onto the crowded Kelly Drive. Buttercup's reassuring words and the effect of the Henny calmed her nerves. She slightly dozed off. Twenty minutes later Buttercup awakens her with a few light slaps to the arm.

"Where we at?" She asks groggily.

"Uptown baby; the Night on Broadway."

"The strip club?" Takia asks alarmed, her light brown eyes alert with suspicion.

"Yes Takia. What the fuck you thought I did for a living? Doctor, lawyer; maybe even a nun?" Buttercup says with short patience.

"I've fucked niggas for plenty of money; I'm not tripping. But dancing naked in a room full of men for money? I don't think I could do that."

"Listen, we control these pussy hungry niggas. We you on stage, you block them out and pretend you're home dancing freaky in your bedroom mirror. At least come in before you knock it."

Takia's inner thoughts were telling her to say no; *runaway and get out of there*, but her pride was boiling to the surface. She refused to look like a nut ass naïve young girl in front of Buttercup. Takia's eyes turned cold. The old hustling bad bitch returned. "Let's go. I need to get this paper."

"I know that's the fuck right!" Buttercup and Takia slap a high five, walking from the parking lot to the front entrance of the notorious Night on Broadway strip club located in Philadelphia's Uptown neighborhood. The playground of drug dealers, perverts, thirsty young niggas, athletes, low life thugs, and your everyday married nine to five man who wanted to escape a life of boredom with a few round asses and perky breasts shaking in their faces. The line was stretched a block long to enter the large dark brown building with a large flashing sign on the roof that read Night on Broadway Gentleman's Club.

"Buttercup, damn you getting all my money tonight! That ass looking ripe." The men in line holler as Buttercup struts by walking real stank with her ass poked out and bowlegs all cocky.

"Shorty with Buttercup thick as shit." Several guys comment on Takia's brick house body, throwing lustful glances her way as she passes.

Two large bouncers the size of sumo wrestlers stand stone-faced, guarding the clubs entrance. "What up Big Mike?! Yo Troy."

"Buttercup, you looking good girl. These motherfuckers are packed in here tonight." Big Mike, a six-five, three-hundred-pound ex-football player says grinning. His speaks with a low baritone voice, and has a massive dark chocolate dome-shaped head, freshly shaved bald.

"I like the sound of that. Tonight them dollars gonna be flowing. Come on." Buttercup motions for Takia to follow her into the club.

"Hold on, not so fast young lady. You have to be twenty-one to enter. I need to see your ID." Troy, the second even larger bouncer said; his gigantic hand blocking Takia from moving forward.

"Hold up Troy with that drawing shit!" Buttercup snaps, sucking her teeth. "This my cousin Iesha; she's twenty-one." Buttercup quickly digs through her Louis Vuitton bag, hands Troy a driver's license.

"Okay, everything straight Buttercup. Baby, I'm just doing my job." Troy says apologetically.

"Yeah whatever, I'm reporting your ass to Manny." She says, flagging Troy.

Takia follows behind Buttercup, entering the dimly lit club. *Face Off* by Jay-Z and Sauce Money is blaring from the deafening speakers. Takia is stunned and astonished by the scene of confusion in front of her. Three naked women with Coca-Cola shaped bodies gyrate on a small black stage in the center of the room surrounded by dozens of sexually charged men of all ages, showering the girls with cash. Guys slap their round asses, slipping crisp twenty dollar bills in their g-strings as their rough hands slipped and fondled their exposed vaginas. The bar area is packed with guys from every social status. Keeping their lustful eye on strippers shaking perky tits, flat stomachs and round asses, as thick thighs move in perfect motion to the music. Night on Broadway is a fantasy for the hot, horny population of Philadelphia. Cocktail waitresses carry trays of chilled drinks wearing black bra tops and spandex booty shorts, revealing oiled up ass cheeks. The girls receive light smacks on their asses as they pass through tables in the center of the room. In exchange they received hefty tips.

Takia tries to take in every detail. She heard about strip clubs, or 'shaky butts' as they are called by some of her hustler homies.

"Follow me," Buttercup orders in her ear over the blaring music. They walk into the back area of the club. Takia has never seen more pussy hungry men in her life. As *Face Off* comes to an end, the club DJ's voice came in loudly, "Gentlemen, give it up for fine ass Kitten, Vanilla, and Barbie, three of Night on Broadway's finest; or as I like to refer to them as, 'Three the Hardway.' With asses that fat, you know they're deadly. But we got a special treat up next for you fellas. I call up to the stage, the sexy Indian princess; Pocahontas. Get them dollars ready, cause she definitely gonna shake a tail feather."

Takia follows Buttercup down a barely lit staircase. A big sign in neon lights read, 'Dancers dressing room, staff only.' A large dark-skinned female security guard with masculine features and shoulder-length dreadlocks sits on a small metal stool; her massive arms are crossed with black leather gloves. Her stern dark-brown face lights up in a bright smile at the sight of Buttercup in front of her.

"Buttercup, Buttercup, Buttercup." She chuckles.

"Yo Sabrina, what it do?"

"Guarding the chicken coop as always."

"Hmmm, are the chickens clucking tonight?"

"You already know these bitches are crazy. I spend more time keeping them from killing each other than I do protecting them from them thirsty ass niggas upstairs." She laughingly says. "Buttercup, who this cutie?" Sabrina says, sizing Takia up. She runs her tongue over her lips in a sexually suggestive manner; Buttercup peeps it and grins to herself. "What's her dancer name?" Sabrina asks. Buttercup stares off into space, deep in thought before a crafty smirk appears on her face.

"Hennessy... her name is Hennessy."

"Ms. Hennessy." Sabrina says. "Baby if you have any problems you let me know. I'm Sabrina, head of security for Night on Broadway Gentlemen's Club." She said it with such an air of pride. Takia simply shakes her head yes and trails behind Buttercup like a puppy trails behind its mother.

"We're entering the cat's layer. These bitches nails and tongues are as sharp as razors." Buttercup whispers. Takia can hear the clucking and continuing laughter of women. Buttercup swings open the dressing room door. The scent of cheap perfume, weed, and cigarettes, mixed with pussy hit her sensitive nose like a hammer. The hype and commotion simmer down as Takia and Buttercup enter the room. Takia's eyes quickly roll over the two dozen naked, or practically naked women in front of her. Some had stretch marks and post pregnancy pouches; others, drooping breast, and cellulite on their asses. They sized Takia up instantly; jealousy and competition flashed in some of their eyes; lust and curiosity in others.

"Listen up everybody, this is my cousin Hennessy; she's brand new. If anybody gives her any problems, you will be dealt with! And I don't think none of you hoes in this bitch want it with me." Buttercup yells, shifting a cold unforgiving grimace on the group of women; silently daring any one of them to test her.

"Hey Hennessy, what's up? I'm Hot Chocolate." A curvy dark-skinned woman in her late twenties says, standing in front of a large vanity table applying her makeup; wearing only a hot pink thong, and a lace bra with a short black Toni Braxton style wig on her head.

"I'm Cinnamon."

"Hey girl, I'm Crystal." Two pretty light-skinned women in their early twenties spoke almost in unison. Both wearing curly platinum-blonde wigs, wearing colorful spandex bodysuits, revealing butterfly tattoos up the thighs, and black paw prints near their vaginal areas; both chain-smoking Newport cigarettes.

"Hey, what's up? Nice to meet y'all." Takia smiles and waves.

"Chill out with them while I go change," Buttercup instructs before disappearing into a private room in the back of the dressing room.

"How long you been dancing Hennessy?" Cinnamon asks, lighting another cigarette.

"This my first night in a strip club ever."

"So you a virgin to the stripping life, huh?" Crystal laughs.

"Well with an ass like that, your cherry's gonna get popped and dollars gonna rain plentiful." Hot Chocolate chimes in with laughter as she, Crystal, and Cinnamon chuckle in an annoying sound.

"Yeah girl, the customers love a fresh face and fat ass; you gonna kill 'em," Cinnamon says, undressing Takia with her eyes.

"Of course she's gonna kill it, I'm co-signing her." Buttercups says, triumphantly re-entering the dressing room looking beyond tasty in a red leather bodysuit with assless chaps like the artist Prince; with red fringes attached to them. Black open toe stiletto sandals made her appear three inches taller. Her body was oiled up to perfection. She looked like the queen of the dancehall. She was gorgeous; Buttercup moved as if she was the *it* girl for the night. Night on Broadway was Buttercup's world, everyone else was just there.

"Come watch me get this money and learn from a pro." Buttercup says, winking at Takia. They walk through the backstage area; Buttercup is regarded with respect and fear that a royal monarch might receive. The other dancers spoke and bowed and quickly got out of her way. She hands a cassette tape to a cocktail waitress who quickly passes it to the DJ who then announces her arrival on the microphone.

"Aw shit! The moment you freaks and dogs in heat been waiting for all night. The baddest, sexiest, mocha-goddess is about the grace the Night on Broadway stage. Give it up and get your dollars ready for Buttercup!" *It Seems Like You're Ready* by R. Kelly begins playing on the sound system. Buttercup slides on stage like a slithering snake on all fours, slowing pumping her round ass to the beat. The men's cheers were deafening. A flood of dollar bills showered her. Buttercup stands to her feet, grabbing a folding chair; she straddles it, flopping her juicy ass in the air. She rides the chair as if it's a man, slowly unzipping her red bodysuit, teasing the horny group with every small gesture. She turns and twists her tiny waist, revealing her full breasts while licking her lips. She faces her audience of slaves; they worship her. Buttercup was their private dancer, their ultimate love fantasy. In all her bare flesh, she slowly lets her bodysuit hit the floor. Now totally nude, she faces the men, closes her eyes as if she's having an orgasm as she begins massaging her clit, moving her fingers in and out of her vagina. This drove the men even crazier, they pressed close against the stage.

They made it rain with cash until it completely covered the stage. Buttercup dropped down to her knees, rolling around on the green bills. They threw even more; this drove her into an intoxicating frenzy; pumping and moving her body as if she was having full sex on the stage. The guys began surrounding her, slapping her ass with $20s and $50s. She allowed some of their fingers to caress her pussy lips. She dances for two more songs keeping pace and control of the all-male audience like a seductive witch who cast a spell over her servants.

"Give it up for the sexiest woman at Night on Broadway; Buttercup! I know all yall got a hard dick, including me," the DJ chuckles. "Next up coming to the stage for your pleasure is the exotic Spanish mami with the thick thighs; Conchita!" A short, chubby brown-skinned guy quickly gathers up all of Buttercup's earnings, throwing them into a trash bag which looks completely full. Returning to the dressing room, Buttercup walks with an extra pep, silently flexing her superiority over the other dancers. A shapely caramel girl was seated at Buttercup's vanity table; a big mistake.

"If you don't get your funky yeast infested ass out of my seat!" She snaps, grabbing the woman by the hair, yanking her off of the stool.

"Buttercup, I'm sorry. I swear I was just doing my makeup real quick."

"Bitch fuck your makeup! You still owe me money from that bachelor party you did last weekend!"

"I had to pay my son's daycare, I'll pay it tonight. I promise; I got table dances lined up."

"You better Sparkle. I'm not playing with your tired ass!" She pushes Sparkle with a force that causes her to stumble back against the wall. Buttercup turns to Takia, "These hoes will try to take your kindness for weakness. I don't take my foot off they necks." Takia remains silent, taking it all in.

"Calm down you lunatic." A husky male voice says from behind them. Takia turns to see a well-dressed dark-skinned man with a headful of salt and pepper wavy hair and fine West Indian features; Jamaican or Haitian Takia guesses. His navy blue double-breasted suit professionally pressed; a pinkie diamond ring with a huge flawless rock gleams off of his finger. He grins at Takia, analyzing every detail of her body like a predator.

"Manny, you know I don't play about my money." Buttercup retorts.

"Enough about your money Buttercup; which you make more than your fair share of. Who is this lovely one?"

"Oh, my bad Manny; this is my cousin, the one I've been telling you about."

"This is the one time I've heard how beautiful a girl was and it actually turned out to be true." Manny snickers in his thick West Indian accent; Takia blushes.

"This is Manny, the owner of the club. Manny, this is Hennessy."

"Hennessy?" He whispers, his eyes lighting up. "Hennessy...now that's a winning name if I've ever heard one. Hennessy, let's have a drink in my office." Takia quickly looks to Buttercup who nods her head in approval. The other girls watch the scene intensely; silently speculating, heads fill with fresh gossip they would begin spreading around the club.

The inside of Manny's office was loud with leopard and zebra printed rugs and sofas, and a velvet stuffed chair with brass arms and legs.

"Have a seat Hennessy." He says politely, and points to the leopard printed couch beside the mahogany desk. "Buttercup tells me you're interested in working at the club."

"Yeah, I guess." Takia says, diverting her eyes from Manny.

"Don't be nervous with me, I want to help you become successful. You have two type of people in this world; successful ones and everybody else. And I can tell you want to be successful. I can see that in your eyes. Am I right?" Manny asks in a tone that only a therapist would.

"Yes, I want to be successful."

"Good girl. Buttercup says you've never danced before."

"I mean, only in my room in the mirror."

"That's exactly what this job is when you're on stage, pretend you're at home dancing in the mirror. Tune those thirsty bastards in the crowd out; you already own them." Manny says, giving Takia a lustful look.

"Think of yourself as a businesswoman; an independent contractor of sorts. All of the women here are my business partners. The house gets twenty-five percent of all the ladies' earnings. In exchange, I offer the best security and protection than any other gentleman's club in Philadelphia. And I have the largest clientele as well. My girls are the finest and they make stacks unparalleled. There are three classes of girls that work here. The superstar; that's Buttercup, Pocahontas, and Conchita. Those are my top girls. They are three to five stacks a night girls. Then there are the second tier girls. They work the stage, they're beautiful, but lacking star quality. They're a stack to $2,500 a night girls. Then there are the table dance girls; she's the lowest next to the cocktail waitress. Her following isn't large enough to command the main stage. She's regulated to giving out lap dances to the pussy hungry bastards who will work her for every penny they're giving her. She's a three hundred to eight hundred girl, and after I take my twenty-five percent they make enough to pay their rent, by a little raggedy car, but have to be right back here like clockwork. Like a hamster on a wheel, But in you, I think I see a superstar. We can make lots of money together. So are you ready for your big debut?"

"Hold up. You want me to dance tonight?" Takia gasps, her light brown eyes closely paying attention.

"Yes. Why not? Sometimes in life you just have to jump in the deep end of the pool and see if you float." Manny laughs, standing from his desk.

Get the fuck up out of here now! Just get up and run. Takia thinks. *But run where? Takia you broke, not a penny to your name. Girl fuck that! You better go for yours.* Her mind wrestles continuously with what decision to make.

"Here, drink this. It'll loosen you up." Manny places a shot glass and a bottle of Hennessy in front of her.

I'm going for mine fuck that! Her final thought before gulping down three shots back to back.

"Come on, let's get you dressed."

Thirty minutes later, Takia finds herself at the edge of the stage, and her stomach in knots. But the liquor relaxed her and the blunt she shared with Buttercup had her mellow. Buttercup had given her a sexy cheerleader outfit to wear; hot pink pleated skirt with a pink thong attached, a pink and white sports bra, thigh high black sheer stockings, and glass platform high heels. The ones Pamela Anderson the star from the show *Baywatch* made popular.

"Remember, don't get naked too fast; tease these motherfuckers; lots of eye contact. Make these niggas think you love them." Buttercup instructs her before embracing her like a proud older sister.

"You up next baby. Show me the star hiding inside of you," Manny says, emerging from the shadows.

Takia closes her eyes. *Just think you're home alone, dancing in the mirror.*

"Up next we have some fresh meat hitting the stage. This is her first time gracing the Night on Broadway stage. From what I'm told she's something special; she'll get you drunk in love with her moves. Show some love and some dollars for Hennessy; just like the liquor, strong brown and thick just how I like it!" *Pony* by Ginuwine starts blasting through the room.

Takia takes one final breath before gaining the courage to walk out on stage. Her adrenaline is rushing. She looks out into the dimly lit crowd; she can feel the dozens of men undressing her with their eyes. She can feel their hormones raging from the stage. She exhales and slowly begins pumping her body to the music;

twisting her round exposed ass to the thirsty men who start hollering and cheering her on; their approval lit a flame inside of her. It was nothing Takia liked doing more than thrilling a man. And she had an entire room full to play with. She turns and faces them; winking her eye and giving them a little tongue action. They go wild. This turned her on. She slowly unzips the cheerleader skirt, letting it drop to the floor. Giving the men a full glimpse of her thick caramel thighs and ass. She then went to the edge of the stage, dropped down to the floor in a doggy style position, and begins moving her ass; each cheek wobbling like a glistening melon.

The guys were putty in her hands, they immediately start showering her with cash; $5s, $20s, and $50s...and even a few fresh Benjamins. And she rolled around in all of the fresh money she made in minutes. She could feel her old self-being resurrected through this baptism of cash.

Yes Hennessy, you're gonna be Takia's new best friend. She thought alone, locked in the bathroom stall, counting the two thousand dollars she made that night after the club took their twenty-five percent. This was too easy. Working these niggas was like taking candy from a baby. Oh yes, being broke was for the birds. Takia loved the direction Night on Broadway was taking her; she was right at home.

Chapter 18

RAVEN: THE GRADUATE

"Ms. Hightower, you want us to believe that this horrendous crime was a simple domestic dispute gone all the way wrong? Haneef Green, also known as Nickels, age twenty-two, kidnapped you at gunpoint, and sexually assaulted you? And Nadir Hathaway, age twenty-one was your knight in shining armor waving an illegal unregistered gun; killing two young men like dogs. Nafis Williams, age eighteen and your ex-were shot numerous times, unmercifully. Are you sure Nadir's motives weren't more centered on taking on Nickels lucrative drug territory?" Detective Samuel Miller says, steadily pacing the small drab interrogation room of the 18th Police District located at 55th and Pine Street. His repetitive questions and robotic nature were beginning to annoy Raven. It was his fifth time questioning her relentlessly about the death of Nickels and his crew. And her answer was always the same. Nickels was obsessed with her, physically abused her for months; she believed in her heart that he planned on murdering her. And if Nadir had not shown up when he did, she would have never left that room alive.

"That's enough detective. My client has told you everything she knows. And let's not forget, she's the victim in this case. Haneef Green was an animalistic, demented thug who physically, and mentally battered Raven Hightower with iron fists. Let's not forget to mention the stalking and statutory rape that Mr. Green is accountable for as well. He started a sexual relationship with my client when she was under the age of eighteen. His actions violated the Pennsylvania state age of consent and his criminal record reads like a list from a crime dictionary; numerous assault and drug possession charges and he has a similar case with an ex-girlfriend. One Tameka Samson filed a restraining order on Mr. Green in January of 1996. Mr. Green was arrested for stalking and assaulting Ms. Samson which resulted in a broken nose and index finger." Raven's defense attorney Terrance Campbell says, taunting detective Miller with a cocky grin on his handsome light-brown face. He knew this rookie detective was no match for his superior oratory skills and knowledge of the law. That made him one of the most sought-after and highest paid attorneys in Philadelphia.

Once he heard about Raven's horrific ordeal, he agreed to represent her, free of charge. Raven is like a second daughter to him, he'd known her since she was eleven years old; he felt it was his duty to represent her. It also made him reflect for the first time. If a smart well-educated girl like Raven Hightower had gotten caught up in the clutches of an abusive gun toting, low-life drug dealer; what has his daughter been up to on those many days he and his wife were too busy with full caseloads? The very thought of Mya being taken advantage of or abused made him cringe. He put his daughter on such a high pedestal; his wife would always say that Mya was a liar and master manipulator. But in his eyes she was angelic. Had he been blind to the world his daughter and her friends were really living in?

"Your client is free to go Mr. Campbell, but we will be in touch. This is very much still an ongoing investigation. You might be in the clear Ms. Hightower, but your boyfriend, Nadir Hathaway will be facing three to five years for the unregistered firearm. Both of you won't have some perfect fairytale ending. One of you will definitely be doing time behind bars. I promise you that." Detective Miller states with a menacing smirk on his middle-aged dark-brown face.

"Detective Miller, if you insist on harassing my client, I'll be forced to file a complaint against you with internal affairs." Mr. Campbell proclaims, escorting Raven out of the interrogation room where her parents sit on a wooden bench.

Maria and Ricky Sr. jump to their feet at the sight of their daughter being returned safely to them.

"Baby are you okay?" Maria whispers, kissing Raven on the forehead squeezing her tightly, enfolding her in her arms.

"I don't know how to thank you enough for all that you've done for us," Mr. Hightower says, sincerely shaking Mr. Campbell's hand. His Septa uniform slightly wrinkled, a hint of worry and fear on his handsome olive-colored face.

"No need to thank me. Raven is family, and when family is in trouble, we all come together. What that monster put her through; he got exactly what he deserved. And trust me, she has nothing to worry about; all of the charges will be dropped in a matter of weeks. I'm going to see what I can do for Nadir Hathaway. He was well within his rights to use deadly force in self-defense. But the DA is going to try hard for a conviction for the unregistered gun. With no permit, the DA's office is going to come after him full throttle. I've looked into his records; he has several arrests for drug possession, and an attempt to distribute to an undercover. He served a nine-month sentence for assault with a deadly weapon in April of 1994." Mr. Campbell rattled off, adjusting his dark burgundy Armani tie. He looks dapper in a grey Giorgio Armani tailored suit; he looks every bit of a high-priced attorney.

"He ain't nothing special but a con artist drug dealer." Mr. Hightower spouts, flagging his hand in the air.

Mr. Campbell looks at his gold Presidential Rolex. "I have to wrap this up guys, I have a meeting that I have to attend in thirty minutes in Bryn Mawr." Mr. Campbell announces.

"Okay, we understand Terrance. Thank you again for helping my baby through this nightmare." Mrs. Hightower says, embracing him.

"Maria, I'm going to do everything in my power to make sure this goes away as quickly as possible. Young lady you focus on your upcoming graduation and your freshman year of college in the fall. And you call me if you need anything." Mr. Campbell says, tenderly kissing Raven on the cheek, then dashes out of the police station.

"Come on, let's go home." Mr. Hightower says, heading toward the exit walking sluggishly from a long day of bus driving.

It was silence in the Hightower's brand new gold Mazda Millennia. Regina Bell's hit *Make It Like It Was* plays quietly through the speakers on the radio station WDAS.

The Nickels ordeal had caused stress and turmoil in the Hightower household; a series of anonymous threatening phone calls from both male and females in the middle of the night saying they would kill Raven, firebomb the Hightower home, and revenge would be dispensed for Nickels' death. Mrs. Hightower filed complaints with the Philadelphia Police Department. They put unmarked cars, stationed in front of the Hightower's home. Mr. Hightower was the most affected. His pride was shattered, he failed to protect his little girl. He felt less than a man. The gory details of what happened to Raven were soul crushing. The thought of her, being kidnapped, beaten, and almost raped; and he was completely oblivious. These revelations made him more overprotective and determined to keep Raven closely under his watch. Raven had begun to fall asleep as Mr. Hightower stopped at a red light at 53rd and Arch Street.

"I hope they sentence that Nadir to five years. His ass ain't nothing but a thug."

Raven was livid on the inside. Her father refused to believe that Nadir had saved her life. Mr. Hightower had his mind made up that Nadir and Nickels were one in the same. Even if that fact couldn't be further from the truth.

"Dad, you don't even know Nadir to judge him. He's the only reason I'm still alive."

"Goddamnit Raven! You ain't have none of these problems when you were dating Jamal. But you had to get yourself involved with a little gangsta. I don't care what you say about that Nadir, he sells drugs like the rest of them no good niggas."

"Dad will you stop being so judgmental for one second?"

"Don't tell me to stop doing shit because you don't know what the hell you doing. Because of the bad decisions you made, I got police sitting in front of my door; motherfuckers calling my house all hours of the night, not only threatening to kill you, but me, your mother, and your brother. Raven you took someone's life. A young man is dead at your hands. Even if it was self-defense, you gonna have to live with that for the rest of your life. Those men you chose to get involved with; your one decision is affecting our whole family. I can't wait until you graduate next week so your grown, 18-year-old ass can get the hell out of my house!" Mr. Hightower shouts, his light olive-skin flushed red; his almond eyes had flames in them. He jerks the car roughly down their street on Callowhill, and quickly parallel parks in front of their house.

"And for once I can say," Mr. Hightower continues, "Kelly would never have done any crazy reckless shit like this. That's the difference between you and your sister." He says it in such a way, it cut into Raven like a dagger.

"Stop this nonsense right now! Both of you." Mrs. Hightower protests.

Raven jumps out of the car, slamming the door with immense force, darting up the front stairs, and entering the house with tears staining her face. Little Ricky, Budda, and Raheem were at their usual places on the sofa playing Madden NFL 98. They looked puzzled at the sight of an emotionally distraught Raven running past them. The boys, young middle school minds had not matured enough to have the capacity to understand what she might be going through. They simply look on in silence as she climbs the stairs to her bedroom. She closes her room door, collapses on her bed, turns on her stereo; TLC's *CrazySexyCool* album begins playing through the speakers as she cries herself to sleep.

A few hours had passed and a loud knock on her door awakens her from her sound sleep. The sun has set and the room is completely dark, only the budding moonlight lit the room through half-open mini blinds. She sits up on her bed, mouth dry as the Sahara.

"Who is it?" She calls out hoarsely.

"It's Kelly, Raven."

What the fuck could she want? Raven thought, standing to her feet, flicking the lights on. The grey D&G t-shirt dress she wore was covered in sweat. She took a long breath, mentally preparing herself for whatever bullshit Kelly was about to bring her way.

"Hey Raven."

"Hey Kelly." She responded dryly.

"Can I come in?" Kelly is as beautiful as ever. Her long wavy dark hair, and soft loose curls lay across her shoulders and hang down her back. Her purple Gap t-shirt and dark denim jeans fit her nicely.

"Sure, come in. What do you want Kelly?"

"I need to talk to you." Kelly enters and sits down on Raven's bed. Raven shuts her bedroom door before joining Kelly. Both sisters are extremely beautiful. Their mixture of ethnicities made both of them blended to perfection.

"Raven, I've come to apologize to you for being such a rotten sister for all of these years." Kelly says sincerely, her light-olive face looking deep in thought. Her almond-shaped eyes staring up at the ceiling. Raven never noticed how much she resembled their father; Kelly was a female replica of him. "I know I've been a super bitch to you for years, but after mom and dad told me you were almost killed, my conscience wouldn't let me sleep at night. Raven I tried my best to be perfect to cover up my insecurities. My conscience has been eating at me ever since we had that huge fight."

"I didn't know you had one of those." Raven huffs, unmoved by Kelly's display of affection.

"I know I've been the devil incarnate to you, but I've come to realize I was wrong." Kelly whispers, barely audible, coughing into her hands.

"What did you just say?" Raven asks, now at full attention.

Kelly faces Raven, their eyes meet and deep in her sister's eyes, Raven sees tears swelling. She saw compassion, regret; and humbleness. The mocking, taunting hatred was gone. Raven's defenses dropped immediately.

"When we came to blows and mom kicked me out, I had a sudden epiphany. I've been taking out all of my anger on you from the years of pressure mom and dad put on my shoulders to be perfect. Being the eldest, I had a huge burden on me to be the best example. The fear of disappointing them and not getting an A-plus on every exam or failing a test; it scared me to the point that I started having anxiety attacks. I isolated myself. That's why I never had any friends over. I became a bitter intellectual and you became my target. The more I could ridicule and point out your flaws, the more heat I could take off of myself. Raven I must admit I've always been jealous of your friendship with Mya and Takia. The closeness and genuine love you shared with those two girls made me envious. You and I share the same blood, but those two girls are more your sisters than I could ever be." Kelly's voice begins cracking, a flush of red rose to her olive face. "Raven I'm asking you to forgive me for being a monster to you. Let's make amends and be sisters, instead of enemies. We have a deal?" Kelly extends her right hand, smirking at Raven.

"I accept. I'd rather have my beautiful, intellectual sister be my friend any day."

"Aw, thank you." They embrace; sister to sister, heart to heart. "Now let's go downstairs and have a real family dinner. And dad could use a little cheering up, he's in a grumpy mood." Kelly says, standing to her feet, outstretching her hand to Raven.

"I'd love to." Raven smiles, taking her sister's hand.

"Since we're building a new sisterhood; why don't I pick you up on Saturday and we go to King of Prussia mall? I was thinking you can help me pick out a few summer looks. I want to start being more stylish and I don't know anyone more stylish than my sister." Raven flutters at the compliment.

"It's a date sis." Raven hugs Kelly gently. "But you gotta buy me some Chick-fil-A from the food court." They both laughed loudly before joining their parents downstairs for a much needed complete family dinner.

The Last Days at Overbrook High School

The thick muggy air hits Raven intensely as she enters the crowded auditorium to join the rest of the senior class to receive their yearbooks, and cap and gowns. She strolls down the aisles, passing the kids she has known for four years. And a few she has known since elementary and middle school. Some looked up at her from their dated hardwood chairs, with the stress from heat and frustration across their young faces. The orange and blue Armani Exchange t-shirt and light A|X jeans she wore were starting to soak with perspiration.

Damn, not an open seat in sight. She thinks, scanning the large room for an empty seat. She sucks her teeth in frustration, sick of being gawked at by her sweaty peers. She was late as always and one of the last students to arrive. She was about to retreat to the last row when Mya raises her hand, right in the center of the auditorium. She heard light snickering as she passes Kareema, Tee-Tee, and their crew.

"Excuse me, excuse me," she says, squeezing past students to get to the empty seat next to Mya.

"Raven you gonna be late to your own funeral," Mya giggles as Raven sits down.

"Bitch, I had gym last period. You know I had to freshen up a little, I can't walk around stinking like the rest of these triflin' hoes."

"I feel you. I hope Ms. Jones don't drawl and make this some long ass assembly. It's took fucking hot! Give me my cap and gown so I can lay up under central air at home." Mya says, fanning herself with a pink folder. She looks top-notch, even while sweating wearing a white halter top, and her hair in a tight bun pulled off of her face. Two large gold Chanel logo earrings dangle from her earlobes and a hot pink Caviar Chanel bag with gold hardware sits on her lap.

Ms. Jones, their petite principal's voice got everyone's attention. She wore a short Jada Pinkett styled haircut, freshly shaped up. The flowing orange shift dress that she wore looks flattering on her.

"Hello class of 1998! You have exactly six-days and counting before you go from boys to men and from girls to young women. I'm extremely proud of you class of '98. You guys are one of the highest graduating classes of last ten years; 998 out of 1,100. Give yourselves a round of applause!" Ms. Jones says excitedly, rising the limp audience to a round of applause. "Also, we have 350 students going on to a higher education at prestigious colleges and universities. Overbrook senior class of 1998 has received over $250,000 in scholarships and grants for our student's higher education. That's outstanding!" That got the auditorium clapping, shouting, and whooping like the audience at *The Arsenio Hall Show.* "I know the heat is becoming unbearable, so we won't be long. We will be giving out your cap and gowns and your yearbooks in groups by programs and advisory; starting by Health Academy,

Motivation, and Scholars and Business Academy. The quicker, more orderly you all line up, and follow directions; the quicker you all will be dismissed.

Raven and Mya wait patiently, perspiring profusely until their advisory is called. They wait in line and are handed their cap and gowns followed by their yearbooks, given out by Lisa Scott and her merry band of nerds who rolls their eyes at them. Her hair is in a greasy updo where you can see the heat had ravaged her hair and the grease was now dripping onto her neck and the back of the white t-shirt she wore.

"Congratulations on winning best dressed and most popular ladies! Everything was done by the book, every vote counted," Lisa says, condescendingly. "We all have our place in this urban jungle called high school. You earned yours," Lisa says before turning away.

"Oh damn, really?" Raven says flipping through her yearbook. "Yeah, whatever to what you was just talking about Lisa."

"Best dressed...most popular; hey!" Mya exclaims.

And there it was in the center of the yearbook, the most popular female of the class of 1998, Raven Hightower. A colored photo of her in a dark denim Guess jean set with the logo in red, a black DKNY t-shirt underneath the jacket, and a pair of red Gucci cat-eye frames sitting atop of her head; cheesing hard in Mrs. Ashcroft's homeroom. The most popular boy was Ziggy Brown and his photo was next to hers. He was wearing a tan Dickies suit covering his bony frame and a red Phillies baseball hat was on his head. His dark-skinned face expressed a cocky smirk. On the next page, best-dressed female, Mya Campbell who is fresh to death in a purple fox vest, purple and pink Moschino printed satin pants with Moschino spelled out largely down the thighs, and dark purple snakeskin ankle boot from Head

Start. Her head in two ponytails with Moschino satin ribbons, keeping her hair in perfect place and her black Prada knapsack dangling freely in her left hand. She looks aloof, beyond conceited, regal and alone; like she was the only girl in the world. And in Mya's world, she was. Best dressed male, went to Reggie of course. He was a sight in colorful Versace.

"Oh yeah, they got this one right. We them bitches for real." Mya says, grinning with pride at Lisa Scott who simply ignores her.

For the next twenty minutes, Mya and Raven learned what members of a platinum-selling girl group must experience during an autograph signing. The majority of their senior class either asked them to sign their yearbook or wanted them to write one last fly message. They were admired in class or from afar as they strutted through the hallways, never knowing the anticipation their fellow students felt awaiting one over the top outfit after another. They were the fashion show at Overbrook, a ghetto-fabulous feast for all to admire. Even students who didn't particularly care about them one way or the other knew that they were truly witnessing an end of an era. These were the last days of Overbrook's infamous baddest chicks, and at this very moment, everyone was paying homage to them. Raven sensed it too. As she and Mya exit the auditorium, she looks at her classmates; many who after graduation she will never see again. She felt a brewing disappointment and sadness overcame her; the rush to get out of Overbrook suddenly went away. She started ninth-grade as a virgin with zero confidence. A shy timid 14-year-old with braces and no tits. She barely spoke to anyone except for the two girls that knew her better than she knew herself. Mya and Takia held a tight circle of protection around her. An image of her and Mya head to toe in Tommy Hilfiger gear and neon green Reeboks, switching down the hallway with a busty 14-year-old Takia wearing a black bandana on her forehead, black shades and a stonewashed Cross Colours jean set, thinking she was Aaliyah from the *Back & Forth* video. Whom she was obsessed with at the time, entering Overbrook on the first day of their ninth-grade year. How naïve those three fresh-faced young girls appeared to the macking pussy-hungry junior and seniors that kicked game as they walked down the corridors.

Those were the days. Raven thinks smiling cheerfully, reminiscing as she stepped out into the dazzling June afternoon.

Brook's let out is in full motion. Hip-hop music video director Hype Williams could not have come up with a more extravagant concept. The usual suspects of street hustlers in shiny BMWs, Mercedes, Lexus trucks, and Expeditions converse with doe-eyed pretty-young things wearing money hungry smiles on their faces. Raven and Mya stand in line at the water ice stand. Blueberry for Raven, and cherry for Mya. They spot Pumpkin and Mario, both dressed in bright green and yellow Polo rugby shirts, posted up in front of his red Lexus having a flirtatious conversation with light-skinned Kiana and Shante. They are two curvy cute juniors, dressed in fitted Armani Exchange and Iceberg gear; both wearing the new style of capri pants called, knickers.

"Hmm, Pumpkin and Mario got their next victims lined up I see. Lame ass niggas. They irk my life." Mya says, licking her large cherry water ice. Mario frowns at her, his handsome coffee-colored face cold and uncaring; his dark-curly hair growing wild and all over his head as he flaunts a shiny gold Jesus piece hanging from his neck. He looked like he could pass for a Cuban.

He taps Pumpkin who stares at them with a shiesty grin on his ugly face.

"Come on Raven, let's go sit on the front school steps. Fuck them dick-heads!" Mya huffs.

Ever since Nickels, and Nafis' deaths, the streets were running wild with rumors that Raven had set Nickels up to get killed for his pounds of weed. Pumpkin had made his feelings known that he felt that she was a part of setting Nickels up; gritting on her every time he saw her, and making vicious remarks loud enough for her to hear. She personally could give two shits; Raven is overjoyed Pumpkin stopped speaking to her. She never liked his crusty ass anyway.

"Can you believe it's all over next week?" Mya asked, pulling her black Jackie O shaped Chanel glasses out of her Chanel bag, placing them on her face; light hazel eyes squinting from the glaring sun. "Four years flew by fast as shit! I remember ninth-grade like yesterday. And now we graduating; without Takia." Mya's voice drops slightly.

"I can't believe it myself. I always thought it would be us three against the world; taking flicks, jumping in the air with our diplomas. I guess shit don't always go according to plan. This year been the roughest ever."

"Raven who you telling?! Takia having a nervous breakdown, losing her baby, and Rell getting killed. Then your situation with Nickels trying to kill you...I swear I played Mary's *My Life* album a million times." Mya sighs. "Thank God you had Nadir riding with you to pull you out of the nightmare Nickels had you trapped in!" Mya shakes her head. "How is Nadir holding up anyway?"

"He's alright, a strong militant Muslim brother." Raven laughs. "He gotta do a three-year bid. He'll be released in 2001."

"Rav, 2001 seems so damn far away. They probably gonna have flying Mercedes by then."

"Mya, you trippin'. There ain't gonna be no damn flying Mercedes! I guess they gonna have video phones too?" They both fall out hysterically in laughter.

"But seriously Rav, you really love Nadir hun?" Raven brightens up tremendously.

"More than anything. He's the one Mya. It's not a minute I don't think about him. I lay in bed at night and cry from missing him. He saved me. I called him and he ran to me like a smoking gun putting his life on the line for mine. That's the most unselfish thing anyone can do for someone they love." Raven becomes emotional; tears welling in her eyes.

"I knew he was special that night y'all met at Gotham; he's a real standup dude. A rare breed and I'm so happy he's yours. If anybody deserves to be happy, it's you Raven." Mya replies sincerely, wrapping her arms around Raven.

"Ugh, let me get out of my feelings. Bitch what's up with you and Mr. Carmello Black?" Raven asks, switching the subject.

"Raven, where do I begin? He's the best; ain't no other nigga like him. He's the epitome of a boss." Mya blushes. "He's instilled more knowledge in me than my four years in high school combined. He can have any bitch out here and he chose me. He's taking me to Miami for my graduation gift."

"Miami! Bitch you serious?" Raven blurts.

"As a heart attack! He booked us at an exclusive hotel and he's taking me to the Versace mansion. Oh and Rav, they have a mall called Bal Harbour that shits on KOP! Raven I wanna marry him and have his babies; can't no other man come after him. He spoiled me to death and showed me the game on so many levels."

"Seems like we both found the men of our dreams." Raven says, chewing on a lemon flavored Starburst.

"Rav, are you excited to start Temple?"

"Yes! I got my acceptance letter. My parents are finally happy we're on the same page and my mom's talking about how we'll decorate my dorm room. I think we're finally closing that Nickels chapter of my life for good. That's a dark twisted fantasy I think we all wanna erase. And yo, I owe your dad so much. He came through for me like no other; I see why he's one of the top lawyers in Philly. When Mr. Campbell strolled into the courtroom in his fly ass Armani suit and Colgate smile; the judge was flirting with him with her eyes. She looked at me and says Ms. Hightower, charges dismissed."

"My dad is all that."

"Yes he is; fine ass old-head. I swear LaTanya lucked up." Mya's gray Nextel begins ringing.

"Hey babe, I'm sitting on the steps directly in front of the school on 59th Street." "Just chillin' with Raven." "Okay, love you too." Mya was beaming with endearment. "Carmello can drop you off."

"Thanks. Where you going to school?" Raven asked, picking up her book bag.

"I got accepted to St. Joes and La Salle; I'm leaning toward La Salle. I also got into Howard and Spelman. My mom's wish list of colleges for me, but being so far away from Carmello is not an option. He started his real estate company, and he has so many big plans. I be damned if I let another bitch creep in after all the work I put in to make that nigga mine!" Mya declares as if preparing for war. "I can't lose him Raven, I would die." Mya's eyes filled with worry.

"Girl, Carmello adores you. You're more than a dime, you're a crisp Benjamin. He'd be a fool to mess up what y'all built."

Mya lets out a heavy breath. "Thanks Rav." Mya hugs Raven tightly, she could sense the distress all over her body.

Mya, what's really going on with you and Carmello? Raven thought and was about to ask, but Carmello pulls up in a new gold Range Rover, blasting *Mo Money Mo Problems* by the Notorious B.I.G. Whatever distress Mya was in would be discovered another day. This conversation was on pause as they climbed into Carmello's new Range.

Part 2: Graduation

Friday, June 20, 1998

Today is the day I say goodbye to Overbrook High School and my childhood forever. Raven says to herself while admiring her image in her white cap and gown with gold tassels with the class of 1998 dangling; her hair bone straight hanging around her shoulders. Four years of high school seemed like an eternity, but September 1997 to June 1998 seemed like a long ass movie. But someone set the VCR on fast forward. In two hours she would start the next phase of her life; Temple University and Nadir would be the center of it all.

"Raven come on, traffic is going to be hectic. You can't be late!" Mrs. Hightower yells up the stairs.

"Okay mom, here I come." Raven takes one final look, bites down on her bottom lip, and then puts on her best fuck 'em girl walk; switching out of her bedroom.

Her family is snapping photos as she walks down the staircase. Her parents, Kelly, Little Ricky, and her grandparents; Richard and Vivian Hightower, all beaming with pride at Raven as she walks down the stairs in her cap and gown.

"Baby you look perfect." Mrs. Hightower says, fighting back the tears. The mint green and pink floral sundress she wore looks striking against her dark-mocha skin, long silky black curls sweeping her face, and dark slanted eyes are overflowing with pride for her daughter. She kisses Raven softly on the cheek.

"Thanks mom."

"Look at my baby girl." Mr. Hightower beams, joining his wife. "Raven, I know we haven't seen eye to eye on a lot of things, but today you graduate. I've never been prouder to have you as my daughter." Words Raven's been waiting to hear most of her life rang in her ear like a symphony.

"Oh daddy,...." she whispered as a flurry of kisses from her father, covered her forehead and cheeks as she wraps her arms around him.

"Aw, say cheese for the camera." Kelly jokes, snapping away on her black Kodak camera. The royal blue cotton jersey halter top and skirt set looked flattering on her. "We have to hurry; my sister has a graduation to get to." Kelly chuckles.

Raven and Little Ricky get into the family's new Mazda Millenia while Kelly rode in their grandparents' new dark gray Cadillac Eldorado. Traffic is clear as they head up 30th and Spruce Street toward the UPenn Irvine Auditorium. Mr. Hightower enters the crowded parking lot filled with cars of families walking toward the auditorium. Boys in black caps and gowns with kente cloth scarfs around their necks and girls in white gowns. Raven slides out of the back seat. She looks up at the beaming sun; exhales, and embraces her moment. As they walk, they finally reach the crowded front entrance with the other well-dressed parents, grandparents , and family friends. All in attendance to bear witness of the class of 1998.

The students are separated from their families and lead into a private entrance. Raven walks into the open corridor; vice principal Howard instructs them to stand in two single-file lines; one for boys and one for girls.

"Be orderly and silent everyone. You'll be taking your seats in the auditorium, and then your next steps into adulthood." His voice boomed throughout the corridor. The tan linen blazer and slacks look dapper on his fit frame.

"We are fashionably late, but here nevertheless." Reggie's high pitched voice echoes behind Raven. She turns to see Reggie and Mya sashaying through the line, both wearing large square shaped Versace shades with large Medusa heads on the sides. She could see the black tube dress and gold Chanel necklace hanging from Mya's neck. Mya was in full diva mode.

Zigga Brown, Rashawn Jones, Tyrese Thompson, and Raheem Sampson all clapped and whistled as she passed them.

"The baddest of 1998. Life ain't gonna be the same without seeing Mya Campbell every day." They chuckled.

"Best hips and legs I've ever seen." Tyrese shouts. Mya throws them a sly grin.

"Settle down! Settle down now!" Vice principal Howard yells at the guys.

"Raven," she laughs as Mr. Howard calls out her name.

"Mrs. Campbell, I think we all know you arrived. Now file in line with the others," vice principal Howard says obvious that she is annoyed.

"Ugh, please. I can't wait until this graduation is over so I can never see her drawing ass again." Kareema sits, a few seats behind them. "But anyway, I'm gonna miss everyone, even the haters," she says in a light playful tone. TeeTee and Amira are cackling beside her.

"What Kareema? You sure you gonna miss me? You spent the last four years of your life earning your PHD. And you know I'm talking about your playa hater degree; not your high school diploma." Mya chuckles really cocky, not missing her last chance to verbally destroy Kareema. Everyone in line in hearing distance burst out into laughter.

"Girl you lucky I got this cap and gown on or I'd be smacking the taste out of your mouth!" Kareema bitterly retorts, her face caked with harsh makeup. She looked frightening and mean.

"Ms. Campbell, Ms. Wallace, we will have none of that today. If you girls can't put your petty bickering aside, we will have no choice but to remove you from the graduating ceremony. And that is my final warning." Mrs. Ashcroft snapped, stepping forward wearing an authentic African dashiki kente cloth, a black floor length skirt, and a red Erykah Badu style headwrap adorned her head. Only her dark brown well-moisturized face was shown. "Put your petty beefs aside ladies and live in this moment. You only have one high school graduation." Her words sank in and both girls put their claws away.

"Everyone take your places; graduation will begin in minutes." Butterflies filled Raven's stomach. Mya squeezes her hand tightly, blush rushes to her cheeks; hazel eyes filled with love for her sister.

"For Takia," she whispers.

"For Takia, " Raven replies. "Now let's graduate!" They walk hand in hand into the auditorium.

The first fifty rows are roped off for the graduates. The balcony and back rows are filled to capacity. Loud applause and clicking of cameras fill the room. Mya, Raven, and Reggie take their seats next to each other in the fourth row. The stage is filled with teachers and faculty members. Some had been employed at Overbrook for decades. The Overbrook senior class choir files onto the stage followed by choir director, Mr. Williams who lifts his arms in the air; his black suit is pressed immaculately. The young female pianist begins playing the opening to Boyz ll Men, *It's So Hard to Say Goodbye to Yesterday*. The two dozen choir members begin singing in harmony rocking side to side, "It's so hard to say goodbye to Overbrook," they sang, getting a round of applause.

They bring the song to a beautiful finale; principal Jones dressed in a black cap and gown approaches the podium smiling brightly.

"Good afternoon, parents, students, and faculty. I welcome you all here on this glorious afternoon for the graduation ceremony of the Overbrook class of 1998. During these four years we have seen this group of young men and women, grow and mature as we send them off into the next stage of life. We will celebrate them here today." Loud applause rings out from the auditorium. "I would like to introduce the class valedictorian Lisa Scott to the audience to read a speech she has written for today's occasion. I might add, Lisa Scott graduates today, number one in her class, with full honors, and a full scholarship to Norfolk University." The applause begins again.

Lisa prances up the stage, her shoulder length hair is done in a fresh wrap, confidence on her brown-skinned face as her white gown flowed in the air. "Good afternoon class of 1998, we have come to the final chapter of high school life. But we will take with us all of the memories like Boyz ll Men says. And this is not the end of our road. This is the beginning of a bright future with endless possibilities. We are the next generation of innovative thinkers and tastemakers who will change the world. We have gained knowledge through our phenomenal educators at Overbrook High School. Can we have a round of applause for the wonderful teachers and faculty members who have guided all of us?" The room erupts into loud applause. "Class of 1998 as we enter the new millennium, the dawn of an amazing new decade; I say, what a time to be alive. To be a young person with a thirst for knowledge and a future we share, so we all can soar higher than an eagle. Class of 1998, as I conclude, you all are the wind beneath my wings. Keep striving, never stop dreaming, and success will come! Thank you all."

Raven and even Mya were moved my Lisa's speech as they clapped. Today had no place for unnecessary bitchiness. Principal Jones returns to the podium where she begins calling the students one by one, giving them their diplomas. Raven watches dozens of smiling kids she shared her high school years with. The most impressionable years of their lives. She smiles as each one receives their diploma, the honor they rightfully earned.

It's amazing they survived high school. She thinks.

And not just any high school; the maze of terror; Overbrook. Statistics and 'hood superstars are made and broken in those hallways every day.

"Tahira Calloway." Raven smirks as TeeTee's bony ass walks across the stage. A fresh pack of Yaki 30 flowing underneath her cap.

Mya and Raven lock eyes with a telepathic inside joke. Raven even claps for her sworn enemy in her moment of triumph. She was maturing by the second. They called the students by last night name in alphabetical order. Mya would be going on stage with the next group.

"Niko Campbell." Niko, a chubby dark-skinned boy with thick full lips grins widely as principal Jones hands him a diploma.

"Mya Campbell." Principal Jones says into the microphone with a new zest in her voice. "Out of 3,000 students, Mya Campbell is definitely the small percent deemed unforgettable." Principal Jones chuckles and the graduating class certainly agreed; applauding and cheering loudly. Mya immediately put on her fuck 'em girl walk.

"Yes Mya, do that shit baby!" Raven screams, immediately receiving a disapproving grimace from a teacher standing nearby.

Mya takes her diploma, flings her long her wildly and smiles; her face turns cocky; boldness at its finest. The next minutes seem like a lifetime as Raven waits for her name to be called.

"Raven Hightower." Principal Jones finally calls out. She rises to her feet, almost gliding up to the stage. More applause erupts as she is handed her diploma. Principal Jones kisses her tenderly on the cheek. "Congratulations Raven, you're one of the special ones. I knew you would make it." At that moment, every drama and obstacle that transpired in her life that past year was demolished. Breaking up with Mally, the physical and mental torture by Nickels, and being forced to take another human being's life. But finally finding a love that was pure bliss with Nadir. She had to walk through fire to be prepared for this golden moment.

Raven Hightower is now officially a young adult. The Overbrook High School chapter of her life is officially closed. After all of the drama of 1998; 1999 will be a stellar new beginning. *Temple University, here I come!* Raven says to herself, staring into her bathroom mirror, putting the final touches on her sultry look moments away from her graduation party. In the main ballroom of First District Plaza at 3801 Market Street, the strapless dark denim Anna Sui tube dress fit her body exquisitely. Strappy Dolce & Gabbana leopard-print sandals are the perfect footwear of choice. Raven is overjoyed at her self-satisfaction.

"Come on sis. You don't wanna be late for your own party. You look gorgeous, by the way," Kelly observes.

"Thanks Kelly. I'm ready," Raven says, giving herself one final look over.

Raven rides in Kelly's Honda. Her parents and grandparents went ahead to make sure that everything is set up perfectly.

"You're a high-school grad now, soon to be a college freshman," Kelly says giddily, bobbing her head to Aaliyah's new single *Are You That Somebody?* As they pass a light on 41st and Market Street, Kelly asks, "How you feelin', Rav?"

"Blessed, Kelly. I thought I would be dead right now, not about to walk into my graduation party."

"Somebody up there loves you girl," Kelly grins, squeezing Raven's hand.

Parking is tight. Kelly parallel parks into a small space on Arch Street. It is 6:40 p.m. just as the sky turns a perfect shade of dark orange, the sun teasingly on the verge of setting. Raven glances up at the beautiful sight, peace, and tranquility take over her spirit.

"Girl, come on," Kelly insists, holding open the large glass door.

Kelly also looks beautiful. She and Raven definitely come from the same DNA. Her red halter dress looks stunning on her well-portioned frame, and her shiny dark locks are draped down her back. Only MAC cherry-flavored lip gloss cover her lips. Without makeup, Kelly is more flawless than most of the girls that Raven knows.

Raven takes a quiet moment to appreciate her sister's perfection. They take the elevator to the main ballroom on the third-floor. As the doors open, they see dozens of pink balloons that line the entrance. A huge banner hangs from the ceiling that reads, "Congratulations Raven, and the entire Overbrook class of 1998!"

Raven blushes, taking it all in. Dozens of teens dressed in brand-new graduation finery are drinking soda and eating the delicious Dominican and soul food, buffet-style dinner layout that her mother and grandmother had worked hours preparing. Raven is greeted like the star attraction that she is. DJ Tuffy Tuff begins spinning *Dangerous* by Busta Rhymes. Kids are on the dance floor dancing to Busta's melodic flow.

"Raven, your party is the bomb, girl," is repeated constantly as she makes her rounds greeting guests. Which consists of eighty percent of the 1998 graduating class, fifty percent of the junior class, and graduates from neighboring high schools such as University City, West Philadelphia High, and Bartram. The rest are neighborhood friends, neighbors, and family. Raven is handed dozens of sealed cards with fresh $50s and $100s folded inside.

"Miss Raven, I believe you have the party of the year on your hands," Reggie says while embracing her, smelling of the essence of Jean-Paul Gautier cologne.

"Thanks for comin' Reg," she giggles in return.

"Child, my mom wanted to take me to Outback with my grandparents. I said, 'hell no, mom, I wouldn't miss this party not even for a fifty percent off sale at Saks!'"

Raven takes in a visual of the flashy fuschia-pink blazer and Versace pants that Reggie wears.

"Graduates in the house," Mya's voice rings out, breaking Raven's gaze on Reggie's loud outfit.

Reggie and Raven turn to see Mya and Carmello approaching. Mya looks like a video vixen in a strapless white-leather tube dress. White and gold Gucci sandals adorn her feet, dark auburn hair pressed bone straight, and her bright red lips look like a soft kissable heart. Carmello looks dapper in a blank and gold Medusa-print silk Versace dress shirt, black pressed-linen pants, and black gator-tipped shoes shined bright enough to see your reflection.

"Baddest chick graduates," Raven responds as she greets Mya, embracing her tightly.

"Let me get a pic of you two," Reggie directs, pulling out a Fujifilm disposable camera. The girls pose away like Naomi and Tyra from *Vogue Magazine*.

"Congratulations, Raven, from me and Mya," Carmello grins, handing her a white envelope.

By the thickness, she could tell that it is filled with money."

"Thanks so much," Raven replies.

"You and her better be passing them exams y'all first semester," Carmello scolds jokingly, pointing his pointer at Mya to Raven.

"You don't have to worry about me passing. All I'm getting is straight A's at La Salle," Mya says with a sassy attitude, sticking her tongue out while shaking her head side to side. They all erupt into laughter.

"Yeah, alright, since you talkin' all slick, I'd better see nothin' but A's at the end of that first semester," Carmello chuckles, playfully smacking Mya on the butt.

"Hello, Raven, congratulations. Can I talk to you for a moment?"

She turns, locking eyes with Mally who is standing so close that their lips are in kissing range. He holds a bouquet of fresh red roses. Every special moment they shared since the age of fourteen flashes through her mind, while a look of nervous self-doubt fills his honey-brown eyes. He looks handsome and alluring to her in a white, black, and red Polo Sport rugby shirt.

Raven picks up on the evident awkwardness. Maya, Carmello, and Reggie look from a distance with confused and curious glances. Anxiously waiting for Raven's reaction. Her heart softens, time for her and Mally to make amends.

"Mally, thank you so much for coming," Raven says with a dazzling smile and genuine hug.

His familiar scent hits Raven's nose instantly. The interconnection they share remains. "These are for you. Congratulations," he blushes, handing her the bouquet.

"They're beautiful. Congratulations to you also, Mya. Good luck with all of your endeavors," Mally says genuinely to his former arch enemy. Raven embraces herself for Mya to give Mally a severe tongue lashing, but to her astonishment, Mya did the complete opposite.

"Thanks, Mally. It's good seeing you. I heard about your mechanic-shop opening down at 61st and Thompson Street. I'm happy for you."

"Thanks, Mya. If you ever need your car checked out, the diagnostic test is on me."

"I'm gonna hold you to that, Mally," Mya chuckles. Raven is left dumbfounded. These two have hated each other for years. But with everything that went down this past year, perhaps everyone has grown up.

"Yo Raven, can we talk someplace private for a sec?" Mally whispers in her ear.

"Sure come on," Raven takes Mally by the hand, moving through the thick crowd. Heads turn left and right. She even catches her parents with shocked expressions as they pass by replenishing refreshments and snacks at a white-linen-clad table in the center of a long hallway. She leads him into an empty fire stairwell.

"You look gorgeous, Raven," Mally says, his eyes sweeping over her head to toe. He smirks mischievously, the way he always does when a freaky thought enters his mind.

"Thanks Mally. You lookin' like a jawn yourself."

Raven is not ego-stroking him either. His soft, wavy hair is shaped up perfectly, as he stands confidently in his fresh tan construction Timberlands tucked under pencil-pocket Guess jeans.

"I mean it Mally, I really appreciate you comin'. I know how fucked up everything went down between us."

"Raven, we good. No need to apologize. I had to come to grips that we're over. Many late nights sippin' Henny and rollin' blunts. Plenty of tears and lots of Mary J. Blige records on repeat."

They both snicker lightly, recognizing the moment.

"I had to pick myself up and put my heart back together," Mally continues. I can't front, I was sick. I ain't just lose my girl, my best friend was gone. When I heard that nigga Nickles kidnapped you and you had to murk one of his pack boys, I wanted to get to you so bad. Just to hold and protect you. Honestly, Raven, I blame myself for you gettin' caught up with that nigga. I should have worked harder to provide for you."

"Naw, Mally. Never, ever blame yourself. You gave me more than I deserved. I was so ungrateful and blinded by money. I've learned the hard way that all money ain't good money."

Mally's eyes begin watering. "I feel like I've failed you as your man."

"No!" Raven's voice noticeably cracks. "I left you thinking the grass is greener on the other side. You know that old saying, be careful what you wish for? I thought that God was punishing me every day for abandoning you."

Raven wraps her arms around Mally—so comfortable, familiar, and safe.

"Mally, you're the best friend I've ever known. My first love. The first man ever to touch my body or know my heart better than I know it."

His lips move lower toward hers, a slow breathing moment passes between them before he quickly moves up to her forehead while rubbing her back. Memories and images of when their love burned unrestricted come rushing back.

"Raven, I have something else to tell you," Mally says while interrupting her sentimental memories.

"You better not be marrying TeeTee," she says, half playing, stepping back from their embrace.

"Hell no," Mally says with conviction, frowning up his handsome face. "That was some quick rebound shit. After a few weeks, she got too clingy and annoying, blowin' up my phone every five seconds. I got away from her ass real quick. I had enough when she started poppin' up in my uncle's garage without calling on some stalker shit. TeeTee's ass is outta here! But I have met a girl and I can see us going somewhere. Her name is Taylor. The first girl who's made me happy since you."

Jealousy creeps into Raven's mind. She quickly suppresses the emotion, knowing that she has no right to be jealous of Mally; she did, after all, choose to give him up.

"We've been together for a few months; we just found out she's pregnant."

Raven is totally unprepared for this news. She and Mally would lay in his bed for hours talking about how many kids they would have—two handsome little boys and a beautiful baby girl. She felt a pain building in her gut, but again masks such feelings.

"Wow! Congrats Mally. You're going to make a great dad."

"Thanks Raven. I had to come here to tell you this news in person and see you face to face because I want us to be friends and a part of each other's life. Always. Taylor probably heard more about you since we've been together. She says you're like the third person in our relationship."

Raven chuckles. "Whoever this Taylor girl is, she must be special."

"She definitely is."

Raven can tell by his rosy blush that Taylor is quite special. Closure is happening and, to her surprise, Raven is building resistance to it. A what-if thought enters her mind. *Did I give up Mally's love too quickly? Was I wrong? He's gotten this new girl pregnant. Did I hand him over like a coupon to a Bloomingdale's sale? Is he the one?*

But then an image of Nadir's face appears and a short feeling of where her heart belongs reassures her. "I'm dating a new guy, too. His name is Nadir."

"Yeah, the dude who killed Nickles. I read his name in the *Daily News* article."

"Yeah, that's him. He saved me from myself. I was on the verge of self-destruction so many times. I thought about death, thought about killing myself. Nadir saved me, Mally," she reflects purely.

Now Mally can feel his own jealousy brewing behind his light-brown eyes. He quickly contains it, instead beams with approval. "That's what's up. If anybody deserves to be happy it's you, the smartest, most beautiful girl in West Philadelphia."

"Mally, let's make a pact right now. No matter what, we're gonna stay in each other's lives. Best friends forever."

"Without question, my dog for life. I love you, Jamal."

"I love you more, Raven." His face appears sad and tender.

Fuck it, Raven thinks, grabbing him by the cheeks, kissing him deliberately on his lips. He returns her kisses feverishly. For a few moments, they are alone in a space that only the two of them understand.

"You're right here forever," Mally draws an invisible heart on his chest.

"I know I am. Now come on, let's get back to my party."

As they re-entered the ballroom, Raven's ears are immediately filled with loud commotion.

"What the fuck is going on?" Mally asks, staring in disbelief.

"Come on." He pulls her by the hand, hurrying through the crowd. He pushes past a group of teens surrounding the refreshment table. Raven's heart sinks at the sight of Takia or what used to be Takia, sweating profusely, a matted brown wig on her head slightly crooked.

"Raven!" Takia yells, her lipstick smeared around her mouth, and black mascara smudged on the side of both her eyes. She resembles a demented beauty-pageant contestant. The red low-cut mini dress and

Fendi sandals are on point, but the whole room could clearly see that she is either drunk, high on drugs, or both.

"Takia, come with me right now," Mya demands, grabbing her roughly by the arm.

"Mya, I told you I was fine. Calm your hype ass down," Takia slurs, yanking her arm away.

"Takia, you don't need to be in here like this. Yo, you're clearly drunk ass hell!" Mya shouts.

"Leave me the fuck alone! I'm 18 years old. Grown as shit. I don't need you tryin' to tell me what the fuck to do."

Takia twists her face in a deranged frown. She and Mya stand eyeballing each other in a stare-down that could have killed the average bitch. But these were the baddest bitches made of steel.

"Come on, babe, just leave her alone," Carmello says, pulling her away.

"Congratulations, Raven, I knew you was gonna graduate at the top," Takia slurs, stumbling toward Raven and embracing her in a shaky hug.

Raven could feel her best friend's broken spirit while holding her in her arms, lifeless and empty as a corpse. The once vivacious free spirit of a girl is now empty. She squeezes Takia tight around her waist as tears fill her eyes.

Takia, my wild, beautiful Takia. What have these streets done to you? Raven thinks, running her hands up and down Takia's back.

"Takia, Takia. Are you okay?" Mrs. Hightower asks, with true worry across her face.

"I'm okay, Mrs. Hightower. You're like the mother I never had. I just drank a little Hennessy before I came in."

"Oh, so you admittin' you got pissy drunk before you came to Raven's graduation party? You're so trifling," Mya roars, confronting her like an aggressive defense attorney.

"Takia, it's okay," I'm happy you made it. Raven attempts in vain to be the voice of reason.

"Hold the fuck up, Mya. Get your fucked-up ass outta my face," Takia shouts at Mya.

"Guess what, Takia, I'm not . Somebody needs to tell you about your 'hood ways," Mya stresses with anger.

"Oh, I guess you the bitch to do it, huh? Mya, don't play with me. I will beat you the fuck up in here," Takia says as she stares Mya up and down.

"So we'll be two rumblin' bitches in here, Takia!"

They're gonna start swinging on each other any second. Raven thinks, trying to come up with a counterplan of action.

Carmello comes from behind Mya and yanks her arm. "Yo, y'all drawlin'. You can clearly see she's drunk. The argument shit ain't gonna get you nowhere. Leave it alone."

"Listen up, young ladies, watch your language," Mr. Hightower says sternly, joining his wife.

Dozens of freshly graduated teens stand around silently, hanging on to every word.

"Both of you chill out! You're being disrespectful to my parents," Raven shouts over both Mya and Takia.

"I'm outta here. Y'all think I'm crazy. Right? Don't you? None of y'all can judge me. I see Rell's head getting blown off every time I close my eyes. You still got Nadir, Raven, even if he's just locked up in a cell. And Carmello's here wit' you right now, Mya. My nigga is gone, forever," Takia cries before breaking down hysterically in tears.

Raven's heart breaks for her, realizing that Takia is still suffering greatly from witnessing Rell's murder. Raven steps forward to embrace her, but Takia suddenly flees the ballroom, running down the front stairwell. Raven goes after her.

"Takia, Takia, wait! Hold up," she hollers. The clicking of Takia's heels on the hard metal floors fills Raven's ears. Out of breath and stumbling, Raven reaches the bottom of the fourth-floor steps and swings open the glass doors, still yelling Takia's name. She sprints to the top of 40th and Market Street but Takia is nowhere in sight. Raven is filled with the permanent feeling that Takia has vanished from her life.

September 15, 1998

At 1:30 p.m., Raven's eyes look down upon her silver-tone Movado watch, tapping her freshly French-manicured nails on the scratched up, and dented metal table in the visiting room at the CFCF Correctional Facility where Nadir is serving his three-year prison term. The noisy sound of unruly children and loud sounds taking place around her irritate Raven to the core. But that is a small price to pay to see her baby, her love. She misses Nadir like crazy. She misses his kiss, his touch, the scent of him all over her, and their long intellectual conversations. Most of all the lengthy sexcapades they so eagerly played and the multiple orgasms that Nadir eagerly gave her. His soft lips between her legs, sucking, and licking her vaginal lips, leaving her soaking wet and then sopping it all up like fresh gravy. Her clit had become his new favorite toy. The six-months that he had been inside felt endless. She went to Condom Kingdom on South Street, investing in two vibrators to please herself in his absence.

Whenever wet dreams of Nadir took over, she kept them in her nightstand safely within arm's reach.

Being an attractive freshman at Temple University, Raven's good looks caught the attention of the hormonal male students; handsome basketball players, quarterbacks, track stars, and young dope boys with a brain all tried to holler at her. Sometimes temptation was too hard to resist, but she willed a grip on her libido, and could not think of betraying Nadir. He would kill for her, and risk his life unselfishly for hers. Betraying him was unthinkable. The least that she could do was to keep her pussy nice and tight for him. She threw herself into the books, putting all of her concentration into passing her exams. She was on a partial scholarship; the rest of her tuition came out of her parents' pockets. Thanks to their careful saving and belief in purchasing only the bare necessities, there was plenty of money to cover her education.

She hears the loud clinking of the barred doors that prisoners walk through. Raven quickly looks herself over in a small Chanel compact, applying more MAC Viva Glam purple lip gloss, straightening the fitted red French Connection sweater dress that she wears underneath a black Armani Exchange motorcycle jacket, and black Spiga knee boots. She placed her brown Fendi tote next to her. Her shiny dark hair is pulled up into a ponytail with her baby hair laying perfectly on her forehead. She always makes an effort to look her best on her weekly efforts to see Nadir. His life is bleak and mundane in prison. The least she could do is to look like beautiful on visit day. She is his light in a dark world.

Two large Caucasian correctional officers with intimidating bulldog faces walk him to the visiting room followed by two-dozen inmates in orange jumpsuits.

Raven's heart flutters when she sees her man. Nadir is sixth in line.

A black coofi covers his head of curly black hair, and a thick fine beard engulfs his handsome face. He gained twenty pounds, but it is all solid muscle. He has not been doing anything but lifting weights and doing push-ups. He is perfectly fit under his orange jumpsuit, while his mind becomes more deeply connected to his Islamic faith. Reading the Quran and making salat five times a day and attending Jumar services every Friday since starting his bid.

Raven has seen a change in Nadir. His spiritual growth is astonishing. He is committed to becoming a better Muslim. He spoke at length to Raven about converting but she would have any of that. She liked eating pork far too much, wearing tight clothes, and flaunting her new hairstyles. Nadir's eyes light up as Raven stands to her feet. He beams with love, wrapping her in his strong arms.

"Nadir, I missed you so much," she whispers lightly, kissing his neck, sniffing, and taking in his naturally masculine scent.

Damn, he smells good, she thinks.

Nadir cups her hands, planting a flurry of kisses on her face and lips.

"Raven, every time I see you is like the very first time!" Nadir's smile is dazzling; even with his full-grown beard and harsh surroundings, he remains gorgeous. His perfectly shaped face, soft lips, and white teeth still put her in a trance. "Come on, baby, let's sit down," Nadir softly suggests. "So how's Miss Temple Freshman doing?"

"I'm adjusting pretty good, but my roommate irks my life. She's still not cleaning up after herself. That chick is trifling as hell. It takes everything in my soul not to beat the brakes off her." Raven sucks her teeth, clenching her fists.

"Slow down, Tyson. We don't need you catching a case and ending up in here with me." Nadir repeats the line he said to Raven outside Club Gossip the very first night they met.

They both chuckle.

"But on a serious note, I'll be outta here in three years. You'll be graduating with your bachelor's degree. The first thing I want us to do is get married."

Raven's dark eyes grow wide. Time stops around her as she stares into Nadir's radiant face. She has never seen him more humble.

"Look, I know I'm asking a lot of you, Raven. Your life is just getting started. Forget I even asked," Nadir sighs, lowering his head into the palms of his hands.

"No, baby, I'll marry you today if you ask me to," Raven's voice cracks as tears form in her eyes. "I could never say no if you asked me."

Nadir's reaction is similar as he is overcome with emotion. "When I get outta here, we gonna have the biggest wedding. I'm gonna work my ass off and put that iced-out baguette diamond ring on your finger that I said was gonna give you that night at Club Gotham."

Nadir becomes closer to her, wrapping her in his arms and kissing her passionately on the mouth. They are connected as one. Nadir is no longer her boyfriend boo or her nigga. He is the man God sent to be her husband and father of her unborn children.

Raven Hightower, a girl from West Philly who escaped death, is lucky enough to find love in a broken place.

Chapter 19

TAKIA: BLOOD ON THE DANCE FLOOR

It's All About Me by Mýa featuring Sisqó, plays as men fill the smoke-filled room of the Night on Broadway Gentlemen's Club. Hennessy is on the main stage, face down, pumping the floor with wild sexual bravado. Her oiled-up round ass glistens like two honey buns. She has become a pro at playing to the horny masses of perverted male customers who flock to the club night after night. She slowly moves her body into the doggie-style position, her ass perched high in the air, rapidly gyrating her derrière while sliding two fingers into her expectant pussy. This gesture gets the men off and to their feet every time. A shower of money pours on top of her. This makes her even wilder as she caresses her clit in aggressive motions causing an orgasm, squirting across the stage. The men are in a heated frenzy, reaching into their pockets and wallets, placing $20s, $50s, and $100s at the chance to feel her dripping wetness. Their fingers fondling her and their cash in mutual tribute. She has them clearly by their balls and wallets.

"Let's give it up for the intoxicating Hennessy," DJ Screwball says over the microphone from the DJ booth. An overweight dark-skinned woman in her early-fifties rushes the stage with a green trash bag to collect the money thrown all over the stage. Hennessy stands, takes a bow, makes her exit to the catcalls and whistles from the men in the audience.

"Up next we have a special treat for you niggas all the way from Brooklyn, New York. It's the deadly and beautiful Poison Ivy."

Hennessy makes her way down the stairs to the dancers' dressing room with groups of semi-nude young women laughing and talking loudly, while applying makeup, wigs, thongs, and garter belts. The smell of weed, cigarettes, and cheap perfume fills her nostrils.

"Hey, Hennessy!" She is greeted with respect from all of the girls whom she passes. In a short amount of time, she earned that respect and climbed up the ranks at Night on Broadway. Gaining affection and admiration from Manny. He became fascinated with her hustler's mentality. Not to mention her ride game is mean, working her sweet pussy walls up and down his dick in his office, condo, and on his sailboat. They spent countless nights sailing around the Schuylkill River fucking from dusk till dawn. He gifted her with a new blue-faced Rolex and a diamond tennis bracelet. Plus use of his cream 750iL BMW and silver 4.6 Range Rover. She had quickly become the top bitch at the club.

The only person that this does not sit well with is Buttercup, who is seething with jealousy at Takia's straight rise. She is nipping at the throne that Buttercup sits upon. Even Takia's performance is the main attraction now. And Buttercup is salty over Manny. She once held him coyly in the center of her small hands, but now he shows no interest, looking at her as just another employee. Buttercup is on the decline. Takia feels that she has repaid Buttercup many times over for bringing her into the club, by doing dozens of bachelor parties for next to nothing in Jersey and New York. Buttercup is a thorough old-head whom Takia looks up to and respects but she is not about to kiss her ass. She makes her way to the center of the dressing room, where rows of long vanity mirrors are aligned. She passes new girls about her age in neon-colored thongs, heads covered in pink and green wigs, and caramel asses covered in baby lotion.

"Hey Hennessy, what's up girl?" they greet cheerfully, just like the girls at Overbrook High School being Joe Familiar. Loud crackling laughter fills the room as she approaches her vanity table. To her surprise, Buttercup occupies her space, uses her makeup, applying her new crimson lipstick, while having an obnoxious conversation with Hot Chocolate, Crystal, Cinnamon, and Pocahontas. Several rookie dancers surround them.

Oh, no, Buttercup. Bitch, you gettin' out of pocket! I'm shutting this down now, Takia thinks, clearing her throat and folding her arms under her full bosom, covered only by a thin sheer bra top. Her actions become more antagonistic. Buttercup's large dark-brown eyes stare at her through the smudged vanity mirror. A cold hatred flashing in her dilated pupils. A cruel, conniving grin forms on her pretty brown face.

"Hennessy, girl, I didn't know you were done your set already. Hope you don't mind me using your new lipstick. With all that money you gettin' these days," she chuckles condescendingly.

The other girls snicker.

Oh, this bitch wanna play games, Takia thinks. "Buttercup, I don't mind givin' to the needy, especially the way your cash counts are getting shorter and shorter. The girls let out an echoing laughter to an embarrassing rage that now covers Buttercup's face.

She snaps her neck, giving the laughing dancers a mean ice grill that silences the group. She jumps to her feet, facing off with Takia.

"Listen here, you little bitch, you gettin' beside yourself! Don't forget it was me who came through the old block and picked your depressed, broke ass up, and put you on this money. Bitch, I saved your ass. You was about to commit suicide after your little boyfriend got murdered," Buttercup yells in a venomous tone, her white teeth clenched. She is vicious and unhinged. Takia knows by Buttercup's body language that this confrontation will end in blows, mentally preparing herself to knock Buttercup the fuck out. Takia grins, unmoved, remaining cool as a fan.

"Buttercup, you did put me on game, but I took it to the next level. That's what real hustlin' bitches do. You just mad I took your spot and ran with it. Face the facts. You're gettin' old, damn near pushin' thirty. The real reason you mad is that Manny isn't checking for you anymore. You thought he was yours and I took the nigga right from you," Takia spits.

Immediately, without a word, Buttercup lunges at her, swing with wild force, landing forceful blows to the center side of Takia's face.

"I'm gonna kill you, bitch," Takia yells, rushing into Buttercup like a linebacker, knocking her off balance and back into the vanity mirror, loudly cracking it. Takia follows up with rapid punches to Buttercup's face.

Buttercup yanks Takia's wig off, trying in vain to get a grip on her hair, held tightly in place under a stocking cap. She begins scratching, digging her nails into Takia's neck and shoulders as Takia delivers punishing blows to her face and chest until blood flows profusely from Buttercup's nose. The other dancers try but fail to pull them apart. Takia yanks Buttercup by the collar of her bodysuit onto the floor where glass shards of the cracked mirror are scattered. Security rushes in, grabbing Takia in a full nelson, but not before she gets off one last punishing kick to Buttercup's face. Blood splatters everywhere. She is immediately taken to Manny's office, who is behind his marble desk putting currency into piles of their respective denominations, placing black rubber bands around each $1,000 bundle. He looks up at Takia's disheveled appearance, a frown on his dark-skinned face. His majestic chiseled bone structure is striking, square-shaped diamond cufflinks gleam against the lapels of the light lavender suit he wears. Dark shiny waves of hair lay against his perfectly shaped head. A diamond and ruby pinkie ring rests in gold on his right pinkie finger. His well-manicured nails glisten under the small silver lamp atop his desk.

"Look, Manny, this shit is not my fault. Buttercup been tryin' me for weeks. This situation was bound to happen. I told you my heart don't pump no Kool-Aid," Takia sucks her teeth and rolls her eyes with force.

"What have I told you about playing the game? *The Art of War* remember rule number three?" 'The supreme art of war is to subdue the enemy without fighting.' "You might have beaten Buttercup physically, but she won the victory by provoking you out of character. Never forget, she's one of my greatest pupils. She knows how to play mind games like a thorough professional," Manny says, his lyrical baritone revealing its musical quality. His Haitian accent adding distinction to his voice. He speaks in the most proper English, but traces of his island roots remain. Having arrived in the states from Port-au-Prince, Haiti, at age eight with his mother, fleeing famine and poverty in 1980. Young Manny—born Emmanuel Pierre Dumas—father Marcel was murdered by corrupt military soldiers for being an outspoken activist, fighting for better treatment and equality for the Haitian people. He was gunned down at a secret meeting planning a protest from the capital city on Haitian Independence Day. Sadly, he was shot fifteen times at point-blank range betrayed by three close confidants. True supporters of the cause swiftly got Manny and his mother out of the country to a small coastal town on the border of the Dominican Republic. This is where they were smuggled out of the country on a small steamboat headed to Florida where a second cousin sent two plane tickets and wired money to get them to Philadelphia.

Young Manny, a good-natured, soft-spoken boy with an above-average IQ, was thrown into the fast-paced world of Germantown Philly. What a culture shock coming from cramped conditions with barely enough to eat to his Aunt Bernadette's huge three-story stone house off of Germantown and Chew Street, filled with cousins, other aunts, uncles, and many extended family members. Bernadette was the family matriarch, a nurse at Pennsylvania Hospital.

Some Haitians are strongly religious people who attend church several times a week. Yet church was not enough to contain the new urban world around Manny. The sound of hip-hop could be heard from speeding cars throughout the neighborhood and from boom boxes owned by fresh-to-death teens. Innocent Manny quickly learned the importance of material status from being laughed at and shunned in middle school, from wearing faded high-water jeans, and corny on-sale sweaters from Sears. He was teased while his classmates wore fresh Adidas top ten sneakers, colorful Sergio Tacchini sweatsuits, Eight-Ball leather jackets, Polo of all kinds, and dope Fila. His one saving attribute was his smooth dark complexion, exotically handsome face, and a head full of fine black wavy hair that was instantly appealing.

He went through a growth spurt at fourteen, from 5'4" to 5'11" tall and lanky with solid limbs. His good grades and charming persona placed him in magnet classes at Germantown Senior High School. He learned the art of manipulation, and willing people to do his bidding. He became obsessed with two books, *The Art of War* and *The 48 Laws of Power*.

By the time Manny became a sophomore, he had transferred to Central High School, a magnet academic school located in Philadelphia's Olney section. He was regularly having sex with senior girls behind the bleachers of the school's football field. He graduated at the top of his class in 1989, receiving a full scholarship to the University of Miami. Eighteen-year-old Manny became a far cry from the innocent eight-year-old who thought that eating a McDonald's cheeseburger was like hitting the lottery. He matured into the suave ladies' man who now had grown women twice his age throwing him the pussy with ease. His older cousin Theo introduced him to check fraud. Manny became a quick study, and the student quickly replaced the teacher. He became a master at recreating perfect bank-issued and certified cashier's checks. He and Theo recruited attractive young Haitian women to infiltrate the banks. In the late '80s, before the sophisticated bank-fraud system was put in place, banks were sweeter than young virgins to hit. Manny's crew was killing them, going on the road to banks in Jersey, Delaware, and Maryland. He was a senior making thousands of dollars, attending high school in $1,500 suits from Boyd's. He wore Gucci sneakers, and loafers in every color, Alpina shades, and custom-leather outfits like his favorite rapper Kool Moe Dee. Even purchasing his first car, a black, fully-loaded 5.0 Mustang.

Manny began attending popular nightclubs after midnight with high rollers, sleeping with women in their late twenties while still attending church every Sunday. The fast-life did not derail his studies. He scored a solid 1520 SAT score with little preparation or even effort. His mother and Aunt Bernadette knew that he was making money illegally, but he did so well in school and was so respectful that they turned a blind eye. He brought them the most thoughtful gifts, expensive Calvin Klein Obsession perfume and $500 Gucci handbags. He also furnished the house with fancy *Art Deco*-style furniture, a large modern television, VCR, and stereo systems. The man of the house, making sure that his aunt's pricey mortgage was paid on time.

By the time he arrived at the University of Miami in the fall of 1990 set to study bioengineering, he quickly grew bored with the juvenile campus life. Immature sorority girls, pump-up jocks, and drunken homecoming parties became stale. He began venturing into the glamorous world of the Miami nightlife where he saw the sports cars from his favorite TV show *Miami Vice* sped by him. He became a regular at Rolexx, Miami's premier gentlemen's strip club. Where he watched some of the finest women he had ever seen pumping and gyrating their asses to the sounds of hip-hop and pop songs as men showered them with cash. Many of the dancers he had seen before in Two Live Crew's scandalous videos on the *Video Music Box* channel. A revelation came to Manny: the two things he loved, money and pussy, merged into one profitable business. The club's owner Tito, a half-Haitian half-Cuban heavyset man with a mane of unkempt salt-and-pepper hair, took a liking to well-dressed young Manny eager to learn the business. Tito liked his driving ambition, impressed with his college pedigree, and took him under his wing. Allowing him to shadow at first, then the title of assistant club manager came that he earned because of his marketing ingenuity.

He doubled the club's profits and raised its profile by attracting major pro athletes from the NBA, NFL, and even a young Mike Tyson frequented the club. While hot R&B acts like New Edition and Bobby Brown would hold parties after their concerts. Taking Rolexx from hot local strip club to a chic playground of the rich and notorious was all part of his plan. After three years, he was second-in-command. After seven years of building the biggest strip club in the south, he missed his family, longing for new challenges. So he moved back to Philly in the fall of 1996 and set his sights on making Night on Broadway Gentleman's Club the premiere urban strip club in Philadelphia. He certainly surpassed his goal.

It was past 5:30 a.m. when Takia and Manny arrived at his loft condo at the luxury Water Works on Delaware Avenue. They listened to Sade's *Love Deluxe* album. While entering Manny's garage, his silver Range Rover pulled into its designated parking space. Takia climbs out of the SUV. Black kitten-heeled Chanel shoes click across the smooth stone garage floor. The light-blue stretch dress jeans and red Moschino t-shirt feel beyond comfortable. She had become accustomed to being naked. Clothing sometimes feels foreign against her skin. A new black Chanel Caviar bag is filled with $11,000. A simple dark-brown bob wig crowns her beautiful caramel face. They take the elevator to the tenth floor. Manny walks ahead of her. She loves watching him walk. He glides like a king and often brags about having royal Haitian blood in his veins.

Takia believes him. She finds herself believing anything that Manny tells her. He was the first man with whom she was completely enraptured since Rell's murder. The first man with whom she did not feel any utter guilt. He was unlike the dozens of common street hustlers with whom she dealt. Her entire young life, they made fast money moving crack cocaine. Manny is different. His intellect is more in-depth than anyone she had ever met. Every move he makes is like a game of chess. His goal is to earn long-term money to build generational wealth. He constantly reads *Rich Dad Poor Dad* by Robert Kiyosaki. Manny does not just own a strip club; he has a thriving real-estate business, owning several apartment buildings in Northeast Philly. He continues to study Wall Street like a professional stockbroker, owning stock in several pharmaceutical companies. Shakespeare's *A Midsummer Night's Dream* is his favorite play. Classic novels by Ernest Hemingway and F. Scott Fitzgerald line his bookcases. He works out regularly while becoming a vegetarian, constantly urging Takia to give up meat. Pork and beef are gone, but chicken and fish she could not dare part with.

Manny's condo is a sophisticated reflection of himself. Freshly waxed hardwood floors and well-crafted *Art Deco* rectangular sofas line the living room. Tall custom-marble lamps and Andy Warhol replica paintings of Marilyn Monroe and Elvis hang on spotless white walls.

Takia turns on the shower, stepping into the large dark-red marble-and glass enclosure. Warm water hits her body and blasts of steam quickly fill the confined space. She washes her skin with black soap. Her washcloth covers her young, agile body, making sure that her most feminine parts are beyond clean. With Manny, her happiness is clearly returning. Her shorn heart is finally being repaired. She misses Rell every day, but God spared her life the night that he was taken. And she has life in her yet.

She steps out of the shower. The cool dryness of the bathroom sends a shiver through her as she dries off and applies Victoria's Secret vanilla body lotion. The full bathroom mirror still has steam on it. Her body is flawless: glistening young flesh. She spends a final moment admiring her feminine perfection before entering the bedroom, where Manny lay naked atop fresh beige satin sheets. His large bedroom is spotless. The scent of jasmine and lavender candles easily fill the room. A bearskin rug lays in front of Manny's four-poster oak king-sized bed. A spectacular bay window showcases the most magnificent view of the Philadelphia skyline. The Ben Franklin Bridge lit up in the distance, while a full moon shines luminously into the room.

Takia crawls onto the bed, gently caressing the bottom of Manny's ankles while making her way between his legs. His heavy Haitian dick stands at half-attention; by the time her hand reaches over it has become enormous. She could barely get her small hands fully around it. She caresses it gently before sinking her mouth around its wide mushroom-shaped head, moving her mouth like a human suction cup. While she expands her jaws as widely as possible.

Manny lets out low moans, thrusting his dick back and forth in her mouth. He turns his body, forcing Takia on her back and straddling her face, moving deeper and hitting the back of her throat until she inevitably gags. Manny's magic fingers slip inside of her wet vagina so that she anticipates his penetration.

"I think you're ready for daddy," he teases, placing Takia's firm 34C right breast in his mouth, gently biting down on her nipple. She lets out a light scream.

"Yes, daddy, I'm ready for you," she gasps in a girlish baby voice that she developed in sexual role-playing with him.

He begins deeply French kissing her, engulfing her mouth in the process. Manny is the first man since Rell's death with whom she feels completely connected, mentally and sexually. Manny is a skilled lover. Not at all lazy putting the requisite work in like the bedroom represents his nine-to-five. He places Takia's legs over his shoulder, slowly entering her. The pain of his thickness expands her walls and rips through her body, but her fulfillment quickly overtakes. Manny's toned body easily melts into her caramel skin. Their sweat and natural juices intertwine as if made for each other. He pins her arms tightly over her head as he does laps swimming in her pussy. She oozes with wetness running down her thighs. He takes the air out of her lungs with every stroke, forcibly gripping her neck and choking her, while thrusting with greater tenacity, hitting Takia's G-spot. He introduced Takia to choking orgasms early on during their lovemaking sessions. She became addicted to the violently explosive way she climaxed.

"Yes, daddy. Yes, daddy," she gasps.

Manny's grip grows even tighter. Takia knows that a big orgasm is coming and feels it building. She could feel Manny's throbbing dick against her bladder: an overwhelming sensation, almost as though she has to urinate. Manny eases up his grip to let her catch a few breaths.

"Daddy, daddy," she yells as a raging orgasm swells inside of her.

His choke returns to her neck as he pounds with animalistic speed. Seconds later, her body shakes with convulsions as a shattering orgasm like an ocean wave flows out of her. She roars.

"Oh my God, oh my God," Manny hollers, gripping her. Takia digs her nails into his sweaty back. His semen rushes deeply inside of her. He gratefully collapses on top of her. They are bound together by the passion, natural sexual urges, and animalistic order that bonds man and woman as one. The next few weeks fly by in a blur of dancing, shopping, being Manny's main girl, and the Night on Broadway's main attraction.

Takia is making more money than she can handle. Her reputation continues to grow. Guys from all over the tri-state region clamber into the club to get a good glimpse of the girl named Hennessy. Is she as sick and bad as the way niggas described her? Or is she just a bunch of hype? Once their weed-clouded eyes catch Takia's wondrous and curvy caramel body, they toss their cash like crisp winter snowflakes. The other dancers worship her, treating her as the undisputed queen of the pole. Any jealousy they feel is concealed behind fake smiles and false compliments. The ass-whipping she put on Buttercup kept the other girls in line. As for Buttercup, she stayed clear of Hennessy. Buttercup's influence and clout have diminished to the point where the other girls openly show their disdain and mock her. Buttercup would never let any bitch slide with disrespect. So she rumbled one or two bottom-feeder dancers who were eating her back out around the club. She remained one of the crowd's favorite but the word was out; Buttercup's days were numbered.

Takia and Manny spent many splendid days together, enjoying dinner at the finest restaurants. He introduced her to sipping fine Cabernets and Pinot

Noirs. She tried to spend time with Michelle, who is heavily involved with New Hope Baptist Church in West Philly and is now more sober than the AA itself. Takia is proud of her mother for the progress she has made. She has a full-time data-entry job for a collections agency in Upper Darby. The house is kept spotless, and she keeps her hair in a freshly-done flowing bob. Monica from Hair Image Salon is her favorite stylist. She has also taken to dressing in stylish business attire. Yes, Michelle has certainly come a long way from the hateful drunken tirades. Her jealously vindictive nature toward Takia had changed. The word of God heals her poisonous heart and she shouts it to anyone who will listen.

Today, Michelle is a fierce lioness protecting her cub. She pleaded with Takia to stop dancing at the Night on Broadway. Buttercup had been spreading vicious rumors throughout the neighborhood to anyone who would listen that Takia had been turned-out stripping, and turning tricks while rampantly using drugs. Takia did not want to hear any of that, so she avoided Michelle. She was not in the mood for prayers and stories of Christ healing. Most days she longed for her sisters whom she had not seen since her blowup with them at the graduation party. She had cut off all communication and hated the way they made her feel, berating her, and coming at her neck in front of all of those people. Yes, she was a little pissy that night but was battling bouts of depression that happen when she has memories of Rell's death and the loss of her baby. Being the good friend that she is, she still went out of her way to be there for those ungrateful bitches. They ganged up on her like she was a stranger, so sorrowful painful thoughts quickly turn to rage.

"Fuck Maya and Raven," she growls. "I don't need them! Manny is now all I need." The big-money plans that he is masterminding will have her set for life.

Hennessy arrives at nearly midnight at the Night on Broadway on a muggy June Friday evening. She parks Manny's Range Rover in the rear of the club in one of his private parking spaces. *Bed Full of Money* by Charli Baltimore plays lightly on the radio. She applies eyeshadow in the driver-side overhead mirror. The new auburn colored shoulder-length wig appears striking next to her caramel complexion. She gathers up her new black and red Fendi monogram bag, slipping out of the high driver's seat. Her favorite kitten-heeled black high mule sandals hitting the dirty concrete as she wears a black tube glass covering her hourglass shape. She makes her way into the club's back entrance.

"Hey Hennessy, you got a minute?" a female voice calls out from the darkness. She turns to see Buttercup standing in the shadows smoking a blunt. She steps forward into the harsh security lights at the back entrance, a blunt-cut black wig framing her milky brown face.

Takia gives her a skeptical frown before replying, "Yeah," dryly.

Buttercup takes another deep inhale of her blunt, inhaling, and exhaling quickly without a choke. She lowers her gaze to gather her thoughts. "Look, things between us got out of control, and I take responsibility for my actions. I let my ego and petty gossip take me off my square. I brought you to the club 'cause I knew you have everything it takes to get this paper. I can admit you roll like a motherfuckin' phoenix! I'll be the first to say I got jealous," Buttercup says humbly. "Far as Manny, I ain't trippin' off that. He was never my man. We just had a lotta good times together. Anyway, I'm

319

coming to you as a woman to apologize, hoping we can move past this petty bullshit."

Buttercup reaches out her hand for Takia to shake. A beaming smile appears on Takia's face.

"Bianca, I don't want no handshake. Girl, gimme a hug. We're like family."

"I'm sorry Takia, forgive me," Buttercup whispers as they embrace tightly the way feuding relatives do after a long separation.

Takia is relieved. Beefing with Buttercup is not on her agenda. After a few weeks, to everyone's astonishment, things between them returned to as before: laughing, joking, and sharing a vanity table. Even crafting a two-girl performance dressed in matching leopard-print thong outfits, both of them onstage naked and grinding—too much for the men attending Night on Broadway to handle. It had become an ass overload. This duo-set paid off big time. They were drowning in cash, which made Manny happy. In no time at all, Takia and Buttercup took their show from the stage to the bedroom. Engaging in several threesomes with Manny, who gladly accepted their invitation.

Takia considers herself freaky and sexually open. She previously participated in threesomes with two guys, but never with another girl. This is a new twist. She lay on her back, sucking Manny's dick like a throbbing Tootsie Roll melting in her mouth. Buttercup spreads her legs open, sucking on her clit, eating her sensitive pussy with a passionately delicate precision that no man ever had. She exploded with leg-shaking orgasm after orgasm. Manny made Buttercup sit on his face, while Takia mounted and rode his massive cock. They form a sweaty animalistic trinity. She and Buttercup French kiss, mingling, and tasting each other's saliva. Three naked torsos became the norm in

Manny's bed. Legs wrapped around each other, arms intertwined, lying in sweet unison.

Part 2

Hennessy is dripping with sweat after a long three-song set on a muggy June night. The young male audience remains restless and horny. The club is beyond capacity. She strips naked out of the sheer leopard-print body suit that she wears. Other dancers make their way to the stage, while others do their makeup at the row of vanities in the dressing room. Hennessy grabs a pink towel, bar of soap from her locker, and snatches off the short mushroom-blonde wig. Revealing her own hair perfectly braided in tight cornrows like Bo Derek. Her inner thighs ached from doing wide splits on the hard stage. Pain shoots through her calves as she walks to the white-tiled open gymnasium-styled shower, eager to wash her body clean. Several girls talk loudly from the shower, annoying cackles echoing off the hard tile, the loud sound of water spraying the floor from the powerful shower heads. Steam rises, filling the room with a cloud of misty air. The inner bathroom area mirrors are ready to be wiped.

"Yo, Hennessy," her name faintly echoes over the noisy chicks and continuous running water.

She turns to see Buttercup approaching in a short black satin robe, the white turban on her head showcasing her striking bone structure and wide eyes.

"Yo, Bianca, come here. I got something to tell you." Buttercup is as giddy as a young school girl about to confess her crush to her best friend. The only time that Takia has seen Buttercup this excited is when money has been involved. She pulls Takia in a corner, speaking in a hushed tone.

"Bitch, I met one of the Philadelphia Eagles at Palmer's last weekend! A fine-ass rookie. A thick-built chocolate boah. I could have ate him up." They both snicker.

"Anyway, he called me last night. He's throwing his boy a bachelor party. He wants me and another dancer to come to the Sheraton Hotel by the airport this Friday. So of course I'm coming to you first. He's given us a $1,000 booking fee each up front before we take shit off. All his homies are college football players, sports agents, and dope boys. So you know we about to get paid?!"

"Yes, girl, we about to get paid," Takia squeals, feeling beyond lucky. She and Buttercup give each other high-fives.

"Listen, Takia, the only thing is, don't tell any of the girls or Manny. You know how jealous he gets when we set up our own gigs outside the club. He'll try to stop your bankroll 'cause he ain't in on it. This money we about to get is ours, fair, and square," Buttercup says in a serious and measured voice, her large brown eyes probing over Takia with a paralyzed caution.

Her face grows blank before shaking her head in obedient agreement.

"Buttercup, you right. Ain't nobody gon' stop this money, not even Manny."

"Fuck that! We goin' for ours," Buttercup retorts, grinning, gleaming white teeth surrounded by full red lips. "I'll call you when I have the time and hotel room number before Friday," she adds before quickly vanishing from the steamy locker room.

Takia does as instructed, keeping Manny in the dark about the upcoming bachelor party. Even covering her whereabouts by telling him that it was Michelle's birthday and she was surprising her with a small party. He accepts her lie without some much as a questionable glance. She is in the clear, smiling at her masterful manipulation, driving Manny's Range Rover onto the Island Avenue exit of the expressway heading toward the airport. The Sheraton Hotel's well-lit sign comes into view. She drives through two more lights before hitting the congested traffic of cars driving to and from the airport. She turns into the half-full parking lot. Brian McKnight's *Anytime* plays lightly on the radio. She finds an empty prime spot a few feet from the main entrance, lowering the drivers-side overhead mirror, applying dark eyeshadow, and a plum Viva Glam lipstick from her cream-colored Chanel tote bag. She pops a piece of Trident gum into her mouth before doing an inspection of the tote's contents, making sure that Secret deodorant, Summer's Eve vaginal wash, J&J baby oil, Victoria's Secret tropical-breeze body spray with matching lotion, multiple thongs, and other costumes were inside. If there is one thing that Takia has learned in her fast young life of having sex for money is that good hygiene is necessary. Always making sure that every crevice of her body is clean and fresh.

Once she completes her self-inspection, she smirks seductively at her beautiful caramel reflection in the overhead mirror.

"You a bad bitch. Now go get that money," she teases as she winks at her own vanity. She slowly steps out of the Range, straightening the lime-green dress that she wears with matching thong, her bare ass on display. Strappy white sandals by Charles Jordan hanging seductively on her feet. A parted shoulder-length honey-blonde wig makes her feel like Ginger from *Casino* as she enters the lobby. Passing the front desk, a middle-aged bald white man is dressed in a navy-blue suit and red tie, his dark eyes giving a close look at her fully displayed body. Pure visual sexual delight eagerly shines through his eyes. She blows him a playful kiss as she enters the waiting empty elevator before pressing floor nine. The doors close, ascending quickly. The ninth floor arrives and she inhales, mentally preparing for the prime task at hand, and making her way down the generic maze of the hallway. Drab beige wallpaper and dreary brown carpet repulse her eyes. Room 921 comes into view. She looks herself over one more time in the oval hallway mirror before knocking. She hears hip-hop music playing behind the door. A handsome light-skinned guy in his early-twenties answers the door, wearing a burgundy-and-white Phillies jersey and matching fitted hat. His bright hazel eyes mischievously look over her firm body.

"Buttercup said you were fine. But good Lord, damn!" he chuckles. A small toothpick sits in the corner of his mouth.

"Are you gonna let me in or keep me standing out here all night?" Takia says in a honey-glazed girlish voice, flashing an all-too-innocent smile.

"Sure, baby girl, come in. I'm Dante, by the way." He towers over her and moves slightly, leaving a small space open in the doorway. She has to press her body against his to enter. The powerful scent of marijuana reeks on his clothes. *How Do U Want It* by Tupac plays loudly in the suite. A dozen men sit on the darkened sofas, drinking Hennessy and Cristal while pressing freshly rolled blunts and dressed in the New York hip-hop style, oversized basketball jerseys, wearing iced-out crosses, and gold crosses pieces hang around their necks. Their boisterous conversation ceases at the sight of her caramel perfection. They look like a pack of wolves watching their prey.

"Baby is stacked," a dark-skinned guy with freshly braided cornrows yells out. His homies burst into laughter. "She has ass for days," a tan-skinned guy in a blue-and-red Sixers jersey adds. While sitting on the edge of the sofa, puffing an oversized blunt, with a slight grin on his round pudgy face. "Buttercup is in the bedroom over there, Cee" Dante says bending down in her ear. His lips and hot breath touch the back of her neck. Takia spins around with a major attitude.

"Nigga, don't be walkin' up on me," she snaps, wearing a tough grimace on her face.

"My bad, baby girl. I don't want no problems."

He laughs, raising his hands in surrender.

"She feisty," another guy yells out. "I know that pussy is good," as she shifts her curvy ass toward the bedroom.

She answers, slamming the door quickly. Buttercup walks out of the adjoining bathroom, only two pasties covering her nipples and a thong covering her vagina. A blonde wig sits atop her head, her rich-skin glistening from applied baby oil. Her entire body is one color, not a blemish or scar to be found.

"Girl, what's wrong with you?" Buttercup asks, looking like Vanessa del Rio, the popular adult porn star.

"Those thirsty-ass niggas out there are pressed as hell," Takia grates her teeth as she flops down onto the bed.

"Fuck them lames! They just the ballplayer flunkies anyway."

"Oh, he's not here yet?"

"Nope, he on his way, gettin' the birthday boy to cooperate. I have the perfect thing to cheer you up," Buttercup smiles faithfully, entering the bathroom.

Takia is now lounging on the bed as Buttercup showers her with fresh $100s. "$1,000 like I promised. Your booking fee up front!"

Takia sits up on her knees like a wide-eyed kid. "You just made my whole attitude change. "Benjamin Franklin is the man I'm most in love with."

They both chuckle. Buttercup's cell phone begins ringing inside her Gucci handbag. She quickly rummages for the black Nextel flip phone.

"Hello? You pullin' into the parking lot now? We'll be ready by the time you get to the room."

"Okay, bitch, let's start gettin' ready. The football player and birthday boy will be here in minutes," Buttercup directs Takia. "We about to get some major tips from these motherfuckers. I need this come up," she confesses, applying baby oil to her body.

Takia rushes to the bathroom to freshen up, changing into a black thong, garter belt, and sheer stockings. Spraying herself down with Victoria's Secret Love Spell body spray and gargling with Listerine while applying her matte lipstick.

A stern knock on the door alerted them that the party is about to begin. Buttercup unlocks it.

"Yo, y'all ready? Let's get this thing started," says the birthday boy, his deep and gruff baritone voice meeting the bedroom door.

"Here put this on," Buttercup says, handing him a CD.

Takia assumes that it is the Eagles player.

"We need something to drink to loosen us up. Bring me a bottle of Alizé and Hennessy." They expectantly brought the two chilled bottles of alcohol to the bedroom.

Buttercup and Takia quickly swallow their poison of choice. Takia takes three shots of Hennessy without blinking. The stinging brown liquor engulfs her entire body. She is now in her zone, pumped, and ready to take control of this party. Buttercup waves her hand outside of the bedroom door, signaling her to get started as Takia mentally prepares herself. Bachelor parties always make her nervous. The men are so close that she can feel the heat of their stale breath, their hands moving like tarantulas, grabbing, and violating every part of her. The alcohol naturally strengthened their libido and boldness. Within the confines of Night on Broadway, the large stage kept a safe distance between the crowd of men and dancers. The beefy security guards always nearby if dudes got out of control. Bachelor parties in a tight hotel room make a dancer feel like Daniel, walking into the lion's den. All a girl has are her smarts and feminine charm, hoping the lions do not maul her to death. She makes a silent prayer that both she and her cash make it out in one piece.

Takia had done a few parties with Buttercup in the beginning but felt uncomfortable with how drunk and belligerent the guys became. This was a unique circumstance: A $1,000 upfront booking fee was too much for her to turn down. It would all be over in two hours, after which she would be back in Manny's arms, safe, and sound. *Nasty Girl* by Vanity 6 begins playing on the stereo system.

"Come out two minutes after me," Buttercup instructs before swinging open the door and striking a hand-on-hip pose. Her hands rest on her thick hips. The noise beyond the door has become louder. She fiercely walks into the living room. Takia pauses behind the open bedroom door. Buttercup's ass looks like a perfectly shaped peach; 10:32 p.m. flashes across the small clock radio on the nightstand. Her eyes dart between that and the crack in the bedroom door. She can see an attractive brown-skinned guy sitting in a chair in the middle of the room. Buttercup is bending over in front of him gyrating. In front of them stands a tall thick-built, dark-chocolate-skinned man with broad shoulders and protruding chest wearing a dark gray short-sleeved Gucci sweater complemented by his enormous gold-and-diamond Jesus piece. He is covering Buttercup with Benjamins.

Bingo, he must be the Eagles player, Takia thinks. 10:38 p.m. flashes across. "Shit, I'm supposed to be out there by now," she says irked. She goes to the doorway repeating Buttercup's pose. There is a pause in the living room as the men take in her delicious feminine wiles before erupting into wild catcalls. The adrenaline rush of their lustful admiration drives her to perform. She walks over to the awaiting birthday boy who displays a wide grin on his handsome face covered in soft elfin features. She straddles him, feeling his throbbing penis through his jeans. He grips her ass as she begins riding him with rhythmic energy closely mirroring the song.

Buttercup begins giving the Eagles player a full-on lap dance as the other guys in the room surround them. Horny as hell, watching her round, oiled-up ass bouncing up and down to the beat of Adina Howard's *Freak Like Me*. The men slap her voluptuous ass with money. An hour later, Takia is sweaty and fatigued, bent over the couch, going up and down on a lanky brown-skinned guy humping her like a jackrabbit. *Stroke You Up* by Changing Faces is coming to an end on the stereo.

She elbows Mr. Power Humper in the ribs, signaling that his dance is over.

The room had become stifling with body heat. Buttercup hands Takia a chilled glass of Cristal champagne, the third that she had given her in the last hour as *12 Play* by R. Kelly begins playing. It is the final song of their set.

This is my last drink, I've gotta drive Manny's truck home, Takia thinks. *I gotta have some water.* She and Buttercup continue to flex and gyrate their bodies till the sounds of R. Kelly's vocals fade out. They retreat to the bedroom, lock the door, and begin breaking down their kits. The jackpot is hit with the booking fee and tips split evenly. They both walk away with a cool $2,500 each.

"Buttercup, thanks so much for putting me on to this party," Takia says, her voice slurring. "I think I had too much to drink." She slumps over the bed, her sheer dress halfway on. "Buttercup, I don't feel well, my head is throbbing."

"Hennessy, you're fine. You just need to lay down for a while," Buttercup's voice sounds deep and distorted, her words echoing in Takia's ear. She stands in front of Takia, who stares back up at her. She blinks, fluttering her eyes and clearing her vision. Buttercup is a fuzzy distorted figure. Takia's eyes cannot come into clear focus.

"Let me help you get into bed." Buttercup lifts her legs and pushes her shoulders into the king-sized mattress.

"Okay," I'ma lay down for ten minutes," she slurs before completely passing out. Buttercup's face transforms into a wicked frown.

"Night, night, bitch," she says, quickly ripping off Takia's dress and panties. "You surprise me, being so damn gullible," Buttercup laughs in a demented way. "I never let go of a grudge until I take the bitch out the game. I made a vow to ruin you." Buttercup grabs Takia's chin roughly in a tight grip before slapping her with force across the face. She then picks up Takia's Chanel clutch from the nightstand, emptying it from all the fresh cash tucked inside.

"You're gonna remember this night forever. Let's see if Manny sticks by your side after this. Bitch, you thought I was gonna let you come into my club, take my spot, take my man, and get away with it? I played you easier than a fixed Atlantic City slot machine. Hennessy, get ready for the all-you-can-eat dick buffet waitin' for you," she chuckles, unlocking the bedroom door and stepping back into the living room.

Guys are scattered on the couches drinking, while still others are on the balcony smoking weed. The Eagles player walks inside, his massively solid frame protruding through the Gucci sweater he wears. Buttercup waves her left hand to get his attention. He takes a long, strong tote of the overstuffed blunt in his right hand, exhaling a bellow of smoke as his bloodshot-red pupils focus on Buttercup.

"I told you, less risky than committing credit card fraud at Neiman Marcus. The bitch will stay knocked out for at least ten to twelve hours. That's more than enough time for you motherfuckers to penetrate every one of her holes at least twice," she purrs like a sadistic kitten.

"Damn, baby, she looks like a corpse. What the hell you give her?"

"Just a little Special K, date rape drug of choice for those white college boys. They use it on those sweet little sorority girls, knocking them out cold before taking some pussy."

"Well I'm goin' first before these niggas," he chuckles before pulling off his sweater revealing his chiseled chest and abs.

"Hold up, nigga, before you stick your dick in, run me my money," Buttercup frowns with wide venomous eyes.

"Chill. Girl, I got you." He begins digging through the black denim jeans he wears, revealing a thick wad of $100s. "Here's three grand. I told you the night we met at Broadway, I'd pay you anything to have my way with Hennessy. And you made it happen. Baby girl, you A-OK in my book."

Buttercup triumphantly puts the three grand into her bag with the rest of her and Takia's stolen funds. "Nice doin' business wit' you. I'm moving to LA in two days. Startin' a new life. If you're on the West Coast don't hesitate to contact me. One more thing. Pound her pussy hard. She's used to being smutted out." Buttercup laughs hastily before callously walking out of the room.

"I got your fine ass all to myself, Hennessy. And I'm gon' get all my money's worth outta your ass," he says, stripping nude, his throbbing and thick erection clearly on display.

"Tear her ass up, big man!"

"I got next!"

"I'm gonna spend an hour inside that pretty pussy!"

The friends excitedly gather around the open bedroom door, eagerly anticipating what comes next. The Eagles player pushes her frame back and mounts her, his immense frame against her small body. He roughly pushes inside of her, beginning rough intercourse while pounding her lifeless body. His friends move slowly into the bedroom, undressing from their own clothes one at a time.

The Next Afternoon

"Aahh, where am I?" Takia groans, struggling to open her eyes. An excruciating headache bursts through her forehead. Her entire body feels heavy and as weak as a newborn. Her mouth is dry, and lips are chapped as her 20/20 vision comes into focus. The familiar hotel room registers. "How long have I been here?" she says while rubbing her forehead. She slides to the edge of the bed, where the stabbing pain between her legs and vagina paralyze her in agonizing discomfort. She begins a frenzied scream. "What happened to me?" She throws back the sheets. The center of the bed is soaked in blood. She is horrified by all of the blood and jumps from the bed, falling from to the floor unable to stand. The soreness and pain between her thighs render her disabled. "No, not again," she cries, the terrifying realization of what happened sinking in. Flashbacks of the bachelor party and group of men whom she had been entertaining come fluttering back into her mind. She had been raped for the second time, her body violated again. Visions of her first rape by mafia men come to mind. *How could I put myself in a situation that this could happen? I thought I had everything under control. Buttercup wouldn't let anything happen to me! Where's Buttercup? Them dudes might have kidnapped her. They had to put some kind of drugs in our drinks. I hope she's not dead.* Takia cries hysterically.

Call Manny. She tells herself groggily, crawling on all fours to the nightstand and pulling the landline phone to the floor. She dials Manny's number before slamming it on the receiver. "I can't call Manny. He's gonna be pissed I lied to him. Not Michelle either. She'll go crazy. I don't want her relapsing again because of me." She says as she closes her eyes, letting out deep sobs laying on the stiff hotel carpeted floor. The pain of her vaginal rawness continues to grate. "They raped me," she screams, her voice cracking. "I need help. I feel like I'm gonna die." She begins frantically dialing a number. "Raven," she quivers. "These guys hurt me really bad. You and Maya have to come. I can't walk, I can't get up. The Sheraton Hotel by the airport. I feel drowsy. I know they drugged me with something. I need you and Mya right now! I feel like I'm dyin', Raven," she sobs before passing out again in shock.

"What room are you in? Takia, Takia, Takia," Raven screams through the receiver before she hears the dial tone.

Chapter 20

FAHEEM'S BETRAYAL

Black thinks he gonna cut me out of the operation after I put in all that fuckin' work helping him build this fuckin' empire. Protectin' his ass on the daily. He's shittin' on me for that hazel-eyed little bitch! She got his ass pussy-whipped. Faheem thinks to himself, pacing back and forth in the living room of his Upper Darby Barclay Square apartment, wearing a silk black Versace dress shirt covered in gold Medusa heads. He takes off his platinum and diamond Presidential Rolex, placing it on his custom-marble black-and-white living-room table while flopping down on his expensive and expansive red-leather couch. *That nigga supposed to be my brother. We been down since high school. I was the only one who was right by his side rumblin' when we got jumped by them Blumberg project niggas. It was more of them but I stood tall and got six niggas off him!*

Faheem reaches over to a small oval glass side table, grabbing a picture of him and Black at the Tyson-Holyfield fight at the MGM Grand in Vegas in '96, both dressed impeccably in red and money-green gator-skinned shoes and silk Versace shirts, both hungry 22-year-old certified North Philly hustlers.

FATALLY FLAWLESS

"When old-head Enrique died and the throne was up for grabs, I was the one bustin' clips out of my Desert Eagle. We started off dead-broke together, ridin' around in a beat-up 1988 Buick doin' stickups with a rusty .38 revolver, runnin' nick bags on the block, hopin' to reach a stack, and runnin' trains on hoes. Our motto was never catch feelings. We M.O.B, money over bitches. Now this nigga settin' up meetings with the connect in Miami without me. When we start doin' sneaky shit like that? Ha Black?" he yells at the color photo. His twisted face softens into a look of despair. His brotherhood included Black and their young gunner Khalid. It was that way for years. Black was the brains, Faheem the enforcer, and Khalid was their muscle. They went from ashy to classy together as a unit. Faheem has surpassed anyone in his family, the oldest and only boy of five siblings. His four younger sisters are his heart, living in their mother's dysfunctional house took a toll on young Fa.

He grew up fast. His money-hungry mother Wanda had big-money ambitions and get-rich schemes aplenty. Often she boosted from department stores, committed bank fraud, and bought expensive merchandise with bad checks. Wanda had a thirst for the finer things in life and pursued them by any means necessary. That resulted in her being arrested and spending multiple stints in various prisons, which left young Fa and his four sisters in the care of his grandmother Emma, or as they called her Emmy for short. She was a part-time barmaid at the Pleasures bar on Broad and Erie Avenue. A short and stout woman who drank heavy, but her saving grace is her beautiful face, with many saying that she resembles the actress Dianne Carroll. She has affairs with multiple men, most of them married, which her grandchildren call, Papa. These men would pull up in their shiny new Buicks or Cadillacs and give all of the kids dollar bills to buy candy from the corner store.

When Faheem was a young buck, he happily went to the store with food stamps and his grandmother's grocery list, But as he grew older, he hardened up, realizing that his family ain't have shit. They lived in a run-down row house that had second-hand furniture, and bedbug infested mattresses rested on the floor in the almost empty bedrooms. Most days there was barely enough food to fill their young bellies. Sometimes the heat would be off in the dead of winter or the electricity in the summer, casualties of the unpaid bills. Grandma Emmy would always call on one of her list of married men to get them out of a jam. But as Faheem grew older he began to see the stress and toll it was having on his dear grandmother. His mom would be released from jail, come home crying, hugging and kissing her kids, swearing that she was done with scheming and stealing. Promising that she would not leave them again. Like clockwork, she would be back up to her old ways in no time, linking up with her wild girlfriends committing felonies. Faheem and his sisters called her crime partners Aunt Stacy and Aunt Barbara. They bought them clothes and sneakers, took them to the movies whenever Wanda was in jail, and she in turn did the same for their children when they were incarcerated. This group of kids became their godbrothers and sisters. A bond that remains strong until this very day. They stuck together through thick and thin. Stacy's two sons Zakee and Troy are Faheem's best friends, brothers, and partners in crime since they could walk. And Aunt Tameka's two daughters, Mercedes and Myesha, were best friends and rumbling partners with his four sisters. When Fa hit thirteen, he had developed into a handsome young man.

He got his dick wet for the first time by fine-ass 16-year-old Spanish neighbor Maria. After busting his first nut, he felt like the man. Even till this day, he still bangs out Maria from time to time. His attitude changed as he grew into a teenager. Waiting on new sneakers was becoming a problem; he needed to get on some paper. Quick. He was the man of the house. By fourteen, he began rolling the streets without supervision. The hard North Philly streets that surrounded him were filled with boys his age playing basketball, listening to hip-hop, and slap-boxing. A rapid street style of boxing. Faheem had quick hands and gained a reputation for having a nice box game, knocking young cats on their back if they stepped to him. He has heart though, never backing down from anyone regardless of their size or if he was outnumbered. The older neighborhood hustlers, Dice and Jim-Jim, big-time drug dealers from Susquehanna and Dauphin Street who drove Porsche 911s and fresh 5.0 Mustangs. They wore flashy jewelry and fucked the baddest women. They took notice of young Faheem and took him under their wing. Paying him a few hundred dollars a week to bag up and fill bags with potent marijuana.

After he mastered that task, he moved up to serving fiends in a deserted back alley of a run-down row house on 23rd and Hollywood Street. By the time young Faheem entered Benjamin Franklin High School in the fall of 1989, he was fresh to death, sporting Sergio Tacchini tracksuits, Pelle Pelle leather jackets, colorful Polo rugby shirts, and multicolored Gucci sneakers from the Atlantic City Gucci store. That was where all of the get-money hustlers copped their designer wear. A hightop-fade haircut lay freshly atop his head. He had grown in height to 6'2" with a basketball player's frame, smooth chestnut-brown skin, kissable full lips, and thick eyebrows. He quickly caught the eyes of the pretty freshmen girls in his class. His attraction extended to the sophomore and junior girls. He was the most fly out of his ninth-grade advisory. That lasted until for months, but that soon changed when a transfer from Simon Gratz High School showed up in a black leather-fringed jacket, rocking a thick gold herringbone chain around his neck, and wearing a shiny two-finger gold ring on his left hand. His fresh black Guccis and a wavy-Gumby haircut like Bobby Brown made him stand out amongst the other students.

The obese advisory teacher, Mr. Handy, announced to the class, "We have a new student starting today, Carmello Samuels." He stood there, eyes grilling and cocky, skin darker than midnight, but the asymmetrical shape of his cheekbones and nose gave his face an almost pretty-boy look. Beyond the handsome face though, was the cold roughness that evident in his demeanor. An air of superiority hovered around him. "Please, take a seat," Mr. Handy directed in his high tenor voice at a time when dark-skinned brothers were not in style. Young Carmello stood out indeed. Girls whom Faheem had crushes on stayed jocking Carmello. Broad, sturdy shoulders and slightly bowed legs gave him the natural muscular frame of a football player. He stood 5'11" in height, and young Faheem immediately felt he was competition. It was underlying rivalry and inferiority upon his first encounter with young Carmello Samuels. Faheem saw the charisma, cunning, and intellect within Carmello that would be a key component of their rise to power.

Their rise to power ten years later quickly led to a friendship that naturally grew into a close brotherhood that would define a decade of their young lives: creepy, co-dependent business and personal relationship that grew more volatile with each day. *I'm tired of being treated like I'm a fuckin' flunky! This shit gonna be deaded.* Faheem foams, pulling back the back cotton Egyptian sheets on his king-sized brass bed. He flops down, throwing his Versace shirt onto the floor like a five-dollar Hanes undershirt. With frustration brewing in his belly, he drifts off to sleep. The next morning, Faheem awakes with a pounding hangover. He begins his daily routine with a long hot shower and popping three Advils to ease his inevitable headache. As the steaming water rushes over his body, paranoia actively lurks in his mind regarding his second-in-command position in Black's organization, a group that he helped build with blood, sweat, and bullets.

He dries off, throws on a navy-blue Nautica sweatsuit and a pair of black number thirteen Jordans. He hits the first-floor gym of his apartment building, where he throws his anger into long rounds of heavy weightlifting, pushups, and cardio. After an hour of an intensive workout, he returns to his apartment, showering all over again and spraying an overload of Dolce & Gabbana over his body. He walks over to his large closet, a white cotton towel wrapped around his firm waistline, and pops the tag on a brand-new caramel-brown Moschino t-shirt, with Moschino sewn-in white nylon letters. He slides on a pair of fresh dark-blue pencil-pocket Guess jeans. He removes his black chukka Timberland boots from the box, and, lastly, his snaps his gold Presidential diamond Rolex on his wrist. He takes one last conceited look into his bedroom mirror, grabs his car keys before walking out of his apartment. His champagne-colored 1997 Acura Legend coupe sits waiting for him in the afternoon sunshine. He affectionately calls his car Penny after his boyhood crush on Janet Jackson's character on the '70s sitcom *Good Times.*

Penny makes him beam with joy: plush dark-tan leather interior, spotless cherry-wood dashboard, custom chrome rims, and six-disc CD changer. He starts her to the sound of a perfectly purring engine, and plays around with the stereo for a moment before *Love For Gillie* by Gillie Da Kid begins playing through an obnoxiously loud sound system. The bright June sun is blaring down. He reaches into his glove compartment, placing a new pair of gold Cartier shades on his face.

Faheem likes flashy things and spends plenty of stacks on high-priced items. He takes great pride in his appearance, one of the few things that he learned from his mother that stuck with him. He believes having the finer things in life is worth the risk. He cruises through Upper Darby, pulling into the IHOP on 69th Street where he eats breakfast several times a week. The older blonde waitress, Karen, always greets him with a warm smile and kind blue eyes. She had to be about 50 years old, but still has a good shape and great legs. Faheem has a few fantasies about dicking her head down. She makes sure that his turkey bacon and scrambled eggs with cheese are always fresh. In return, he religiously leaves $100 tips on the table.

He heads up toward North Philly, pulling off a tight little block at 30th and Myrtlewood Street. "Yo I'm outside your aunt's crib," Faheem says into his black Nokia cell phone. A moment later, a busty girl wearing a white halter top barely holding her large breasts in and black spandex shorts so tight her camel-toe is bulging. Her platinum-blonde wig crowns her seductive face, as she appears in the doorway. "What's up, Kamisha?" Faheem greets with a cheeky smile at his well-built passenger. "Nothin' much, chillin' Fah. So what's up? Why do you need to see me so bad?"

"I need a favor," Kamisha says, licking her full bottom lip.

"Oh really, what's that?"

"I need $500 for summer school so I can get my diploma from Dobbins."

"Kamisha, ain't you like twenty? You ain't graduate yet?" Faheem chuckles.

"First of all, I'm nineteen Faheem. No, I had to stop goin' to school when I had my son. I only need two credits. The classes are $250 apiece. Can you give me the money?"

"Sure. But you know what you gotta do for it," Faheem says slyly.

"Yeah, I know what I gotta do," she chuckles.

Faheem turns into a back alley filled with abandoned garages. He reclines his driver seat all the way back. Kamisha leans over and unbuttons his pants, pulling out his thick curved penis. She gently kisses the brown tip while massaging his hairy balls. Without warning, she swallows his dick like a python around its prey, sucking and gagging on it with a crazed speed.

"Damn, girl, slow down," Faheem moans while sliding two fingers into her moist vagina inside her shorts.

Kameesha begins sliding her hands up and down his immense dick, back and forth, using her spit as lubrication, using her tongue and jaws like a tight rubber band. Fifteen steaming minutes passed before Faheem's toes curled inside his Timberland boots.

"Fuck, fuck," he shouts, as the wave of semen fills her mouth.

She continues sucking away until he literally cannot take any more. He pushes her off.

"Goddamn, Mish, I swear you're the best, yo. I wish I could marry your mouth."

He laughs, peels of six one-hundred dollar bills, placing them with an extra hundred, for a well-earned tip.

"Thank you, daddy," she says victoriously, hopping out of the passenger side.

Faheem watches her slowly wiggle her curvy ass into her aunt's house. His mind quickly turns back to business, driving quickly to the underworld lair, one of Carmello Black's secret warehouses. The center of his drug empire, hidden in a cluster of abandoned factories under twenty-four-hour surveillance. Faheem does the coded door knock. The metal slit opens and two menacing brown eyes peer at him. The large metal-secured door opens and eight large Pit Bulls that guard the entrance to the den stand at alert attention as their keen ears hear his approaching footsteps. But the dogs become coy and playful as he comes into their full view.

"Beretta, Uzi, Cannon, Smith, and Wesson," he says tenderly, each affectionately named after firearms.

He enters a code into a keypad built into the wall. The black iron door quickly opens. It always amazes Faheem watching the door fly open, reminding him of some space-aged Star Trek shit. He enters the den. Dozens of worker bees, as he and Black call then, men and women stripped down to their underwear, fill thousands of crack vials with their precious product. The den is run like a precise business, efficiently like any other factory in America, except their product is a little bit more potent.

Faheem's presence insights immediate fear. If any worker bee is slacking, he will not hesitate to put his foot in their ass.

"Yo, it's the first of the month, you motherfuckers better put some pep in y'all step. Fiends been waitin' to be served. We got money to stack. Khalid growls, waving a black TEC-9 wildly at the frightened workers who begin scrambling, working at a more rapid speed.

Khalid, or as Black and Faheem, refer to him, as the young gunner is America's worst nightmare. He is a young, black, and cold-blooded killer. He is a 20-year-old shooter that Black took under his wing after his crack-addicted mother left him in a roach-infested, run-down row house with no heat or running water in the middle of a freezing winter.

Faheem took a liking to Khalid. He reminded him of himself when he was a young buck. He is blindly loyal and will kill anyone who gets in Faheem's or Black's way. He was initiated when he was seventeen, put to the test when carrying out a drive-by on 18th and York Street. Sabir Muhammad, a mid-level hustler with a lot of mouth, wanted to build his rep by robbing one of Black's corner boys.

Sabir takes $3,000 in cash. Black and Faheem are fuming. Khalid was eager to pull the trigger and prove himself. Faheem and Khalid crept up on Sabir and his crew in early July 1994 in a tinted black Jeep Cherokee. Khalid cracks the rear passenger window and sprays up the sidewalk in a hail of bullets. When the smoke clears, a pool of blood stained the concrete. Sabir was laid out dead with two shots to the head. Another nigga named Tone is left paralyzed from the waist down. That is how Khalid got the name 'young gunner.' He earned his stripes and became one of Black's and Faheem's most trusted henchmen. And he has shed more blood and taken out more men since then. Murder 101 was one class that he passed with a bloody A-plus.

"Yo Fah," Khalid says, his voice booming, a wide grin on his dark-brown face. A fresh green white and orange short-sleeved Coogi fits him well. A platinum and diamond cross proudly hangs around his neck. A row of waves crowns his freshly shaped-up head.

"Yo, Lid," Faheem addresses him as the two shake hands. "How's the output lookin'?"

"It's cool, it's time to distribute product to the corner boys and row houses. We can't keep enough product in there. But I'm on top of it. I got Turk and Sayeed makin' runs, deliverin' product, and collectin' money."

"My man. That's what I'm talkin' about. You stay on top of shit." Faheem grins, patting Khalid on the back.

"I'm just holdin' my niggas down," Khalid owns, like a student receiving praise from his favorite teacher. Is Black around?" Faheem asks.

"No, OG ain't been here yet." I'll be in the office if you need me."

"Aight. It ain't no lunch break. Back to work," Khalid screams at the worker bees.

Faheem walks down a hallway into the back office and flicks on the light. Carmello's large marble round desk sits cold and ominous. Several security cameras show all that is happening within the underworld. Faheem pulls out the custom black leather and mahogany armchair from behind the desk, flops down, puts his feet up on the desk, and folds his arms across his Moschino t-shirt. He lets out a sigh.

"I could get used to this. Maybe it's time for a new king." His brown eyes open in wide astonishment at this revelation into his mind. "Maybe it's time for a new king," he whispers again. "Black is gettin' soft. He's reigned long enough. Young Fah, underworld king. I like the sound of that." A sinister grin appears on his face, his thick dark eyebrows arched. He spins around widely in the chair, laughing like a scavenging hyena. The look of a brewing Judas betrayal eradiates from his sinister grin.

Chapter 21

MYA: NO WAY OUT

June 29, 1998

"Ladies and gentlemen, we will be landing at Miami International Airport in twenty minutes. The local time is 11:30 a.m. The weather is a sunny eighty-eight degree. Thank you for flying with Delta Airlines. Prepare for landing and please keep your seatbelts fastened. Enjoy your stay in beautiful Miami." The giddy flight attendant's voice says over the intercom system. Mya is ecstatic: her first trip to Miami on vacation with her man. This was Black's graduation present to her along with along with a pair of three-carat flawless round diamond earrings. She is used to flying, having attended many vacations with her parents: Barcelona, London, Paris, Jamaica, and Hawaii, among others. Mya Campbell's passport has plenty of stamps on it. But this is her first adventure into womanhood. Once they land, the passengers are grabbing their overhead luggage. Black takes hold of their two Louis Vuitton luggage bags as they stand in the aisle impatiently waiting for the crowd to move. Mya smirks while observing him. *Ain't no nigga like the one I got,* she thinks, adjusting the large turquoise-colored oval-shaped Gucci shades. Black looks delectable to her. His frame looks perfect in the white Versace shirt he wears, biceps busting out from the sleeves. White Ralph Lauren pants nicely fit his firm ass. His white gold Presidential Rolex hangs on his left wrist. Just watching him delights her.

"Come on, babe," he says nodding at Mya. She slowly slides from her window seat, looking magnificent. A black Dolce & Gabbana halter top and white miniskirt are topped off by black four-inch open-toed D&G mule sandals. D&G bold-patterned letters are written across the front. They slowly walk through the plane's rows.

"Enjoy your vacation," the bleached-blonde flight attendant says smiling at them.

Black and Mya walk through MIA along with travelers throughout the world rushing to and from flights. They exit at the arrivals gate and the air feels refreshing against their skin. A young Spanish man in his late twenties holds up a sign that says "Mr. Carmello Samuels" in front of a red Bentley Azure. Mya beams with delight. Black cannot help but cop a smile knowing that he keeps his girl impressed at all times.

"I'm Mr. Samuels," Black addresses the driver.

"Hello, sir. I'm José your driver. Let me take your bags," José says in a thick Cuban accent, with his dark tan a marker of his island people. Once he loads the luggage in the trunk, he opens the back passenger door. Black and Mya load into the plush Bentley. Mya had never been inside one before, just had seen them in flashy hip-hop music videos. This is some next-level shit in her book; Black has certainly set the tone for their trip in the right way. She rolls down the window, letting the intoxicating breeze hit her, gusts of wind blowing through her long dark hair. The sun is laminating while palm trees whip passed them as they coast down the highway.

"This is paradise on fucking earth," Mya says with wide hazel eyes. Black chuckles.

"Baby this ain't nothin'. We got five days of lounging in nothin' but luxury."

They cruise gently down the Palmetto Expressway. Ten minutes later, José gets off at the South Beach exit. The sophisticated ambiance gets Mya going. They hit Collins Avenue, with their rows of Art Deco boutique hotels and well-dressed people eating at chic sidewalk cafés sipping martinis behind large tennis shades. Bikini-clad girls hold onto tan muscular guys on mopeds zooming by them. Porsches and Lamborghinis fly by like Pathfinders back in Philly.

"Here we are, the Delano South Beach hotel, 1685 Collins Avenue," José says happy pulling into its main-entrance pathway. The immense white hotel is classic and modern all at once, with an enclave of palm trees giving shade to arriving guests. A young Cuban bellman with darker skin than José opens the rear passenger door.

"Welcome to the Delano," he says in almost inaudible English. They exit the Bentley and stroll into the impeccable all-white lobby. Spotless waxed marble floors and Art Deco styled sofas and armchairs grace the lobby. While fresh orchids sit in polished crystal vases around the front desk where two attractive women in dark-blue uniforms await them with warm Colgate smiles. Both dark brunettes have their hair pulled back in tight buns to display their beautiful faces.

"Welcome to the Delano," they greet in lush exotic accents that Mya could not place.

"Reservations for Mr. Samuels," Black says while pulling out his driver's license and platinum American Express card.

After a few moments, one of the brunette attendants does some light typing and Black is soon handed the key to Suite 1025. A chipper white bellhop in his mid-twenties carries their bags and leads them onto the elevator. The doors open onto the tenth floor to wide hallways with crystal chandeliers. And more marble floors so clean that one could eat off of them.

"Enjoy your stay," the bellman says joyfully, opening the door to their master suite overlooking the Atlantic Ocean. From drapes of fine white lace, the breathtaking skyline is revealed as Mya rushes out onto the open balcony. The smell of the ocean and beauty of waves splash against each other. Dozens of bodies line the beach in relaxed harmony.

God outdid himself with this paradise, Mya thinks as she is absolutely blown away.

"You're impressed I see," Carmello whispers in her ear stepping behind her, engulfing her in his arms.

She bites down on her bottom lip, feeling his erect penis against her ass. She instantly becomes wet, winding her hips back and forth against him. His tongue begins moving up and down on the back of her neck. She closes her eyes, moaning gently. Carmello's hand reaches under her skirt and he moves her panties to the side, sliding his right middle and index fingers inside her wet pussy. She is now completely enraptured, her body tingling. Black rubs and teases her clit before dropping to his knees and ripping her panties off. The open-air breeze glides over her naked genitalia. He squeezes and slaps her ass and she lets out a playful cry. Black begins putting his tongue around the right side of her vagina, sucking and planting kisses as her wetness fills his mouth. Mya grabs the balcony's rail as Black's tongue slides to the crack of her ass. He sucks on her clit from behind as Mya stands bent over, knees buckling. In his own lustful fury, Black reaches into his linen pants and grabs his throbbing dick while still sucking every part of Mya's womanly anatomy, teasing her thighs in slow massaging strokes with his strong hands. He stands to his feet, grabbing her breasts while licking her earlobes and neck. Mya bites down on the inside of her cheeks. Black slowly enters her from behind and holds her by her hips. Mya grabs the balcony railings tighter as she buckles from the pressure of Black's pounding, opening her walls with force.

"Fuck me, fuck me, fuck me, Black!" she yells.

He lets out a deep groan, sweat dripping from his brow. He grips her hair as she fills the orgasm building deep inside.

"Fuck, fuck," she shouts, as she comes, exploding, hot liquid running down her legs.

"I'm about to nut," Black swoons before shooting a thick load of semen inside of Mya.

Both sticky and hot, they retreat to the white marble bathroom, stripping what remains to take a joint shower, washing each other's back with vanilla opal soap. They dry off with the softest of towels, slipping on tan Egyptian cotton robes. Black leads Mya into the master bedroom, pulling back the white satin sheets of the king-sized bed. She collapses on his chest, both easily falling into deep slumber. The next few days roll by the with most blissful of tender moments ever shared between Mya and Black.

Miami is a great adventure that they explore with vigor. Black rents a medium-sized luxury yacht that takes them into the middle of the Atlantic. He had the crew set up jet skis. With life-jackets on, Black takes the wheel with Mya holding onto him fearfully, the crushing blue waves guiding them. At one sharp turn, Mya digs her head into Black's shoulder, thinking that they were about to flip over. But with calm finesse, Black avoids the misfortune with ease, going deeper and faster into the ocean, while Mya relishes her adrenaline.

Back on the yacht, they eat fresh lobster, oysters, and sea bass prepared by a local gourmet chef. Mya sits across from Black on a small white linen-clad table with fresh red roses in the table's center. She wears a pink-and-white Gucci two-piece bikini under the blazing sun beaming down. Black boasts about being a jet-ski expert from his many trips to Cancun and Miami. Mya feels like she is living larger than life. If this is the start of what her life with Black is going to be, she cannot wait to say, "I do." At the tender age of 18-years-old, she is making moves that old-head hoes a decade older could not comprehend. As the sun sets, they decide to go skinny dipping and make love in the Atlantic Ocean under the star-lit sky.

Mya is overwhelmed as she holds onto the yacht's ladder, with her legs wrapped around Black. As he drives his dick deeper into her, the ocean is their bed, and the moon and stars are their audience. The rawness of their bare natural sensuality makes her orgasm volcanic. The next day, they hit up the shops at Bal Harbour, Miami's to explore the designer boutiques and gaze at the large black marble waterfall filled with colorful exotic fish of all sizes. They begin blowing money like it grew on trees. Three thousand at Versace. Another four thousand at Gucci. And six thousand at Prada. Black lets Mya go bat-shit crazy in Chanel, dropping seven grand like it was Monopoly money. They have so many shopping bags the Bentley's trunk and back seat could barely contain them. Black takes her salsa dancing at Club Samba on Ocean Drive with its live Mariachi band. He spins her around, grabs her back into his arms, and holds her off balance. Yet she is always secure in his grasp. She stares into his dark brown eyes. All she wants or needs is him. They take pictures on the steps of the legendary Versace mansion and The Villa Casa Casuarina, where the iconic designer Gianni Versace was killed less than a year earlier.

On the fifth evening of their Miami adventure, Mya lay in the master suite half asleep, enjoying a cool breeze billowing from the open balcony where Black stands looking out over the night. The sounds of ocean waves crashing onto the shore sound so peaceful. His cell phone rings and Mya sits up in bed, eager to eavesdrop.

"Hector... hola amigo. Yeah, I'm enjoying Miami, but I'm ready to get down to business. I came down here with my eye on the prize. Dom Cartagena arrives tomorrow, at 9 p.m. The Palm Springs estate. Hector, chill out. I know how to be punctual," Black chuckles. "Tomorrow night then." Black ends the call.

Mya drops down as if she had been in uninterrupted sleep. Black enters the bedroom and drops his robe to the floor, snuggling up close to her. Mya's eyes are wide open in the dark. *We need to connect, prepare the last run, then the wedding day,* she thinks as Black caresses her back.

The next morning, they have an early breakfast on the balcony. She sips fresh-squeezed orange juice and looks at Black intensely through dark Fendi sunglasses. She can tell that he is deep in thought, unusually quiet and biting slowly on brown turkey sausage. He had several heated arguments with Faheem during phone conversations in hushed tones since 6:30 a.m. Those two were clashing more and more. Mya's mistrust of Faheem continues to grow. She views him as a conniving jealous snake who wants Black's throne. Whenever they were in the same space, Faheem's dark hateful eyes focused on her with alternating lust and open contempt. Mya had confronted Black several times about her suspicion of Faheem's shady behavior. He silently took note, like a sulking panther. He and Faheem's arguments were becoming more frequent. She could feel the power struggle brewing ever stronger each day.

"Why don't you just off that nigga? Put him in the dirt." She had dared to once ask Black while the two were having dinner at the Shark Bar in Manhattan. Carmello's dark brown eyes cut through her like an ax freshly cutting down a tree. His jaw clenched. He had never looked at her with such disgust. He hated her at that moment and she knew it. For the first time in their relationship, she was terrified of him.

"Why don't I just off him? Don't you never some bullshit like that to me ever again!" He says sternly from across their center booth, his fists pounding the table. The gold and onyx Movado watch clinking against his wrist. Fah done rolled with me until the wheels fell off. Been a loyal soldier. Put his life on the line for me many days. We been broke together and counted millions. You tell me to just kill my brother? Fah got some shit with him. He can be a real dickhead but I believe his loyalty to me is unbreakable. Killing him is not an option," Black says, taking a big gulp from the glass of chilled champagne in front of him. His sincere look turns into a solemn expression of doubt.

After that intense confrontation, Mya decided to keep her feelings about Faheem to herself. She would rather make love than war. Nonetheless, she knew in the back of her mind not to trust Faheem. As the day went on, she and Black visited the Delano's spa, getting deep-tissue body massages. Mya got a facial, mani, and a pedicure. They had lunch by the pool. Mya looks at her platinum Rolex. *It's 2:15 p.m, seven hours until the meeting with the connect*, is her thought. All Mya cares about is getting it over with so that she and Black can start their new life together. *8:15 p.m. on the dot,* Mya says to herself looking at the large white oval-shaped clock hanging on the wall in the spacious bathroom. Mindful of the time as she put the finishing touches on her look for the meeting, adjusting the spaghetti straps on her red Calvin Klein mini dress. An exact version that Cher wore in the 1995 hit movie, *Clueless.* Mya's four-inch Prada sandals made her vivid burgundy colored pedicured toes look edible. Her suntan-skin gleaming from Donna Karan skin moisturizer, as she flaunts her three-carat flawless diamond studs in her earlobes. Dark hair pulled into a bun off of her face, her hazel eyes are clear, and her confidence is at its peak.

"Babe, are you ready?" Carmello's baritone says, gently knocking on the bathroom door.

"Yes, here I come." She throws her black Nextel phone and a pack of Doublemint gum into a small red Caviar Chanel clutch. As she turns the knob to re-enter the suite, she locks eyes with Black, analyzing the perfection they continue to see in each other.

"You look like you stepped straight out of *Vogue Magazine,*" he says blissfully, staring with love in his eyes as if seeing her for the very first time. He makes Mya feel like a little girl. She blushes. *God, I'm in love with this perfect image of a man standing in front of me,* she thinks. If Carmello thinks that Mya is *Vogue*-worthy, then he is a *GQ* cover boy in a perfectly tailored and coordinated cream-linen shirt and pants. Gold lion head Versace buttons are sewn into the top pockets of his shirt. The freshly polished brown gator loafers on his feet, canary-diamond pinkie ring, and Rolex are impeccable on his right hand. A shiny deep wave spins on top of his head. His perfect bone structure and dark-chocolate skin is smooth absent of any bumps or blemishes. He looks every bit the leading man who arrived to save the girl in those romantic movies that Julia Roberts and Gwyneth Paltrow typically starred in. She wanted her to become a Kodak camera and capture this moment to remember Carmello just as he is.

"Come on, let's do this," he says, smirking. "We about to set ourselves up for the rest of our lives," he continues as his cell phone begins ringing deep inside his pants pocket. "Okay, we'll be right down, José."

He grabs the room key and heads out of the door, with Mya following behind. They enter the elevator. As the door closes they read each other's eyes.

I'm not a hustler's dream, I'm what he might be, Mya thinks looking at Black standing strong and powerful. Never in Mya's wildest dreams did she imagine playing her cards so well and finding the ace. So many other girls tried to lock down Black and had failed. But Mya is the lucky one. She is the girl that will be by his side, helping him count his riches being his wife, and part of his plans for world domination. She was never previously one to believe in fate, but she accepted whatever conspired to bring them together.

They step off the elevator as hotel guests and employees stop to stare at them as if two Hollywood stars wandered into their midst. Mya and Black ignore the attention, heads held high, walking with perfect posture.

I'm definitely that bitch, she thinks as Blacks holds open the hotel door. The Miami heat feels alluring.

"Good evening, sir and madam," José says while holding open the red Bentley door.

"This feels like prom night all over again," Mya whispers to Carmello.

The Best of Luther Vandross... The Best of Love plays softly over the radio as they drive into the dark Miami night. Black reaches to Mya's thigh as she leans her head on his firm right shoulder. She closes her eyes as Luther's *Here and Now* soothes her into a nap. Thirty minutes later, Black nudges her.

"Mya, wake up."

She sits up, her eyes slowly coming into focus. They sit outside an enormous mansion behind large black iron gates. Two dark-skinned guards in tailored black suits approach the car. Black rolls down the left rear window.

"Carmello Black. I'm here to see Dom Cartagena."

The guard peers into the car, his long black hair pulled into a tight ponytail and cold black eyes with two tatted teardrops under his left eye. He pulls out a gray cell phone.

"Okay, you have clearance," he says in hushed Spanish. "Antonio, open the gate," he yells to the other guard.

The tall iron gates with gold lines down the center slowly swing open. José drives through, turning down a winding road surrounded by lush well-trimmed gardens. The Spanish-style Mediterranean mansion comes into view.

This place makes my parents' house look like a damn shack, Mya thinks as José pulls up to the front of the house. A dark-brown marble and gold fountain sits in the center of the welcoming circle.

"Carmello, my friend, welcome to La Costa del Sol," says a short Spanish man with shoulder-length jet-black hair, oily skin, and soft feline features.

He's almost as pretty as me, Mya thinks, observing the beautiful stranger whom she had overheard on several phone conversations with Carmello. She had expected Hector to be a 6'5" hard-bodied goon. Instead, he looks like the pretty-boy male models in a glossy Calvin Klein underwear ad.

"Hector, my man," Black chuckles while getting out of the car. They embrace. "Hector, this is Mya. My woman," he beams. Hector turns to her, his soft-brown eyes covered by a flurry of long eyelashes.

"Senorita Bella," he says, taking Mya's right hand and gently kissing it.

She blushes instantly at Hector's display of charm.

"Carmello, you sly dog, where on earth did you find this rare beauty? Come on, let's go inside," Hector says, leading them up the shiny waxed gray-marble steps into the grand foyer. An enormous crystal chandelier hangs above them, lit like a miniature sun suspended in its own orbit. The opulent style of the mansion is breathtaking. It takes a lot to impress Mya Campbell; she is completely in awe. Large oil paintings in brass frames line the hallway. Louis XIV classical French furniture fills the room. Just as Mya takes in views of the luxury around her, a husky male voice calls to Carmello.

"It's been a very long time since our last face-to-face meeting."

Mya turns to see a large imposing man walking down the staircase wearing a red and black satin-trimmed smoking jacket in the style of Hugh Hefner. He has a well-trimmed tan Yorkie in his arms, salt-and-paper hair, and a beard perfectly trimmed. Flanked by two young guards dressed in black suits with Uzis strapped to their shoulders. He displays a hawkish look on his bronze-colored face.

"Dom Cartegena," Black says quickly as he goes to kiss his diamond-and-ruby pinkie ring.

Mya is stunned. This is the first time that she ever saw this, quickly taking a mental note that for every powerful man in the world, there is a man with yet more power than him.

"You look well, Carmello."

"Thanks Dom. Look at little Pepe," Carmello approached the Yorkie in Dom's arms attempting to pat him on the head. The small creature immediately begins barking, viciously trying to bite Black's hand. They all erupt into laughter, which echoes off the acoustic high ceilings.

"Take this as a small bit of advice, Carmello. The softest, most beautiful creatures can be lethal," Dom Cartegena says looking over at Mya with dark probing eyes. His stare makes her uncomfortable. "Come to my office. I know you didn't come to Florida to hear an old man speaking in riddles." They move down an open corridor. "How's business in Philadelphia?"

"Couldn't be a better product for my king to distribute," Mya responds.

Dom turns to Mya and smirks. "Gentlemen never discuss business in the presence of ladies. Hector, show this lovely one to my private drawing room. Have Conchita prepare beverages and hors d'oeuvres."

"Follow me, my dear," Hector says, standing beside her. She reluctantly moves, giving Black a hesitant stare.

"Go ahead, I won't be long," he says reassuringly, following Dom Cartegena down the corridor.

Hector escorts her to a drawing room draped in royal-blue satin curtains, plush suede sofas, and high-backed chairs. The porcelain statues of characters from Greek mythology, whom Mya recognizes from her English literature classes align the wall. Pan, the gold-leafed god of wild shepherds and flocks, Cupid, god of desire and erotic love, Venus, mother of Cupid and goddess of love, and Apollo, god of sun and light all sit around the room in glorious splendor.

A young maid in her mid-thirties comes in with a silver tray filled with small gourmet desserts: cheesecake, chocolate crumbles, and sorbet. It sat in front of Mya, who is too nervous to eat a thing. An hour and a half pass according to the oval-shaped brass clock hanging above the fireplace. She paces back and forth. *What the fuck is taking so long?* Midnight strikes as she hopes that nothing went wrong, and moments of terror pass through her body. Just as tears are beginning to form in her eyes, the doorknob turns, and Carmello walks in smiling.

"Babe, come on, we out." She throws her arms around him in a frantic manner.

"Whoa, slow down, Mya! What's wrong?"

She lets out a deep sigh of relief, refusing to let him go.

"It's okay, baby girl, it's okay," Black says while massaging her back and shoulders.

Part 2: Mya Has No Way Out

Black pulls his Navigator in front of Mya's house. The lawn is freshly cut, the looming June sun beaming over the Bala Cynwyd skyline. Mya feels sluggish from the 7 a.m. flight back to Philadelphia. But in reality, she could not have boarded the plane fast enough. Black's meeting with Dom Cartegena leaves her fearful and suspicious. He takes notice and tries to reassure her that she has nothing to worry about. He had been doing business with Dom and his crew for years.

"Back to the burbs," Black chuckles, grabbing a dozen bags from the back seat. *Money, Power & Respect* by the Lox featuring DMX and Lil' Kim starts to play as Mya exits from the passenger side into the glaring ninety-degree heat. Her black tube top is soaked with sweat and her tan Gucci shorts feel stuck to her skin. Which was a deep bronze from the Miami sun. Black follows her up the red brick path to the front door.

Bright pink roses line each side of the pathway. Mya searches through her black Prada shoulder bag for her house keys. Black drops her bags to the ground by her feet.

"Yo look at me," he commands, placing his hands on her shoulders. She peers into his ruggedly handsome face, his skin now the color of onyx from baking in the Florida sun. "You been actin' weird as shit since we left Dom Cartagena's. I told you to stop worrying! We straight. Hector is gonna fly into Northeast Philly Airport next week on a chartered plane with two million dollars worth of product. We give him cash and do an even exchange. I'm gonna flip the coke at a reduced price, flood the streets, and distribute the kilos all over the East Coast: New York, DC, VA, Boston, and Jersey. I'm gonna make so much fuckin' cash, you gonna be able to swim in it! I've already trademarked the name of my construction company: 'Samuels Custom Construction.' After I move the last of it, we'll be set. I'll be retired out of the game at twenty-five. You'll be on campus at La Salle and our new life will begin. I just need you to be strong. Don't play God with me. Mya, the finish line is straight ahead. Get focused."

Black stares into her eyes with extreme intensity. "I'm gonna ask you one last time, Mya. Are you a hundred percent down with me on this last run? If not, we can end everything right now. You can go ahead and live your life and keep playing a little rich girl from the 'hood. I don't need weak motherfuckers around me. My girl or not?" The cold bluntness of Black's tone tears through her.

She begins to tear up. "How could you ever say such shit to me, nigga?! I love your black ass more than I love my damn self! Ain't nothin' pussy about me. You should know that by now," Mya fumes, breaking out of his grasp. She turns to put her key in the dark cherry wood front door. Black's hard frown turns into a cocky smile.

"There's my soldier," he boasts. Mya's fire is back. With all the molding he had done with her mentally and physically, his kitten was now a lioness. He grabs her in a tight bear hug. She tries in vain to break out of his arms but it was impossible.

"Get the fuck off me! Let me go Black," she hollers. She stops fighting, both communicating with their eyes. Suddenly Black kisses her on the lips with a flurry of passionate wet kisses. Intense passion erupts inside of Mya.

"Yes, I'm down, baby, I'm down with you until death," salty tears staining her cheeks.

"Don't cry, Mya." Black's tone is now soft and soothing.

"I can't live without you, Carmello! You're my whole world."

Black wipes her tears away with his thumbs. "We gonna get through this. We a unit. Fuck the world. It's just us. You hear me?"

She nods her head yes. Black's cell phone starts ringing inside his royal-blue khaki shorts. "Khalid, I'm just getting back from the airport. You tellin' me the same issues are still happenin' from the time I left? Y'all niggas is like toddlers. Yo I'm not tyin' to hear that shit right now. I'm wit' my girl," Black says annoyed, wiping sweat from his brow.

Mya wants to escape to the sanctuary of the familiar landscape inside of her home. She is mentally drained and relieved when Black is in a rush to leave. They had been in each other's presence for six days straight and a break is needed. She loves herself from Black, but Mya is an only child and feels comforted in the silence of her own world. And after years of being left alone due to her parents' hectic work and travel schedules, she craves solitude. She watches Black speed off with the Navigator and enters her house. Nostalgia and a familiar sense of safeness rush over her. Looking at her parents' worldly possessions, the pink vases that line the entrance to the foyer, lovely custom-made furniture inspired by 1930s Hollywood give the living room an air of regality. Her mother had spared no expense making sure that their home is luxurious, a reflection of her social status. The dining room table is encrusted with marble and gold-plated inlays with tall silver candlestick holders strategically placed. A large oil painting of Mya with her parents done by a famous Rittenhouse Square artist hangs in a brass frame in the center of a wall. Black and gold Versace plates, forks, and knives adorn the table.

Mya drags her bags up the stairs, heavy with all of her new designer pieces. She collapses on her fuschia and pink satin-covered bed. She slips off her Gucci shorts, and the central air cools her body. She grabs the remote from the nightstand, turning to *Video Jukebox*, on channel sixty-five. Will Smith's new *Miami* video was playing. Mya is feeling the song and loves the video, especially since she was just down there living in a dream. Before the next video plays, she hits mute on the remote, dropping her head onto the soft cool pillows.

Part 3: Are You Still Down?

It is exactly 5 p.m. when Black and Mya reach the underworld. The immense warehouse, the heart of Black's drug empire. It is only two days away from the big exchange with Hector. Black is making all of the necessary arrangements for the meeting. He becomes wary and distrusts every person in his organization, including his right-hand man Faheem. Things between

Black and Faheem had not been the same for months. Mya knew eventually shit would blow up between them...it was only a matter of time. The late afternoon sun is tiger-orange in color. The muggy heat is deplorable. Mya is becoming immune to it. She wears a white tube top, black fitted Guess jean shorts, and black Chanel cat-eye sunglasses bedazzled with the letters written in shiny crystals. Her hair is in a messy side ponytail. She gets out of Black's Mercedes and senses a tense restlessness in Black the closer the time approached the meeting with Hector. He looks like a panther waiting for a fight with another predator. The dark red Moschino t-shirt fits him perfectly. He uses the secret underworld code to gain entry. Mya is always astonished by the deft vastness of his operation. The flesh-eating Pit Bulls trained to kill on sight once terrified her, and now greet her like puppies, panting, and wanting to be petted.

Dozens upon dozens of men and women are wearing only undergarments, filling crack vials by the hundreds with the product to be distributed. Black's operation is like any professional business. Crack houses are given a certain amount of product. Every rock is counted and calculated. Ledgers are kept with accounts of each of the houses' inventory. A profit and loss statement is drafted detailing the numbers down to the penny. In case of shortage of cash or product, house managers, as Black calls them, would be responsible. There was not any room for error. Any mistakes resulted in the house manager and the workers would be fined. A second offense guaranteed a beating. And if anyone dared to fuck up the accounts again, they could find their wig pushed back.

They walk into the center of the underworld and their presence is immediately sensed. Workers stop their robotic assembly-line frenzy of filling an endless overflow of small, clear crack vials. Staring at them with interest, brown and black eyes under white surgical masks, they are back to work with a heightened vigor. Three medium-brown-skinned men in their early thirties stand guard over the room. They are holding Black's semiautomatic weapons on their shoulders, each positioned at the warehouse's three fire exits. They display cold and uncaring grimaces on their faces. The voice of Khalid, Black's young gunner, bounces off of the warehouse walls.

"Yo, it's the first of the month. Y'all motherfuckers movin' slow as shit! Put some pep in your step. All our corner boys meet at re-up. I bet if I bust a cap in one of you motherfuckers, you assholes will start workin' faster."

Carmello pauses, chuckling. He always finds Khalid's brutal animalistic behavior intriguing. He has no home training or couth. His imposing six-foot stocky build carries a small bead of sweat on his camel-brown face. The bright pink, orange and aqua-green short-sleeved Coogi sweater fits him nicely. Black calls him America's worst nightmare; young, black, and ready to kill. Mya likes Khalid, one of the most ghetto niggas she had ever met. His crude unapologetic sense of humor leaves her laughing in tears. He is simple with no manners. Even when speaking in a vulgar manner, he has no clue that he is offensive. He begins waving the black Uzi in his hand wildly at a worker, his blackened lips turned up as if he smells a pile of shit.

"Fuck you, punk ass! Time is money. Start baggin' up faster," Khalid seethes, spit flying out of his mouth. The small man shrinks back in fear.

"Yo, Lid, chill. Don't hurt him. We need them to be comfortable doing their jobs." Black laughs, lowering the Uzi with the two of his right fingers. At the sight of Black, Khalid becomes demur and calm. He goes from a deranged killer to a son overjoyed at the presence of his father.

"Yo, B, when you get here?"

"I been here a minute in the cut watching you."

Khalid's total dedication to Black is his most endearing quality to Mya. He would die for Black, no questions asked.

"New inventory been hittin' the blocks like clockwork. Samir and Hasan been doin' drop-offs and collectin' money all day.

Where Faheem?" Black asks abruptly.

"In the back office going over the accounts with Aunt Tameeka."

"I need to holler at him," Black says sternly. "That's a wild little nigga," he smirks to Mya, who follows behind him to his office in the rear of the warehouse. Aunt Tameek and Faheem are seated counting thousands of dollars, dividing the denomination of bills into hundreds, fifties, twenties, tens, and five-dollar bills. Some of the cash is crisp and new, while the other bills are wrinkled, dirty, and faded. No matter what, cash is king. Aunt Tameeka runs stacks of money through a gray electric money counter. Faheem would quickly wrap a rubber band around a fixed wad of money, throwing it into a pile, so that every ten thousand dollar stack is separated.

"Nephew, my love, welcome back," Aunt Tameeka giggles, her hand rapidly moving money into the counter. Her dark skin, is shiny, and well-moisturized; barely looking her age. The red, green, and black African tribal gown with matching head wrap look magnificent on her.

"Yo Black," Faheem says, barely lifting his head from his task, cutting his eye at Mya in a shady twist of his face that only she could catch. A mean expression is forming on his brown face.

Fuck your bitch ass, Mya thinks while going over to greet Aunt Tameeka with a big hug.

"Hey beautiful," Aunt Tameeka says, kissing Mya on the cheek. "This week has been flowing with payroll, supplies, product re-up, and utility payments on all of the properties. The grand total is $89,000."

A clever smile appears on her face, adding numbers on her large industrial calculator.

"That's good shit," Black laughs while running his hands over the piles of neatly organized money.

Just seven days of work hitting the street—Mya's pussy gets wet thinking about all of that profit.

"I gotta get home and get dinner on the stove. Your cousins turn into wild animals when they're hungry. Here are the expense reports and receipts. In about six months it's going to be time to file your 1998 business taxes," Aunt Tameeka says rapidly, gathering her things.

"Auntie, you the best," Black says, kissing her on the cheek as she walks past him to leave.

"Good night everyone." She says as she exits the door.

"Don't forget to put me up a plate. Your cooking is the best," Faheem says, a smile finally returning to his face.

"Start bagging this money up," Black directs Mya, handing her a small duffel bag from the closet. She goes to work, throwing the cash into the bag, filling it so much that it is impossible to zip close.

"Fah, what been up my nigga? You been radio silent," Black snickers, adjusting the bezel of his gold Presidential Rolex.

Faheem sucks his teeth. "I been a good soldier holdin' the underworld down, makin' sure business is gettin' handled while you been on vacation laid up on the beach. Must be nice, B," Faheem says sarcastically.

Black's dark eyes are squarely transfixed on Faheem. Mya watches intensely.

"Faheem, when you sit at the head of the table and feed everybody, makin' sure every nigga in your faculty eats, you have the perks of deciding when and where your presence is needed. But you wouldn't know about being the head of shit," Black laughs condescendingly, picking up the duffel bag up off of the floor. "I gotta run to make. I'll get wit' you later, Fah."

"Black, I need to talk to you about somethin' that's been on my mind before you roll out."

"Take this bag and wait for me in the car." Mya obediently shakes her head yes, taking the heavy duffel bag. She has to hold it with both her hands. *Man, this bag is heavy as shit*, she thinks, walking out of the room. Her gut instinct is telling her to stay put and ear-hustle. She listens very closely.

"Fah, wassup? I ain't got all day." Black's smooth dark face fills with annoyance. Faheem stands to his feet, his six-foot-two stature overshadowing Carmello at six feet even. Cold disdain flashes in his eyes. "Wassup at the Colombian situation? Word got back to me about the secret meeting you had down in Miami that I somehow wasn't invited to. Look, Fah, honestly, I'm thinking about taking things in another direction."

"What direction is that? When you start makin' major decisions without including me?" Faheem's nostrils flare.

"Nigga, discussing decisions with you?" Black's face twists in a dangerous frown. "I might ask your opinion on things, but the last time I checked I built this empire."

"And I done put in a lotta work, too, Black," Faheem spits back while waving his hands back and forth. "All the grindin' I did seems to have been forgotten along the way."

"Fah, I ain't tryin' to hear that shit," Black smacks, flagging Faheem with his backhand. "Fah, I look at you as my brother. But don't you ever question me about moves I decide to make concerning my business. I *am* the underworld! You hear me?"

Faheem's jaw clenches, a look of utter disgust on his brown-skinned face. "B, I'm just keepin' it real wit' you. Lately, you been slippin'. I know you in love with that pretty little bitch or whatever, but we got way too much paper at stake."

"What you just call her?" Black fumes.

"A bitch," Faheem says nonchalantly. "We know all these bitches out here are the same."

Black reaches for his 9mm tucked in the back of his jeans, grabbing Faheem by the collar of his gray Iceberg t-shirt, slamming the gun to his temple. "Nigga, don't you ever disrespect my girl again! You gettin' beside yourself. You think you big enough to fill my shoes?" Black yells in his face. "You can never be Carmello Black. You hear me?!"

Faheem grunts in pain from the hard metal gun slapping him on the side of the head. "Yo, B chill. Put the gun down," Faheem whimpers. "It's me, Faheem, the same nigga that was by your side gettin' rolled on by ten motherfuckers at Franklin. When we went to war with them Blumberg niggas, I was the first one bustin' my gun to make you king. How could you ever question my loyalty?" Faheem speaks in a broken tone on the verge of tears.

"That's all good, Fah. But there's only one hip nigga in charge here! I'm me not Nino Brown," Black shouts in Faheem's ear, referencing Wesley Snipes' character from *New Jack City.* "My brain and hustle is what made this business grow!"

Mya places her hand over her mouth, shaking with fear. She backs away from the office door, not wanting to be caught witnessing the explosive situation between them. So she quickly heads for the car but bumps into young gunner in the process.

"Where you sneakin' off to?" Khalid asks her while eating a butterscotch Krimpet, his Uzi dangling over his right shoulder. She ignores him, feeling unsafe until she is back inside Black's Mercedes.

Mya pulls down the passenger overhead mirror, hazel eyes wide full of fearful disdain. *Bitch, what did you get yourself into? Mya, you're trapped inside the devil's triangle. You in so deep, and there's no way out.* Her thoughts are quickly interrupted by Black opening the driver's side door. He says nothing, but slams his fists with rage on the leather steering wheel.

"Babe, what's wrong?" she sits up and asks Black in a faint whimper.

"Nothing you have to worry about. Change is coming down the pipeline. A big one," Black says cryptically. "I'm starvin'. Let's go eat," he announces. " I gotta get the fuck outta here." He starts the car and moves so quickly that Mya is thrown back into her seat. She cuts her hazel eyes at him; he is so focused on his thoughts that she sits in silence not wanting to bother him. As they drive through North Philly she glances at the run-down abandoned row houses and crackheads getting high in playgrounds, with graffiti-splattered walls. Groups of shirtless boys play basketball on crowded courts that have rims without the nets attached. Foreign cars pull up on pretty, well-dressed women sitting on the steps of Richard Allen housing projects.

Mya takes in the moving motion picture that is North Philly. West Philly is known for fly girls, South Philly is known for boosters and credit-card scammers, Uptown is known for pretty boys in nice houses, but North Philly is the pulse of the city. Black continues to ignore Mya as she passes the silence between them with Mary J Blige's *Share My World* album. *I Can Love You* blares out of the perfect sound system.

Days later, Black gives Mya a sexy grin as he pulls up to the valet at Ruth's Chris Steak House. He has a hearty appetite, and ordered a well-done quarter steak, fresh asparagus, mashed potatoes, and lobster bisque. In contrast to Mya who picks over her grilled salmon.

"Stop tryin' to be cute," Black chuckles while chewing on a big chunk of his steak.

"Actually, I don't have an appetite," she smiles while feeling their chemistry return for the first time in days.

"I know I've been aggressive and distant lately, but things are about to change. The monkey shit that's been happening has left a bad taste in my mouth."

"More trouble with Faheem?" Mya blurts out eagerly.

His dark eyes move over her with cunning delight as if he had known that she was listening outside his office door during that confrontation.

"Fah has changed, or maybe we drifted apart. The outlook you have at fifteen changes at twenty-four. What that nigga Nas say, "Best friends become strangers." I feel that shit happenin' before my eyes." Black's voice drops, his eyes lowered and a group of sadness on his dark face. "Cheers to my day-one nigga, my brother Faheem," Black laughs with a slight sense of pain in his voice. For a split second, Mya thought that she saw tears within his eyes. The entire time that she had been his girl, she never saw him this vulnerable. He has only been strong, and measured. Within seconds his tears rescind and his eyes turn cold and unforgiving.

"Cheers to you, Fah," Black raises his champagne glass from the white linen table.

Mya watches in wonder. *What does that gesture symbolize,* she questions herself. After dinner they drive down the New Jersey Turnpike to Black's Maplewood condo. He drives with reckless abandon, waving his Mercedes in and out of traffic, and almost causing several accidents. Drivers honk their horns in panic.

Black couldn't give two shits. Tupac's *All Eyez on Me* blasts on the stereo.

He's about to snap, Mya thinks, watching the lanes of traffic flashing past them.

They arrive at Black's complex and the elevator ride takes an eternity. He turns the key to his condo door and they move through the pitch-black living room into Carmello's bedroom. Black presses on the remote, to close the drapes that are controlled by his state-of-the-art system. The bathroom door opens, and a blanket of steam flows into the bedroom. Mya sits down on the four-poster bed clad with fresh satin sheets. A large movie poster with Al Pacino in *Carlito's Way* hangs above the bed. She kicks off her Chanel flats, grabs the remote off of the black marble dresser, and turns on Carmello's fifty-two inch Panasonic television. She settles on an episode of *Real World Seattle.* Fifteen minutes later, the bathroom door swings open and Carmello comes in wearing only a brown towel, his face and eyes blank, and unreadable.

Mya hops up to take her hot shower to clear her mind. After she is dried off and freshly moisturized, she joins Black in bed. They wrap their arms around one another in a cocoon of love, drifting soundly to sleep.

A few hours later, Mya is jolted awake by voices in the living room. She sits up and grabs her senses, trying to make out the muffled voices coming from the living room. The bedroom door is cracked open, illuminating the otherwise dark room. *Bitch, just lay down and mind your own business! No, fuck that,* she thinks and jumps out of bed, tiptoeing over to the cracked door. Khalid's image sitting on Black's living room sofa comes into focus in Mya's squinting eyes.

Black paces back and forth wearing his dark-burgundy Versace bathrobe and slippers.

"Damn Black. What's so important that I had to rush up here? It's 5 a.m. I was chillin' with this bad little bitch. She was givin' me some serious head," Khalid laughs.

"I told you, stop being so pussy whipped. This conversation won't be long. Then you can get back to the pussy."

"So what's the big emergency," Khalid asks.

Carmello pauses standing directly in front of him, covering Mya's view. She can only see Carmello's back.

"Khalid, you was what thirteen or fourteen when I met you?

"I was fourteen, B."

"Damn, you sure was fourteen, looking pitiful as shit locked outside your crib in the freezing cold."

"My mom left the crib, no food, the heat was off, and she was high as shit in a crack house somewhere. I was crying like a little bitch when you pulled up. And you said, 'Young boah, what's wrong? Take this ride with me."

"You took me to your nice-ass apartment on City Line Avenue. You fed me, gave me some clean clothes, taught me how to be a man, and stand on my own two. B, I'll never forget what you did for me."

"I'm glad to hear that you ain't forget those things. I've always told you loyalty first. The reason I called you here is because a certain situation has come to my attention. The day might come when I need you to eliminate one of my own." Black says cautiously. "Who, B?" A twinge of apprehensive comes into Khalid's voice.

Black pauses for a few seconds, moving to the sofa beside Khalid, rubbing his hands over his face. Mya strains to see Black's face.

"Faheem," Black whispers. "It's getting to the point where he can't be trusted and this underworld chain can't have any weak links. This machine gotta keep rollin'. So Faheem might have to get rolled over. Khalid, you're the only one he trusts enough to let his guard down. And you're the only one besides me to pull the trigger on a nigga you love, and blow his brains out." Black's tone is ruthless and unforgiving.

Mya feels a sense of doom as she rushes away from the door unable back to hear the conclusion of Black's and Khalid's conversation.

As the next few days pass, she masks her deepest fears lurking inside when in Black's presence. She greatly dislikes Faheem but would never wish for his death. The steamy humidity of summer is looming over Philadelphia. A sweltering ninety-five degree is a backdrop against a city otherwise pulsing with life. Guys pushing freshly waxed SUVs and sedans cruise through sunny streets looking for shapely, well-dressed, pretty young women to impress. The heat highlighted the lust and polluted the air. Mya is in no cheerful mood. The rival of summer 1998 fills her mind with dread. After hearing about Black's and Khalid's conversation about killing Faheem, it only added to her anxiety. She and Black would be meeting Hector in two days for the big drug exchange. She looks at Carmello differently, knowing that he could be treacherous when his business is threatened. But she had never been directly faced with the brutal nature of the world that he controls. Her blinders are off; she now recognizes that the game she is playing is bloody. The fun is over. She had been so caught up in Black's power, playing her part as his young bitch. The stench of ugliness that lurks underneath the flashy materialistic underworld is now demanding her attention. Whenever Mya Campbell is in doubt or overwhelmed by life, she turns to the one thing that brings her comfort: shopping. The jubilation of swiping her credit card or handing a saleswoman crisp cash for luxury clothing is her sanctuary. Mya's shopping habits are excessive and she could spend a small fortune within a few hours.

She calls Raven, whom she had not seen since before her Miami trip, needing her best friend's company more than ever. They hit their favorite store, Toby Lerners, and Head Start Shoes, both located at 17th and Sansom Street. The salespeople know them on a first-name basis, smiling as they walk through the front door. They know that they will surely get a fat commission from the high-priced transactions.

Groups of fresh-to-death fashionable girls stand at the sales counter handing the salesgirls fresh $100s as they receive their glossy shopping bags. A few chicks browse the racks, cutting their eyes at Mya and Raven with curiosity. Hate and jealousy by others were always typical. But who could blame them? The girls are CoverGirl ready. Mya is ravishing in a neon-yellow Fendi double-F logo halter top and matching pants. White Gucci open-toe mule sandals, her favorite *Mary J.*

Blige white Fendi shades, and her hair freshly pressed by her hairstylist Coco flows down her back. A white Caviar Chanel bag hangs loosely off of her left shoulder, with long red manicured nails, and a diamond tennis bracelet adorns her left wrist.

Raven is equally stunning in a leopard-print Dolce & Gabbana fitted mini dress with the name written boldly in bright red. She is wearing a pair of black Prada wedge sandals, silky black hair pulled off of her face in a ponytail, gold hoop earrings, and has her black Prada knapsack. Mya is in no mood for shady bitches. She rolls her eyes with great force. Ramondo, the flamboyant salesman, greets them with air kisses. He has on the essence of Platinum Chanel cologne, prancing through the boutique in a finely tailored beige satin suit. He shows the girls several fabulous new items from Moschino, Versace, Iceberg, Valentino, Gianfranco Ferré, and Coogi. Mya's mouth waters with fashion thirst. She and Raven pick out a dozen or so colorful spring items, and head to the dressing rooms in the rear of the boutique. She is filled with joy looking at her well-developed body in a pink neon-green and black Coogi dress, as she spins around looking at her round ass. After trying on her options, she decides on three Versace shirts, a floral Valentino sundress, two pairs of Iceberg jeans, and a monogram Ferré sheer shirt. She notices that Raven had put most of her items back. Only deciding on a pair of Moschino pants with Moschino printed all over them, and two Iceberg t-shirts. She is deep in thought, as though going over numbers in her head. Since her escape from Nickels, Raven's money situation has been tight. She is not working and had been pinching off of the graduation money she received from family and friends. But it is dwindling by the day. Raven is humble, outwardly proud, and would never complain to Mya about her hardships. They have known each other since they were eleven-years-old. Ramondo and the saleswoman wrapped their items in soft-pink wrapping paper.

"Mya, my dear, your total is $1,775." Ramondo smiles, his pearly white teeth on display.

"Add my friend's items to my total," Mya says, handing him her Platinum Visa.

She turns to Raven who is standing behind her, with her eyes wide and full of surprise.

"I owe you a graduation gift. Here you go," Mya smiles, feeling internally noble with doing such a good deed.

"Yo shorty, what's up with those Fendi pants? They look painted on. Yo leopard print, I like pretty kittens," two young brown-skinned guys flirt, pulling up alongside them as they walk toward the E-Class Mya has for the day. The guys are in a new white Ford Expedition truck. The passenger hangs out of the window grinning, the huge gap in his buck teeth protruding in front of acne-scarred brown skin. He is unattractive, borderline ugly. Mya and Raven ignore them as they reach Latanya's Mercedes parked in the middle of 19th and Sansom Street. She opens the trunk as she and Raven put their shopping bags inside.

"I see y'all pushin' the dope Benz. Follow us, we gonna take y'all out to eat. Hang with some real niggas," the passenger shouts. The driver who remained silent leans over. "We got some paper to spend, too." His shiny dark, bald head perspires.

Mya boils. She cannot take one more second of these clown-ass niggas as she opens the driver's side door. She snatches her Fendi shades off, looking at them with her hazel eyes like daggers.

"Cocksuckers, beat it! We would never go out with you corny-ass niggas. Y'all followed us for three blocks but we've been on mute. Take a hint," Mya yells, with her head moving back and forth.

"Damn, sis, you ain't gotta get like that," the driver yells back.

"Yes I do! You been stalkin' us."

"Get the fuck outta here! Ain't nobody stalkin' you. What the fuck you talkin' about," the passenger snaps.

"Mya, come on, forget them," Raven says from the passenger seat.

"See this is why niggas can't never be nice to bitches," the passenger chuckles.

"Nigga you need to take your money to the dentist and get your rotten bucked teeth fixed." Mya replies without hesitation.

"Bitch, I'll smack the shit outta you!" He replies angrily.

"Do you know who my boyfriend is? Smack me? And that'll be the last thing your ugly ass does." Her nostrils flared.

"Mya, come on, stop arguing with them." Raven pleads.

"Yo Buck, pull off before I put hands on this bitch," the passenger snarls, his hard features twisted in a hideous frown. The driver hits the pedal as they speed off and disappear in the traffic.

"I had to check their punk asses," Mya hisses, finally continuing to drive.

"Bitch, I thought we was gonna have to jump out," Raven bursts into laughter."

"We was about to go Tyson and Holyfield on them niggas," Mya retorts, cruising down the street. She needed a good laugh. They cruise down South Street and grab cheesesteaks from Jim's Steaks at 4th and

South Street before heading back to West Philly. Mya blasts Foxy Brown's *Chyna Doll* album. The Schuylkill Expressway is congested as no one wanted to sit in the house on this perfect summer day.

Mya navigates her way through traffic with an arrogant swagger, spinning the wheel quickly with one hand. She drives aggressively and reckless like a dude. But measured at the same time. They stop at Overbrook Water Ice, directly across from their beloved alma mater. Raven orders a large blueberry, Mya settles for a medium lemon and cherry blend. They devour the mouth-cooling treats that make Philly summers better; one of their favorite pastimes. They converge on Raven's front porch watching the sunset. Children chase each other up and down the street. Laughing and teasing each other, innocent of the painful hardships sure to come. Girls played double-Dutch in the middle of the street while older neighbors converse sitting on plastic lawn chairs on their porches. Everyone is relaxing and enjoying the perfect summer breezes...blissful urban tranquility.

"Raven, I know you can't wait to move into your dorm room at Temple. You had your eye on Temple since ninth grade," Mya says sitting beside her. Little Ricky and his friends are yelling loudly, their voices carrying through the open screen door. Rounds of NBA Live 98 is causing debates and rematches.

"They are so damned annoying," Raven sighs. "My brother and his drawling friends are one of the main things I'm *not* gonna miss when I move into my dorm. "Mya, are you excited about La Salle?"

"Kinda, sorta. I pray I don't get no triflin'-ass roommate. You know I'm not used to sharing. I tried to request a single a single room, but students aren't allowed to get one till sophomore year," Mya says in disgust.

"I'm not sweating the roommate situation. As long as she cleans up after herself and never touches myself, I'll be cool as a fan," Raven snickers. "I spoke to Michelle." Her tone changes slightly.

Mya takes a deep breath. She was guilt-ridden that she had not visited Takia more since she and Raven found her drugged up in the hotel room, raped for a second time. Mya had been so caught up with Black and his master plan that she neglected her other best friend. "What did Michelle say?" Mya asks in a concerned tone.

"Takia is making progress at the rehab center. She's in Langhorne, PA, getting counseling for her drug and alcohol problem, and psychiatric treatment for her shaky mental state after her second rape. Michelle said she's on antidepressant meds and seems to be returning to normal."

Mya lowers her head in disbelief. "Sometimes I just lay in my bed and cry thinking about all that's happened to Takia. She always had a hard life. The way Michelle treated her, losing both of her brothers, running the streets, and dealing with shady-ass niggas. Why couldn't guys give Takia a break? She was so happy with Rell and finally had some peace. She wanted her baby so bad, then Rell is murdered in front of her face. If I were in her shoes, I'd probably have committed suicide by now. My heart breaks for her every day," Mya says slowly, holding back her tears.

Raven sighs, her deep-mocha face solemn. "I feel like a piece of me is missing without her. I always admired her strength. She thugged her way through life and always found a way to survive. I still remember the night in eighth grade when she ran to my house crying hysterically. Her hair was all over the place, and she had on dingy clothes. Michelle had beaten her up badly. Takia had a bloody nose, and scratches all over her face. All because she told our teacher that one of Michelle's boyfriends was touching on her. Michelle flipped, accusing Takia of flirting with her man. Of course he denied it, but Michelle took his side over her own fucking child!"

It was Raven now choking back tears. "I remember my mom was so upset. My dad was ready to step up to Michelle's boyfriend. He never played that man-touching-little-girl shit. My mom cleaned her up, put peroxide and Band-Aids on her bruises, and fixed her dinner. Then she held Takia in her arms. She got her to confide in her about all of the nasty details that had happened. She stayed with us for a week before Michelle showed up, trying to play the victim, painting herself as a struggling single mom with a wild out-of-control daughter. My mom saw through her act and got at Michelle's ass. They had a woman-to-woman conversation in my kitchen that Michelle would never forget. She threatened to report the abuse and molestation to DHS and Family Services. And if her boyfriend didn't leave their house, she would make sure that Michelle was put behind bars. Michelle walked out of our front door crying. To this day, my mom still refuses to speak to her."

The two take a few silent moments to reflect on Takia, visions of her vibrant, sassy, and beautiful in her prime. Talking slick to niggas, full kissable lips glossed, seductive honey-brown eyes alert, and full of fun and mischief. Always strutting her curvy body on the street. They reminisce about the days when their lives were carefree, and wore badges of invincibility. Mya finally broke the silence.

"So how's Nadir up at CFCF?"

"Girl, he's alright. He's liftin' and studying the Quran. Our Sunday visits are our happy time. He's gettin' husky as shit," Raven giggles. "Girl, weights have the niggas lookin' right. All they do is work out, so Nadir's lookin' right. He's perfect. It kills me every time I have to leave him. I wake up in cold sweats from dreams of holdin' him in my arms, and protecting him. Then I wake up alone in my bed. I just lay there and cry. I can't wait until he's back home with me." Raven's voice twinges with grief.

"Aww, Raven, he'll be home soon. That small bid he's doin' is gonna be before you blink." Mya gently rubs her back.

"You're right. Nadir keeps tellin' me to toughen up, to not be so sensitive." She takes a deep breath as her calm disposition gradually returns. "Enough about Nadir. How was Miami? I haven't seen you since before you left."

Every pent-up emotion that Mya was holding inside burst out of her. She begins crying, a mournful stream of tears flowing down her cheeks, her face flushed red.

"Mya, what's wrong?" Raven panics, wrapping her arms around her. "Mya talk to me! Did Black do something to you in Miami?"

Mya leans her head on Raven's shoulder sobbing. Black molded her to be a soldier, to never show fear. She is beyond conflicted. Black's actions scare her and she would like to back out of the meeting with the connect. But she feels trapped.

"Mya, what is it?" Raven is now alarmed.

She leans on Raven's shoulder, trembling like a child.

"What did Black do to you? You know you can trust me."

Mya breathes deeply, biting down on the flesh inside her left cheek. *Bitch, pull yourself together,* she thinks, sitting up, and wiping away her tears, regaining her composure.

"I've been knowing you my whole life. You don't cry often or easily," Raven whispers, rubbing Mya's hands. "Some bullshit is goin' down, Mya. I need some answers," Raven presses more aggressively.

"Nothin' is wrong, Raven. I just got emotional thinking about Takia. We're both goin' off to college startin' our lives, while she's living the best years of her life in a mental hospital." Mya is lying without a blink of an eye."

Raven's suspicious inquiries turn back to Takia. Mya knew that the Takia card would calm her down.

"It's so unfair," Raven shakes her head in sorrowful disdain. They sit perfectly still in silence as the sound of the ice-cream truck approaches Raven's street. Kids yell, asking their parents for money. After an hour of what she considers boring conversation passes, Mya makes her escape, heart full of restless confusion, whipping her mother's Mercedes through the empty streets of their Bala Cynwyd neighborhood. *Butta Love* by Next plays lightly on the radio.

Part 4: The Long Kiss Goodnight

Mya lies on her bed face down, rapidly flipping through pages of *Vogue Magazine*. The clock on her VCR switched from 9:59 p.m. to 10:00 p.m. Carmello will be arriving at any moment. It was no turning back. She made her pact with him a while time ago. Her Nextel phone begins ringing beside her. For the first time, she did not jump to answer Black's call on the first ring. She sits holding the phone as it rings in her hand. She answers on the sixth ring.

"Hello," she says timidly. "You outside? Here I come." She says as she slips on a pair of tan Gucci sneakers, blue Guess jeans, and a tan halter top. Mys has on lip gloss, she is fresh-faced and makeup-free, looking like a little girl forced to go to a family outing against her will. *Bitch, stop being weak*, she tells herself. She steps in front of the full-length mirror in the far corner. Her lovely face turns into an icy grimace. "Weak bitches don't sit at the king's side. Just get past tonight. Mya, pull it together," she sighs, rubbing her forehead. "Always remember, you're Mya fucking Campbell! Mya fucking Campbell," she whispers again, smirking before walking out of her bedroom. Her parents are at a charity dinner at the Bala Cynwyd Country Club. A nice breeze hits her body as she closes the front door, walking toward Black's Mercedes. His Versace cologne fills Mya's nose as she enters the passenger seat. Big Pun featuring Joe hit song, *Still Not a Player* plays on the stereo.

Black greets her with a confident grin. A simple black Polo Sport t-shirt fits him perfectly. His gold Rolex and diamond pinkie ring sparkle in the shadowy Benz. Mya stares ahead as Black gets onto the expressway at the City Line exit. "After we make this last exchange with Hector, no more arguing, and no more stress. Just me and you chillin' out, enjoying life ole' girl," he teases jokingly, reaching over to squeeze the back of her neck. Her guard drops instantly as a smile forms at the corner of her lips.

"I want a tropical vacation for the stress I'm under."

"Pick a place! Bahamas, Puerto Rico, Virgin Islands, baby pick anywhere on the globe and we're there." Mya giggles. She loves when Black talks heavy.

"Aight, I'm holding you to that. When I see your first-semester grades, then we'll talk about vacation," he chuckles.

They reach the Northeast Philadelphia Airport. He pulls into a small motel parking lot two blocks away. His cell phone rings. "Hola, Hector. I'm at the spot now."

Two black Lincoln town cars pull into the deserted motel parking lot. Mya's stomach gets tight. "Come on in," Black whispers, opening the driver's side door, placing his black 9mm in the back of his pants and pulling his shirt over it. Mya has never been religious, but at this moment she closes her eyes and prays for God to keep his hand over her and Black. She slowly opens the passenger door.

"Carmello, my friend, the weather in Philadelphia is caliente," Hector laughs in his melodic, thick Columbian accent, leaning against the Town car looking as dapper as she remembered, his long black hair loose around his shoulders. He wears a white and gold silk Versace shirt, his soft elfin face looks flawless. Three bodyguards dressed in black suits stand nearby.

"My Bella, so good to see you again," Hector addresses Mya. She smiles, nodding approvingly. Dom Cartagena sends you his best wishes.

"When you get back to Miami, please give him my best regards," Carmello replies, opening the Mercedes trunk and pulling out two large duffel bags containing two million dollars in cash. Black hands one to Mya. The sheer weight of the bag pulls her down. She follows Black and puts the bag on top of the Town car that Hector leans on. Carmello unzips the bag, revealing endless $100s wrapped tightly with rubber bands.

"Very nice, Carmello, very nice indeed," Hector says, running his hands through the money and looks at Mya, winking, a satisfied smile on his handsome face. He then snaps his finger. Two of his bodyguards walk over to the first Town car, returning with four duffel bags, placing them next to the bags of cash. "Carmello, your heart's desire, one hundred and fifty kilos of the best Colombian cocaine."

A look of triumphant delight takes over Carmello, who starts examining the large kilos wrapped neatly in clear plastic and duct tape. He looks happier than a kid on Christmas morning, Mya observes, feeling relieved that the deed had been done. Black glances at her, silently saying, *We did it. We fucking did it.* He keeps his composure steady in front of Hector and his guys. If you decide that your retirement is too boring, you know how to find us, Carmello. You have earned us a great deal of money and have always been a solid, good soldier." Hector extends his hand to Black.

"Hector, you've been a brother to me. I'm forever in your debt."

They embrace, patting each other on the back in brotherly solidarity.

"Our business is concluded. Let me get back to my plane. I can be back in Miami just in time for a late-night rendezvous," he snickers. "I expect you two will have your own celebration. Carmello, take good care of this precious beauty." He approaches Mya, gently kissing her on the cheek. She and Carmello carry the heavy bags of kilos, placing them in the Mercedes trunk. They all get into their cars under the dark shadow of night, moving like bad guys in mafia movies, only this is real life. Mya's adrenaline is high as they pull out of the hotel parking lot. Black puts on Jay-Z's *Reasonable Doubt* album. He leans over, kissing Mya passionately on the lips. "Tomorrow is a new fuckin' day," he says joyfully, pulling to the right onto the expressway entrance.

Black's Mercedes is behind Hector's two Town cars, waiting for the light to turn green. Mya pulsates with wild energy. She wants to stand up, put her body through the sunroof and scream to the top of her lungs. She wets her lips with a swipe of her tongue, giggling at her thoughts when the distant sounds of sirens penetrate her ears. The flashing lights come into view as a dozen federal and local police cars approach at full speed. Carmello hits the gas, flooring the Mercedes. Mya turns to see them surrounding Hector's vehicles. Her heart sinks as Carmello whips through traffic maneuvering, using his driving skills to lose the Feds and police.

"Go faster, they on our ass! This can't be fuckin' happening," Mya cries.

"Calm the fuck down, I got this," Black hollers, getting off at the Hunting Park exit, turning the car wildly into oncoming traffic when a minivan cannot avoid slamming into the rear of the Mercedes. Black loses control as Mya screams in horror as their car jumps the curb onto the pavement and collides into the porch of someone's house. Mya bangs her head on the dashboard, throbbing pain shooting through her body. Black groans beside her, blood running down his forehead. Mya's vision is blurry.

"Turn your car off now! Put your hands out of the window and get out slowly," a deep-voiced FBI agent orders, approaching the car as backup, with guns drawn. "You are now under arrest by the United States federal government," a female agent yells, yanking Mya out of the car stumbling, roughly handcuffing her as a large black agent slams Carmello on top of the 'hood of his car, placing handcuffs on him.

"We waited a long time to put your ass away," the male agent growls, his elbow deep in Carmello's back.

"You're two-bit low life drug dealing ass will be off the streets for good. Carmello Matthew Samuels, you are now under arrest by the United States federal government of America. Anything you say can and will be used against you in a court of law."

Carmello looks at Mya on the hood of the car, a cheeky grin on his dark face. His eyes blink, full of sentimental regret. Mya brings down tears. She wants to break out of the handcuffs and throw her arms around him. She struggles against the strong grasp of the female agent holding her. A fury bursts through Carmello as a second agent grabs him by the shoulder, dragging him to the waiting SUV.

"Don't cry in front of these suckas. They ain't nothing to be afraid of. Remember Mya, ain't nobody built like us," Black hollers before being pushed into the back of the truck.

"Get her into the next transport car," the tall, intimidating agent instructs the female agent holding Mya. In a blur of tears, Mya is placed into the back of a blue Chevrolet Caprice, with a thick clear fiberglass divider that is found inside any standard police car. She is thrown from side to side. Her mind is filled with panic and fear. Shocked to her core, she simply lays her head against the window. She weeps, not for herself but for Black. Being separated from him is like her eyes being ripped from their sockets. She is left blind without her beloved. She is dragged into FBI headquarters, where she is booked, fingerprinted, and a hideous mugshot is taken. Then placed in a foul-smelling and damp holding cell. Mya places her head in her lap, cradling her knees tightly, vainly praying that she awakes from this sadistic nightmare. She and Black would be reunited as if this was a figment of her imagination. That comforting thought disappears as the cell door opens. The female

SALEEM ROBERTS

FBI agent who arrested her stands in the doorway. A tall thin redhead with dark emerald-green eyes, ivory-white skin, and an attractive oval-shaped face sprinkled with freckles. A silent assertive power radiates, her red hair pulled into a tight bun. A black fitted FBI t-shirt, and slacks cover her slender frame. She is armed with a brown leather gun holster around her waist, where her gold badge, and silver gun sit boldly, confirming her power.

"Ms. Campbell, I'm special-agent Winters. Please come with me. I have a few questions that I would like to ask you." Her voice echoes through the cell.

Mya picks up on the thick South Philly accent, Italian or Irish she thinks. Standing to her feet and gathering her wits, her mouth as dry and hollow as the Mojave desert. She is led down a long stretch of corridor, where other interrogations are in progress. Hector and his two henchmen sit handcuffed to wooden chairs, being grilled by two much older gray-haired agents. Their eyes turn to daggers at the sight of Mya. Hector yells out a threat in Spanish that Mya cannot quite make out. She knows by his tone that it was nothing nice. Agent Winters leads Mya into a small interrogation room, where the tall black agent who slammed Carmello on top of the hood sits stone-faced, not a smirk on his dark-skinned face.

"I'm Agent Johnson, Ms. Campbell," he introduces himself. Dark-brown hawk eyes watch her with cold contempt, arms folded tightly underneath his chest. The black bullet-proof vest protrudes over his large chest, his gray hair in a buzz cut like an army private. His dark eyes cast over Mya, calculating every fiber of her being.

"Are you thirsty?" Agent Winters asks, propping herself on top of an adjoining desk.

Mya shakes her head yes. Agent Winters stands to her feet, walking over to the water cooler to fill a plastic cup, then grabs a manila folder. She hands Mya the water, which she slowly sips. Agent Winters skims through the folder's contents. "Mya Campbell. Age eighteen. Recent graduate of Overbrook High School. Both parents are attorneys at prestigious law firms in the city. No prior arrests or juvenile history. She is clean." Agent Winters' thick accent rings out, a smirk on her freckled face.

"Mya, tell us everything we want to know, and we'll go easy on you," Agent Johnson's deep baritone declares calmly.

Agent Winters leans over into Mya's personal space, her green eyes gleaming. "Ms. Campbell, this situation is very serious. The amount of narcotics that Carmello Black and his Colombian cohorts were attempting to import into the city is at such a level that, honey, you're guaranteed to do twenty years easily. But if you cooperate, we can make sure you get a reduced sentence."

Agent Winters grabs a rusty metal chair and sits down right beside Mya, who shrugs her shoulders and rolls her eyes, expressing a defiant frown on her beautiful face. "Mya, think about your future. Carmello Black is a low life scum bag who doesn't care about anybody but himself."

"Yeah, whatever," Mya whispers, taking another sip from the cold water in front of her."

"Believe me, honey, he's not thinking about you. Help us out, so you're not spending the best years of your life behind bars being somebody's sweet young girlfriend."

"Please, you Feds don't scare me. My father is one of the most respected attorneys in Philadelphia. He's friends with the mayor and the D.A. I'll be out of here tonight. You have nothing to hold me. I'm not your average teenage girl. Now can I get my fuckin' phone call?" Mya says coolly, her hazel eyes defiant. Agent Johnson grins at Agent Winters.

"Oh, you're feisty I see. But you can be broken." Agent Johnson's grin turns back into a hard frown. "Mya, wake up. You think Black is your Romeo? Two young lovers against the world. I think Ms. Campbell needs a wake-up call," Agent Johnson says in a smirky tone, leaning against the large reciprocal mirror. His looming frame has wide solid shoulders. He is touched by age but well preserved. Fifty, Mya guesses his age. *Why does he keep grittin' on me*? Mya thinks, taking another sip of water. Agent Winters shakes her head in agreement and exits the room. She reemerges, a triumphant grin on her ivory face. She stands in front of Mya, pulling out several photos from the manila envelope, throwing them on the scraped-up table. She slowly picks them up.

Carmello is with several different women in the black-and-white FBI photos, kissing several of them, and leaving hotels. One photo is of a girl giving him head in his Navigator. Mya stares in disbelief. Her mind races with sorrowful despair that quickly turns to rage. The agents silently collect their files, their calculating eyes speaking to each other, knowing that the photos of Black's secret romances would break Mya. The door slams behind them. She immediately breaks down in tears, trembling hands covering her face.

"Fuck, Black! How could you do this to me," she sobs. "What have I done? Mya what have you done? My parents are going to kill me! I thought it was us against the world? But you out here creepin' with some bitches?! If I get convicted of a felony, I can't go to college. I won't be able to get a job at fuckin' McDonald's," she screams, banging on the table. "Calm down, Mya, calm down, and pull yourself together. You're gonna get out of this. Remember one thing. You're, Mya fuckin' Campbell," she whispers, desperately trying to reassure herself.

After two more hours, it seems like an eternity. Agent Winters reemerges. "Your parents are here," he says tauntingly. LaTanya and Terrance enter the interrogation room. They appear in complete contrast within the room, both dressed in sophisticated evening attire, Mr. Campbell in a black tuxedo, white dress shirt, and bow tie. His diamond cufflinks sparkling from his lapels. LaTanya is ravishing in a black-and-white silk taffeta gown, with an ivory and pearl-embroidered bodice, a pearl choker around her neck, and her dark auburn hair pulled back in a tight bun. She has fiery disbelief in her hazel eyes. Mya jumps to her feet with open arms to greet her savior, her father. But instead of reciprocating the embrace, he gives her a stinging slap to her face. She instantly feels excruciating pain, and stumbles back against the wall, looking at him in tearful shock. In her eighteen years of life, he never raised a hand to her. Looking deep into his dark-brown eyes, she sees sadness and betrayal. His handsome face locked in a mournful expression, the look that a father gives his daughter during times of disappointment.

"Mya, this can't be reality?! You've been arrested for drug trafficking? We rushed here from a charity event at the country club. "We're going to be blackballed because of your reckless actions," LaTanya yells, shaking her head, her light face flush red.

"I finally see what your mother has been trying to tell me about you all of these years, Mya," shouts Terrance. "How can you disgrace our family like this?"

He points his index finger in her face and steps closer as if to strike her again. She sees tears in his eyes as she backs away in fear. "I don't know who my daughter is anymore. Involved with drugs? I busted my ass to get my family out of the ghetto! Mya, we spoiled you rotten, giving you every luxury, no matter the price. My entire law firm will be laughing at me when the press breaks this story. I'm the first black partner at my firm. That's history. Do you know how those white people look down on us? I worked so hard to break their stereotype that we're all not just degenerate criminals and drug addicts. And my only daughter an alleged accessory to drug trafficking with a punk drug dealer," Terrance cries, hot tears flowing down his cheeks.

"Daddy, I'm so sorry. I'm so sorry," Mya sobs, never seeing her dad so hurt or emotionally broken in her life. The fact that she is the cause of his grief is too much for her young heart to bear. She rushes to him, throwing her arms around him.

"Mya, get away from me," he gruffs, pushing her forcefully away from him.

"I can't even look at her," he says to LaTanya shaking his head, heartbroken, and shame reflected in his eyes as he storms out of the interrogation room.

LaTanya glares at Mya. "How could you hurt your father in this way? You ruined everything! You just never know when to stop. We gave you everything and that still wasn't enough. You had to keep playing your little games. Now you've thrown gasoline on the fire and burned the whole bitch down," LaTanya utters, staring blankly, her hazel eyes frozen as a pair porcelain dolls.

Agents Johnson and Winters return twenty minutes later. "Mya, your parents certainly have the right connections. You're free to go, for today. So don't get too comfortable. We'll be in touch soon. Really soon." Relief washes over her. The ride home in the back of her father's Jaguar is one of stone silence. Not even the radio plays.

God, wake me up from this nightmare. This can't be real, she thinks, laying across the back seat. They arrive at the sprawling house on the Main Line, the Campbells' pride and joy. Their status symbol that reassured them they had made it successfully out of the ghetto. Ironically, Mya's safe haven is now her prison.

Her parents ransack her bedroom, taking the stereo system, her cordless landline, cell phone, credit cards, forty inch television, and piles of her extensive wardrobe. They order her to only leave her room for food. She feels completely alone, cutting off the lights, and lying down on the bed crying herself to sleep. By the beginning of July, the *Philadelphia Daily News* is running front-page stories of North Philly's underworld kingpin and girlfriend caught with millions of dollars worth of drugs. There had been a leak at FBI headquarters. Mya's pictures are plastered on every major news platform top story.

Raven rushes to the house, but is angrily turned away by Mr. Campbell. LaTanya informs her that Carmello's warehouses were raided, and members of his crew were arrested, including Aunt Tameeka. Indictments are coming down left and right. Her parents along with Agents Winters and Johnson attempt in vain to get her to flip on Black. She refuses, and rather dies before turning snitch. Yes, she was angry about Black cheating on her, but would never betray her love. Being separated from him hurts her the most. She misses his voice, his touch, and their intimate talks. Her man was snatched away. She stares at photos from prom night and their trip to Miami. Mya's hair had grown wild and untamed from lack of salon maintenance. She began keeping a diary, writing down all of her intimate thoughts, suffering from depression, and cabin fever. Being confined to her parents' home twenty-four hours a day force her to face her innermost demons. She had been selfish, cruel, materialistic, and unkind. She reflects on many instances in which she had wronged people, and had done many shady things to her parents and friends.

Terrance had even hired private security guards to surveil the house twenty-four hours a day. He wanted there to be armed and ready in case any of Carmello's crew wanted to permanently silence Mya. She knows information that could put Black away for good if she testified against him. This made her a prime target for murder. By the beginning of August 1998, her mother eases a little, letting Raven visit the house. Mya is also holding a secret that is confirmed when Raven sneaks in a home pregnancy test. The results read positive and Mya gasps with joy, knowing that part of Black would now be hers forever. "Carmello, I'm having your baby," Mya says smiling, lying in bed rubbing her belly. *I have to be about three or four months pregnant*, she guesses, thinking about the new life growing inside of her. She hides her pregnancy by wearing oversized clothes, t-shirts, and sweatpants. She figures it is pointless to get dressed in designer clothes when she has nowhere to go.

Her parents are as busy as ever, their full caseloads keeping them occupied and out of the house. As long as she stays in the house, that is all the information they need. She watches summer turn into fall. Leaves begin falling from trees and daylight savings time is has returned. While all of her former classmates are starting their first semester of college, trade schools, and new jobs, Mya Campbell is awaiting trial because she refused to cooperate with the Feds. They offered her many plea deals that would provide her with immunity, but she refused them all. She would be tried in a federal court of law for conspiracy, aiding and abetting a felon, and drug trafficking. Each charge, if found guilty, carries a heavy sentence that would be served consecutively. Mya prays to God for mercy. She is nearly six months before her pregnancy is discovered. Her parents are furious. If the scandalous drug charges were not enough, she is about to be a teenage mother. The pristine, upstanding reputations that her parents built are now shredded because of the scandal. The constant media coverage of the case keeps the Campbells' wealthy Caucasian neighbors, country club acquaintances, and counterparts at their respective law firms whispering. No matter how high they climbed out of the ghetto, their skin is still black.

The Campbells had been so successful, educationally and financially, they thought they had grown beyond race. But Mya being arrested and romantically linked to the largest drug lord in Philadelphia, has put their black skin under a glaring spotlight in the well-to-do white world that they had occupied for decades.

LaTanya takes Mya to her prenatal appointment, nearly six months pregnant when she receives her first ultrasound. When that strong resounding heartbeat fills that examination room, Mya and LaTanya both become filled with emotion. They hug in a tight embrace. A pure, untainted bond between mother and daughter has formed again.

Terrance on the other hand is utterly devastated and he could not bear to look at Mya. He walks past her like she is invisible, barely speaking two words to her since the night of her arrest. Mya is crushed as her father is her hero, her provider, the man who kissed her bruises, and tucked her in at night. Their bond had been so special and yet she destroyed it with her careless disregard for the morals and values he had instilled in her.

As Mya's belly grows, so does her appetite. She craves seafood pasta, hot sausages, grapefruit, and chocolate. And spends her days overdosing on MTV's *The Real World, The Simpsons, Beverly Hills 90210, The Fresh Prince of Bel Air,* daytime talk shows and soap operas like *Ricki Lake, Jerry Springer, Oprah, The Young and the Restless, All My Children,* and *Guiding Light.*

It is late December. Mya is almost nine months pregnant with swollen feet and unable to fit any of her old clothes. After gaining almost forty pounds, she could only wear sweatpants and loose sneakers. Her sore breasts are swollen and filled with milk. Every painful kick her baby delivers humbles her instantly. She is growing with love, constantly rubbing cocoa butter on her stomach to keep the stretch marks to a minimum. Her core vanity could only be shaken but so much. Her happiness is that she would always have a part of Carmello with her. God had taken pity on her, knowing that her inconsolable broken heart would never mend. So he blessed her with Carmello's son.

His final court appearance was nearing. Mya knew that the judge and jury were going to throw the book at him if he was found guilty. She was unable to be present for the other court dates, but she would be in the courtroom to lock eyes with him on this day no matter the cost.

Part 5: Carmello's Trial, Never Say Goodbye

December 20, 1998, the last day of Carmello's trial at The U.S. District Court on Market Street, resumes on an unbearably cold winter afternoon. Mya shakes with nervousness underneath an unbuttoned black mink coat and thick cotton Iceberg sweat suit, walking through the metal detectors. Raven is behind her. Her sister would not dare miss being by her side during a time like this. The entryway is crowded with police, press and gawkers, all coming to see Carmello's verdict. She scans the area behind huge aviator Gucci sunglasses, her hair pulled back into a tight ponytail, wanting to be incognito. Mya would rather be shot to death than miss Black's last court appearance. This would be the last time for her to see him in a space outside of a prison. She had not laid eyes on her beautiful love since their arrests. Her own trial would begin in February, just a few months away. The cruel reality that she would have only one month with her baby if she is convicted overwhelms her. She had to see Black as her spirit could not rest. At this moment, he does not even know that she is pregnant with his child.

Mya and Raven enter the crowded elevator about to see Black one last time. The stench of someone's foul body odor fills her sensitive nose, turning her stomach. They are pressed like sardines in the small elevator. Finally, the silver metal doors open to the eighteenth floor. The pile of bodies spill out into the corridor leading to the numbers 1830, Black's trial room. The place is packed, leaving little room to walk through. Reporters eager to report the verdict to all of the various media outlets are huddle outside of the courtroom. Policemen with stern faces stand immobile against the dark gray marble walls. Young boahs who ran the corners for Black in the underworld, whom Mya recognizes, huddle together in deep conversation. All are bundled in dark Woolrich coats and pea coats with fur collars.

Other older hustlers and goons post up, all curious about the fate of North Philly's king. Mya and Raven manage to squeeze in the back row. She noticed Khalid and a few of the underworld underlings. They are seated a few rows behind the lawyer's table on the defense's side. Some of Black's family are directly behind them. Mya scans a few rows ahead, recognizing one of the bitches from the photos they showed her in the interrogation room that was creeping with Black. She snatches off her Gucci shades to closer examine the bitch. A competitively jealous feeling sweeps over her. She is a typical light-skinned chick, cute but not beautiful, with a large round nose, and full-sized lips. Her stiff shoulder-length wrap needed to be pressed. *This bitch couldn't touch me if she was leaning on my shoulder,* Mya thinks, studying her rival with cold hostility.

"All rise. Court is now in session. The honorable Judge Maureen Shriver presiding," says the slim, middle-aged, shoulder-length brunette bailiff. The entire courtroom rises. A dignified white woman in her mid-fifties appears. She has a silver-gray hair cut in a short bob, and her black robe flows against her thin frame. She majestically sits in her chair, towering above everyone in proximity.

"You may be seated," she says into the microphone in the center of the dark cherry wood bench. The collapse of bottoms into their respective seats echoes within the confined space.

"The proceedings may begin with The Commonwealth of Pennsylvania versus Carmello Matthew Samuels docket number 431 Pa. 353 . I'll let the prosecution begin followed by the defense. Mr. Salvino, I understand there's been a delay with the transfer of your client from holdings."

Black's defense attorney Lorenzo Salvino is a smooth-talking, Italian South Philly defense attorney known for getting mob bosses, gangsters, and shady criminals off in high-profile cases. His fee is a small fortune, but his track record has proven itself worth the money.

"Yes, your honor, there seems to be an issue with the transport, but my client should be here momentarily," he addresses, a thick South Philly accent rolling off his tongue; more of a mafia associate than an attorney. His heather-gray suit fits impeccably, his black hair combed back, and trimmed perfectly. A cocky confidence rests on his dark Sicilian tanned face. Seconds later, two stocky black male bailiffs enter from the court's holding room followed by Carmello.

Mya's heart sinks at the sight of her beloved, shackled like a field slave. He is wearing a wrinkled orange jumpsuit with its black ID numbers across his chest. His always-precise head full of shiny deep waves is now shaved bald. A thick beard covers his face, an unreadable look on his dark chiseled face. He is placed beside his lawyer, then unshackled.

"Mr. Salvino, I see your client has arrived. If the prosecution does not have motions these proceedings can now begin."

"No motions, your honor," the middle-aged dark brunette female state prosecutor answers in a high soprano voice. Her deep-burgundy pantsuit fits her figure decently.

"The prosecution may proceed," Judge Shriver orders.

For the next two hours, Mya listens with sorrowful ears to Black being described as a ruthless drug dealer and vicious cold-hearted killer. A menace to society, the deadliest of cancer who needs to be removed from daily life. He was also accused of being responsible for countless deaths. His long ties to the Columbian drug cartel have played a major part in the crack epidemic plaguing Philadelphia, leading to drug wars over territory in the city.

"Carmello is the king on a chess board, full of minions and underlings, distributing his product, money laundering millions of dollars in offshore accounts to banks in the Cayman Islands to one Dom Cartegena, a ruthless Colombian drug lord whose reputation has continued to grow. Additional information was revealed in confiscated IRS records that Carmello operated sham businesses he used to wash his dirty drug money clean." The prosecutor claims, speaking directly to the jury.

She then places five easels on display in front of the multicultural jury made up of four Caucasians, two middle-aged men in their early forties, one dark-blonde and tan, the other a lighter complected redhead with a buzz cut, two young white women in their late twenties, one heavyset with oval-shaped reading glasses, short brown hair, the other an attractive blonde with shoulder-length hair, and bright blue eyes. Then two Asians, one Chinese man, thin-built with a plain face, and the woman is dark-tan in her mid-thirties. She appears to be Cambodian. One Latino grandmother, heavyset with long stringy gray hair in her early sixties, and the other five are African-American, two men and three women. They seem to be educated and hard-nosed.

"This defendant clearly has blood on his hands." The prosecutor states as she sets photos of five black men brutally murdered in the most gruesome way on easels. Some are strangled, others have multiple gunshot wounds to their heads and faces. One body was placed in a meat locker and had to thaw out for three days before the medical examiner could conduct an autopsy. A twinge of terror streaks through Mya as the prosecutor reads off the names of the fallen young soldiers. She instantly recognizes a few names. They were corner boys working in Black's stash houses. *Could he have ordered their murders?* The thought enters her mind for the first time.

The prosecution then parades two of the grieving mothers and one grandmother on the stand, waling with tears, choking on kind words of a bitter life without their boys. In detail they described how they think about their sons and grandson every hour, whose lives were stolen by the hands of the 'black devil,' Carmello himself. As the last upset family member leaves the stand, the prosecutor throws Black and Salvino a smug grin, basking in an internal victory before saying, "Your honor, the prosecution rests."

Mr. Salvino follows with charisma and style, smiling and winking at the jury, painting a portrait of Carmello as a kid from the wrong side of the tracks, growing up in a foul and impoverished neighborhood. "Carmello's father was murdered by the police while robbing a liquor store when he was only eight-years-old. His mother, Casandra Samuels, suffered from schizophrenia since her teens, and began snorting cocaine and shooting heroin in the late '70s. Desperate for money, she began turning tricks to make a quick buck, leaving Carmello with his grandmother and aunt for weeks on end. That was until her body was discovered and identified. She was strangled to death by one of her clients in a filthy hotel room on Roosevelt Boulevard in the Northeast. He had become the product of his bleak environment." Mr. Salvino stresses to the jury.

Mya is overcome with grief, hearing the details of Black's early life. He had kept all of this a secret from her. She knew that his parents were dead and that he was raised by his grandmother. But he would completely shut down and grow silent whenever she would press him for details about his childhood years.

"Ladies and gentlemen of the jury, my client is also a victim in this dark web. He is a low-level player with petty connections to the Cartegena drug cartel. His co-defendant Hector Montega threatened his life. He told him that they would kill his entire family if Carmello did not agree to distribute their product. My client does not own any planes or boats. Ladies and gentlemen of the jury, the prosecution would have you to believe that this one man born into extremely poverty-stricken circumstances is the head of a multimillion-dollar drug syndicate. That is completely preposterous! This one man could not have all of that power." A confident grin begins to form around Mr. Salvino's mouth. "As for the homicides presented by the prosecution, they are very sad and unfortunate. However, there is not an inkling of concrete physical evidence linking my client to any of those murders. There is not any audio or surveillance showing my client interacting with any of the deceased or giving orders to anyone to carry out those murders. Yes, my client does happen to be from the same neighborhood as those men. However, should Carmello Samuels be sent to prison for the rest of his life just because he was unfortunate enough to be raised in the same poor environment as the victims? This case is about facts and the prosecution has not provided any evidence implicating my client in those murders. When you go back to the room and deliberate, remember a young 24-year-old man's life is on the line," Mr. Salvino says before taking a long dramatic pause before resting his case.

Judge Shriver calls a lunch recess. Everyone leaves out of the courtroom and the hallway is littered with bodies. Khalid approaches Mya as she and Raven head to the elevator. He kisses her on the cheek. He is shocked and pleasantly surprised by her pregnancy, beaming with happiness. Their blessed legacy will live on. He gently rubs her belly. She told him that she is having a boy. "A little fuckin' Mello is just what the world needs! I'm the godfather. Not even up for debate," Khalid chuckles. "Look, I'm runnin' shit now. If you ever need anything at all, don't hesitate to give me a call."

"I won't. I promise," Mya answers as they embrace.

"Oh yeah, I put that snake nigga Faheem in the dirt," Khalid whispers in her ear. She is shocked and happy all at once. She and Raven have a quick lunch at Olive Garden, eating lasagna at a rapid pace, opting to return to the courtroom early so that they can find seating. Mya says a silent prayer hoping that God would send an intervention to help Carmello. She knows that he is accused of being a horrible person but even cynics deserve a second chance. The tension in the room is thick as she and Raven return to the courtroom. They manage to squeeze into the third-to-last row.

"All rise for the honorable Judge Maureen Shriver," the aging Asian bailiff commands.

"Jury, have you reached a verdict?" Judge Shriver asks, focusing on the jury foreman, the dark-blonde and tan man in his late forties.

"Yes we have, your honor," is the response of the foreman.

"Please read the verdict on the count of drug trafficking."

"We the jury find the defendant Carmello Matthew Samuels, guilty." A collective gasp of shock rings out from the courtroom.

"On the charge of racketeering. How do you find?"

"Guilty."

"On the charge of money laundering. How do you find?"

"Guilty."

"On the charge of first-degree murder. How do you find?"

"Guilty."

After hearing the verdicts, the judge proceeds and says, "Mr. Samuels you have been tried and found guilty on all counts by a jury of your peers. These convictions carry a combined minimum sentence of not less than life in prison. Mr. Salvino immediately turns to Carmello and says, "Stay strong. Don't worry we'll file an appeal."

"The jury has spoken. Court is now adjourned," Judge Shriver says flatly, slamming down her dark-brown wooden gavel.

"No, no" Mya cries. She literally feels her heart pounding inside of her chest. *My God! Life? Fuckin' life?! They might as well kill him*, Mya thinks as Raven rubs her back and tears pour down both of her cheeks.

The courtroom is in an uproar. Some of the murder victims' family members loudly thank Jesus. Journalists are in a frenzy, rushing out of the courtroom to get the guilty verdicts to their respective newspapers. Khalid and the underworld crew are snapping, screaming profanity-laced threats to the DA.

"Order in my court! Order in my court," Judge Shriver screams, slamming her gavel repeatedly. "Bailiff, please remove the defendant from the courtroom."

Two bailiffs walk over and shackle Black. Mya cannot take it anymore. She leaps to her feet.

"Black, Black, Black!" she yells at the top of her lungs. Once she has his attention she shouts, "I'm pregnant! I'm pregnant with your son!"

The entire courtroom focuses on her. Carmello turns to see her full pregnant belly heading toward him.

"Mya!" he shouts, breaking out of the bailiffs' grip.

"Order in the court right now! Young lady, you will control yourself," Judge Shriver yells. "Bailiff, remove the defendant and this woman right now!"

They grab Carmello with force, but not before he embraces and kisses Mya one last time. He is shackled and pulled out of the courtroom as two female bailiffs seize Mya.

"Mya, remember what I told you. Nobody is built like us! Be strong for my son," Black wails as he is dragged forcibly from view.

"I love you! I love you Carmello!" Mya hollers, as the two bailiffs force her out of the courtroom.

"Don't be so rough with her! She's nine months pregnant," Raven insists, trailing behind them.

Mya feels an excruciating pain erupting in her stomach. She collapses, unable to walk any farther. "My water broke," she whimpers.

"Call a fucking ambulance," Raven screams kneeling beside her.

Moments later, paramedics rush Mya on a stretcher from the courthouse to nearby Thomas Jefferson University Hospital. The emergency room nurses undress her and place a hospital gown over her body. Raven notifies Mya's parents. Mya cries out in severe pain as her contractions are now coming quickly. The emergency room doctor examines her.

"Nurses, prepare for delivery. She has fully dilated" The doctor exclaims.

Mya is placed on a gurney, profusely perspiring. Her mouth is dry and the lower portion of her body feels as though it is being pulled apart. The nurses prop her up as her legs are spread and placed in metal clamps. Her pain feels worse than being stabbed or shot. A nurse administers a local anesthetic through a catheter to subside the excruciating pain.

"Mya, your baby is almost here. I'm going to need you to push with all of your strength." A nurse commands.

Mya screams in agony.

"Mya, push!" the doctor yells as she bites down on her teeth, pushing her vaginal muscles to the brink. "That's good, he's halfway out. I have his shoulders. I need one more big push."

"I feel lightheaded and woozy. I can't," she whimpers in exhaustion. A nurse places ice chips in her mouth.

"Mya, one more big push," the doctor demands.

"Mya, be strong for my son!" Black's last words before being ripped away from her grasp fill her mind.

She musters her last bit of strength, pushing with every fiber of her being. She screams a frightening howl.

"That's it! That's it," the doctor says in delight. Seconds later, her baby's roaring cry fills the room.

The sound of her son's strong lungs overwhelms her with joy. The nurses clean him off, wrap him in a sky-blue blanket, and then place him in her arms.

"He is a little angel, a healthy eight pounds and seven ounces," a jolly and smiling nurse says.

He struggles to open his hazel eyes, the same color as his mother's. He is alert and inquisitive, with a head full of black hair. He will be strong like his father. Mya instantly becomes in love with him. She covers him with kisses, feeling unworthy of such a gift. He is worth more than any Chanel bag or designer pair of shoes. He is a prince, created out of his parents' love. A gift so great that only God could create. She feels a calming peace as her son, Carmello Matthew Samuels, Jr., lay on her chest.

Mya's life had always been about her own selfish wants and needs, but this child in her arms would take precedence over everything else in her life. More than wonderful. More than amazing. Her son is now the irreplaceable love of her life. Her parents and Raven are allowed to visit. The sight of baby Carmello brings tears and healing to her father, holding his grandson in his arms.

"Mya, he's beautiful," Terrance says, bonding with his grandson. Baby Carmello brings hope and sunshine, lifting the dark cloud over their family since her arrest. At this moment, the past is irrelevant. Their bloodline would continue. This little baby, not even eight hours old, was already healing his suffering family. The smallest feet leave the biggest footprint. The world's sweetest joy is a brand-new baby boy.

Part 6: Lockup

Mya sits on her bunk wearing her prison uniform inside Munchy State Correctional Institution, a white Chanel scarf wrapped around her head. She writes her personal thoughts in a black-and-white composition book. Posters of Jay-Z, Lil' Kim, and Aaliyah cover the walls. She reaches underneath the mattress, pulling out the photo of her and Black the night of her senior prom. She then reaches for a picture of their son. He is fat-cheeked and grinning, looking more like his father every day. Young Carmello is just five months old, his bright hazel eyes filled with innocence. Mya could not wait to kiss and hold him when her parents bring him to her next visit. They come every Sunday evening. She kisses her baby's photo, and tuck both pictures back under her mattress. She picks up her ink pen, and starts writing.

"This is the fourth month of my year-long sentence. My father pulled a few strings and got my sentence reduced. I thought I would be doing five to ten, thoughts of dying in prison filled my mind, but I realized I'm too young and beautiful to die. I've let my parents down beyond comprehension. My mother goes back and forth, writing me nasty letters using every four letter word in the book. Then, the next one I receive would be filled with uplifting Maya Angelou poems and Oprah Winfrey quotes. But hurting my dad, filling him with shame is what's killing me the most. I've learned to stay strong, that's how Black molded me. I've forgiven him for his indiscretions with those stank ass bitches; any man in his position of power is gonna have easy pussy thrown at him. I know he ain't love those hoes, and I always had his heart. I bet my life on that. Besides, we made something special out of our love; our son. Black has no other children, so I'm selfishly happy that I'm the only woman who can say she has his child.

I'm growing bored out of my mind. The days and nights in prison linger like eternities. But I have chalked it up and faced the fact that I'm gonna have to do this little bit of time standing on my head. My poor love, Carmello just turned twenty-five a few weeks ago. He's going to be trapped like a caged animal for the rest of his life. Another good black man caught up in the system he couldn't control. "You can't hate the roots of the tree and not hate the tree," as the great Malcolm X would say. I read his autobiography three times. Look at me kicking some knowledge.

I'm down and out right now, I miss my girls. Raven writes me regularly. She put me on three-way with Takia a few weeks ago. She seems to be in good spirits trying to get her life back in order. Some days, late at night when I'm in my bunk, I dream about all of the fun we had. All of the places we've been, and all of the niggas we've played. Just living in stress-free days, and not a care in the world. Now, we are all living our separate lives. We lost our friendship because of foolish pride, but we're slowly healing. When I step foot out of this jail, I swear on everything, I'm going to stay that bitch! I might be missing this summer, but summer 2000 is mine! The resurrection of Mya Campbell."

As Mya continues writing in her diary, a conceited smirk forms on her face. A heavyset Hispanic correction officer in her early fifties walks past her cell.

"Lights out ladies!" She says in a thick Spanish accent.

The cell block lights cut off. Mya sits alone, with the gloom of the dark prison all around.

"I'm always going to be the baddest bitch." She whispers before curling up on the thin mattress in a fetal position and slowly rocking herself to sleep.

Saleem Roberts, of Philadelphia, is a true creative who takes an interdisciplinary approach to his craft. For over ten years he honed his talents in the fashion and entertainment industries of Philadelphia and Hollywood. With his debut novel, *Fatally Flawless*, he began his foray into the literary world as an author of non-fiction and mainstream fiction. Using his professional expertise and life experiences Roberts creates exciting and compelling stories focused on charismatic and captivating characters.

If you or someone you know struggles with an additction to alcohol and/or drugs, please contact The Substance Abuse and Mental Health Services Administration (SAMHSA) at **1-800-662-HELP (4357)** or visit their website at *www.samhsa.gov.*

If you or someone you know is a victim or survivor of sexual assault, please contact RAINN (Rape, Abuse & Incest National Network) at **1-800-656-HOPE (1-800-656.4673)** or visit their website at *www.rainn.org.*

If you or someone you know is a victim of domestic violence, please contact the National Domestic Violence Hotline at **1-800-799-7233** or visit their website at *www.thehotline.org.*

CPSIA information can be obtained
at www.ICGtesting.com
Printed in the USA
BVOW08s1029251117
501042BV00002B/2/P